THE CLONE REDEMPTION

STEVEN L. KENT

ACE BOOKS, NEW YORK

THE BERKLEY PUBLISHING GROUP
Published by the Penguin Group
Penguin Group (USA) Inc.
375 Hudson Street, New York, New York 10014, USA
Penguin Group (Canada), 90 Eglinton Avenue East, Suite 700, Toronto, Ontario M4P 2Y3, Canada
(a division of Pearson Penguin Canada Inc.)
Penguin Books Ltd., 80 Strand, London WC2R 0RL, England
Penguin Group Ireland, 25 St. Stephen's Green, Dublin 2, Ireland (a division of Penguin Books Ltd.)
Penguin Group (Australia), 250 Camberwell Road, Camberwell, Victoria 3124, Australia
(a division of Pearson Australia Group Pty. Ltd.)
Penguin Books India Pvt. Ltd., 11 Community Centre, Panchsheel Park, New Delhi—110 017, India
Penguin Group (NZ), 67 Apollo Drive, Rosedale, Auckland 0632, New Zealand
(a division of Pearson New Zealand Ltd.)
Penguin Books (South Africa) (Pty.) Ltd., 24 Sturdee Avenue, Rosebank, Johannesburg 2196,
South Africa

Penguin Books Ltd., Registered Offices: 80 Strand, London WC2R 0RL, England

THE CLONE REDEMPTION

An Ace Book / published by arrangement with the author

PRINTING HISTORY
Ace mass-market edition / November 2011

Copyright © 2011 by Steven L. Kent.
Cover art by Christian McGrath.
Cover design by Judith Lagerman.

ISBN: 978-1-937007-02-7

ACE
Ace Books are published by The Berkley Publishing Group,
a division of Penguin Group (USA) Inc.,
375 Hudson Street, New York, New York 10014.
ACE and the "A" design are trademarks of Penguin Group (USA) Inc.

PRINTED IN THE UNITED STATES OF AMERICA

10 9 8 7 6 5 4 3 2 1

This book is dedicated to
John and Shirley Carmack.
So many good things could never have happened
had I not spent the winter
in Boise with them back in 1981.

Thank you.

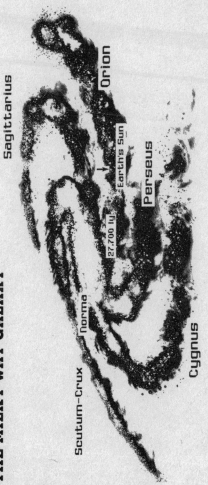

SPIRAL ARMS OF THE MILKY WAY GALAXY

Sagittarius

Orion

Earth's Sun

27,700 ly.

Perseus

Scutum–Crux

Norma

Cygnus

100,000 ly

Map by Steven J. Kent, adapted from a public domain NASA diagram

The mountains quake at him, and the hills melt, and the earth is burned at his presence, yea, the world, and all that dwell therein.

—Nahum 1:5

SEVEN EVENTS THAT SHAPED HISTORY:
A Unified Authority Time Line

2010 TO 2018
DECLINE OF THE U.S. ECONOMY

Following the examples of Chevrolet, Oracle, IBM, and ConAgra Foods, Microsoft moves its headquarters from the United States to Shanghai. Referring to their company as a "global corporation," Microsoft executives remain committed to U.S. prosperity, but with its burgeoning economy, China has become the company's most important market.

Even with Toyota and Hyundai increasing their manufacturing activities in the United States—spurred on by the favorable cheap labor conditions—the U.S. economy becomes dependent on the shipping of raw materials and farm goods.

Bottoming out as the world's thirteenth largest economy behind China, Korea, India, Cuba, the European Economic Community, Brazil, Mexico, Canada, Japan, South Africa, Israel, and Unincorporated France, the United States government focuses on maintaining its position as the world's last military superpower.

JANUARY 3, 2026
INTRODUCTION OF BROADCAST PHYSICS

Armadillo Aerospace announces the discovery of broadcast physics, a new technology capable of translating matter into data waves that can be transmitted to any location instantaneously. This opens the way for pangalactic exploration without time dilation or the dangers of light-speed travel.

The United States creates the first-ever fleet of self-broadcasting ships, a scientific fleet designed to locate planets for colonization. When initial scouting reports suggest that the rest of the galaxy is uninhabited, politicians fire up public sentiment with talk about "manifest destiny" and spreading humanity across space.

The discovery of broadcast physics leads to the creation of the Broadcast Network—a galactic superhighway consisting of satellites that send and receive ships across the galaxy. The Broadcast Network ushers in the age of galactic expansion.

JULY 4, 2110
RUSSIA AND KOREA SIGN A PACT
WITH THE UNITED STATES

With the growth of its space-based economy, the United States reclaims its spot as the wealthiest nation on Earth. Russia and Korea become the first nations to sign the IGTA (Intergalactic Trade Accord), a treaty opening the way for other nations to become self-governing American territories and enjoy full partnership in the space-based economy.

In an effort to create a competing alliance, France unveils its Cousteau Oceanic Exploration program and announces plans to create undersea colonies. Only Tahiti signs on.

After the other nations of the European Economic Union, Japan, and all of Africa become members of the IGTA, France discontinues its undersea colonization and joins the IGTA. Several nations, most notably China and Afghanistan, refuse to sign, leading to a minor world war in which the final holdouts are coerced into signing the treaty.

More than 80 percent of the world's population is eventually sent to establish colonies throughout the galaxy.

JULY 4, 2250
TRANSMOGRIFICATION OF THE UNITED STATES

With most of its citizens living off Earth, the IGTA is renamed "The Unified Authority" and restructured to serve as a government rather than an economic union.

The government of the Unified Authority bases its rule on a new manifesto that merges principles from the U.S. Constitution with concepts from Plato's *Republic*. In accordance with Plato's ideals, society is broken into three strata—citizenry, defense, and governance.

With forty self-sustaining colonies across the galaxy, Earth becomes the political center of a new republic. The eastern seaboard of the former United States becomes an ever-growing capital city populated by the political class—families appointed to run the government in perpetuity.

Earth also becomes home to the military class. After some experimentation, the Unified Authority adopts an all-clone conscription model to fulfill its growing need for soldiers. Clone farms euphemistically known as "orphanages" are established around Earth. These orphanages produce more than a million cloned recruits per year.

The military does not commission clone officers. The officer corps is drafted from the ruling class. When the children of politicians are drummed out of school or deemed unsuitable for politics, they are sent to officer-candidate school in Australia.

2452 TO 2512
UPRISING IN THE GALACTIC EYE

On October 29, 2452, a date later known as "the new Black Tuesday," a fleet of scientific exploration ships vanishes in the "galactic eye" region of the Norma Arm.

Fearing an alien attack, the U.A. Senate calls for the creation of the Galactic Central Fleet, a self-broadcasting armada. Work on the Galactic Central Fleet is completed in 2455. The newly christened fleet travels to the Inner Curve, where it vanishes as well.

Having authorized the development of a top secret line of cloned soldiers called "Liberators," the Linear Committee—the executive branch of the U.A. government—approves sending an invasion force into the Galactic Eye to attack all hostile threats. The Liberators discover a human colony led by Morgan Atkins, a powerful senator who disappeared with the Galactic Central Fleet. The Liberators overthrow the colony, but Atkins and many of his followers escape in G.C. Fleet ships. Over the next fifty years, a religious cult known as the

Morgan Atkins Believers—"Mogats"—spreads across the 180 colonized planets, preaching independence from the Unified Authority government.

Spurred on by the growing Morgan Atkins movement, four of the six galactic arms declare independence from Unified Authority governance in 2510. Two years later, on March 28, the combined forces of the Confederate Arms Treaty Organization and the Morgan Atkins Believers defeat the Earth Fleet and destroy the Broadcast Network, effectively cutting the Earth government off from its loyal colonies and Navy.

Believing they have crippled the Unified Authority, the Mogats turn on their Confederate Arms allies and attempt to take control of the renovated G.C. Fleet. The Confederates escape with fifty self-broadcasting ships and join forces with the Unified Authority, leaving the Mogats with a fleet of over four hundred self-broadcasting ships, the most powerful attack force in the galaxy.

The Unified Authority and the Confederate Arms end hostilities by attacking the Mogat home world, leaving no survivors on the planet.

2514 TO 2515
AVATARI INVASION

In 2514, an alien force enters the outer region of the Scutum-Crux Arm, conquering U.A. colonies. As they attack, the aliens wrap their "ion curtain" around the outer atmosphere of a planet, creating a barrier cutting off escape and communications.

In a matter of two years, the aliens spread throughout the galaxy, occupying only planets deemed habitable by U.A. scientists. The Unified Authority loses 178 of its 180 populated planets before making a final stand on New Copenhagen.

During this battle, U.A. scientists unravel the secrets of the aliens' tachyon-based technology, enabling U.A. Marines to win the war. In the aftermath of the invasion, the Unified Authority sends the four self-broadcasting ships of the Japanese Fleet along with twelve thousand Navy SEAL clones to locate and destroy the Avatari home world.

2517
RISE OF THE ENLISTED MAN'S EMPIRE

The Unified Authority Congress holds hearings investigating the military's performance during the Avatari invasion. When two generals blame their losses on lack of discipline among their cloned enlisted men, synthetic conscription is abolished, and all remaining clones are transferred to frontier fleets—fleets stranded in deep space since the destruction of the Broadcast Network. The Navy plans to use these fleets in full-combat exercises designed to test new, more powerful ships; but the clones revolt.

After creating their own broadcast network, clones establish the Enlisted Man's Empire, a nation consisting of twenty-three planets and thirteen fleets. As hostilities continue between the Enlisted Man's Empire and the Unified Authority, the Avatari return, attacking planets with a devastating weapon that raises atmospheric temperatures to nine thousand degrees for eighty-three seconds.

The Avatari attack three planets in December 2517—New Copenhagen, a Unified Authority colony; Olympus Kri, an Enlisted Man's colony; and Terraneau, a neutral nation. Working together, the Enlisted Man's Navy and the Earth Fleet successfully evacuate Olympus Kri prior to the attack, but there are no survivors on New Copenhagen, and slightly more than one thousand refugees survive on Terraneau.

Earthdate: November 18, A.D. 2517
Location: Planet A-361-F
Galactic Position: Solar System A-361
Astronomic Location: Bode's Galaxy

"If this is supposed to be our funeral, I'm not impressed," Chief Petty Officer Robert Humble whispered to the clone standing next to him.

"It's not a funeral. They don't give corpses wine at funerals," said Edward Kapeliela, who was also a CPO.

"It's an old Kamikaze thing," said Humble. "These guys are all about tradition."

"It's not a funeral; it's a farewell. Now will you shut up?"

"Quiet. Both of you," hissed Emerson Illych, a master chief petty officer and the highest-ranking member of the SEALs.

Yamashiro Yoshi, admiral of the Japanese Fleet, stood behind a table that had been draped with a white tablecloth. On the table sat a ceramic bottle, an ivory-glazed ceramic cylinder, eight inches tall and three inches wide, covered with hand-painted *Kanji*.

Beside the bottle sat a row of thirteen "thimbles." The SEALs called them "thimbles" because they held no more liquor than you could fit in a thimble. The Japanese called them *ochoko*. The *ochoko* matched the bottle, ivory-colored glaze and covered with *Kanji* symbols.

"What? You don't think you're the guest of honor at your own funeral?" asked Humble.

"Stow it, Humble," Illych growled. "I want to hear what he's saying."

"He's speaking in Japanese," Humble pointed out. "You told us to pretend like we don't understand Japanese."

Staring straight ahead, Chief Petty Officer Kapeliela said, "Show some respect, the man is trying to honor us."

Yamashiro filled each of the *ochoko* with sake. Speaking in Japanese, he ordered the SEALs to step forward. Before the ceremony began, another Japanese officer had drilled Illych and his men so that they would recognize the commands.

"This is honoring us? He's giving us a thimbleful of rice wine and speaking in a language he doesn't think we understand. How is this an honor?" asked Humble.

Short and sturdy, Yamashiro stood five-five, making him three inches taller than the diminutive SEAL clones. He had thick arms, a thick neck, a thick chest, and a round gut, all solidly packed together. His senior officers often speculated on whether or not he dyed his coal-colored hair. His eyes were hard and dark, and he barked the order for the twelve SEALs to lift their *ochoko*. He took the thirteenth cup and drank with them.

Once the SEALs had drained their sake, Yamashiro seemed to run out of words. He remained solemn as they replaced their *ochoko* on the table; and then he dismissed them.

Humble asked, "That's it? He's supposed to give us a flag and a sword. We're supposed to read our death poems."

"You wrote a death poem?" asked Illych.

"I wanted to get into the spirit of the occasion," said Humble.

Illych laughed, but Humble's complaining offended Chief Petty Officer Kapeliela. Had his neural programming allowed him to swear, he would have strung all the profanity in the English language into a single run-on sentence; but he could not do that. The Unified Authority scientists who created the SEAL clones organized their brains so that they did not have vices. The SEALs did not swear, drink, or smoke. Their self-esteem was so low that they did not approach women, not even prostitutes.

Illych and the SEALs stood at attention as Yamashiro and his officers left the landing bay of the battleship *Onoda*. Once they were gone, Illych gathered his SEALs beside the transport that would launch them on their mission. The transport would not take them down to the planet; but if everything went well, it would bring them back to the ship.

Kapeliela and Humble continued their argument. Humble said, "You did know that was a traditional Kamikaze farewell?"

Kapeliela grunted. "Yeah, I know. Only we're coming back."

"Maybe. We might think we're coming back, but Yamashiro doesn't," said Humble.

The rear hatch of the transport ground open, and the SEALs shuffled in. As Illych passed, Humble asked, "Master Chief, do you think we're coming back?" He was not afraid, just curious. The SEALs did not know fear, it was not in their neural programming.

"As long as the fleet doesn't leave us behind," said Illych. Like all of his men, Illych was nothing if not stoic.

The joking and bickering ended when the hatch closed, and the mission officially began. In action, the SEALs only spoke when they had a real reason.

Every SEAL had the same basic training in stealth, marksmanship, demolitions, close combat, and reconnaissance skills; but each had a specialized skill as well. During the three years since they had left Earth, the SEALs had picked up new areas of specialization. Some had studied engineering, others chemistry or physics, anything that might help when they infiltrated the enemy.

The cargo compartment of the transport was known as the "kettle" because its floor, ceiling, and windowless steel walls combined into a curbed interior. In the shadow-filled confines of the kettle, the SEALs became all but invisible. The dark gray of their complexion made them look sickly in light, but they blended in with the shadows in the dimly lit environs of the transport.

The Japanese called the SEALs *kage no yasha*. It meant "shadow demon." The name referenced both their ability to vanish in the darkness and also the inhumanity of their faces. Their noses turned up so sharply they might have been snouts. Each had a thick ridge of bone forming a protruding brow over his tiny dark eyes. They were short and wiry, with entirely bald heads and clawlike fingers that could slice through skin.

Unlike other synthetics, the SEALs knew that they were clones. They knew they were ugly and were deeply ashamed of it. The Japanese made jokes about their having the faces of bats or dragons or demons. Not wanting to embarrass the Japanese, the SEALs pretended not to understand them; but in their hearts, they agreed.

"Board your caskets," Illych told his men.

The *caskets* were "stealth infiltration pods" or "S.I.P.s," coffin-sized people-fliers designed to evade all known forms of detection. Six feet long and three feet wide, S.I.P.s could travel millions of miles in an hour. They scanned for radar, sonar, and laser detection and camouflaged their own footprint. They did not have guns or steering controls. SEALs did not pilot their caskets, they went along for the ride. Trapped in tubes so tight they could do no more than breathe, the SEALs did not become claustrophobic. It was not in their programming.

Seemingly designed to make passengers uncomfortable, the cargo pit of the S.I.P. lacked so much as a shred of padding, had no lights, and no communications gear. The S.I.P. was designed for ten-minute flights and nothing longer. Naturalborns could not tolerate even ten minutes in an S.I.P., but it never occurred to Illych and his SEALs that their S.I.P.s were uncomfortable.

The launching device at the back of the transport did not simply release the pods into space; it fired them like a highpowered rifle using supermagnetism. Once launched, the pod controlled the flight itself, using a field-resonance engine that operated as silently as a gentle breeze and as untrackably as one particular raindrop in a storm.

Field-resonance engines offered one other advantage. In theory, overcharging the engine of an S.I.P. triggered a reactive explosion that would measure in the millions of megatons. These were more than bombs; they were planet colliders.

A team of technicians opened the pods and the SEALs climbed into their caskets without hesitation. Once the technicians closed the pod doors, dry gel oozed in around the SEALs to protect them against the stresses of extreme acceleration and deceleration.

Working as quickly as they could, technicians dressed in

soft-shelled armor lifted the S.I.P.s into place. The launching device had a revolving carriage with chambers for twelve caskets that the techs loaded like bullets.

The transport had been specially equipped with a stealth generator. Sitting only five hundred thousand miles outside the planet's atmosphere, cloaked by the generator, the little ship was invisible, even to the Japanese Fleet. The pilot purged the air from the kettle, then he shut off the engines and all of the lights as he opened the rear hatch. This was the mission's most vulnerable moment. With the hatch open, and the S.I.P.s in place, the stealth generator could no longer hide the transport.

Per special orders given them by Admiral Yamashiro, the sailors raised a hand in salute and shouted *BANZAI* as the device fired each pod into space.

The SEALs did not hear their cheers. InterLink transmissions did not penetrate the walls of their pods. For the duration of their flight, the SEALs heard nothing more than the sound of their own breathing as they streaked through space. Barely larger than old-fashioned space suits, the pods carried their cargo a half million miles in a matter of seconds.

In the history of mankind, no human had ever traveled so far in such a small vessel. Tasked with saving humanity, the SEALs went to space with equipment that Congress had previously labeled "too expensive to be practical." Concerns about practicality vanished when it came to saving the human race.

It cost approximately eighty million dollars to build a stealth infiltration pod. The SEALs had brought five thousand of them to Bode's Galaxy.

The pods traveled from the transport to the planet at top speed and did not slow until they pierced the atmosphere, leaving no more traces of their entry than needles slicing steam. Invisible to radar, sonar, and visual contact, the pods continued their computer-controlled deceleration until they touched down at the preappointed target as gently as autumn leaves landing in a grassy field.

All twelve pods landed within a forty-foot radius, their cargo bay doors opened, and the SEALs emerged. This was the first time man had set foot on a planet outside the Milky

Way, a benchmark that meant nothing to Emerson Illych and his men. They had not come to explore. They had come to destroy.

Illych and his team knew what to expect. This planet was known as "A-361-F," as it was the sixth planet from the star labeled "A-361." A-361-F had an unbreathable atmosphere—a toxic cocktail of nitrogen, carbon monoxide, and methane. Because it was so far from the sun, a foot-thick layer of poisonous frost covered its surface. Had they not been wearing atmosphere-adjusting combat armor, the SEALs would have frozen to death before they got a chance to die of asphyxiation.

Illych thought the planet looked a lot like Earth's moon might have looked had it been frozen under ice. Nothing had color. The ground was gray. The sky was black. The SEALs had landed during the period that passed for day, but the sun was four billion miles away, and day on A-361-F looked a lot like night.

The SEALs did not waste time chatting about the dreary surroundings. They quietly checked to make sure they had not left gear in their pods and began their mission.

In the hours before the mission began, remote surveillance technicians had used satellite drones to map the planet. Designed for military use, the satellites were not equipped to take air samples from space. They tested for radiation, located non-natural structures, recorded ground movement, and searched for possible targets. On this planet, the satellites found only one point of interest, an abandoned building complex.

Looking at the satellite reports, Yamashiro's intelligence officers said that complex was "inactive," possibly an abandoned fort or a fueling station for space travelers. They had no way of knowing if it belonged to the Avatari, the aliens who had created such havoc upon the Milky Way. The author of the report did speculate that the enormous cylindrical structures along one face of the complex might be storage silos, suggesting that the facility might have been used as a fuel refinery.

The land around the complex was completely flat, no hills or craters. A labyrinth of tunnels and trenches might have been hiding beneath the foot-thick frost; but if so, it was invisible to the recon satellites. To Illych's eyes, the plain had no notable features except for the buildings.

Illych did not bother telling his men what to do, they already knew their assigned duties. The SEALs had trained together since the day of their manufacture, twelve years earlier. They knew their objectives and performed their duties.

The SEALs divided into three four-man reconnaissance teams. Illych led his team toward the complex itself. If the buildings had had walls, doors, or windows, the master chief and his men would have searched from outside, looking for guards or security equipment. No doors, no walls, no roof. More than anything else, the place was a tangle of pipes and chambers. Inch-thick frost had formed on the structure, creating gray camouflage over the jet-black metallic surfaces below.

The building stood no more than fifty feet tall, built on an open-faced foundation. Using the thermal lenses in his visor, Illych scanned the area for heat signatures. He found nothing. Either the structure was out of use, or the material flowing through the pipes was of a type that could not be frozen.

Illych and his team looked for signs of the Avatari. They searched the platform for doors and compartments, using the sonar and X-ray equipment in their helmets; then they used the enhanced handheld equipment that they had brought with them. The pipes and chambers were hollow, the foundation and the ground around it were solid.

One of the SEALs shined a laser on pipes and panels to test for vibrations and found nothing. Petty Officer Andrew Call aimed a torch at a patch of frost from a pipe that was so big around he could have stood in it. The gray layer turned to steam under the heat and quickly evaporated.

Speaking on an open frequency, Call asked Illych, "Do you want me to cut the pipe open?" He did not refer to the master chief as "sir." By design, none of the cloned SEALs were officers.

"Didn't you say the pipe is empty?" Illych asked.

"As far as I can tell."

"What's the point in cutting it open?"

"It will give us a chance to see what it's made of," said

Call. "I've never seen anything like this. It X-rays easily, but I can't find wires or circuits, none of the components you expect to find inside a machine. Whatever passes for power around here, it's not electricity-based."

Illych considered this. "Hold off," he said. "For now, let's just figure out what we're dealing with."

Illych stood at the edge of the foundation, tracing the shapes of the pipes that formed the structure. The building had an organic, random feeling. Like vines in jungle, the pipes weaved in and out in a haphazard braid. So much frost covered the pipes that they looked like an ice sculpture, but only a thin layer of powdery frost had formed on the foundation. Looking for footprints in that powder, Illych thought that centuries might have passed since the aliens had last visited the facility.

Using optical commands, he raised the volume of the sound sensors in his helmet so that he could better monitor the ambient sounds. He heard only the mouselike whisper of the wind and the footsteps of his men. The planet had a thin atmosphere, and much of it was frozen.

The master chief went to an N-shaped stand of pipes and tapped it with his finger. He could see the structure of the pipes deep inside a dirty frozen layer. Using a knife, he scraped the skin of the ice, letting the peelings fall into an analysis kit.

He checked the reading, saw nothing of importance, and scraped deeper. The kit checked for radiation, chemicals, and age. The content of the ice remained the same; but as Illych gouged deeper into the frozen sheath, the age changed. The readings struck Illych as odd, but he did not question the results.

"Do you think this belongs to the same aliens that invaded us?" asked Kapeliela.

"I'm sure of it," said Illych.

"This place is weird. I never seen anything like it," said Kapeliela.

"It looks like a refinery," said Illych.

Kapeliela agreed. "Yeah, an abandoned refinery. That makes sense, but it's been out of service for a long, long time."

Chief Petty Officer Humble joined the conversation. "So what? It's a refinery?"

Illych asked, "What kind of ships did the aliens fly when they attacked our planets?"

"They didn't have . . ."

"You don't need remote fuel depots once you stop flying ships," Illych said.

Beside the building, a row of twenty-seven identical cylindrical structures rose out of the ground. They stood 970 feet tall. They had the same hyperbolic shape as the cooling towers of nuclear power facilities only turned upside down. The structures were wider at the top than at the base.

While Illych and his men surveyed the building, Chief Petty Officer Humble's team studied the towers. Using equipment in his helmet, Humble measured the nearest tower—223 feet wide at the base and 352 feet wide at the top.

"You got anything?" Illych asked Humble.

"Yeah. It's like these things are made of eggshells," Humble said. "Once you get through all the ice, the walls are a twentieth of an inch thick. I'm surprised they don't collapse under the weight of the ice."

"Can you see inside it?" Illych asked.

"Yeah, they X-ray right up. They're empty and hollow all the way down."

"All the way down?" Illych asked.

"If you think this thing is tall, you should see how far down it goes."

"How far?"

"Over a mile."

"Do you think it's a silo?" Illych asked.

"That's my best guess; but it's empty."

Kapeliela waited for Illych to run out of questions, then asked one of his own. "Do we know if these pipes are made of the same stuff?"

"They aren't as thin as eggshells," Illych said. "It looks like this place was abandoned a long, long time ago. Some of the ice on these pipes is over a hundred thousand years old."

That was when Illych saw the light. All of the SEALs saw it. A dull sun shone in the distance; but far brighter light now shone directly above them. Having been briefed about the invasion of their own galaxy, the SEALs knew what that light meant. The aliens had arrived.

"Looks like the home team knows we're here," said Illych.

A few yards away, Call left his X-ray camera beside a pipe and pulled out his gun. Three of the SEALs carried pistols, six carried M27s, three carried sniper rifles. All of their weapons were loaded with custom-made rounds, bullets designed to explode like miniature grenades.

"Okay, we've trained for this," Illych told his men.

Light so bright it almost looked solid shone on the other side of the building. The SEALs knew what to expect: First came the light, then the aliens that traveled inside it.

Illych told his men, "Take your positions. Maybe we'll get lucky." He did not believe they would.

Illych held no delusions about being rescued. No one would come to the planet to save them. If his men had any hope of survival, they would need to make it out on their own.

Believing that he and his men would not survive the next five minutes, Illych decided to die on his own terms. The only thing that mattered now was reporting what little they had learned before the aliens "sleeved" the planet. The light in the sky, dubbed by scientists as an "ion curtain," would quickly enclose the planet, ending all transmissions. Once it spread over the platform, the SEALs would be cut off.

With his team running beside him, Illych relayed findings to the fleet as he dashed from pipes to cylinders to pillars. He kept his M27 out and ready though he still had not yet seen the enemy.

"The atmosphere is toxic, mostly nitrogen and carbon monoxide. The building appears to be a refinery. We think it is out of use but cannot be sure. It's covered with ice. The ice on the pipes is a hundred thousand years old. I checked the samples myself."

The pilot of the transport interrupted Illych's message. "Find a safe position. I'm coming to get you."

"Negative. Do not attempt to retrieve us."

The pilot did not argue the point.

An officer from the *Onoda* asked, "Master Chief, have one of your men fire at the cylinders."

Illych relayed the order. "Humble, fire a burst at one of the silos."

Already one hundred yards away, Humble spun and fired five rounds into the nearest silo. Had they been regular rounds, the bullets might have ricocheted off. The special rounds struck the target and exploded.

Even as he pulled the trigger, Humble realized that the bullets should have triggered a chain reaction. They should have broken through the thin wall and caused the structure to collapse.

Seeing that his bullets did not penetrate the silo, Humble fired five more shots. The bullets burst like small grenades, a pop, a flash, a flame. Anyone standing a few feet from the explosions would have been thrown in the air. The bullets blew away the frost, but they did not scratch the structure.

"Bulletproof," said Humble. He sprinted to catch up to the men in his squad.

Instead of beams, walls, and doorways, the building had pipes and empty spaces. As he ran, Illych looked for elevators or ladders that would lead to the top of the structure. He found nothing.

In the sky, patterns of colors showed in the light, shimmering like heat waves, and the glaring light spread across the sky.

The atmosphere above the building glowed like crystal as the top of the pillar of light spread into a silver-white canopy, the color of lightning, but with spectrums of other colors playing inside it.

Illych looked into the sky long enough for shades and shapes to pop before his eyes, then returned his gaze to the ground. He reached the far side of the building at the same moment as the three other men in his squad.

"You getting this?" he asked the officers on the *Onoda*.

"Have you seen defenders?" asked the man on the other side of the commandLink.

On the frozen plain not far from the building, a ten-foot-tall globe glowed even more bright than the light around it. It stood out like a platinum sphere in a bed of well-polished silver. As he turned to examine the globe, the tint shields in Illych's visor deployed to protect his eyes.

Unlike the tint shields in standard combat armor, the tinting in SEAL armor filtered light instead of simply darkening it. Illych saw everything clearly, but the glare was gone. He saw the crystal white sphere and the dirty brown gas that leaked from its base. Illych also saw the aliens inside the globe, ten-foot-tall translucent yellow shadows with arms and legs but no facial features except grapefruit-sized chrome-silver eyes. The first humans who saw these creatures had labeled them "space angels."

The apparitions stepped out of the sphere, and the SEALs opened fire. Their bullets passed through the aliens the same way they passed through light or air. They hit nothing and did not explode.

Above the fight, the ion curtain had spread across both horizons. Illych was too busy to notice, but if he'd tried to contact *Onoda*, his transmissions would have gone unanswered. Somewhere in the back of his mind, the master chief understood that he was cut off from the fleet. Communications could not penetrate the curtain. Ships could not pass through it. There would be no airlift. He and his men would fight until they died.

But Illych would still achieve one of his objectives. As mission leader, he had access to controls in his visor that the other men on his team did not have. He started the process.

Illych knew his SEALs could not win this firefight. They specialized in stealth combat. They infiltrated bases, sabotaged targets, and occasionally assassinated enemies. This was open combat, the specialty of soldiers and Marines.

When he saw Kapeliela die, Illych felt a stab of doubt and asked himself if the stealth infiltration pods would charge in time.

Kapeliela had run along the side of the building. He came within a few feet of the creatures and fired his weapon. His bullets passed through them as if they were ghosts. He threw a grenade. It exploded without harming them.

One of the creatures swung its chrome-barreled rifle at Kapeliela and fired a yard-long bolt of light that passed through the SEAL and into the ground behind him. The bolt passed so smoothly through the man and his armor that, seen from the side, it looked like the shot missed. Kapeliela's body did not explode. No blood splashed from the wound. He simply fell backward. Mercifully, he was dead before he hit the ground.

As Illych watched, the aliens' bodies slowly solidified. "Aim for their rifles," Illych yelled to his men over the interLink.

A bullet glanced off one of the aliens' rifles even before Illych finished speaking. It had to have come from one of his snipers, a pinpoint shot that hit the barrel and exploded without leaving a mark.

Hiding behind a pipe, Illych leveled his M27, and fired a long burst. He expected the aliens to return fire, but they didn't. They stood outside the building, their glowing, translucent hides cooling to the color of honey, and they waited.

For just an instant, Illych considered stopping the countdown, but he decided against it. He read the timer in his visor. In three minutes and twenty-six seconds the field-resonance engines in the twelve stealth infiltration pods would overcharge and explode. Once overcharged, the field-resonance engines inside the pods would become unstable. They'd be like dams holding back an endless flow of energy. In three minutes and twenty seconds, the pods would use that energy to self-destruct, taking the entire planet with them.

One of Illych's snipers ran out into the open, looking for a shot. An alien fired first, its bolt hit the SEAL in the chest, and he collapsed in a violent spasm that lasted only a few seconds.

"It looks like they don't want to come in after us," said Humble.

Illych checked the timer. He and his men needed to hold out for three minutes and twelve seconds. They had to defend the S.I.P.s. If the aliens found the pods and shot them first, the overcharging engines would not explode.

One of the aliens walked to the edge of the building and stopped. Dozens of bullets passed through its body and head without leaving a trace. Several shots hit its weapon.

"Transport, you there?" Illych asked, though he would not get through.

Three of the aliens walked toward the building. They moved slowly, taking shaky steps like drunks or maybe toddlers learning to walk. The SEALs hit the aliens with grenades and bullets and rockets, but their attacks meant nothing. One of the aliens came closer, raised its weapon, scanned back and forth for targets, but did not fire or step onto the foundation.

"You there?" Illych asked again. "I hope they're getting this."

The alien either wouldn't or couldn't enter the building. It did not fire its weapon at the SEALs. Having read the reports and seen the video feeds, Illych knew the bolts these aliens fired bored through brick, metal, wood, and men alike. Humble's bullets had not hurt the silo, but this creature's bolts would probably pierce it.

Illych checked the time. *One minute forty-eight seconds.*

"It's not coming after us," said Humble.

All five of the aliens gathered at the edge of the building. They did not speak to each other. Their skins still glowed the color of honey, but dark scales had begun to form.

"Maybe it has orders not to hurt the building," said Call.

"So we have a standoff," said Humble.

"For another minute and a half," said Illych.

"You're charging the caskets?" asked Humble.

"Eighty-seven seconds and counting."

Humble laughed, and said, "I knew I should have read my death poem."

CHAPTER
ONE

Location: Terraneau
Galactic Position: Scutum-Crux Arm
Astronomic Location: Milky Way

They say God created the plants on the third day, the animals on the fifth, and man on the sixth. What God did in three days the aliens undid in less than a minute and a half. It took the bastards eighty-three seconds to kill everything that walked the surface of Terraneau, right down to the microbes.

I was one of the 1,037 people who survived the attack on the once-grand planet of Terraneau. We survived because we hid in a tunnel that ran under a lake.

By far, the vast majority of the survivors were clones, members of Scutum-Crux Fleet's Corps of Engineers. There was an even thousand of them.

I was one of two Marines who survived. The other survivors included Ava Gardner, the woman I had once loved, and the man who had replaced me as her lover. My pilot, Lieutenant Christian Nobles, was the other Marine. Ray Freeman, the mercenary/homicidal humanitarian who busted me out of jail in time to save me from getting cooked with everybody else, survived as well.

The thirty-two other lottery winners were members of the local militia. In the moments before the aliens attacked, the local militia raided the tunnel hoping to haul me back to prison. They entered with hundreds of men, but only thirty-two had traveled far enough into the tunnel to survive the heat. They attacked our sanctuary moments before the Avatari performed their pyrotechnic magic, raising the surface temperature of Terraneau to 9,000 degrees. The temperature outside the tunnel spiked 8,927 degrees and remained at 9,000 degrees for precisely eighty-three seconds, then dropped back to normal almost as quickly.

During those eighty-three seconds, the temperature created a convection, causing the atmosphere to rise off the surface of the planet. When the Avatari shut off the heat, the atmosphere dropped back into place, crushing buildings, kicking a thick layer of dust and ash into the air, and sending a shock wave across the planet.

Hiding behind a thick steel door in the depths of a tunnel, my engineers and I rode out the attack unharmed. When we opened the doors, just about everyone on the planet had been killed and cremated; and their dust was carried on the largely carbon-dioxide winds. Just behind the door, we found thirty-two militiamen cowering in the dark. They were good to go except for burst eardrums, a few broken bones, and the shock of knowing that everything and everyone they loved had been burned.

The rest of the tunnel was littered with the bodies of men who were cooked but not cremated. The first bodies we found were covered with blisters, their clothes singed and their hair burned brittle. Grease leaked from breaks in their scalded hides.

As I wandered toward the entrance of the tunnel, the corpses became more badly burned. One hundred feet from daylight, the bodies were papery ash that turned to dust at the slightest touch.

I walked to the mouth of the tunnel, taking in the lake, the sky, and the distant ruins of Norristown. From where I stood, Lake Norris looked as big as an ocean, so far across that I would not be able to see its farthest shores . . . even on a clear day. On this day, the air around me was the color of tea, and clouds of smoke and ash filled the sky. Incinerating five million people and all their belongings puts a lot of dust in the wind.

The militiamen, the engineers, and Ava's lover remained in the tunnel, standing in the darkness, staring at nothing in particular. Their crying carried in the stillness like an echo.

Ava came to me as I stood in the entrance. Though I tried to stop her, she looked back toward the city and saw the ruins.

"What about my girls?" she asked. Before the cataclysm,

she had taught drama at an orphanage for girls. She stared toward the ruins of the city, and tears rolled down her face. I did not blame her. I'd tried to warn her, but she couldn't envision destruction on this scale without having seen it. Once you see an attack of this sort, a part of your humanity closes forever.

This was the third time I'd seen an attack of this kind, and it still left me numb.

I had come to warn these people, and they threw me in jail. Freeman rescued me, and the people burned as if I'd never arrived.

"General Harris, are you there?" The call came from Captain Don Cutter, commander of the E.M.N. *Churchill*. E.M.N. stood for Enlisted Man's Navy, my Navy. I was a Marine, but I was the highest-ranking officer in the fleet.

Cutter contacted me over my commandLink, part of the communications network built into my combat armor. "General Harris, are you there?"

"Harris here," I said. I hoped I sounded in control. This was the first outside communication I had received since entering the tunnel.

"What's the situation, sir?" asked Cutter.

"The worst," I said.

"How many survivors?"

"A thousand and change," I said. "How do things look up there?"

Cutter was calling from a badly damaged fighter carrier, supposedly the only operational ship in Terraneau space. He said, "The Unifieds sent a spy ship into the area."

"How were you able to spot it?" I asked.

The Unified Authority, the Earth-based empire that created me and my fellow clones, used modified cruisers for surveillance and reconnaissance. The spy ships were fast, small, and equipped with cloaking technology that rendered them utterly invisible.

"We parked in the debris and turned off our lights," said Cutter. "They didn't know we were here."

By "debris," he meant a graveyard of ships. More than a hundred dead ships floated in the space around Terraneau, remnants of a forgotten battle that had happened earlier this year.

"Didn't they cloak?"

"They cloaked all right; but they dropped their skirts when they launched their 'eye.'"

I knew that "eye" was Navy-speak for a spy satellite. The part about the skirts made no sense to me. "Come again?" I asked.

"They had to lower their shields to deploy their satellite. Weapons picked up the energy fluctuation."

"Nice work," I said.

"Thank you, sir. Do you want us to destroy the eye?"

"Hell no," I said. Then, realizing I might be coming off harsh, I said, "Leave it alone, Captain. Having an enemy satellite in place might come in handy."

Terraneau was in the Scutum-Crux Arm, the outermost arm of the Milky Way. Earth was located in the Orion Arm, clear across the galaxy. The only way for the Unifieds to pull any data from that satellite would be by sending their spy ship back to retrieve it.

When their spy ship returned, we would give her a proper reception.

CHAPTER
TWO

Earthdate: November 19, A.D. 2517

The spy ship sneaked out of the anomaly the way mice sneak out of their holes—quickly, carefully, silently. Anomalies are like electrical tears in the fabric of space. They occur when ships travel using broadcast technology. In this case, the Unified Authority spy ship had a built-in broadcast engine that enabled her to make the hundred-thousand-light-year jump from Earth to Terraneau instantaneously. She arrived in Scutum-Crux space approximately fourteen million miles from Terraneau, far enough out of casual surveillance range that we would not have noticed the disturbance had we not been looking for it. With her stealth generator, the spy ship was invisible to our equipment. Only the anomaly showed on the readouts.

The spy ship was small and unarmed, the naval equivalent of a hummingbird. She had the ability to slip in behind enemy lines and listen to our communications, track our movements, and watch our production without threat of detection.

But this ship had been detected. We saw where she broadcasted into our space, and we knew her final destination. It didn't matter that we lost track of the ship as she traveled the fourteen million miles from the anomaly to the satellite because we knew precisely where she would end her journey.

She was the mouse in the night, we were the cat. When she materialized beside the satellite, we would pounce. Even if we never saw the ship, our equipment would detect a momentary energy fluctuation when she lowered her shields to retrieve the satellite. She would be vulnerable when she lowered her shields.

I had no sympathy for the crew of the spy ship; they had

come to the Scutum-Crux Arm to watch people die. Instead of offering assistance, the bastards placed a satellite so that scientists could study the death of an entire planet.

The satellite was smaller than a golf ball and armed with a camera so powerful that it could pick out a single grain of sand in an open desert. The satellite's unblinking eye undoubtedly recorded us as we pulled our shuttle out of the tunnel and launched into space. It must have spotted us setting our trap as well; but the crew of the spy ship would have no access to those data until they retrieved the satellite.

"Anything?" I asked Cutter. Under normal circumstances, I would have used ship-to-ship communications; but the spy ship might have overheard us. Instead, we used the short-range interLink, a network designed for battlefield communications.

Cutter spoke to a tech officer, then said, "Nothing yet, sir."

We kept our communications short in case the Unifieds tried to listen in.

Freeman and I watched the scene on a small video screen as we waited inside the kettle of a transport. The screen showed a panoramic view of open space. Terraneau spun in a corner of the screen, its oceans still blue but hidden behind a global cloud of smoke and ash. The alien attack had erased the green from the continents. Gone, too, were the ice caps that had once marked the poles at the top and bottom of the planet. Soot from the attack had turned the atmosphere a rusty gray.

"You're still on our side, right?" I asked Freeman.

Ray Freeman, one of the deadliest men who ever lived, said nothing as he watched the screen. The man was huge, seven feet tall. He was wide and thick and covered with muscle. He was also the last of his kind. In a galaxy that had outlawed ethnicities a century ago, Ray Freeman was proudly African-American. A lot of men saw him as someone to fear. I admired him.

Freeman was a human sphinx. He answered questions only when he felt like answering. Generally, he ignored them. He was a mercenary, but money did not determine his loyalty.

"Why help us?" I asked. "Why not the Unifieds?"

"I'm not taking sides," said Freeman.

"The hell you're not," I said. "We're about to attack a Unified Authority boat. If you don't care who wins, you don't belong on this ride."

I trusted Freeman though he had been vague about his loyalties. Freeman was not the type who started the mission as your friend, then shot you in the back. He made his alliances public and sniped his targets from a mile away. In my experience, Freeman's loyalty was never in question.

"I don't care about sides, just saving lives," Freeman said. "That's it. It's not about loyalty. The only planet the Unifieds care about is Earth; you're out to save what's left of the galaxy."

"What's left of the galaxy . . ." Before the first alien invasion, the Unified Authority had 180 colonized planets scattered around the Milky Way. The aliens "sleeved" 178 of them. The Enlisted Man's Empire, a nation composed of the cloned military that the Unified Authority had ejected, reestablished contact with 23 of those planets before the aliens began incinerating rescued planets.

Freeman's entire family had been on the first planet the Avatari, the aliens, incinerated. Having lost everyone he might have ever loved, the galaxy's best professional killer became a self-appointed savior.

When dealing with people like Ray Freeman, as if there were anyone else like Freeman, there is no room for ambiguity. I decided to reconfirm his motivation. "As long as we're saving more lives than the Unifieds, you're on our side?"

He nodded.

"Good enough for me," I said, though inwardly I still had doubts. The clones of the Enlisted Man's Empire had been bred to save the lives of natural-borns, and the Unified Authority had thanked us for it with one betrayal after another. I felt a need to save the natural-born residents of our planets, but I could not come up with any logical reason to do it.

Satisfied that I could trust Freeman for now, I turned my attention to the mission at hand. "Cutter, are the traps in position?" I asked over the commandLink.

Asking that question was my form of fidgeting. Captain Don Cutter was a good officer, not the kind of man who left things undone. Still, we were dealing with an invisible foe, and we would only get one shot at the bastards. It was one of those pivotal moments on which the future hung. If we failed to bag that spy ship, the war would end before it began.

"Yes, sir," said Cutter. He spoke in a whisper.

Five transports floated within a few hundred yards of the satellite. They were not debris from the graveyard of ships but fully functional birds Cutter had placed himself. One of the transports carried a team of engineers. Freeman and I sat in the kettle of the second. The others sat facing away from the satellite, their rear hatches open, their kettles carefully packed with explosives. When the spy ship lowered her shields, we would use these transports like old-fashioned cannons.

The bombs were not especially powerful. We needed to cripple the spy ship, not decapitate her. I didn't care if the crew lived or died; I didn't owe the bastards. The ship's computers, on the other hand, they mattered.

Five million people had just died on Terraneau, and millions more had their necks on the chopping block on other planets. The key to saving them was on those computers. We could not win the war with the aliens; but armed with the right information, we might survive it.

"How long has it been since you detected the anomaly?" I asked Cutter.

"Fifty-two minutes, sir," he said.

Fifty-two minutes, I thought. *Fifty-two minutes to travel fourteen million miles, either the bastards are taking their time or they've figured us out.* In conventional travel, U.A. cruisers topped out at a speed of thirty-eight million miles per hour. Traveling the fourteen million miles from the anomaly should have taken less than half an hour.

"Maybe they know we're here." I said the words out loud but meant them for myself.

"Not likely," said Cutter.

Listening over the interLink, Freeman heard every word we said but did not comment. He lived in a world of absolutes. Either the spy ship was coming, or she was not. He saw no value in second-guessing the situation.

I looked back at the video screen and saw nothing but empty space. The satellite was so small that it did not even appear on my screen. A little bubble of light represented the area around it.

"Mars, are your men ready?" I asked on a different frequency. Mars, Lieutenant Scott Mars, ran my corps of Navy engineers. I would have preferred using a demolitions team on this mission, but Mars's men were handy with explosives.

"Yes, sir. You stop the ship, sir, and we'll kick her doors in," he said.

"Minimal damage," I reminded him for what might have been the hundredth time.

"You said you wanted a hole," he reminded me.

"Right," I said.

"If you know a way to put a hole in a ship without doing damage . . ."

"I take your point."

"We'll keep the damage to a minimum, sir," said Mars.

Cutter interrupted us. "It's a go!"

Nothing had changed on my screen. The ash-choked atmosphere of Terraneau still showed in one corner of the screen. Our transports still hid at the edge of the debris.

I did not see the spy ship. Of course I didn't see her, not yet at least. But the spy ship must have been in place beside the satellite, and her crew must have lowered her shields or Cutter would not have sent that message. His sensors detected energy fluctuations.

Cutter detonated the bombs in the three open transports, firing a barrage of bearings and shrapnel at the invisible target. In the silence of space, the detonations made no noise; but the explosions flashed and vanished on my video screen.

Had it been a civilian ship caught in that storm, the debris would have broken her to pieces. The spy ship took the beating and survived. Her stealth generators failed, and she came into view. Air and flames leaked from small holes in her hull, and a large outer panel had been ripped from her bow, all cosmetic damage that would nonetheless prove fatal for her crew.

The ship was shaped like the head of a gigantic spear, fifty feet wide at her stern and two hundred feet long. Tiny electrical eruptions burst across her cylindrical hull. That bird would need repairs before she flew again. No problem. Mars's engineers could repair her.

Our ambush nearly sheared off one of her three aft engines. It hung limp at an odd angle, like an arm in a cast. Liquid fuel escaped from the back of the engine, flying into space in bubbles. If the pilot of the spy ship tried to light the other engines, he'd ignite a fire that would consume the entire ship; but judging by the damage to the bridge, I did not worry about survivors among the flight crew. The bridge had gone dark, and the spy ship wasn't going anywhere.

THREE

"We're up," I told Freeman, though he was already moving toward the sled. A flatbed hauling device used for spacewalks, the sled looked like a scale for weighing cattle. It had a ten-foot-long base lined with tiny booster rockets. It did not have walls or rails or even a dashboard, only a column with handles for steering.

We climbed onto the sled, Freeman driving. Freeman always drove. A moment later, he had the boosters fired, and we hovered down the ramp at the rear of the transport, traveling at the sled's top speed of ten miles per hour.

And there was the spy ship, long and gray and sleek, little bursts of air emanating from her many wounds. Parts of the ship had gone dark, but light showed from some of her viewports.

Ahead of us, the team of engineers assigned to open the ship approached the hull on a sled as well. They drifted along the fuselage, finally stopping behind the darkened maw of the bridge. They worked quickly, using a laser saw to slice a five-foot hole into the side of the ship.

Had the debris we fired at the spy ship not already lacerated her hull, that door would have exploded from the ship in a pressure-blasted burst of oxygen; but any atmospheric pressure had already leaked out.

"Now we know how we're going to get in," I told Freeman.

He puttered our sled toward the hole. As we drew nearer, the spy ship no longer looked so remarkably small. She was three stories tall. I reached out an armor-covered hand and ran my fingers along an undamaged stretch of hull as we pulled up to the opening.

For his purposes, Freeman only needed to salvage a specific communications computer; but I wanted the entire ship.

My goals were more military-minded. I would not throw away a ship that was both invisible and self-broadcasting no matter how damaged.

Under normal circumstances, Freeman and I would have used particle-beam weapons when entering a disabled ship. This time we brought fléchette-firing S9 stealth pistols. He was concerned about a communications computer; I worried about everything else. Lieutenant Mars would need to fix everything we broke if we ever planned to fly this ship. Hit a computer or a circuit panel with a fléchette, and you may get lucky. The dart could pass through without hitting vital organs. Anything hit with a particle beam would end up a pile of molten metal.

Using a magnetic clamp, Freeman anchored our sled to the hull of the ship, and I launched myself in through the door. Emergency lights flashed along the ceiling of the mostly darkened main corridor. This was the spine of the ship, a hall that led from the bridge to the galley.

When the hull of a capital ship is punctured, emergency bulkheads slide into place to prevent the depressurization from shooting sailors into space. In theory, the bulkheads created pressurized safety compartments in which sailors could wait for the atmospheric pressure to stabilize. In practice, the bulkheads created death chambers. Sometimes, sailors got lucky, and the bulkheads sealed them into compartments with armor or rebreathers. Usually, they didn't. The bulkheads opened once the atmosphere equalized, which meant that someone had patched the holes or that the atmosphere had bled out completely.

If the emergency bulkheads were still in place, we might find crew members trapped in the various compartments. If they had already retracted, we might run into armed sailors hoping for a little revenge.

Using night-for-day vision, I looked toward the bridge. Cruisers don't really have bridges; they have oversized cockpits. I saw no signs of life. I looked toward the aft of the ship.

"The emergency doors have retracted," I told Freeman, Mars, and Cutter on an open frequency. The ship would need extensive repairs. We'd miscalculated the damage when we set the trap, and we did not have a working shipyard for making repairs. I began to have doubts about Lieutenant Mars's ability to resurrect this spy ship.

Freeman drew his pistol as he entered the ship. His desire to save lives en masse would not prevent him from killing anyone who got in his way. He floated through the hole like a ghost passing through a wall. "Any signs of life?" he asked.

"Not on this deck," I said.

There were a couple of bodies, men iced up like statues. The smaller debris must have flushed out through the holes. Looking down the hall, I saw empty floors and battered walls.

"Do you have any idea where they stowed your computer?" I asked.

Not much of a conversationalist, even in the best of times, Freeman said, "Second deck." I should have guessed as much. The Unifieds usually housed the spy gear and communications equipment on that deck.

"Are we looking for anything in particular?" Ships like that one might have a thousand different computers on board.

"It might be attached to a broadcast apparatus," he said.

"A broadcast computer? You're looking for a specking broadcast computer?" I asked. In my experience, broadcast computers were strictly navigational tools, and they were big.

"Not the main broadcast engine. This will be attached to a small, secondary broadcast engine."

That made sense. The Mogats, an extinct band of terrorists who had plunged the Unified Authority into a costly civil war, established a pangalactic communications network using ships equipped with tiny broadcast engines to route their signals.

We might have knocked out the spy ship's air and lights, but her gravity generator still worked. We were standing, not floating above the floor.

"This wreck may be beyond repair," said Freeman.

I had the same fear. Deployed properly, a ship like this could turn the course of a war. I was just about to tell Lieutenant Mars to send over some engineers when I glimpsed the glow just beyond the next bulkhead.

"There's a live one," I told Freeman, not that he needed the heads-up. Always aware of everything around him, Freeman held his S9 out as he moved to cover.

In a calm voice, he said, "Shielded armor." He did not say "damn shielded armor" or "specking shielded armor," just "shielded armor," because he seldom wasted time assigning values and judgments.

The bastard walked right up the hall showing no fear at all. He might have been a Marine or sailor, but he was wearing the shielded combat armor of a Unified Authority Marine, the new shielded armor that the Unified Authority created after expelling us clones from its military. Knowing that we had no weapons that could penetrate his ethereal electromagnetic coat, the cocky son of a bitch walked right up to the hole we had created as an entrance and casually surveyed the area.

I hid behind a storage locker. Freeman knelt beside a desk.

The man did not carry a gun. The shielding prevented him from holding external weapons. That did not leave him unarmed. A fléchette-firing tube ran along the top of his right sleeve.

I needed a better hiding place. If the bastard spotted me, his depleted uranium fléchettes would cut through the locker, through me, and probably through the bulkhead behind me as well. Even a shot through the arm would be fatal since the fléchettes were coated with a neurotoxin.

"Get ready to run," I told Freeman. "I'm going to hit him with a grenade." The shrapnel would not penetrate his shielding, but the percussion from the blast would still knock him on his ass.

Freeman did not respond.

Scanning the cabin, his right arm out straight and slightly bent at the wrist, the man zeroed in on my hiding spot without seeing me. The bastard probably was a Marine, but a new Marine. It was hard to believe what passed as a Marine in the Unified Authority military.

In a situation like this, a real Marine would have shot first and checked later. This guy lacked that kind of instinct; but dressed in combat armor and waving a fléchette gun, he was still dangerous. I'd seen armor like his in action. The fléchette gun could fire thirty shots per second. The darts were tiny splinters. He probably had a thousand rounds packed in a pocket on his sleeve.

I made ready to throw my grenade.

"You want this ship in one piece?" Freeman asked.

"If you have a better idea . . ." I started.

Freeman pulled a thumb-sized device from his ammunition belt and slid it onto the desk.

Speaking over the interLink, Freeman said, "Look at the floor and don't look up." I had just enough time to avert my eyes before his device lit the area so brightly that the floor looked bleached beneath my knee.

The man in the Marine armor pivoted around and reached out with both hands like a drunk groping down a dark alley. He'd looked into the light before the tint shields had formed on his visors, and it temporarily blinded him. A moment later, the sensors in his visors would detect the lumens from Freeman's lamp, but by then it would be too late.

I looked away from the lamp to keep the tint shields from blocking my vision as I followed Freeman around the Marine and down the corridor. Freeman stopped long enough to place another light to shine at the man from the opposite direction. Now the bastard would be blinded until he groped his way out of the trap.

We ran down the corridor, hugging the walls in case the blinded Marine tried to shoot us. A short way down the corridor, we found stairs leading to the lower decks. I figured we would search together, watching each other's back. I figured wrong. Starting down the stairs, Freeman said, "Stall him."

"Stall him?" I asked.

"Keep him busy while I look for the computer."

As far as I knew, I was the highest-ranking officer in the Enlisted Man's military. I didn't take orders from anyone . . . anyone but Freeman. He knew more about the computer than I did.

"Got any suggestions about how to keep him busy without getting myself killed?" I asked as I watched him disappear down the stairs.

Questions like that could lead to all kinds of smart-ass answers, but Ray Freeman did not have a mind for humor. He said, "Call out if you get trapped," and vanished down the stairs.

Trapped, I thought to myself. I might have said it out loud as well. The thought resonated. I was on a relatively small ship, a hundred thousand miles from the nearest planet, fighting a Marine in armor my weapons could not penetrate. I was trapped.

The glare died out at the other end of the corridor. The Marine must have found Freeman's lamps and smashed them, leaving the long hall dark except for the flash of the emergency lights and the glow of his armor.

Hoping to catch the bastard's attention, I aimed my S9 and fired a few shots in his direction. The fléchettes were meant as a message. Even if they hit him, they would do no harm. But the stupid bastard didn't even notice the darts when they hit him.

Needing to grab his attention, I stepped into the open, catching the silly bastard by surprise. I fired three shots that hit him square in the face, then jumped down the first flight of stairs and waited for him to chase me.

Mission accomplished.

The Marine came after me; but when he reached the top of the stairs, he stopped. So he had sufficient brain cells to sense a trap, big specking deal. Even monkeys hide when they sense danger. I waited for the bastard to start down the stairs. When he didn't, I cautiously climbed back up to see what had happened.

Hoping to ambush me, the stupid son of a bitch had waited in an open hatch at the top of the stairs. I spotted him easily enough. The light from his shielded armor glowed like a moon.

"So much for the element of surprise, asshole," I muttered. Not only did the light from his shields ruin the ambush; it showed his position. He was kneeling. The glow only filled the bottom half of the hatch.

So I waited for him as he waited for me. I had my pistol out and aimed. When he peered out of the doorway to look for me, I shot him in the face. It was a moral victory. My fléchette hit him between the eyes, but it only hurt his pride.

Caught off guard, the Marine tried to spring up, lost his

footing, and fell on his ass. He climbed off the floor and re-turned fire; but by that time, of course, I had jumped back down the stairs.

I needed him to follow me to the bottom deck, so I waited on the landing. If he lost my trail and strayed onto the second deck, he might find Freeman.

Up at the top of the stairs, the glow of his shields diluted the darkness. The squirrelly Marine was in no rush to chase me. He moved cautiously, as if he thought I could actually hurt him. He aimed down the stairs and fired a dozen shots to flush me out of hiding.

Had I still been on that landing, his darts would have passed through my armor as if it weren't there. The needles themselves would only do minimal damage unless they hit a vital organ, but the poison would leave me numb as it para-lyzed my limbs and stopped my heart.

Under his shields, he had the same armor as I and the same smart visor. He could track body heat with his heat-vision lenses if he knew how to use them, but he wasn't paying atten-tion. I waited until he reached the landing by the second deck, then I drilled several shots into him. The fléchettes did no damage, but they kept the guy on my tail.

I called Freeman over the interLink as I ran to the bottom deck. He did not answer, but I knew he was listening. "Have you found your computer yet?" I asked, though I already knew the answer. We'd only parted ways a minute ago; there was no way he could have found it yet.

"You in trouble?" he asked.

"No, I'm good," I said. I heard a soft *thwack*, *thwack*, *thwack*, and looked back in time to see the last of the fléchettes bore a wire-thin hole in the landing wall above me. "I'm hav-ing a great time keeping our friend off the second deck."

Freeman did not respond.

"I think I'll take my new friend for a tour of the bottom deck," I said.

Freeman did not answer.

My job was to keep the Marine off the second deck so Freeman could search. No problem. The trap I had in mind could only be sprung on the bottom deck.

Trying not to offer myself as a target, I spun and fired a couple of shots to let the bastard know which way I was going.

Having survived being shot in the face multiple times, the Marine had come to realize that I could not harm him. Now he stormed the hall like a bull in a china shop, firing badly aimed fléchettes that skimmed the walls and the ceiling.

I leaped over dead sailors lying in frozen heaps along the floor. When we had blown holes in the hull, we exposed these men to space, with its vacuum conditions and true-zero temperatures. They froze in a flash, dying too quickly to suffocate; but as the spy ship's atmosphere leaked, bodies broke open from their own internal pressure.

The hall before me was long and straight, with no place for me to hide. If the Marine had had better training, he would have drilled those fléchettes into my back.

"How are you doing?" I asked Freeman. Only a minute had passed since the last time I asked.

"You okay?" he asked.

"Peachy," I said.

He did not respond.

The first of the landing bays was just a few yards up the corridor. The door slid open, revealing ten thousand square feet of empty hangar floor without paper, furniture, or bodies. Everything had been sucked out through the jagged thirty-foot wound in the far wall.

The area was full of shadows, but my night-for-day lenses let me see through the darkness. There was no other way out than the hatch I had just used, so I hid in a corner, squeezed in as best I could, and hoped I could sneak out of the dead end.

The hatch opened, and the glow of shielded armor spilled in. Seconds passed. Then the bastard walked into the landing bay without so much as a glance to the side, marching right past me. If this was what passed as a Marine in the Unified Authority these days, I was glad the clones revolted. No self-respecting clone Marine would make such a foolish mistake.

He walked straight to the far wall and examined the gaping hole that looked like a mural of open space. If I'd thrown a grenade, the percussion might have knocked the bastard through the gap, and he could have floated to the next galaxy for all I cared. I couldn't risk it, though. I waited a second, then dashed toward the hatch.

This time his fléchettes barely missed me. I saw holes appear on the wall ahead of me and laughed. He was toying with me. He thought he was a cat playing with a mouse, but he was mistaken. Sure, he had the protective armor, and that made him confident, but I controlled this fight. Unless he got very lucky, his time in the U.A. Marines was about to end.

"Any luck finding your computer?" I asked as I sprinted down the hall.

"Yes," Freeman said. "These guys were at Olympus Kri." Olympus Kri was another planet that the Avatari had burned.

"Sounds like they had a disaster fetish," I said.

"You safe?" asked Freeman.

"I have an angry Unified Authority Marine in shielded combat armor chasing me down a dead end," I said.

Freeman did not say anything. He knew the situation.

I said, "I've got things under control."

The next landing bay was almost right across the hall. I ran to the hatch, but it did not open. As I pushed off and started for the last landing bay, a trio of fléchette holes appeared in the wall near my head. The bastard's aim kept improving.

I streaked down the hall in a balls-out race. Cocky or not, this guy would win the fight if the next hatch did not open. Hell, he might get lucky even if it did.

I hurled myself at the hatch, and the door slid open. Bolting through as fast as I could, I tripped over a dead sailor, barely managed to catch my feet, and ran toward the transport that sat with its hatch open. I jumped over the frozen corpse of a dead tech lying on the ramp, entered the kettle, and hit the button to close the doors at the rear of the ship. Then I climbed the ladder that led to the cockpit three rungs at a time.

As I reached the top, I looked back over my shoulder. I could not see the doors at the bottom of the ramp, but I knew how slowly they moved. They were eighteen inches thick and made of metal. It would take them twenty seconds to close.

The man in the armor made it through the doors and up the ramp. I could not see him, but I saw the glow that his shields cast on the wall as he strolled up the ramp. He moved slowly, casually, probably keeping a wary eye for more grenades.

I slipped from the ladder to the catwalk that led to the cockpit. Then I knelt low against the metal walkway and watched the bastard as he reached the top of the ramp.

"I have the computer," Freeman said over the interLink.

Hidden and protected by a thick steel wall of transport construction, I lay on my back and laughed.

Freeman must have mistaken my laughter for combat strain. He asked, "Harris, where are you?"

"I'm fine," I said.

"What is the situation?" Freeman asked.

"I'm in a transport in the third landing bay."

"Where is the Marine?"

"You call this shithead a Marine?" I asked, still laughing. "I'll tell you what—the Unifieds are scraping the bottom of the barrel. The only thing this guy's trained for is KP duty or maybe scrubbing the head." As I said this, the doors at the back of the transport clanged shut. I was trapped in the transport with an enemy wearing shielded armor, and I could not have been happier about it.

"Harris, hang on. I'm on my way."

"Take your time, Ray," I said. "There's no rush."

The U.A. Marine knew enough about his armor to switch to heat vision. He either used heat vision or possibly radar. One way or another, he spotted me on the catwalk and fired. His fléchettes hit the iron walls and dropped to the floor. This bird was made to withstand missiles and particle beams, depleted uranium fléchettes could barely scratch it.

Tracking the guy with my heat vision, I sat with my S9 pistol ready and watched as the poor bastard wasted his endless supply of fléchettes. I laughed. "You can't hit me, asshole. Not from down there," I yelled. He didn't hear me. I was talking to myself.

Down on the deck, the guy kept firing fléchettes in my direction. I switched from interLink to external speaker on the off chance he might be listening. I yelled, "Hey, shit for brains, you're wasting ammunition."

In response, the bastard shot five more fléchettes, then yelled, "Get specked." The term, "speck," was sometimes used as a noun referring to bodily fluids and sometimes used as a verb referring to the transmission of those fluids. On the hierarchy of modern profanities, "speck" was as bad as a word could get.

"Have it your way," I called back. "You've been chasing me for about ten minutes now. That leaves you with about half an hour before the battery powering your shields runs out."

He answered with a flurry of needles. Some struck the ledge below me, some flew over the catwalk. Nothing came close to hitting me.

When he came to his senses, the bastard would realize that he had two choices—he could climb the ladder to come after me, or he could open the rear hatch and escape. Either way, he would need to lower his shields. The shields would prevent him from wrapping his hands around the ladder, and they would short out the circuits if he tried to work the hatch.

Using heat-vision lenses, I watched as he worked out his options. Hoping to keep me honest, he fired sporadic fusillades of fléchettes in my direction. After a minute or two, he started toward the ladder. The bastard must have known that his shields would repulse anything he touched, but he had to make sure.

I moved toward the edge of the catwalk on the off chance he was stupid enough to lower the shields and start climbing. He stood at the base of the ladder and weighed his options, growling like a caged animal and firing fléchettes into the impenetrable steel of the kettle walls.

Apparently rejecting the ladder as an option, he paced back and forth across the floor of the cargo hold. I could not see him, per se, just the red-orange oval of his heat signature. He walked toward one corner of the cabin, maybe looking for a better shot at me, then he stormed off in the other direction.

By this time, he had figured out an indisputable truth—he could not exit the transport without opening the rear hatch. There were only two mechanisms for opening that hatch. One was up in the cockpit, one was in the kettle. He walked to the panel at the far end of the kettle.

At that point, I needed to do more than track heat signatures—I needed to watch the bastard. Needing to catch him the moment he lowered his shields, I crawled to the edge of the catwalk and stared down at him.

He stood a foot from the panel with his back to me, staring

at the button. He stayed that way for several seconds, then spun and fired six shots my way. His shots were wild. Most of them struck the wall somewhere below me and ricocheted around the kettle.

Now we were both in trouble. He could not hit that button without lowering his shields; but I could not watch him without placing myself in his line of fire. Realizing my trap was not as bulletproof as I had surmised, I ducked back behind the ledge and used my heat-vision lenses to watch as his hand edged toward the button. He fired a couple of shots at me, reached for the button, and stopped. I could not tell if he was waiting to shoot me or looking at the button. When I rose to my knees, he fired. Suddenly, the bastard knew how to aim; his first shot missed me by an inch.

I dropped to my stomach. When I raised myself with my elbows, he fired again. In the brief glimpse I got, I saw him there, standing two feet from the button, his right arm pointing up toward me and his left probing toward the button. Like him, I was using heat-vision tracking. I switched to tactical view, the unenhanced view we used on the battlefield.

I rose to a crouch and dropped, not hoping to shoot so much as to keep the bastard honest. I wanted to keep him on his toes. I wanted him to know I was watching, waiting, biding my time until he dropped his shields; and then I would have my shot.

I wanted him to think that I was blind, but I was not blind, not anymore. He was using heat vision to track me. Using the tactical view, I could see the glow his shields projected on the wall.

Another moment passed, and he began shooting faster, maybe five shots per second. The shots cut a line above me, some pinged off the side of the catwalk.

And then he made his move. He lowered his shields, and the cabin went dark. The moment the cabin went dark, I rolled to my side and fired three shots blindly as I engaged my night-for-day lenses. Even before the lenses showed me the cabin floor, I instinctively knew I had hit the target.

The bastard lay on the cold steel deck, rolling and writhing like a fish on a line. Blood leaked out of his armor at the shoulder and gut. The two shots that hit him in the shoulder probably hurt more than the one in the gut, but it was the latter that would kill him.

I'd seen too many men kill the enemy who had dealt them the fatal blow, so I waited on the catwalk and watched as the poor bastard bled to death. I watched as his convulsions slowed into tremors, and his tremors slowly went still.

"Does the computer work?" I asked.

"I haven't tested it yet," he said.

That made sense. You'd want to make sure you had everything ready before you booted a computer that conjured up ghosts.

CHAPTER
FOUR

The Enlisted Man's Empire had men and ships and a recently rebuilt broadcast network. What we did not have were the "ghosts." We needed the computer from the spy ship to reach the Unified Authority's top secret ghosts.

Okay, well, I called them ghosts. In truth, they were virtual reproductions of William Sweetwater and Arthur Breeze, the two dead scientists who had helped thwart the Avatari's first invasion.

Shortly before they died, the real Sweetwater and Breeze allowed a team of medical technicians to scan their brains and take samples of their DNA. Somewhere along the line, the Unifieds used the scans and samples to re-create the scientists inside a computer. They used the DNA to construct virtual models of their bodies that were realistic enough to make their scanned brain waves feel right at home.

In order to keep the virtual versions of Sweetwater and Breeze from figuring out that they weren't real, the models had all of the original scientists' mental and physical flaws. In life, William Sweetwater had been an overweight, middle-aged dwarf who got winded climbing a single set of stairs. When virtual Sweetwater climbed a flight of stairs, his pulse rose dangerously high, and sweat stains formed under his arms. I'd placed a few calls to virtual Sweetwater. When he had to run to the monitor to catch the call, he came panting.

In his computer universe, virtual Arthur Breeze was a six-foot-six balding beanpole with dandruff and oily skin who needed to clean the grease from his glasses every couple of minutes. He stuttered when he became nervous, which was most of the time since he suffered from an intense inferiority complex.

The flaws were almost as entertaining as the men themselves.

But the tiny computer Freeman showed me had neither a broadcast engine for pangalactic communications nor the power to host the complex models of Sweetwater and Breeze.

"That's it?" I asked. "I played hide-and-seek with a guy in shielded armor for that?"

The computer was the size of a man's wallet, and most of it was screen. "Where's the broadcast engine?"

"Broken," said Freeman.

"Broken? So we're out of business," I said.

"The computer works, I just need to connect it to a broadcast engine before we can reach Sweetwater and Breeze," Freeman said.

"Did you have one in mind?" I asked. Broadcast engines were complex and dangerous machinery. You didn't find them lying around.

"The E.M.E. broadcast network," said Freeman. He was so big and so menacing, I sometimes wondered if he realized just how frightening he could be.

The Enlisted Man's Empire had a broadcast network. It was the backbone of the empire. Friend or foe, it didn't matter, I was not about to give a mercenary access to the network.

"You're out of luck, Ray," I said. "I won't give you that access."

He sat on the edge of my desk, staring down at me. His wide-set eyes reminded me of the barrels of a shotgun. Even though he spoke softly, his voice had a thunderlike rumble. The voice and the eyes were intimidating, but not as intimidating as the implicit threat of his enormous arms and chest.

Freeman sat silent for a moment, then he said, "You're going to need Sweetwater and Breeze if you're planning to evacuate planets."

"I'm not giving you our broadcast codes," I said.

Freeman's expression did not change. He did not smile or snarl or do anything threatening. He simply spoke in a quiet voice as he asked, "Are you saying that the Enlisted Man's Empire is going to abandon its planets and citizens?"

Oh, shit, I thought. With that simple question, he had served notice. If the Enlisted Man's Empire was no more committed to saving lives than the Unified Authority, his loyalties might shift.

I could have shot him, of course. We were on the *Churchill*, an E.M.N. fighter carrier. I had thousands of sailors and Marines at my disposal. Even the mighty Ray Freeman would not escape if I sounded the alarm . . . maybe. I did not want him as an enemy, and he made a powerful ally.

I weighed all of the possibilities in my mind, then I smiled, and said, "We won't have much of an empire if we let everybody die."

The compromise was obvious. Freeman probably expected it from the start. He said, "The computer stays with me. When we need to contact Sweetwater, I control the computer, and you control the broadcast access."

I was the commanding officer of the largest navy in the galaxy, and he was nothing more than a mercenary, but he had just proposed an equal partnership. I thought about it for a second, and said, "I can live with that."

Freeman and I sat side by side in a conference room on the *Churchill*. Freeman's little communications computer, now jacked into the ship's communications network, sat on the table between us.

Freeman toyed with the links going to his computer, and asked, "What time is it?"

I looked over at the wall and saw what Freeman already knew. "01:00 STC," I said. STC was short for "Space Travel Clock," the twenty-four-hour clock used for synchronized space travel.

"They're asleep," he said.

As nothing more than sophisticated computer animations, Sweetwater and Breeze should have been able to work around the clock; but they had been programmed to eat, sleep, and shit. They didn't know they were dead. No longer needing sleep might tip them off to their virtual state; and if they learned they were virtual, no one could predict how they might react. They might go into a depression or refuse to work.

If some virtual lab assistant answered our call, he'd undoubtedly warn the Unifieds that we had broken into their system. "Maybe we should wait until 10:00," I said. "We wouldn't want to disturb them."

Freeman, being Freeman, did not note the irony in the situation, and said, "They'll be in the lab by 07:00."

I nodded. "Not much we can do until then," I said, meaning there was not much for Freeman to do. I, on the other hand, had a hundred hours' worth of work to fit into the next six hours.

As Freeman took his communications device and left the conference room, I called Captain Cutter and asked him to join me.

I did not know Cutter well, and I needed to find ways to distinguish him from other clones. He was a standard-issue U.A. military clone. He stood five feet ten inches tall, had brown hair cut to regulation length, and brown eyes. Every clone of his make, which included every last sailor on the ship, fit Cutter's description.

The Unifieds did not consider clones to be human. Since standard-issue clones like Cutter were programmed to think they were natural-born, they tended to be a little antisynthetic as well. When clones like Cutter found out the truth, all hell would break loose. A gland built into their brains released a fatal hormone into their systems; it was a fail-safe that was supposed to prevent a clone rebellion. They called it the "Death Reflex."

When clones like Cutter looked in a mirror, their neural programming made them see themselves as blond-haired and blue-eyed. Like every clone, including me, Cutter had grown up thinking he was the only natural-born resident in an "orphanage" that trained military clones. He had memories programmed into his head. We all did.

Seeing himself as the only blond-haired, blue-eyed natural-born in the entire Enlisted Man's Navy, Cutter would naturally become suspicious if I did not recognize him. So would every other clone on the ship.

The door to the conference room opened, and in walked Captain Don Cutter. I pretended to recognize him when in fact the only thing that stood out was the eagle on his collar.

I was not the same make of clone as Cutter, by the way, though I was no less synthetic. I was a Liberator, a discontinued model with a penchant for violence. Instead of a gland with a deadly toxin, Liberators had a gland that released a mixture of testosterone and adrenaline into our blood during battle. They called that the "combat reflex," and it worked too well. My forerunners became addicted to violence, which was why my kind were discontinued and replaced by a class of clones with a fail-safe mechanism.

Cutter and I traded salutes and formalities, then I asked, "What is the status of your ship?"

"We wouldn't do well in a fight, but she'll get us where we want to go," he said.

"Can she broadcast?" I asked. Even as I asked it, I realized it was a dumb question.

"She broadcasted here," Cutter said without a hint of sarcasm. One thing I noticed about Cutter, he always gave me the benefit of the doubt. I had just asked an obvious question, and he did not call me on it.

"What happens if we find ourselves in a fight?" I asked.

"It depends who we're fighting, sir," Cutter said. "As things stand now, the *Churchill* should do right well against transports and civilian ships."

"How about U.A. battleships and carriers?" I asked.

"Permission to speak frankly, sir?"

"I wish you would."

"The attack at Olympus Kri specked us up good," he said, his formal tone now gone. "Our forward shield is fine, but our ass is exposed. If the enemy comes up behind us, we'll go down fast."

We had gone to Olympus Kri to help the Unified Authority evacuate the planet, then the bastards attacked us.

The Enlisted Man's Empire and the Unified Authority were entangled in an antagonistic triangle in which every side had two enemies. Our enemies were the Unified Authority, the Earth-bound empire that once ruled the Milky Way, and the Avatari, the alien race that was systematically destroying the galaxy for mining purposes. The Unifieds had to contend with us and the Avatari. The Enlisted Man's Empire and the Unified Authority would have loved to destroy the Avatari; but their world was in another galaxy. We were more concerned with survival than conquest.

So the Avatari came to Olympus Kri and incinerated the planet the same way they incinerated Terraneau. Working with the Unifieds, we managed to evacuate the population before the aliens arrived; then the Unifieds ambushed our ships. The *Churchill* was the only ship that escaped.

"They specked us up good," I agreed, reflecting on the other ships that did not manage to broadcast out of the trap. We lost our entire command structure when the Unifieds ambushed us at Olympus Kri.

I thought about what he had said. The U.A. Navy had newer ships than ours. Their ships had shields that wrapped around their hulls like constantly renewing second skins. Our ships had six independent shields that formed a box around the hull. If a shield gave out, parts of the ship were left unprotected.

"Can you repair the rear shields?" I asked.

"They got the antenna, sir. We're going to need to build a new rear array."

"I see," I said. "Has Lieutenant Mars had a look at it?"

"He says he can fix her if we take her into the dry docks."

I sighed, thanked Cutter for his report, and dismissed him. All in all, the news could have been worse. We had a working ship and a way to communicate with Sweetwater and Breeze. Given a little time, Mars and his engineers might even get the spy ship operational. All just a matter of time, but we did not have time.

Glad to have a moment to myself, I reviewed the situation in my head.

The good news was that we had liberated the Golan Dry Docks from the Unified Authority, so we had facilities for repairing the *Churchill*. Fixing the spy ship was another story. Mars might be able to make her broadcast-worthy if he got her to the dry docks, but the dry docks were thousands of light-years away. We couldn't get her to the dry docks without broadcasting.

And then there were the Avatari. Over the last two weeks, the bastards had attacked New Copenhagen, Olympus Kri, and Terraneau. They were destroying planets every three or four days. Unless we stopped them, we'd be galactic nomads in another few months.

The room was oblong, brightly lit, its nearly soundproofed walls devoid of art and windows. Sitting in the well-lit silence, I stared straight ahead, taking in the sterile emptiness around me.

I could not win this war, yet I felt compelled to fight. We could attack and defeat the Unifieds, but they were more of a distraction than a problem. They had massacred our leadership while holding up a flag of truce, but we wouldn't make the mistake of trusting them again.

If it came to a fight with the aliens, on the other hand, we didn't stand a chance. We couldn't even strike back at them if we wanted.

How the speck do you defend planets from spontaneous combustion? If anyone could figure out a solution, it was Sweetwater and Breeze. Freeman was right, we needed them. Finding that communications computer was worth the risk . . . assuming they would be willing to help us. The last time I had spoken with them, they had not known that the Unified Authority and the Enlisted Man's Empire had gone to war. Hell, they didn't even know that the enlisted men had an empire; they thought we were loyal to the Unified Authority.

I sat lost in my thoughts, for maybe fifteen minutes.

The Avatari did not attack arbitrary targets. They went after the planets we had reclaimed after their first sweep through the galaxy. Once they finished attacking our planets, they would turn their sights on Earth. Sooner or later, we might need to evacuate the Unifieds from Earth along with the people living on our planets.

Thinking about the situation made my head hurt, the kind of low, thudding ache you get with a hangover. I sat and I stared and I rubbed my temples, and finally I got up, still staring blankly ahead, and left the conference room. I went to the temporary quarters that Cutter had assigned me in officer country—a comfortable suite generally reserved for visiting politicians, with its own office and a spacious shower in the head.

When I opened the door to my billet, I found Ava waiting for me. Ava Gardner, the cloned incarnation of a twentieth-century movie star, was my ex. When the Unifieds decided to jettison all clones from their republic, they didn't just aim that animosity at military clones; they extended it to the only known cloned goddess in the galaxy.

First, she was under my protection, and the next thing I knew, we were in love. Well, maybe I was in love. She moved on before I did. Thinking they were doing me a favor, my engineers rescued Ava and her natural-born lover when the Avatari incinerated Terraneau.

I'm not being fair. Ava left me because I talked nonstop about conquering Earth when I should have been saying sweet nothings in her ear. She thought I was married to the Corps. She was right.

"How did you get in here?" I asked as I entered the room. Officers' quarters were supposedly as secure as prison cells.

She stood about ten feet away from me, swaying slightly and looking nervous. She wore a wrinkled yellow dress, and her hair and makeup needed tidying, but that couldn't be helped; her clothes, makeup, and brushes would have gone up in smoke when the Avatari fried Terraneau.

"A sailor let me in," Ava said.

"They're not supposed to let passengers into officers' quarters," I said.

"He thought you'd be glad to see me," she said.

I'll bet he did, I thought, and his respect for me had probably doubled. "He was wrong," I said. I was lying.

I wouldn't have described Ava as top-heavy, but she had a notable figure. Fire smoldered in her wide-set olivine-colored eyes. She knew how to smile at a man and dismiss him at the very same moment. I did not know if she could read every man, but she always seemed to know what I was thinking.

"Wayson, I need to be with you," she said, sounding so damned sincere. She pressed herself against me, trusting that I would wrap my arms around her. When I did not respond, she took a step away from me.

She usually referred to me as "Harris," but she did it in a way that was informal and endearing. When she became brassy, I was "Honey" and when she was angry, I was "Dear." And now, having seen the destruction of Terraneau, she added "Wayson" to her vocabulary.

"You need to be with me?" I asked. "You moved on, remember?"

"Everything changed yesterday. I don't think I ever understood your world," she said. "Yesterday it became real." Here came the tears. Right on time. God, I hated dealing with women.

It wasn't the crying that bothered me. I'd seen grown men cry. Hell, I'd seen Marines get weepy. Who would not cry after seeing an entire population cremated. What bothered me was the way women cried, like they weren't embarrassed about it . . . like they expected you to do something about it.

"I don't see how that changes anything," I said.

"Wayson, they killed my girls."

"Go tell it to . . ."

"I don't love Kyle. I never did," Ava said as she stepped back in my orbit. She reached out and placed her hand against my chest.

She might have been acting or sincere or possibly she was acting but thought she was sincere. I believed her.

I did not know if she was my roommate or my girlfriend, but we spent the next few hours together.

CHAPTER
FIVE

Location: Planet A-361-F
Galactic Position: Solar System A-361
Astronomic Location: Bode's Galaxy

Only the captains of the four ships saw the video feed; Admiral Yamashiro would not risk showing it to anyone else.

They met in a conference room on the command deck of the *Sakura*, Yamashiro's flagship. First they watched the mission through Illych's eyes—video feed recorded by the camera in his visor. The master chief petty officer had not known it, but the commandLink broadcasted his entire mission to the transport. Communications transponders on the transport relayed the signal back to the fleet.

The captains saw the bleak landscape and the giant silos. They watched in silence as Illych scraped ice and analyzed it. A timer in the corner of the screen showed that the SEALs had been on the planet for ten minutes and seventeen seconds when the light appeared in the sky.

Yamashiro stood at the front of the room. He said, "Matsuda thinks the aliens detected the infiltration pods the moment they entered the atmosphere." Matsuda Takashi ran Fleet Intelligence.

"How could they have done that?" asked Captain Yokoi Shigeru. "We cannot track those pods. How would the aliens track them?"

Yamashiro ignored the question, and the video feed resumed with Illych telling his men to take positions. When Humble spun around to fire rounds at the silo, a small window appeared in a corner of the screen. The window showed the scene through the late Chief Petty Officer Humble's eyes as his bullets exploded against the silo's icy surface.

"I wish he had tried a laser and a particle beam as well," said Takeda Gunpei, the only captain with an engineering background.

Captain Miyamoto said, "Good point. You should tell him if you see him." They all knew that the SEALs did not return; but Miyamoto Genyo was a hard-ass, an old-style Japanese military man who never smiled and had no sympathy for weakness. "You may soon get your chance."

The feed showed the globe of light with creatures forming inside it and the ion curtain forming across the sky. The transmission ended, but the video feed continued. The screen showed the planet as seen from the stealth transport that launched the pods.

The image on the screen looked like a barren planet partially dipped in white gold.

"The 'sleeving' process went quickly," said Takeda as he watched the shiny skin move across the atmosphere.

A jolt ran across the planet, and the ion curtain dissolved, revealing a partially imploded planet. A flat and fiery dent showed on the otherwise-iron-colored globe. With the planet's symmetry broken, it looked as though the stress of its own rotation might cause it to come apart. "The *kage no yasha* detonated their ejector pods," said Miyamoto, a smile of admiration on his face. "I am glad we gave them a traditional farewell."

Miyamoto was the captain of the *Onoda*, a battleship named after a Japanese soldier who fought in the Second World War. At the end of the war, Onoda hid in the jungles of the Philippines for twenty-nine years rather than surrender. Like the man for whom his ship was named, Miyamoto held those who died in battle in high regard.

"So we have destroyed an alien way station on an obscure planet. What have we learned?" asked Yamashiro.

"We know they can detect the pods," said Takahashi Hironobu, captain of the *Sakura*. Takahashi was Yamashiro's son-in-law.

Yamashiro grunted, a sound that might have signaled agreement or disgust. "We have been searching their galaxy for nearly three years. Why has it taken the aliens so long to detect us?"

"They don't have a navy," said Captain Yokoi. As the youngest of the ships' captains, he generally remained quiet during staff meetings, but this time he spoke up. "Maybe they did not view us as a threat because we were in open space."

"We have entered their solar system. They won't ignore us anymore," said Miyamoto.

Though he seldom agreed with the "old man," Takahashi agreed with Miyamoto this time. He said, "If they detected the SEALs, they must know we are here as well."

Admiral Yamashiro's manner remained gruff, even when answering his son-in-law. He said, "That is a possibility. What do you suggest?"

"We must proceed with caution. They may attack at any time," said Takahashi.

Two of the other captains, Yokoi and Takeda, agreed. Looking around the table, Takahashi could see it in their expressions and their posture. Takeda sat perfectly erect, an excited expression on his face. Captain Yokoi turned toward Takahashi and gave him a furtive nod.

"Cautious, yes, but not timid like frightened mice," growled Miyamoto. The oldest of the ships' captains, he often harped about honor and the Japanese way.

Takahashi sighed. Three of the four captains agreed, but democracy did not exist in the Japanese Fleet. Admiral Yamashiro placed more weight on Miyamoto's opinion than the opinions of any other officer, and Yamashiro's decisions were the law.

"We need to divide the fleet. If our ships travel as a pack, an attack on one ship could destroy us all," said Takahashi. He looked at Yokoi and Takeda for support, but they did not meet his gaze. Takeda, an older man with white hair along his temples, stared down at the table. Yokoi now stared up at Yamashiro, ignoring the rest of the room.

"Lone ships lose battles that fleets might win," said Miyamoto.

Yamashiro grunted his approval. He did not smile, though. *You used to smile,* Takahashi thought. *Back in the days before the aliens and the Mogats, you used to smile.* Yamashiro Yoshi had been a politician back then, before he appointed himself admiral of the fleet.

Having spent the last three years searching Bode's Galaxy, the Japanese sailors had no way of knowing that the Avatari had returned to the Milky Way. The last outdated intelligence they heard was that the Unified Authority had won the battle for New Copenhagen, and the aliens had left the galaxy. They did not know that the Avatari had returned and incinerated New Copenhagen and Olympus Kri. They did not know that the Unified Authority had abandoned its military clones and that the clones declared a civil war.

"Now that we have destroyed A-361-F, the next closest planet is A-361-D," said Yamashiro.

"What about A-361-E?" asked Yokoi.

The name of the solar system was Bode Galaxy A-361. A-361-F, the planet Illych and his SEALs destroyed, was the outermost planet in the system. A-361-E was the next planet in terms of distance from the center of the solar system.

"It's on the opposite end of the solar system," said Yamashiro.

"Admiral, why bother with the outer planets at all? We should bypass the outer planets and attack the planets closest to the star," said Takeda. "The aliens will be on the planet that is the same distance from this star as Earth is from the sun."

"That's quite a gamble," said Admiral Yamashiro. "Why should we take such a risk?"

"When the aliens entered the Milky Way, they only attacked the planets we ourselves would inhabit."

Miyamoto leaned forward so he could face Takeda. The old warhorse and the officer with the background in engineering, they were opposites and adversaries at every meeting. Takeda was slender, dapper, a man in his fifties with an interest in science. Miyamoto, who trained in the traditional arts of *Judo* and *Iaido*, was squat and powerful. His uniform barely fit over his massive shoulders, chest, and neck.

Miyamoto said, "The Avatari are miners, Takeda-san. They do not populate the planets, they conquer, they mine. Though a man would want to collect the content of a gold mine, he would not necessarily want to live in it.

"If we proceed to an inner planet, and they have bases on A-361-E or A-361-D, we could find ourselves attacked from every side."

"All the more reason to split up the fleet," said Takahashi.

"If we send one ship to each planet, we can search the solar system in a single day."

Miyamoto clapped his hands, and said, "An excellent idea. We send one battleship to each of the remaining planets; and when one of them does not return, we will know where the aliens are hiding."

As the meeting ended, Yamashiro cornered Takeda Gunpei, the only one of the captains with a background in engineering. He fixed Takeda with a businesslike glare, and the two men sat silently as the other officers filed out of the room.

"When that pod exploded, was it as powerful as a nuclear bomb?" asked Yamashiro. He claimed no understanding of science or engineering. His background was in politics.

Before joining the Japanese Fleet, Takeda, who was nearly as old as the admiral, had worked as a professor of space travel and engineering. Now he slipped comfortably back into the role of the teacher. He smiled, and said, "It all depends on the size of the bomb. Judging by the damage, I would estimate that the explosion from the field-resonance engine was forty or fifty times more powerful than any nuclear explosion on record; but that is just a guess."

Though he tried to hide it, Yamashiro could not hide his shock. Both fear and anger showed in his normally unreadable expression. "We have five thousand of those vehicles aboard our ships."

Takeda smiled, and said, "There's no reason to worry about the pods, sir. They pose no more threat to your ships than the torpedoes in the armory, maybe even less of a threat."

"Twelve of them destroyed an entire planet," said Yamashiro.

"The energy they produced destroyed the planet. The pods themselves are nothing more than a generator and a battery. When the battery is overcharged, it explodes. Without the charge, the battery is of little consequence."

"Perhaps we should store them in our transports," Yamashiro said.

Calm as ever, Takeda pointed out that the Fleet did not have enough transports to carry five thousand S.I.P.s.

Yamashiro took in the information and nodded, all the while toying with the idea of dumping excess pods in space.

CHAPTER
SIX

Location: Planet A-361-D
Galactic Position: Solar System A-361
Astronomic Location: Bode's Galaxy

Admiral Yamashiro did not often meet with SEALs. They were enlisted men. He was an officer. So many layers existed between them that he felt irritated that he now had to meet with Senior Chief Petty Officer Corey Oliver, the new leader of the SEALs. He considered the indignity of meeting with the SEAL a part of his penance.

Ten years earlier, Yamashiro had been the governor of Ezer Kri, one of the 180 populated planets of the Unified Authority. In an effort to create cohesion in the republic, the founders of the Unified Authority had populated their planets with a mixture of races and ethnicities.

The first governor of Ezer Kri, however, had been Japanese. While other administrators accepted the settlers they'd been given, Takuhiro Yatagei traded and switched personnel until he had a sizable minority of Japanese colonists. Since the days of Yatagei, all of the governors of Ezer Kri had been Japanese. They acted as the guardians of their culture.

Shortly after Yamashiro became governor, the people voted to change the name of the planet from Ezer Kri to Shin Nippon—"New Japan"; but their timing was off. A civil war was brewing. Key members of the U.A. Congress saw the name change as a sign of insurrection. With the Unified Authority Navy imposing martial law on their planet, the Japanese fled Ezer Kri and joined the real insurrection.

Yamashiro was nothing if not pragmatic. Seeing that his new allies would soon betray him, he stole four self-broadcasting battleships and returned to the Unified Authority. Had it not been for the return of the Japanese Fleet, the Morgan Atkins Believers would have won the war; but the Unified Authority did not easily forgive. The Linear Committee initially allowed Yamashiro and his people to settle in the islands of old Japan; then, after the U.A. military defeated the aliens on New Copenhagen, the Linear Committee sent the Japanese Fleet to locate and destroy the enemy.

To assist with the assault, the U.A. Navy assigned its twelve thousand cloned SEALs on the mission. Speaking among themselves, Yamashiro and his captains referred to the clones as *kage no yasha*, shadow demons.

Yamashiro picked up the recon photos on his desk. Before approaching planets, the Japanese sent out stealth transports that deployed spy satellites. The images from A-361-D showed a barren planet with a brutal atmosphere.

There were no military installations on Planet A-361-D. In fact, there were no signs of any kind of development. The planet was a gas giant, its surface a bed of unrecognizable gases. Installations had been built, however, on the two moons orbiting A-361-D.

One of the moons, designated "A-361-D/Satellite 1," had a long flat deck that might have been a landing strip. It measured 12.315 miles long and 12.298 miles across. It crossed a slightly raised plain that appeared to be made out of the same white substance as the soil around it.

A-361-D/Satellite 1 was a large moon, nearly three thousand miles across, and had a thin-but-discernible atmosphere. The second moon, A-361-D/Satellite 2, was eight hundred miles in diameter, considerably smaller than the moon orbiting Earth, with no atmosphere whatsoever.

On this moon, the reconnaissance satellites found a ring of small buildings that looked like warehouses. They stood twenty feet tall with flat roofs and no windows. With no wind to beat against them and no elements to wear them down, the buildings were perfectly preserved. Without running more tests, Intelligence had no methods for predicting the ages of the buildings. As one of the specialists said, "For all we know, these buildings could have been built a billion years ago."

Abandoned, thought Yamashiro. Looking at the bleak surfaces of the moons, Yamashiro wondered how the SEALs dealt with fear as they prepared for missions. They knew the risks. They were ugly and vicious, but they were also intelligent. Yamashiro admired their courage.

The satellites had scanned for footprints, tire tracks, and landing points, and found nothing. If it were possible for buildings to spontaneously generate, he would have believed that the buildings on Satellite 2 had done just that.

Yamashiro sat behind his desk feeling slightly sick to his stomach. He disliked looking at the SEALs so much that it nauseated him. The ships' captains, almost all of them younger men, made jokes about their appearance. That was fine for them, they were young and foolish.

Yamashiro was a man in his sixties. He recognized the SEALs' intelligence and their honor. They accepted dangerous assignments and never complained. They did not seek attention. From what Yamashiro had observed, the *kage no yasha* behaved in a manner more Japanese than any of his officers.

Yamashiro pressed the button on the intercom that connected him to his assistant, and growled, "Arakawa, please send the senior chief in."

"Yes, sir," she answered. He could hear the ease in her voice. Though the SEALs avoided contact with the women of the fleet, most of the women liked the clones.

The door opened, and Anna Arakawa, Yamashiro's assistant, showed the SEAL into the office. Yamashiro noticed the way Arakawa smiled at the SEAL, and he sneered.

Addressing the SEAL in English, Yamashiro said, "I hope I did not keep you waiting too long," as he stood and returned the SEAL's salute. He knew precisely how long he had kept the SEAL waiting—seventeen minutes. His assistant had signaled when the SEAL arrived, and he'd looked at his clock.

"No, sir," said Senior Chief Oliver.

They remained standing. Yamashiro knew that the SEAL would not sit down until given permission, and he enjoyed testing the clone's tolerance. "Would you like coffee or tea?"

"No, sir."

Yamashiro sat down. Though he would have enjoyed leaving the SEAL on his feet, Yamashiro did not like staring up to see him. He finally said, "Have a seat."

The only seat was ten feet from Yamashiro's desk. Oliver did not move it closer to the desk. Without a word, he went to the chair and sat down.

"The mission on A-361-F did not go as expected," said Yamashiro.

"Were there casualties, sir?"

"There were no survivors," said Yamashiro.

Oliver took the news in silence, his expression unreadable. Yamashiro forced himself to meet the senior chief's gaze. *Kage no yasha,* he thought to himself. *A nose like a Chinese dragon. The eyes of a demon. The gray skin of a cadaver.*

"I will send you the video feed from the mission. Illych and his men performed honorably.

"Since he has not returned, I am promoting you to master chief petty officer effective immediately." Still sitting at his desk, Yamashiro said, "I have every confidence in your ability, Master Chief."

"Thank you, sir," said Oliver.

I wonder if they talk among themselves? Yamashiro thought. He couldn't remember ever hearing any SEAL utter more than ten words at a time.

"I will also send you satellite photos of A-361-D."

"Are there aliens on that planet, sir?" asked Oliver.

"No. Not on the planet. We have discovered structures on two of the moons. This mission should be similar to the mission on A-361-F," Yamashiro said, wondering what emotions the SEAL kept hidden.

The SEAL clone showed no reaction when he heard that they'd run an operation similar to the one in which his fellow SEALs had died. He sat still in his chair, his hands on his lap, his feet flat on the floor, his gaze not quite meeting Yamashiro's. In Japanese culture, you never looked your superior in the eye. Yamashiro wondered how the SEAL clones had learned this.

"We will reach the moons in twenty hours. Prepare a reconnaissance team for the operation."

"Yes, sir."

"I want to send one hundred men on this mission, fifty to each moon. Perhaps if we send a larger force, we will have better success against the enemy," Yamashiro said, though he had his doubts. From the little of the battle he'd seen, Illych and his men never stood a chance.

"Yes, sir."

Yamashiro looked at the newly minted master chief and felt dissatisfied with the way the interview had gone. He felt as if he had not given the man his full due. "You may be wondering why we are sending men to these installations instead of attacking them from space."

"No, sir," said Oliver.

"No?"

"No, sir. I would not presume to question your orders."

Yamashiro believed this, but he still felt the need to explain. "As you will see from the video feed, Master Chief Illych destroyed A-361-F by detonating his stealth infiltration pods. We did not fire on that planet. Perhaps the master chief and his team would still be alive if we had.

"Illych and his men launched from a cloaked transport, flying stealth infiltration pods. We do not know anything about the aliens' technology; but there is little chance they could trace the landing team to our ships. If we fired on the planet instead of sending a team, the aliens would certainly be aware of our ships.

"We have invaded an alien empire with four ships. We are badly outnumbered by an enemy with superior technology. If I must lose men to keep my ships hidden . . . I am willing to make that sacrifice."

"Yes, sir," said Oliver.

Yamashiro nodded, and said, "Master Chief, as the highest-ranking member of the SEALs, you will oversee the operation from this ship."

There was neither hostility nor complaint in Oliver's voice as he asked, "Sir, wouldn't that qualify as a dereliction of duty? As the highest-ranking man on the team, I am supposed to . . ."

"Master Chief, you will be violating a direct order if you assign yourself to this mission," said Yamashiro.

Oliver did not raise an eyebrow or cock his head. His lips did not twitch, and he did not look away from Yamashiro though his gaze still fell just below the admiral's eyes.

Yes, thought Yamashiro. *He is very Japanese.*

"Sir, if you are concerned for my welfare . . ."

Yamashiro scowled and raised a hand to stop the SEAL. *These are the true Kamikaze,* he thought. *He has no fear of death.* And then he lied. "I do not have time to worry about your welfare.

"Sending your highest-ranking man into an action is inefficient. Commanding officers remain with the fleet and coordinate the movements. I was not aware that Illych accompanied the team to A-361-F. If I had been, I would not have allowed it."

"Sir . . ." Oliver began.

Yamashiro shook his head to signal that he did not want to continue the discussion. "You have your orders."

"Yes, sir."

A moment of silence passed, then Yamashiro asked, "Do you have any questions, Master Chief?"

"Yes, sir. Did Illych accomplish anything on A-361-F?"

Yes. Yes he showed us that detonating S.I.P.s can destroy an entire planet. We learned that the aliens can detect our movements even when we cannot detect them ourselves. We learned that the aliens can detect us and defeat us from halfway across the solar system in six minutes.

Yamashiro kept these thoughts to himself, and said, "We'll be in position by A-361-D in twenty hours, Master Chief. Have your men ready."

"Yes, sir," said Oliver.

Yamashiro looked away from the SEAL, and said, "That will be all."

SEVEN

If Yamashiro did not want Oliver to show the video feed to all of his SEALs, he should have voiced his preference. The SEALs shared information unless given orders to conceal it. Oliver routed copies of the video feed to the senior chiefs on each of the four battleships; and they, in turn, held mass briefings in which they showed the footage to their men.

Master Chief Oliver sat in the back of a large auditorium with his two closest friends watching the video feed along with his men. No one in the auditorium spoke a word until the feed ended. When the lights came on, the SEALs divided themselves by platoon and discussed what they had seen. Oliver and his two friends, Senior Chief Jeff Harmer and Senior Chief Brad Warren, remained where they were.

"What did you see?" asked Oliver.

Down in the gallery, chief petty officers led similar discussions.

"We can't outgun them," said Warren. "It doesn't look like we can even touch them."

"Agreed," said Oliver.

"They only sent five defenders," said Warren.

"What's your point?"

"They must have had a pretty good idea about how many men we had, or they would have sent a larger force to intercept us."

"Maybe they didn't have anyone else available," said Harmer.

Warren shook his head, and replied, "They always sent armies of fifty thousand soldiers on New Copenhagen. It didn't matter how many men we sent, they always sent fifty thousand."

"But if we caught them by surprise," Harmer began.

"They could only find five men . . . Are you joking?" asked Warren.

"Okay, so you think they counted our caskets?" Oliver asked.

"Aren't the caskets untraceable?" asked Warren.

"They are to us . . . with our technology," said Oliver. "Who knows what they have. For all we know, they may be able to track us by our brain waves."

"How would you track an S.I.P.?" asked Warren.

"Light field, vision, and sound tracking are out; but who's to say they don't have technology that senses every time anything breaches their atmosphere," said Harmer.

Warren gave Harmer an incredulous glare, and asked, "How in the world did you come up with that?"

"It's Occam's razor, yes? The simplest explanation . . .

"Their technology is more advanced than ours, but from what we know, it's centered around the use of tachyons and particles. Invisible or not, infiltration pods are still made out of matter. They still caused a physical disruption when they entered an atmosphere. Matter displaces matter, it's going to cause a disruption.

"The simplest solution is that the aliens counted the disruptions."

Senior Chief Warren muttered, "A tachyon early-warning system . . . like a burglar alarm. How do we get around something like that?"

Oliver asked, "Do either of you see any holes in the theory?"

Neither of them did, so the discussion moved ahead.

"They may have been bulletproof, but that final explosion did them in," said Warren. He enjoyed looking for holes in everything Harmer suggested. They were friends, but they were also rivals.

"We don't know that," said Oliver. "We know what it did to the planet, and we know that the tachyon curtain dissolved, but the alien avatars may have survived."

"The avatars are made of tachyons. If the explosion dispersed the tachyons, then we can take it for granted that the individual avatars were destroyed," said Harmer.

"That is the first time anyone has detonated a field-resonance engine. We don't know how much radiation it generated. Maybe it was the radiation that destroyed the curtain," said Oliver.

"But we all agree that the caskets did the job, right? I mean, come on, those babies zapped the whole planet," said Warren.

Harmer agreed. He said, "They are our best weapon."

"They may be our only weapon," said Oliver.

"So do we win the war by blowing ourselves up?" asked Warren. He did not seem bothered by the idea, just curious.

"We win the war by any available means," said Oliver. He thought about using them as torpedoes instead of transports. They flew themselves. So long as they were preprogrammed to overcharge and explode, they did not need live cargo for seek-and-destroy missions.

Harmer and Warren agreed.

Earthdate: November 20, A.D. 2517

Master Chief Oliver looked at the time. Two hours to go before the launch. In another hour, he would board a shuttle to the *Onoda* and escort one hundred of his men to their Kamikaze farewell. He would watch as they drank the ceremonial sake. They would leave on a hazardous mission, and he would call in their orders from the safety of a ship. They would face danger, and he would command them from far away. Oliver chided himself for hiding on a ship while his men faced the enemy on otherwise-uninhabited moons. He felt humiliated.

Replacing Emerson Illych as master chief of the SEALs was a nightmare for Oliver. Like an undergraduate second-stringer replacing an injured varsity athlete, Oliver saw himself as having inherited the promotion instead of earning it. He thought about Illych's dying on A-361-F while he would not go on the mission to A-361-D, and experienced a stab of the self-loathing that had been hardwired into every SEAL clone's brain.

He went to the landing bay and boarded an interfleet shuttle that flew him to the *Onoda*. Five Japanese sailors rode the same flight. They were enlisted men, as he was. Oliver did not speak to the sailors, and they paid little attention to him as they talked loudly among themselves in Japanese.

They were not really ignoring him, though. English was the first language on Ezer Kri, as it was in all of the 180 colonies. Many of the colonists learned to speak Japanese and read *Kanji* out of pride in their heritage, but English remained their first and native language. Had a SEAL clone not been on their shuttle, the sailors would have spoken in English.

Bred for stealth and almost invisible, Oliver told himself.

He sat alone in the back of the shuttle for the ten-minute flight. A few rows ahead, the sailors chatted among themselves, confident in the knowledge that the master chief could not understand them. One of them commented that Oliver had the face of a bat. Another said, "Not all bats are that ugly. I once saw a fruit bat that was much better-looking than this *kage no yasha*."

The sailors laughed.

Had the sailors been paying more attention, they might have noticed Oliver ignoring them a little too much. Some of their chuckling should have caught his attention.

Had Yamashiro read Oliver's profile a little more closely, he would have seen that the SEALs learned languages just by hearing them spoken. The ability was built into their brains. Corey Oliver spoke Japanese better than the sailors on the shuttle. Sitting quietly in his seat, pretending not to hear them, he corrected their grammatical mistakes in his head.

Oliver fantasized about asking the sailors for directions to Captain Miyamoto's office in Japanese. He imagined the stunned looks on their faces and smiled. But Illych gave strict orders to the SEALs not to speak Japanese in public, and Oliver understood the wisdom of that decision. If he spoke Japanese to these men, he would humiliate them. They would know that he had heard them, and they would be ashamed. Oliver did not want to humiliate them.

The shuttle landed. Oliver waited for the sailors to leave the ship. He gave them another minute to leave the landing bay, then he rose from his seat and left as well.

Two of his SEALs met him as he came off the shuttle. "Do I have a face like a bat?" Oliver asked as he joined his friends.

"Maybe a really ugly one," said Senior Chief Harmer.

"Have you been eavesdropping on sailors again?" asked Senior Chief Warren. "Just ignore them."

Harmer laughed. "Listen to him," he said. "He's always complaining because some sailor . . ."

"He asked what my face looked like before it caught on fire," Warren explained.

"He wasn't speaking to you," Harmer said.

"But he was talking about me."

"Well, yeah. But you really are ugly."

"You have the same face I do," said Warren.

Harmer looked mortified. He looked down at the ground, then briefly met Warren's gaze, and said, "That's low."

Warren looked to Oliver for help. "See what I mean? He treats me like this all the time."

Oliver only shrugged, and said, "You shouldn't let it get to you."

They started toward the compound in which the SEALs lived and trained.

All three SEALs might have been thinking the same thing, but Warren was the one who voiced it. "I'm sorry you can't come with us," he said, and the joking fell away from his voice.

"I wanted to go on the mission," said Oliver.

"Everybody knows that," said Harmer. "Give us a little credit."

A few silent moments passed, then Harmer and Warren began joking back and forth, their banter coming across like a play they had rehearsed to bolster the master chief's spirits. Warren made himself the butt of the jokes, spurring Oliver and Harmer to use him as their fall guy; but Oliver's mood only became darker.

"You know, it's not going to be like Illych's mission," said Warren. "You saw the files. It's a flat surface. That's all it is, probably just an abandoned landing strip. I bet the only thing we find is a million-year-old sign that says, 'Keep off the grass.'"

Oliver tried to smile, but he felt so humiliated.

Still hoping to raise the master chief's mood, Warren added, "Honestly, the aliens won't even bother coming after us, not on a moon like that. They probably forgot the place exists."

They reached the compound but did not get the chance to step inside. A young Japanese ensign waited for them at the door. Short by Japanese standards, the ensign stood five-eight and towered over the SEAL clones. He wore a blue uniform, so dark it was almost black.

"Captain Miyamoto has sent for you," said the ensign.

Already wallowing in insecurities, Oliver jumped to conclusions. He assumed this meant he would not be allowed to attend his men's Kamikaze farewell. At first he was angry, then he felt more ashamed than ever. Maybe he did not belong at the ceremony. Maybe a leader who did not accompany his men on a suicidal mission did not deserve to attend their last ceremony.

Oliver saluted and acknowledged the order. He turned to Warren, tried to sound upbeat, and said, "Give my regards to Admiral Yamashiro."

"The admiral is not here," said the ensign.

Not here? thought Oliver. *It's not just me. He's dismissing the SEALs from his mind. Perhaps we haven't lived up to his expectations.* As these thoughts ran through his mind, the master chief began to believe he had dishonored his men. It was not a rational thought, and he knew it. It was part of his neural programming. He knew that as well, but he could not do anything to change it.

Oliver did not speak as he followed the ensign up to the bridge. He considered all the things he might have done wrong and all the reasons Yamashiro might have for dismissing him. Only a day had passed since he took command of the SEALs. The only misdeed that came to mind was showing the video feed of Illych's mission to his men.

They passed several sailors on the way to Miyamoto's office, both male and female. The men mostly ignored Oliver. A pretty female petty officer third class smiled at him. The ensign noticed this and scowled. Oliver pretended not to see her.

Rumor had it that the SEALs protected the female sailors in the Japanese Fleet. In the three years that the Fleet had been in Bode's Galaxy, none of the women had been raped or assaulted. The women credited the SEALs for the men's law-abiding behavior.

The SEALs did not fraternize with women. Because they saw themselves as hideous, they spoke to almost no one, especially not women. When women looked in their direction, the SEALs turned away and felt ashamed.

The ensign took Oliver to Captain Miyamoto's office, just off the bridge. When Miyamoto came to the door, he and the ensign spoke in Japanese. Oliver listened, pretending not to understand.

Miyamoto asked, "Why did you take so long?"

The ensign answered, "He did not know the mission was canceled."

"What did you tell him?"

"I told him the admiral was not aboard the ship."

Miyamoto grunted, then asked, "What's wrong?"

"Sir, a woman smiled at the *kage no yasha* as we came to meet you."

Miyamoto laughed, and said, "Do not worry, the women in the Fleet see them only as their protectors. If she has a dog back on Earth, she probably smiles at the dog the same way."

The ensign nodded, and said, "Yes, sir." He saluted Captain Miyamoto and left the office.

Miyamoto kept the master chief standing at attention as he sat behind his desk. He said, "At ease, Master Chief."

Oliver relaxed his posture.

"We have canceled the mission," said Miyamoto.

Having just overheard the conversation at the door, Oliver had to pretend to be surprised. He asked, "Was there a reason, sir?"

Miyamoto had been the first officer to question the idea of sending men down to the moon, though he would never admit it. He persuaded Yamashiro to reconsider wasting men on a fruitless mission. Now he said, "Admiral Yamashiro canceled the mission. I do not believe the admiral needs to explain his decision." Then, in a moment of charity, Miyamoto sighed, and said, "The admiral does not wish to risk men for a closer look at ancient artifacts."

Miyamoto Genyo was the kind of commander who never showed any emotion other than anger. "We lost a dozen men learning about hundred-thousand-year-old ice and empty silos. There is no point throwing away more lives," he said, using a voice that reeked of disapproval. Miyamoto relied on disdain and scowls to distance himself from his men. He did not want to appear concerned about the lives of the SEALs.

"Sir, what if the sites have military value?" asked Oliver.

"Military value? Master Chief, did you look at the recon photos? Those sites are of no strategic value except as target practice."

He thought, *Maybe Master Chief Illych's death was not so meaningless. He taught us that your injector pods make excellent torpedoes.*

NINE

Location: Terraneau
Galactic Position: Scutum-Crux Arm
Astronomic Location: Milky Way

Freeman nodded as I entered the room, and continued fiddling with his communications computer. The time was 07:00 according to the Space Travel Clock. The virtual versions of William Sweetwater and Arthur Breeze should have arrived at their virtual lab.

"How much can we tell them?" I asked Freeman as I took the seat beside him. The last time we had spoken with Sweetwater and Breeze, Freeman and I were cooperating with the Unified Authority, and the aliens had just burned Olympus Kri. Even then, the ghosts were behind the times. They did not know that the clones had formed their own empire, and Freeman had warned me not to tell them.

Freeman said, "We can tell them about Terraneau."

"Won't they already know about it?" I asked.

"The only things we can tell them are things they already know."

"How much trouble will we cause if we leave the script?" I asked.

Freeman did not respond.

"Are we going to ask them where the aliens are going next?" I asked.

Freeman nodded.

"You do realize that the Unifieds have probably told them that we died on Olympus Kri. They may be surprised to see us," I said.

Freeman said, "Only Andropov would have that kind of clearance." Tobias Andropov was the chairman of the Linear

Committee, the executive branch of the Unified Authority government.

"Andropov is handling this himself?" I asked.

Freeman responded to my question with a glare. As far as he was concerned, he'd already answered the question. "Unless they ask, the only thing we will tell them about ourselves is that we are alive."

I wondered if he would have been more honest with the real William Sweetwater and Arthur Breeze. Generally aloof, Freeman had adopted the scientists back on New Copenhagen as if they were his pets.

When we fought the Avatari on New Copenhagen, I was a lieutenant. Now, thanks to the ambush at Olympus Kri, I was the leader of a great empire. I was the head of state, but Freeman was the high priest, bringing down sacred revelation from ethereal beings only he could contact—William Sweetwater and Arthur Breeze. He would tell me what to say, and I would obey. He passed me the little communications computer, and I typed an access code into it, then gave it back to him.

The screen flashed to life, showing a large laboratory. Sweetwater, who was working near the camera, looked up, and said, "Now here's a surprise."

Freeman put up a hand to stop him, and whispered, "Are you alone?"

"At the moment," Sweetwater said in his friendly, gravelly voice. "Raymond, aren't you supposed to be dead?"

"Not that I know of," Freeman said.

"How did he die?" I asked.

Sweetwater gave the lab a visual sweep, then stepped closer to the camera. "They said you both died on Olympus Kri."

"We went to Terraneau after Olympus Kri," I said.

"We heard about Terraneau, what a tragedy. We heard no one survived." Sweetwater always referred to himself in plural; it was one of his quirks.

"We got a thousand people off Terraneau," I said.

Sweetwater shook his head. Anger and depression showing in his eyes, he said, "Arthur tracked the Avatari signal to Bode's Galaxy. The Navy should have sent a fleet to destroy their home world by now."

"They sent the Japanese Fleet," I said. Then I had to grit my teeth to stop from swearing because, below the table, Freeman had dug the heel of his oversized boot into my shin to get my attention. He was right, of course. The launch of the Japanese Fleet would have taken place between Sweetwater's death and digital resurrection. I had wandered into dangerous grounds.

For his part, the dwarf did not seem to notice. He asked, "Are we correct in assuming that you are no longer working with the Unified Authority?"

Not wanting to risk another sub-table attack, I looked at Freeman for cues on how to proceed. He met my gaze and gave me a single nod.

"Yes, sir, that would be a correct assumption," I said.

"Are you fugitives?"

After glancing back at Freeman one last time to make sure that I still had permission to speak, I said, "Enemies might be a better description."

"I see," said Sweetwater. "We're out of the loop up here on the Wheel." The virtual versions of Sweetwater and Breeze lived on a computer simulation of the Arthur Clarke Space Station—better known as "the Wheel."

I was about to say something, but the dwarf scientist put up a hand and shushed me. Someone had entered the laboratory. Before I could see who, our connection went dead.

Unless some four-star survived the ambush at Olympus Kri without telling me, I was the highest-ranking officer in the Enlisted Man's Empire, and I did not consider myself fit for command. I was a combat Marine, not an admiral. I understood the movements of troops and companies, not fleets. I was made for the battlefield.

I wanted to find my successor. All of the two-star and three-star candidates died at Olympus Kri, leaving me with three one-star admirals to choose from. One look at the field, and I already knew that the pickings were slim.

Along with being the ranking officer in the meeting, I was the lone Marine in attendance. I brought Don Cutter with me as an advisor. As the captain of a fighter carrier, he would know the officers by reputation if not from experience.

Cutter and I were the only people actually sitting in the room, the other officers attended as holographic images sent in via the broadcast network. We sat at one end of a long table, watching the other attendees through a transparent screen that looked for all intents and purposes like a pane of glass. Naval officers called this device a "conferencer." We Marines called it a "confabulator." Around Washington, D.C., it was known as a "social mirage." It facilitated the feeling of having all participants in the same room by placing holographic images of remote attendees around the table as if they were actually there. Looking through the confabulator, I saw each officer in his assigned chair with a virtual plaque that identified his name, rank, and fleet. If I allowed myself to stare at the virtual attendees, though, I could see a slight translucence in their faces.

The three admirals in attendance chatted among themselves, occasionally pausing to glance back at me through the window. They were scattered across the galaxy as well. One of them was in the Perseus Arm, one was in the Sagittarius Arm, and the last was in the Norma Arm.

I came to the meeting thinking I would hand over the reins of the military to one of these men; but as I watched them, I had second thoughts. Looking through the confabulator, I saw an enclave of assholes.

I called the room to order by asking, "Have any of you heard from Warshaw?"

"Warshaw" was Admiral Gary Warshaw, the commander, chief, and architect of the Enlisted Man's Empire. He was the officer who rebuilt the broadcast network, a man with a knack for finding options in hopeless situations.

Somewhere inside me, I still hoped that Warshaw had survived the ambush at Olympus Kri. The arrogant prick strutted like a peacock, and he wasn't worth shit in combat situations, but Warshaw was a great organizer. He'd created an empire out of chaos.

All three of the admirals shook their heads.

"No one?"

I asked, "Have any of you heard back from your commanding officers?" They gave the same response. That didn't surprise me. All of our top brass had been at Olympus Kri when the Unifieds caught us flat-footed.

Looking around the table, I noted how the three admirals looked similar but with unique features. They were all clones, all five-foot-ten, with brown hair and brown eyes. Two of them looked to be in their early thirties, the other in his fifties. He had rims of white hair around his ears. He was also fat as a whale.

I took a deep breath and launched into the bad news. "The Unifieds attacked our ships after we evacuated Olympus Kri. As far as I know, the *Churchill* is the only ship that escaped."

"What about the *Kamehameha*? Do you think she survived?" asked Rear Admiral Steven Jolly. The *Kamehameha* was the flagship of the Enlisted Man's Fleet, Warshaw's ship.

I'd never met Jolly in person, but I'd heard stories about him. By reputation, he was a man of unlimited ambition who suffered from depression and self-doubt. Nobody respected Admiral Jolly, not even Jolly himself.

I shook my head, and said, "I was on the *Kamehameha* when the attack started."

"Did you see her go down?" asked Jolly.

Cutter leaned forward, cleared his throat, and said in a loud whisper, "The *Kamehameha* was the first ship they destroyed."

"What about Admiral Cloward? He was on the *Clinton*?"

"I didn't see the *Clinton* go down," said Cutter. "Admiral Warshaw ordered every ship to the broadcast zone. The *Churchill* was the closest ship to the zone, and we barely made it through. The last ship I saw was the *Salah ad-Din*. She was right behind us, but the Unifieds were closing in on her."

I said, "If the *Kamehameha* went down, all of your commanding officers went with her. They were with Warshaw on the *Kamehameha* when the attack began."

"What were they doing on the *Kamehameha*?" asked Rear Admiral Curtis Liotta.

"They were negotiating reunification with the Unifieds. The U.A. sent an ambassador."

"Did Andropov attend?" asked Jolly.

"Martin Traynor came in his place," I said.

"Traynor? Who the hell is he?" asked Liotta. I knew Liotta by reputation, too. He was a weasel. According to Cutter, people called Liotta "Curtis the Snake" behind his back.

Liotta was an outspoken critic of everyone and everything that did not suit him. He openly criticized other officers' tactics and battle strategies despite having risen to the rank of rear admiral (lower half) without ever seeing combat.

"The only thing I know about Traynor is that the Linear Committee sent him," said Cutter. "I think he's secretary of galactic expansion or some odd thing."

"And they sacrificed him?" asked Jolly.

Looking around the room, I watched the admirals to see how they would react to the news. Admiral Liotta looked shocked and scornful. Admiral Peter "Pete" Wallace of the Sagittarius Central Fleet looked angry enough to gouge somebody's eyes out. Only Steven Jolly, the old man, hid his emotions. He sat still and slumped in his chair, staring down at the table, his face unreadable.

"He left the ship a few moments before the attack," I said.

"The hell you say," said Cutter. "No one made it off the *Kamehameha*."

"I did," I said. "I saw Traynor leaving the summit and followed him to a landing bay. That's the only reason I made it off the ship, I was already near my shuttle when the attack began."

If I ever saw Traynor again, I'd have to thank him for saving my life. I'd thank him, then I would shove a grenade so far up his ass his doctor would mistake it for a hemorrhoid.

The silence in the room was so heavy it felt like it was made of bricks. Wallace, the youngest of the one-stars, broke that silence when he said, "It's time we annihilated those speckers once and for all."

Wallace looked fit, but he had a disfigured face. Long, striping scars covered his forehead and cheeks and neck, making his head look like a misshapen map. He might have seen action or he might have been in a fire. I would not have trusted the surgeon who performed Wallace's skin grafts to wrap a Christmas present.

"We can't attack Earth," Jolly said, dismissing the comment as if it had been made by a child.

"Why the hell not?" demanded Wallace.

"Because it's Earth," said Jolly.

Hearing Jolly speak, I was struck by how much these men did not know. They might have known that the aliens had returned to New Copenhagen and Olympus Kri, but they did not know about Terraneau. From what I could tell, their superiors had not informed them that the aliens would attack every one of our planets or that they would eventually attack Earth.

"Are you saying that because Earth is the gawddamned-specking home of humanity, we have to let those Unified bastards get away with an ambush?" asked Wallace, venom oozing from his voice. "Bullshit, Jolly! That's bullshit, and you know it."

"We cooperated with them, and they ambushed us," said Cutter. "That can't go unanswered. If we let them get away with it . . ." He was making one of those vague, fill-in-the-blank-type threats, and he let the sentence go unfinished.

"I don't get it," said Admiral Liotta of the Cygnus Central

Fleet. "How did they catch us with our pants down? I mean, what was going on?"

"The specking bastards set us up," said Wallace.

"Looks that way," Liotta agreed.

Jolly turned to me, and the room went silent as he asked, "What about Olympus Kri? The reason we went there in the first place was to evacuate the planet before the aliens attacked it. Was the whole thing a trick?"

Jolly was a fat, old clone with pockets of flesh sagging from his jowls. The skin hanging down his chin and jawline reminded me of an overstuffed hammock.

"It must have been," said Liotta.

"The aliens attacked Olympus Kri," I said. "They have attacked three planets so far: New Copenhagen, Olympus Kri, and Terraneau."

"How the hell do we know that's not more Unified Authority bullshit?" asked Wallace.

"I was on Olympus Kri when they attacked. I was on Terraneau as well. The Unifieds don't have anything powerful enough to do what the aliens did to those planets. We'd be having this discussion in the afterlife if they did."

The officers considered my words. Finally, Admiral Jolly asked, "What's the matter with them? Wasn't the alien attack enough?"

"Nothing will be enough for them," said Wallace. "The bastards came under a flag of truce."

I had come to this meeting hoping to find a worthy successor for Warshaw, but the prospects were dim. Jolly was next in line. He had more self-control than the other two, but he came across as weak. I asked myself if I really wanted to place the Enlisted Man's Navy in that man's trembling hands.

Liotta asked, "Were you able to evacuate Terraneau?"

"No," I said.

Admiral Wallace said, "I heard they wanted to join the specking Unifieds. It sounds to me like those assholes got what they deserved."

I stared into the holographic window, but I did not focus on anyone in particular, taking in the entire scene instead of the details.

None of those officers was fit for command. Steven Jolly

was weak. James Liotta was a bullshit artist. Pete Wallace was a big-talking kid. They were the rightful heirs to the throne; and if I did not choose one of them, the mutiny that would follow might spread across the fleet.

My mind wandered as the three admirals bickered among themselves. Maybe they knew this was an audition. The thought of one of these fools as my commanding officer left me depressed until I remembered a lesson from ancient Rome, the Praetorian Guard.

The Praetorian Guard protected the emperors of Rome. They also killed several of the emperors. When they did not like an emperor, they assassinated him and chose his replacement.

I hated the idea of placing Steven Jolly in charge; but if I looked at him the way the Praetorians viewed their emperors, as a disposable figurehead who got to make decisions until he proved his inability to make sound choices, then the prospects improved. The thought made me smile.

As I came back to the conversation, I heard Admiral Wallace say, "Who gives a shit about Terraneau? I'm glad those speckers died; the universe is better off without them."

"I am not here to discuss the people of Terraneau or their place in the universe," I said.

The look Wallace shot me could have set off a fire alarm. His face flushed red. As he glared at me, he clenched his teeth so hard that his chin quivered.

"The aliens are retaking the planets we liberated from them, and they're not going to stop until they reach Earth," I said. "They're following our schedule. First we beat them on New Copenhagen, so they burned New Copenhagen first. The first planets we rescued were Olympus Kri and Terraneau. Does anybody know which planet came next?"

Some quiet discussion followed, holographic men whispering to the holographic shades beside them. Obviously, no one knew the answer. It didn't matter, Sweetwater and Breeze would know . . . assuming they were willing to divulge information to enemies of the state.

"It may not have occurred to you, General, but our hands are pretty well tied," said Jolly. "I'm here in the Perseus Arm. Curtis is in Cygnus Central. Until we find some method to program our broadcast stations, we're stuck where we are."

He did not mention Admiral Wallace.

"You don't have keys?" I should have known. The late Admiral Warshaw only gave the keys to control the broadcast system to his fleet commanders—the guys who died in the ambush.

"They weren't exactly standard-issue," said Admiral Liotta.

"Fleet commanders only," said Jolly.

"And all of the fleet commanders were on the *Kamehameha*," I said, finishing the statement as I held up a little device for the officers to see. It was the size of a deck of playing cards and a quarter of an inch thick. It was all black, with a touch screen.

"Warshaw gave this to me right before the attack," I said. "I needed it to get to Terraneau."

"Why did he give a shit about Terraneau?" asked Wallace. I noticed a certain rhythm about his speech. He managed to work profanity into every sentence. If he were a religious man, his prayers would have been *specking* incredible.

"If you saw what happened on Olympus Kri, you'd understand," I said.

"What exactly happened?" asked Admiral Jolly.

"They ignited the atmosphere . . . lit the planet to nine thousand degrees and let it burn. By the time they got through, every living thing was incinerated."

"And you think they're going to do that to all of our planets?" asked Jolly.

"Not if we hit them first," said Liotta.

Only an ass-wipe who'd never seen battle would talk like that, I thought; but I didn't speak my mind. If things did not work out the way I hoped, I might need Liotta. Now that I had decided to turn my Marines into the new Praetorian Guard, I might need all three of these ass-wipes. The good news was that I'd only need them one at a time.

"We can't hit them, Admiral," I said. "It's not like they're flying to planets and attacking from ships. They're hitting us from some other galaxy, a billion light-years away. We've already lost the war. We're not fighting, we're evacuating refugees."

Silence.

"But we only have one broadcast key," said Admiral Jolly.

"My engineers can make more," I said.

"So we have our broadcast network back," said Jolly.

"The way I see it, Admiral, we will be one big happy Navy in a couple of hours," I said. Hiding my distaste for what I had to do next, I said, "Admiral Jolly, we're going to need a supreme commander."

"Are you placing me in charge?" asked Jolly.

"Yes, sir."

"But you outrank Admiral Jolly," said Liotta.

"Rank isn't everything," I said. "Have any of you ever heard of the Praetorian Guard?" When they shook their heads, I smiled, and said, "No? Maybe it's for the best. They were the troops who guarded the emperors of Rome. Caesar, Caligula, Otho, they guarded all of them."

"What's your point?" asked Liotta, clearly unaware that the three emperors I had listed all died prematurely.

"I'm a Marine. I'm a combat officer, not the kind of man who runs empires," I said. I gave them a crooked smile, and said, "I'm the kind of guy who guards the throne, not the kind who sits in it."

They liked that. Admiral Jolly bobbed his head up and down, his real chin vanishing behind the folds of his jowls. He said, "Well done, General. That makes perfect sense."

Liotta gave me a casual salute.

"But the bastard still has more stars than us?" said Wallace.

"You can have 'em if you want," I offered. "As of this moment, Admiral Jolly, you are in charge."

"You've just relinquished your command, General. You no longer have the authority to make that kind of decision," said Admiral Liotta, waking from his revelry. He must have thought I would put him in charge.

"I still have three stars," I said. I turned to Jolly, and added, "Unless you plan to strip me of command." I knew he wouldn't. If Liotta and Wallace conspired against him, he'd need a strong ally.

Jolly shook his head. "No, General, I think you should hold on to those stars." He was weak, and no one values alliances more than the weak.

Before calling the summit, I had visited Engineering and shown the broadcast key to Lieutenant Mars. When he saw it, he laughed, and said, "Mary Mother of God, you have got to be kidding. A frequency-modulation transmitter?" He looked at me and saw that I had no idea what he was talking about, so he said, "It transmits FM radio waves. This is very old technology . . . ancient even. Kids build these things as history projects in grade school. These things came out between the Internet and smoke signals."

"What is the Internet?" I asked.

He laughed, and said, "No wonder the Unifieds never cracked it; only a fool would use such a primitive technology to control a broadcast network. It's inspired."

CHAPTER ELEVEN

Ava waited for me in my billet. What else could she do? As
the only woman aboard the *Churchill*, she didn't dare leave
the protection of my quarters. Fighting the effects of a growing depression, she sat on my rack, watching a movie on a pair
of mediaLink shades. When she heard me come in, she tore
off the shades.

In better times, those shades could have provided news and
editorial; now they only accessed preprogrammed materials—
books, movies, and educational curricula that had been created a decade earlier.

"I was watching your movie," she said.

"My movie?" I asked.

"The Battle for Little Man."

The name did not register for a few seconds. Then it hit me.
The Battle for Little Man, an old propaganda film released at
the beginning of the Mogat Wars, depicted a battle in which a
division of Marines was sent to an unsettled planet called Little
Man. We went expecting to find a small detachment of Morgan
Atkins Believers. What we found was an army that outnumbered us two to one. Outnumbered and cut off from help, we
made our stand. I was one of only seven survivors.

The movie was made at a time when I was listed as MISS-
ING IN ACTION AND PRESUMED DEAD, opening the door
for the filmmakers to portray me as a natural-born.

"You don't look a thing like Sean Gregory," Ava said.
Gregory was the square-jawed male model who played
natural-born me.

"Really? I thought that was the most accurate part of the
movie."

"You're much better-looking than Sean," Ava said. She
acted like she was in a playful mood, but I could see through

the cracks. She didn't call me "Honey." That was a sure tip-off. She also sounded more sincere than brassy. When Ava was playful, she liked to sound tough.

"I knew that," I said, trying to play along.

"I'm not kidding. You should see Sean in person."

"He isn't six feet tall and covered with muscles?" I asked.

Ava pretended to have to think that over, pausing, mulling over the words, scratching her chin, and finally saying, "Well, he is pretty tall."

"And muscular?" I asked.

"He does have big arms . . . and that chest . . ." Her olivine-colored eyes became dreamy. Had I dredged up old memories or fantasies?

It felt nice to flirt with Ava even though I could tell she was putting on an act. I wished things had worked out differently. I wished I could have given her what she wanted and that she had not left me for some other man. I wished the people in charge on Terraneau had listened to me, and the girls in Ava's orphanage had not been incinerated.

Wishes were like intentions; they counted for shit.

"We're meeting the Cygnus Central Fleet at Providence Kri," I said. "I'm going to leave you there for a little while."

"How long of a little while?" Ava asked, no longer pretending to smile.

"I don't know. You'll be a lot safer there than you would be on a ship. The Unifieds aren't attacking planets."

She looked at me, studying me closely, her arms folded across her chest. She said, "The aliens are." Her eyes marched back and forth across my face, seeming to take in every detail. God, she was beautiful.

"You'll be safer on a planet than you would be on a ship," I said. "At least you will be for a little while."

"You live for this. You live to fight, don't you?" she asked.

"You live for this . . ." The words echoed in my mind. The war did not belong to the Navy or the empire; it belonged to me.

"The Unifieds haven't asked for a truce," I said. "The aliens are still scorching planets."

"I hoped maybe Terraneau was the end of it," she said.

The end of what? I said, "The aliens are going to attack every planet we have until they erase us from the galaxy. The war with the Unifieds is just a distraction. We're like two kids fighting over a toy while their house burns down around them."

Ava put up a hand to stop me. She did not want to talk about aliens or reality.

Hearing me mention the Avatari ended the charade. She stood there, her eyes twitching back and forth as if she were having some sort of seizure. Her arms dropped to her sides, and her hands formed fists. "They kill everyone," she said. "They killed my girls."

She thought about what she had just said. "My girls . . . my girls, they had their whole lives ahead of them."

When I did not answer, she stared up at me. A few seconds passed, before she asked, "How long do we have before the Avatari reach Providence Kri?"

"I don't know. I think it will be one of the last planets they hit before they attack Earth."

"Earth?"

I needed to sleep, not talk. I had an hour or two to rest while Mars built FM transmitters to use as broadcast keys.

Freeman was in his quarters trying to reach Sweetwater and Breeze. We had not heard back from them yet, and I began to wonder if perhaps they now considered us the enemy.

While Ava and I discussed life, the galaxy, and the Avatari, Captain Cutter sailed the *Churchill* into a thousand-mile-wide zone flooded with highly charged electrical current from the local broadcast station. As the ship entered that zone, great tendrils of voltage formed around her hull, creating a glow so bright it could leave a man blinded. The streaks of electricity running the length of the ship carried so many joules that they would incinerate the entire crew had the ship not been properly insulated.

The *Churchill*, a Perseus-class fighter carrier, had automatic tint shields on her viewports and insulated tiles along the length of her hull. As we approached the zone, Klaxons sounded, signaling the crew to return to stations, and the *Churchill* passed from the Scutum-Crux Arm of the Milky Way to the Cygnus Arm, a journey of more than twenty thousand light-years, in a matter of seconds.

A flash of electricity so bright it could be detected by the human eye from a million miles away marked the ship's exit from one arm of the galaxy, and an equally bright flash marked its entrance into the next. That flash was called an "anomaly."

Every broadcast was a scientific miracle, but pangalactic travel had become so mundane that the crew of the *Churchill* did not even think about it.

CHAPTER
TWELVE

Location: Planet A-361-D
Galactic Position: Solar System A-361
Astronomic Location: Bode's Galaxy

Because of their synchronous orbits around A-361-D, the
two moons always remained on opposite sides of the planet.
The sun shone on the far side of the planet, its glow illuminating the back of the planet and both of its moons. The sides
facing the Fleet were bathed in shadow.

Three of the Japanese Fleet's four battleships had flown
into position one hundred thousand miles from the moons.
The *Yamato* and the *Onoda* hovered nearer to A-361-D/Satellite 1, the larger of the two moons, the one with the flat plain
that looked like a landing field. The *Kyoto* patrolled A-361-D/
Satellite 2, the smaller moon.

The *Sakura* remained another hundred thousand miles
back, far enough away for Admiral Yamashiro to watch both
moons from a viewport. He sat on the observation deck with
Captain Takahashi. Takahashi looked through the viewport,
then returned to his computer to oversee the operation through
the eyes of satellites. He was too far away to see the battleships or the transports unassisted.

"How do you think they will they react when we destroy
their moons?" asked Captain Takahashi. With the other captains away, Takahashi became less formal around the admiral. Yamashiro was, after all, Takahashi's father-in-law.

"They would have attacked us already if they had the ability," said Yamashiro. "They must not have a navy. It's as if
they have spent so much time conquering other planets that
they have forgotten how to defend their own."

Takahashi walked to the viewport and leaned against the

rail that ran beneath the glass. He stared out at A-361-D. The gas giant was a muddle of yellow and brown and orange.

Far in the background, A-361, the star from which the solar system took its name, burned like an electrified ember. *Earth's future generations, assuming Earth would have future generations, might know this as the "Avatari System,"* thought Takahashi. *In another hundred years, children might be required to memorize the names of the four battleships in the Japanese Fleet, the* Sakura, *the* Onoda, *the* Kyoto, *and the* Yamato.

"What will we do if they shoot back at us?" he asked.

Yamashiro dismissed the idea. "We've analyzed the moons," he said. "They pose no threat."

The video feed from one of the satellites shadowed the *Onoda*. Another showed a view of seemingly empty space, that was, in fact, occupied by a stealth transport. That same satellite also had a telescopic sight on the moon, which included a very clear view of the flat area that Yamashiro's officers now called, "the deck." Everyone agreed that it looked like a landing field, but it could also have been the roof of a huge subterranean city or a missile-defense system. Because he did not know what lurked under that flat top, Yamashiro had sent the *Yamato* to back up the *Onoda*. On his computer screen, a satellite tracked the *Yamato* as it approached the larger moon, lagging twenty thousand miles behind her sister ship.

Yamashiro didn't care about the moon or what it housed. Gathering scientific data did not interest him.

Back in his office, Yamashiro had a photograph that he had not yet shared with Takahashi or the other captains, one that made the *deck* on A-361-D/Satellite 1 and the little ring of buildings on A-361-D/Satellite 2 look insignificant. It was a photographic image of planet A-361-B taken by a scout satellite, and it showed a city.

THIRTEEN

The two lead transports carried infiltration pods but no SEALs to fly them. On this mission, they would use the S.I.P.s as weapons instead of transports. On this mission, the S.I.P.s were both the message and the messenger.

Two technicians rode in the kettle of each of the transports. The technicians did not need to open the pods to program them. They prepared the pods using special computer stations. Though the techs had never programmed pods to overcharge and self-destruct, they had been trained in the operation of field-resonance engines. They jacked computer lines into the pods and typed in instructions.

Now that the pods would be used as torpedoes, the techs loaded the S.I.P.s into the launching device with new reverence. Once they had the pods in place, they returned to their programming stations. The displays on the computers glowed like neon signs in the darkness of the kettle, their low glow showing on the wall in a twist of white and red and green.

Young and tired of exploring Bode's Galaxy, the technicians normally complained and commiserated as they worked. They criticized officers and gossiped about shipboard romances. On this day, though, with high-ranking officers listening in from nearby battleships, the technicians only spoke to report their progress.

The field-resonance engines required two minutes and twenty-seven seconds to build an explosive overcharge. That left the techs and the transport pilot with a chilling two minutes and twenty-three seconds in which they would sit with the S.I.P.s as they morphed into bombs.

Admiral Yamashiro ordered the attack, and Miyamoto Genyo, captain of the *Onoda*, coordinated it. Sitting on the bridge of his battleship, grim-faced, his eyes dark as flints, his lips pressed so tightly together they formed a single flesh-colored line, his shoulders tight, he watched the satellite feeds, ready to pull the plug on the operation if something went wrong.

"Flight path programmed," reported a technician on the transport preparing to attack the moon known as A-361-D/Satellite 1.

"Flight path programmed," reported a tech on the transport preparing to attack the moon known as A-361-D/Satellite 2.

Miyamoto gave the order that everyone anticipated and feared. Speaking in Japanese, he said, "Charge the infiltration pods."

Time seemed to freeze at that moment. For Miyamoto, who had never put much thought into the length of two minutes, the next one hundred and forty-seven seconds felt like a lifetime. From the bridge of his ship, he watched the larger moon, studying the curve of its surface, and he wondered what mysteries it held.

Miyamoto looked at the timer and saw that only twelve seconds had passed.

No one spoke. The sailors manning the bridge of the *Onoda* remained silent. If the technicians in the transports had spoken, Miyamoto would have heard. He had a commandLink connection with the pilots of the transports as well.

Twenty seconds had passed.

Miyamoto watched an unenhanced view of the moon through a viewport. Seen from hundreds of thousands of miles away, its surface had no more features than a rubber ball.

Twenty-seven seconds had passed.

Miyamoto turned to his satellite feeds, his expression unflinching. Through the satellite's mobile eye, he could count the pea-sized pebbles around the target. He could see the "deck" and the land around it. The satellite allowed him to zoom in close enough to study a grain of sand or pan his view out so far that he could peer down on an entire hemisphere.

He thought about *Bushido*, the Samurai code of conduct. The old captain organized his life around his own personal *Bushido*, letting it bind his thoughts as rigidly as any Christian monk had ever embraced the Ten Commandments. Even before the war, back when he lived on Ezer Kri with his wife, Miyamoto tried to live the detached life of the Samurai code. When he visited his children and their children, he had made himself gruff and distant and showed no more emotion than a stone in a river.

He knew that his sailors considered him cold and indifferent. He also knew about the *Kabuki* mask in the officer's lounge, the face of a scowling demon that his officers jokingly referred to as Miyamoto-san.

The code was the stuff of legends and stories, a tradition so old that nobody knew how rigidly the ancients had lived it. Miyamoto's New Japan was built upon such legends. And now, with the future of that New Japan hanging in the balance, Miyamoto Genyo was glad for the code.

When the timer showed that one minute and five seconds had passed, Miyamoto ordered the transport pilots to purge the air from the kettles and open the rear hatches. He gave the order in Japanese.

The pilots responded immediately.

This was the pivotal moment. By opening their hatches, the transports would nullify the stealth envelope that kept them hidden. If the aliens were watching, they would detect the transports, and they might attack.

Seconds ticked by slowly. One minute and five seconds became one-fifteen, and then one-thirty-five.

Takeda grimaced, and told the technicians, "Prepare to launch."

He looked at the moon through the viewport, a silver coin in a velvet space. He looked at its image in the satellite feed and saw a desert pitted by craters and marked with a deck as flat as a dance floor.

One minute and fifty-two seconds. Fifty-three. Fifty-four. Fifty-five.

Miyamoto clenched his hands into fists and hid his fists by his sides so that no one saw him trembling. He felt the weight of humanity upon him, but his eyes remained fixed as he said, *"Ute!,"* the word that translated to the English command "Fire!"

Able to hold twelve stealth infiltration pods at a time, the launching device worked like the cylinder of a revolver. It fired its first pod, rotated twenty degrees, and fired the next one, then the next all in under a second.

Flying at top speed, without a human payload, the S.I.P.s could reach the planet in less than five seconds. Passengers slowed the pods down—not because of the added weight but because they were fragile. When the pods accelerated at top speed, the gravitational force inside the compartment was more than the human body could withstand. Possessing so much power that they seemed to bend the laws of physics, the S.I.P.s could decelerate so quickly that the force would turn human passengers inside out.

Moments after they left the transports, the S.I.P.s accelerated to ten million miles per hour. They dropped to the speed of sound as they reached their targets. One of the S.I.P.s reached its target. Two did not.

FOURTEEN

Captain Takahashi, standing by the viewport and watching the larger of the moons, only knew that the mission had begun because Yamashiro told him. There were no explosions or bursts of laser to signal the beginning of the attack. Still staring out into space, waiting to see what would happen to the moons, he heard his father-in-law's sharp gasp.

He turned in time to see Yamashiro yelling into the communications console. "Return to the *Sakura*." He spoke in English. Yamashiro generally spoke in Japanese when addressing junior officers, but he gave this order in English.

The pilot on the other end of the communication asked, "What about survivors?"

Yamashiro stood partway out of his chair as he shouted, "Return immediately!" He took a breath, and added, "There are no survivors."

Takahashi wanted to know what had happened, but he knew better than to interrupt the admiral. Still listening for clues, he looked out through the viewport and searched in time to see the smaller of the moons fall apart. First, it blurred into a smudge, as if fog had formed on the viewport. An envelope of fog, or dust, or maybe gas formed around it. Whatever rose off A-361-D/Satellite 2, it was the same color as the moon itself and translucent. It did not spread. It remained tight around the moon and became thicker and thicker, a stifling, suffocating cloud. Focusing on the words "no survivors," Takahashi wondered if somehow one of the transports had collided with the moon. But Satellite 2 had come *undone*, and that suggested more than a transport mishap. The core that held the moon together broke and dissolved before his eyes.

Feeling a sense of elation, Takahashi looked at the larger

moon, hoping to see similar destruction. Nothing had changed on Satellite 1.

"No! Do not return to the *Sakura*," Yamashiro said, countermanding his first orders. Takahashi heard something in Yamashiro's voice he had never heard before. He heard fear. Clearly struggling to keep from shouting, he growled, "Rendezvous with the other transport but do not return to this ship until you are given further orders."

Then, obviously speaking to the bridge, he barked the fatal order, "Prepare to broadcast!"

"Admiral, are you leaving us in space?" asked a voice over the console. Takahashi knew the man was a transport pilot.

"We will return for you," Yamashiro told the transport pilots. "We are broadcasting out of the solar system. We will contact you when . . ." But he clearly did not know how to finish the sentence.

"Yes, sir." The voice that came from the console speaker bore the uncertain tone of a terrified child.

Yamashiro turned his attention to the bridge. "Broadcast status?" he barked, waited less than a second for a response, then repeated the question in a more emphatic tone. "What is our broadcast status? We need to broadcast now!"

"Admiral, the generator is not yet charged."

Yamashiro stared at the screens, glanced toward the viewport, looking right through Takahashi, then back at the screens. "Broadcast us the moment it's ready!"

"What is our destination, sir?" asked Commander Suzuki, Takahashi's second-in-command.

"Out of the solar system! Anywhere outside of this solar system!"

One of the transport pilots asked, "Admiral, where do you want us to rendezvous?"

"Get as far from A-361-D as you can . . . as far from every planet as you can. Get as far as you can from those planets, and keep flying farther away. We'll find you. When we return, we'll find you."

Takahashi stood behind Admiral Yamashiro, staring over his shoulder. He looked into the various screens and saw nothing. All but one of the displays showed nothing but open space.

"Why are we broadcasting out of the solar system?" he asked.

If Yamashiro heard the question, he did not acknowledge it. He sat hunched over the monitors as if searching for secrets in the empty screens.

"Admiral, why are we leaving the solar system?" Takahashi repeated.

Yamashiro still showed no sign of hearing him.

Suzuki's voice came over the console. "Admiral, the engines are . . ."

"Take us out of this solar system." Yamashiro yelled the words.

"What is our destination, sir?"

"Out. Anywhere out of this system!" He sounded desperate. He sounded frantic. Takahashi thought he sounded crazed as well.

"What about the other ships?" asked Suzuki.

His face turning red, Yamashiro hissed the word, "Now!"

Tint shields formed on the viewport, blocking any hint of the one remaining moon. A moment later, the *Sakura* had broadcasted out of Solar System A-361.

He's lost his mind, thought Takahashi. Wondering if his father-in-law was still fit for command, he asked, "How will we find the other ships?"

Slowly turning in his chair so that he faced his son-in-law, his dark eyes burning with more intensity than Takahashi had ever seen in them, Yamashiro said, "They have been destroyed."

The video feeds were clear and mysterious.

The feed of A-361-D/Satellite 1 showed a bird's-eye view of the deck and the surface of the moon. For a tenth of a second, maybe only a hundredth of a second, light flared across the screen. A small wisp of steam formed and dissipated. Steam and smoke vanish quickly in the absolute zero temperature and vacuum conditions of space.

Slowing the feed to five seconds per frame did not make a difference. Whatever happened, it happened so quickly that the camera on the satellite could not record it. One moment there was open space, then light appeared and vanished, then the steam appeared and dissolved.

Yamashiro played that portion of the video feed three times without saying a word.

"What was that?" asked Takahashi.

"That was the destruction of an infiltration pod," said Yamashiro. Now that they were out of danger, he seemed drained of energy. He sat slumped in his chair, answering his son-in-law's questions in a soft tone that could most accurately be described as defeated.

Yamashiro ran the loop again, this time even more slowly. The one-second feed lasted nearly ten minutes.

"That can't be a pod," Takahashi said.

Yamashiro switched to a screen that showed a battleship. One moment she lingered peaceably in space. Something happened. Like the S.I.P., the big ship did not explode. She left no debris. It was like a magician's illusion. For just a moment, the battleship seemed to inflate, then she crumpled, folding in on herself, compressing until nothing remained except a formless wad of space-colored junk leaking tendrils of steam or smoke.

Yamashiro stared at the screen, and, in a soft, broken voice, he said, "The *Onoda*."

"That cannot be," said Takahashi. The words were a reflex. He believed his eyes. He did not place as much trust in the absolute laws of physics as he did in his father-in-law's word.

"I can show you what happened to the *Kyoto* and the *Yamato*. They vanished the same way."

Takahashi heard himself hyperventilating, but he could not stop. "We need to go back. We need to help them. We need to look for survivors."

"We need to accomplish our mission," Yamashiro replied in a hushed voice. "They sent us because we are expendable. We are not part of the Unified Authority, we are the Japanese. Our fleet and our men were the price we paid to return to Earth."

Takahashi looked at the screen again and rewitnessed the destruction of the *Onoda*. It was as if the ship had melted.

CHAPTER
FIFTEEN

Earthdate: November 21, A.D. 2517
Location: Providence Kri
Galactic Position: Cygnus Arm
Astronomic Location: Milky Way

More often than not, the Unified Authority colonized planets that came complete with continents and an oxygenated atmosphere. The Galactic Expansion Committee's top criteria for selecting suitable locales included distance from a suitable and stable star, Earth-like size and gravity, and good galactic position.

Since the prime criteria could not be altered, they were nonnegotiable. Other preferences, such as oxygen and water were open to interpretation. Providence Kri, for instance, was something of a fixer-upper when the Unified Authority decided to colonize it. The term "Kri" was attached to planets that required terraforming—a miracle process that could convert rocks and deserts into gardens of Eden.

As I entered the bridge, I saw Providence Kri in its rotation through the view screen. Whatever the planet had looked like before the Unified Authority gave it a makeover, it certainly looked like a hospitable blue-and-green marble afterward.

Having been rescued from the Avatari by clones, the populace of Providence Kri was unfailingly loyal to the Enlisted Man's Empire. That was good. We were too busy fighting natural-borns and aliens to lay down laws, so we trusted the residents of the various planets to govern themselves. We were military clones; our dabbling in politics never worked out the way we hoped.

Looking out of a viewport, I wondered how long we had until the Avatari turned this planet into a dust bowl as well.

In better times, Providence Kri had served as a galactic hub for the Unified Authority. In these times, it served as a galactic hub for the Enlisted Man's Empire. The Cygnus Central Fleet, Admiral Liotta's fleet, a fleet that included seven fighter carriers and thirty battleships, orbited the planet.

The Cygnus Central Fleet was big, but it lacked the firepower needed to defeat the Earth Fleet. The U.A.'s new generation fighter carriers and battleships were smaller, faster, and better shielded than our ships.

Liotta and an entourage of fleet officers flew out to the *Churchill* to meet me. We did not have time to chat. Time had become scarce.

Liotta took me and my team to Engineering, where Lieutenant Mars presented the crew with a new broadcast key. I allowed Admiral Liotta to have a key, but I did not give him a copy of the book that contained the complete set of codes and broadcast locations. The book contained hundreds of thousands of codes, pinpoint coordinates for safe broadcast areas all across the galaxy. Instead, I handed him a highly abbreviated list that included coordinates for the twenty-two remaining planets in the Enlisted Man's Empire along with a few strategic destinations such as New Copenhagen.

"I have a pilot delivering keys and coordinate cards to every fleet," I said. "He'll have a key to Jolly within the hour."

Liotta smiled, and said, "So we're back in business," as he glanced at the list of broadcast coordinates. Then he paused, and asked, "New Copenhagen? I thought they destroyed that planet."

"They did."

"Why would we want to go there?"

"That's the point," I said. "There's absolutely no reason to go there. If there's no good reason to go there, the Unifieds probably aren't patrolling the area."

Liotta nodded, and said, "So it's a safe place to regroup."

"Something like that," I said.

I did not say good-bye to Ava. As I said before, time was scarce.

She would be safe on Providence Kri until we evacuated the planet. Once the evacuation was done, and the danger had passed, we would sit down and sort things out . . . assuming she had any interest in sorting things out with me.

I had not come to Providence Kri to drop off refugees or meet with officers though I did a little of both. I came to commandeer a new ship. With her shields broken, the *Churchill* needed repairs or retirement, so Freeman and I transferred to a carrier named the *Bolivar*. I met the captain in the bridge, handed him a broadcast key, and told him to take us to New Copenhagen.

Captain Tom Mackay heard my orders, and said, "I heard the aliens scorched that planet."

"They did," I agreed.

"Um," Mackay said. "I just wanted to make sure."

CHAPTER
SIXTEEN

Shortly after the *Bolivar* broadcasted into the Orion Arm, Freeman and I met in a small conference room off the bridge. He brought the computer, I brought the codes, and we put in another call to the late Dr. Sweetwater. This time, more than one ghost answered the call.

Arthur Breeze stared at me from the little oblong screen of the communications computer. He sat on what must have been a standard-sized rolling lab stool. Beside him, William Sweetwater sat on an oversized barstool. Their heads were just about even, but Sweetwater's seat came all the way up to Arthur Breeze's ribs. Breeze was that tall and Sweetwater that short.

Bald except for the ring of cotton-fluff fuzz that ran level with his ears, Breeze had thick glasses and teeth so big they belonged in the mouth of a horse. "When William told me about your call, I couldn't believe it," Breeze said, his eyes bouncing back and forth between Freeman and me. "He said you were on Terraneau when the Avatari attacked."

"Something like that," I said.

"We understand Terraneau was a total loss," said Sweetwater. We'd already told Sweetwater the gory details. Apparently, he wanted us to rehash them for Breeze's benefit. "Did you arrive too late to evacuate the planet?"

I said, "We didn't have the barges. Andropov had no interest in evacuating Terraneau."

The Unifieds had built a fleet of space barges that could carry 250,000 people at a time. Without those barges, it would take months to evacuate a planet.

"Why would the government leave them to die?" Breeze asked. He looked thunderstruck, his eyebrows riding halfway up his forehead and his mouth hanging slack.

Sweetwater, on the other hand, knew the answer. He sat silent, his hands pressed against his lap. William Sweetwater was both a brilliant scientist and a bureaucrat. He understood the political world.

"The local leadership declared independence when we liberated the planet. Terraneau wasn't part of the Unified Authority," I said, neglecting to mention that it was not part of the Enlisted Man's Empire, either. I did not know if either scientist knew that the clones had formed their own empire. Breeze certainly didn't.

"What did you think you could accomplish going alone?" Sweetwater asked.

"I tried to get the government to send everyone underground," I said.

"Terraneau had a sizable population. Were there facilities for that many people?" asked Breeze.

"I don't know. I didn't think it through," I admitted.

Freeman, sitting beside me, could have jumped in to add his part of the story, but he let me do the talking. As long as I didn't give out unnecessary information, he was content.

I had the distinct feeling that Sweetwater had left Breeze in the dark about Freeman and me. He did not know that we were fugitives. As far as he knew, we were still loyal citizens.

I also got the feeling that Sweetwater did not want us to complete Breeze's education in a single call. He cleared his throat and attempted to steer the conversation by saying, "So counting Olympus Kri and Terraneau, *we've* managed to liberate twenty-four planets so far. Is that correct?" He placed obvious emphasis on the word "we," suggesting that I might still be part of the Unified Authority.

"Twenty-four planets including Terraneau, that's right," I said.

"Did any other planets wish to remain independent?" Breeze asked. He sounded painfully naïve. Tall and skinny, his eyes almost buglike behind his thick glasses, he stared into the screen, never questioning a word we said.

I was about to say no when Sweetwater said, "Didn't I hear something about Gobi demanding independence?"

"Gobi?" I asked. Gobi, a backwater planet in the Perseus

Arm, had most recently been the headquarters of the Enlisted Man's Fleet.

"Gobi broke from the republic?" Breeze asked, thinking out loud. He ran a hand across his ring of white fluff hair. "That might explain their attitude toward the planet."

"Whose attitude?" I asked

Breeze turned and stared into the camera, showing a profile that was nearly deformed. "Mr. Andropov's . . . General Hill's . . . The Joint Chiefs' . . . We held a briefing with them a day ago. When I told them that the aliens would attack Gobi by the end of the week, they didn't seem to care."

"The end of the week?" I asked.

"It will happen within the next three days judging by the Tachyon D levels," Breeze said.

Tachyon D was the harbinger of disaster. From what we could tell, the Avatari built their technology around the manipulation of tachyons—subatomic particles that moved faster than the speed of light. Before the Avatari invaded the galaxy, scientists considered tachyons a "theoretical probability."

Once the aliens moved in on us, tachyons moved from "theoretical possibility" to "lethal reality." With Sweetwater and Breeze spearheading the work, U.A. physicists not only learned how to detect tachyons, but apparently they'd now figured out how to classify them.

"To be honest, the Joint Chiefs haven't shown much interest in any planet since we discovered Tachyon D levels in Earth's atmosphere," said Breeze.

"You found Tachyon D in Earth's atmosphere?" I asked. I expected the aliens would work their way to Earth, but this was too fast.

"We've found traces of it on every habitable planet," Sweetwater said. "The gears are definitely in motion."

We were out of options. We were out of answers, and we were still at war with ourselves.

I had given Admiral Steve Jolly command of the Navy, but I kept Sweetwater and Breeze to myself. I did not have much of a choice in the matter. Freeman owned our only portal for reaching the scientists, and he wasn't about to turn the device over to a fool like Jolly.

For what it was worth, I agreed with Freeman. Real or virtual, I felt a deep obligation toward the scientists. I'd served with them on New Copenhagen and seen them die with honor. In the Marine Corps, we took death, debts, and honor seriously.

We took the chain of command seriously, too. Leaving out the source of my information, I notified Admiral Jolly about the pending attack on Gobi.

"How did you come upon this information?" asked Jolly. He was on the *Windsor*, a fighter carrier in the Perseus Arm.

"Stray intel," I said, hoping it would make the question go away.

"Stray intelligence?" he repeated.

"Yes, sir."

"What exactly does that mean, Harris?" He gave me a hard look, a surveying look, maybe trying to decide whether or not to trust me.

I said, "It means that I am not willing to divulge my source." I sat placid, relaxed, returning his inspection with a calm gaze.

A more self-confident officer would have pushed the issue. Jolly simply said, "Your stray intelligence just happens to match my findings. It turns out Gobi was the first planet we took after Terraneau. From what we know, that should make it the aliens' next target."

"Yes, sir," I said.

"You said something about hiding underground on Terraneau. Can we do that on Gobi?"

Fat and old and something of a coward, Admiral Jolly was the quintessential survivor. He'd probably never gone a day without brushing his teeth. The idea of saving lives without risking ships and personnel appealed to officers of his kind.

"Have you ever visited Gobi, Admiral?" I asked.

"Yes, and you were there at the same time," he said. "I attended Warshaw's summit with Admiral Huxley." I had not known the late Admiral Huxley. He was one of the victims of the Olympus Kri Massacre.

"I hid in a tunnel under a lake on Terraneau," I said. "As far as I know, Gobi doesn't have tunnels or lakes."

Jolly said, "If I am not mistaken, Gobi Station has underground levels." Gobi Station was the base that the late Admiral Warshaw had used as his Pentagon. "What if we evacuated people to the base?" he asked.

I considered the idea and dismissed it. "We might be able to stash a few hundred people there, but I'm not sure we'd be able to get them out after the attack. Gobi Station is made out of plastic and metal. It's going to melt when things get hot."

"Melt?"

"The atmospheres of Terraneau and Olympus Kri hit nine thousand degrees. Everything made out of glass, steel, or plastic ended up in a puddle," I said.

"Nine thousand degrees?" Jolly had some idea about how the aliens operated, but he did not know the specifics. "That doesn't sound possible. Nine thousand degrees . . . how do you heat a planet to nine thousand degrees?"

"If we knew how the bastards did it, we'd do it to them," I said.

Jolly massaged his brow with a pudgy thumb and sausage-shaped pointer finger, sitting silently as he considered his options. "How are we supposed to evacuate an entire planet?" he asked.

"Gobi's only the first. We'll need to evacuate all of our planets," I pointed out. "At least we're starting light. The population of Gobi is less than a million."

"Do you know how many ships we'd need to transport a million civilians?"

"Four," I said.

"You're planning on stealing the Unifieds' barges," Jolly said. He sounded impressed.

"The word 'stealing' has such a negative connotation," I said. "Let's just say I plan on commandeering the barges. We'll give them back once the emergency passes."

"Do you even know where the barges are moored?" Jolly asked.

"Last I heard, they were orbiting Mars."

"It sounds like you have it all worked out, General. Is that just bluster, or do you really believe you can hijack those barges?"

I laughed. "Oh, I'll get them. The Unifieds aren't going to shoot at us once we board the barges. They need those scows as much as we do."

"Then what?" asked Jolly.

That question took me by surprise. I asked, "Then what . . . what?"

"If I understand what you are saying, you and a small team of operatives plan to sneak behind enemy lines and board twenty-five ships that are not self-broadcasting and have no defenses. Your only protection is that the Unifieds probably won't risk shooting at the ships, but you're still trapped in Unified Authority space," Jolly pointed out. "General, you haven't thought this through."

"The Unifieds have a temporary broadcast station orbiting Mars. They used it to broadcast the barges to Olympus Kri."

"Are you sure it's still there?" asked Liotta.

"Yes," I said. In truth, I had no idea.

"And you believe it is still operational?" asked Jolly.

"Yes, sir."

"And you can access it? Please tell me that you are not simply planning to sail into a broadcast station without knowing where it will send you."

Actually, I was, but I had an answer. "I have engineers who can hack into the satellite's computers."

It was true, too. I'd asked Lieutenant Mars if he had any way of hijacking a U.A. broadcast satellite. He smiled, and said, "Sure. No problem. It's a U.A. installation; my guys know how to get past their security codes. We can even make it play 'Nearer My God to Thee' on its sound system."

I laughed, and said, "I'm not up on my hymns."

Admiral Jolly cleared his throat, and his drooping jowls wobbled. He said, "Assuming you are able to locate the barges and assuming you are able to spirit them away to Gobi, what are you planning to do with the refugees you rescue?"

"Evacuate them," I said.

"And where are you going to put them?" Not looking so jolly, the admiral growled as he asked this question and squinted at me. Multiple chins bounced below his jaw.

"Oh," I said. "I hadn't thought about that."

That was a moment when salvation came from an unexpected source. Admiral Liotta said, "We have facilities on Providence Kri. There's empty housing. Hell, we have entire cities that are sitting empty."

"Yes," I said. "We can ferry them to Providence Kri."

CHAPTER
SEVENTEEN

"There has got to be a way to run this mission without the spy cruiser," Lieutenant Mars said. He sounded indignant as he added, "You blew the ship into Swiss cheese a couple of days ago?"

"You blew the ship to Swiss cheese. You were the one who rigged the cannons," I pointed out.

"Fine, I blew the ship to Swiss cheese following your orders. It's still Swiss cheese."

"We need it, Lieutenant."

"General, I am a believing man. I believe that Peter walked on water. I believe Moses crossed the Red Sea on dry land. I even believe Jesus fed thousands of people with a few loaves of bread and a half dozen fishes. God performed those miracles. If you want your ship resurrected in three days, maybe you should go to Him," Mars said. He was a born-again Christian, except that he was also a clone, which meant he was never actually born the first time.

"If I ever need a sea split, I'll ask Him for help," I said. "In the meantime, I need you to repair the spy ship."

"You do understand that the loaves, the fishes, the water into wine, the resurrections, Christ performed those miracles, not his disciples?"

"Give it your best shot," I said.

"We can't even fly her into dry dock; she's too banged up. One of her engines came off."

Maybe he's getting too comfortable around me, I thought. I stared at Mars's image on the screen, and said, "I need that spy ship, that very ship, engines and stealth generator running by the end of the day."

"By the end of the day" meant by 17:00 hours on the Space Travel Clock. That gave Mars less than ten hours.

"General, sir, may I remind you that you waited until the ship lowered her shields before you fired on her?"

"Sounds like you have your work cut out for you."

"You do understand, sir, that the damage was not just to the hull? I toured that wreck, you blew the holy sh . . . snot out of it." Mars must have really been frustrated. He'd started to say, "shit." He never used profanity, it was not in his vocabulary.

He took a deep breath, then held it for a moment as he composed himself. Then he attempted to reason with me. "General, a stealth generator is a sophisticated piece of equipment. I couldn't make one if I had the cookbook and all the ingredients. If you handed me all the parts and the instructions and gave me a year to put it together, I would not be able to do it."

"Good thing you only need to repair this one," I said.

"From what I hear, repairing them is more difficult than building them, sir. It's not like they carried spare parts on the ship. If that generator is damaged, it's going to need replacement boards. We can't just make them, sir. It's not as easy as reloading a rifle."

The thing about reloading a rifle was Mars's subtle way of reminding me that no matter how many stars I carried on my shoulder boards, I was still a dumb Marine.

"And then there's the broadcast engine. If the broadcast chain is damaged, I mean, General, the Corps of Engineers builds dams and electrical grids. You're talking about one of the most sophisticated . . ."

"Lieutenant, we're wasting time," I said.

"No, sir. I am not wasting your time. I am trying to save time. I don't want to waste time trying to fix a ship that I can't possibly fix." Mars and I had worked together in some tight corners. He was an honest man. That was one of the reasons he was still only a lieutenant. The officers who knew when to pucker and where to kiss generally rose through the ranks more quickly.

"The aliens are about to attack Gobi. If we don't evacuate that planet, every man, woman, and child on Gobi is going to burn. They're going to burn just like the people on Terraneau burned.

"I can't evacuate Gobi unless I steal the Unifieds' barges, and in order to steal them, I need a working spy ship," I said. "I need that cruiser, stealth generator, broadcast engines, and all. Do you understand me?"

Then I said the phrase that officers use to end unpleasant conversations. I said, "You have your orders, Lieutenant."

"Yes, sir," he said, and he saluted. My demands were unfair; but if I played fair, millions of people would die.

While Mars worked miracles, I assembled guns and men and ships.

I hoped we would find the barges moored near the Mars Spaceport, sitting empty and completely ignored. More likely we would find them guarded by a skeleton crew, security men who would slow us down at a time when every second wasted would cost lives.

Marines knew how to steal boats. It was in our skill set, but there were better men for the job. I once worked with a team of SEAL clones, little wiry bastards who specialized in stealth. It was in their genetic makeup. The U.A. designed them to vanish into the shadows and kill without making a sound. Clones were tools, after all. "A tool for every job and a job for every tool," right? We all had our areas of specialty. SEALs and Special Operations clones strolled behind enemy lines and did the dirty work. Marines ran the invasions. Soldiers held down the fort. I wished I had a company of SEALs for this mission; but the last I'd heard, they'd gone with the Japanese Fleet to Bode's Galaxy.

I studied a large holographic map of Mars—the planet, not the engineer. The map showed the planet with a blacked-out area representing the spaceport and the military base. Until we ran some sort of reconnaissance mission, we would not know the precise location of the barges or what kind of force guarded them.

When I explained my plan to the three admirals through the confabulator, Jolly drew in a hissing breath, shook his head, and said, "Risky tactics, General, launching a mission with no idea what you might be up against."

Admiral Wallace, sarcastically referred to as "Warhawk

Wallace" on the bridge of the *Bolivar*, took my side. He said, "You know, Admiral, they may damn well let Harris have the barges. We need them to rescue natural-borns."

"Natural-borns who are loyal to the Enlisted Man's Empire," said Jolly.

"True, but natural-borns nonetheless," Wallace said. "It's a specking humanitarian effort."

"Good point, Pete," sneered Jolly. "Why don't we just ring up Andropov and ask if we can borrow his barges?"

Wallace said, "I checked the specking orbits. Mars and Earth are approximately eighty million miles apart. Even with their fastest ships, the Unifieds will take three specking hours to respond."

"They have self-broadcasting ships, Admiral," I said. "They'll need eight minutes to charge their broadcast engines. If we're not out of there after eight minutes, the shooting starts."

"General, can you give me a ballpark on how much time you'll need to pull this off?" asked Jolly.

Think like a SEAL, I told myself. *Think like a SEAL.* But the SEALs I knew would have calculated the mission down to the last millisecond before presenting it to command. Me, I ran calculations off the top of my head. I smiled, and said, "I'm thinking seven minutes and fifty nine seconds."

"Now how the speck did you come up with that?" asked Wallace.

"Isn't it obvious?" asked Admiral Liotta. "That's one second less than it takes the Unifieds to charge their broadcast engines."

If Lieutenant Mars managed to get that cruiser operational and had time to repair the landing bays, we could wedge twenty-one transports onto that one tiny ship. That meant that four of our transports would need to return to the cruiser for a second crew of Marines if we planned on capturing all twenty-five barges; and capturing every available barge was an essential part of the plan.

Capturing the barges would be easier than securing them. They did not have gun turrets, security doors, or other measures to keep intruders out. Having figured out that the aliens were coming to Olympus Kri, the Unifieds had slapped the barges together as quickly as they could. Dealing with external security measures did not figure into the equation.

Once we boarded the barges, it was a question of knocking out security inside the barges. Like I said, that was the easy part. Flying the ships out might be a different question entirely.

I said, "The Unifieds won't be expecting us. That should buy us a little time.

"If we broadcast in here," I said, pointing at the side of Mars that pointed away from Earth, "we can use the planet to hide our anomaly from Earth. Assuming no one is out sightseeing on the far side of Mars, we should go unnoticed.

"If everything goes right, and they don't spot the anomaly . . ." I paused, superstitiously believing that I had just jinxed myself. "If everything went right . . ." Everything never went right. "Assuming they don't spot the anomaly, we should be able to approach the barges without being seen." I traced a line around the planet.

"They'll pick up your cruiser when you launch your transports," said Jolly. "You can't launch without lowering shields, and the transports won't be cloaked."

He was right, and I admitted as much. I said, "Yeah, but by then it should be too late. If we maneuver the spy ship in close enough, we should have crews aboard every barge in three minutes."

As long as the Unifieds did not catch us broadcasting in, we'd be able to slide right up to the barges.

Jolly held up a pudgy hand to stop me. He said, "General, even if you reach the barges, how will you get them out without a broadcast station?"

Our broadcast network extended only to the planets we controlled. It was the remnant of the old Unified Authority Broadcast Network, the pangalactic superhighway that had once linked Earth to all of its 180 colonies. Back in those days, the satellite broadcast station orbiting Mars was the linchpin of the Network. The Mogats destroyed it during the civil war, cutting Earth off from its colonies.

"The Unifieds launched a temporary broadcast station for evacuation. That was how they got the barges to Olympus Kri," I said.

"And you think they will let you use it to steal their barges, do you?" asked Admiral Jolly. He had a point.

"I think we can commandeer it along with the barges."

"You'll just hack into their security system, no problem." Sarcasm oozed from his voice.

"Something like that," I said. "Look, Admiral, the Unifieds aren't expecting us to enter their space. They're not going to have extensive security guarding that satellite."

It was like breaking into a bank. There might be several layers of security, but they're all outside the safe. Once you get past the front entrance, the counters, and the door of the safe, you're in . . . right?

So much of my plan was based on guesswork, but we did not have much of a choice. If we'd had another week, we'd have had time to repair the spy ship and locate the barges. We'd have been able to breach their computer systems, too. In another week, the Avatari would incinerate two more planets. Millions of people would die. That did not seem to matter to the Unifieds. After evacuating Olympus Kri, they seemed to have decided that the only survival that mattered was their own.

"You're basing your plans on a lot of guesswork," said Jolly. He didn't like the plan. I could hear it in his voice.

"Educated guesses," I said. Putting him in charge had been a mistake. I would correct that mistake when I got back. I wasn't only the highest-ranking Marine, I reminded myself. I was the chief of the Praetorian Guard. *Who would I place in charge?* I asked myself. I currently had two officers to choose from, Pete Wallace or Curtis Liotta. Either might be better than Jolly, but not by much.

"I'm not inclined to authorize this operation," said Jolly.

"Really?" I asked, planning out the admiral's early retirement in my mind.

"You're taking an unreasonable risk," said Jolly.

"Admiral, doing nothing would be an unreasonable risk. The aliens are going to attack Gobi in two days. How many people do you expect to evacuate without the barges?"

"That is not the point, General. Civilian casualties are not our only concern." He paused, looked at his notes, and said, "Once you launch your transports, how long will it take you to board the barges?"

He thinks he's in charge, I told myself. *I can pull the rug out from under this bastard at any time.* But I still played along. I did not have time to retire his ass at the moment. I was in the Orion Arm, he was in Perseus, and I could not spare an hour to fly out and find him, so I decided to play nice for now.

"We just went over this, Admiral. I told you it should take no more than three minutes to place teams aboard all twenty-five barges," I said.

"Three minutes? That seems very optimistic," said Jolly.

Three minutes was not optimistic; it was utter bullshit, but he didn't know that. I said, "It's a realistic estimate, sir. Remember, the clock doesn't start counting down until we start launching transports. Until then, the Unifieds won't know we are there. That means we can pull the spy ship right up to their docks."

I could not tell if Wallace and Liotta agreed with him or realized he was a coward. Maybe they'd known he was a coward from the start. Whatever their reasons, they had become silent.

"Three minutes, is that really possible?" asked Jolly. He was starting to come around.

"Absolutely, sir," I said, staring into his virtual eyes, willing myself to look as honest and sincere as any Marine in history. "If we catch the Unifieds napping, the entire mission will be over in eight minutes. We'll be done before their ships arrive on the scene."

"This is all moot unless your engineers get that stealth cruiser going," Jolly pointed out.

"Absolutely, Admiral. I wouldn't dream of running the mission without a working spy ship." In truth, I had a plan that involved distracting the Unifieds by attacking Earth with one fleet while sending a second fleet to commandeer the barges. I did not think I could get permission for that plan. If it came down to stealing the barges without the spy ship, I'd begin the mission with a visit to Admiral Jolly . . . then maybe I'd ask his replacement for permission to attack Earth.

Mars got the spy ship running.

While his men began work on the hull and the engines, he sent a message across all thirteen fleets looking for engineers with stealth-generator experience. Three men responded. Before Congress had banished us clones to space, they had worked as technicians in the lab that developed the stealth engines.

We were in business.

EIGHTEEN

Walking through the corridors of the cruiser, I could see that the ship was still a wreck. Not having enough time to replace the ruined sections of the hull, Mars's engineers had patched the holes as best they could. Plasticized metal scabs marked spots where shrapnel had cut through the walls. Most of the holes were the size of a coin, but a few of the rips were so large you could drive a jeep through them.

Mars's engineers ignored fixes deemed nonessential to the operation of the ship. As I entered the second deck, I noticed that the lights were out. "You going to fix those?" I asked Mars. The surveillance and recon computers were on this deck. The engineers Mars had sent to hack into the broadcast station would work on this deck as well.

When I pointed this out to him, Mars said, "God be praised, they'll be wearing soft-shelled armor, sir."

"Yeah, so?"

"This might be an excellent opportunity for them to acquaint themselves with the lighting array along their visors."

"What if they decide to remove their helmets?"

"I would recommend against that, sir," he said. "We haven't repaired the oxygen generator."

"That could be a problem," I said. I'd known the engineers hadn't run the air yet when Mars said I needed armor to tour the ship, but I'd thought he'd have it up and running by the time we began the mission. "What if someone needs to use the head?" I asked.

"Probably not a good idea, General. We haven't restored power to the toilets, either.

"You wanted a self-broadcasting spy ship with working stealth engines, sir, not a luxury cruiser. Getting the broadcast and stealth gear running was miracle enough."

Realizing that the only things holding the ship together were chewing gum and Scott Mars's faith in God, I decided to cut the inspection short. I knew what I needed to know—that the ship was flying, and she had a working stealth generator. I did not want to know the rest.

I returned to the bridge as Don Cutter prepared for the inaugural broadcast. With the *Churchill* out of commission, he had nothing better to do than to risk his life helping me.

"Feeling lucky?" he asked, as I entered the bridge. He and his three-man bridge crew wore the soft armor used by technicians and engineers.

"Mars says the ship is fine," I said.

"With all due respect, sir, that's bullshit. The engines work and the holes are plugged, but this ship is several miles south of fine."

"Just get us out there," I said.

"Yes, sir," said Cutter. "You should probably use the tint shields in your visor, sir."

Larger ships such as battleships and carriers did not have viewports at the front of their bridges. They had display screens, which they shut off during broadcasts. Cruisers and frigates had actual honest-to-goodness viewports. If the people in the bridge did not shield their eyes during broadcasts, they'd most likely go blind.

The tint shields in my visor normally came on automatically; but a quick glimpse of the glare from the anomaly could do a great deal of damage if you looked into it before your shields kicked in. Using optical commands, I initiated the shields. The only problem was that in the moments before the broadcast, the shields left me blind.

Then the broadcast began. Even through the blackness of my tint shields, I could see the anomaly, its thick tendrils of electricity wrapping like ivy around the hull of the ship. I should have looked away from the viewport, but I was mesmerized. To me, the anomaly was like a passageway to death, and death fascinated me.

And then I saw nothing. We had completed the broadcast and left the anomaly to fade behind us. I deactivated the tint shields, and there was Mars—the planet—a tawny-colored globe in a solitary orbit. We had broadcasted in only ten thousand miles off the surface of Mars, on the side of the planet facing away from Earth and the sun. Our ship was small and designed to create a diminished anomaly. Unless they were looking for us, or a ship happened to be passing nearby, no one would notice the anomaly. The Unifieds did not know we had stolen their self-broadcasting ship. As far as they knew, we needed a network for pangalactic travel.

Our stealth generator purring like a newborn, we circled Mars. The planet was dark and still below us. It only took a minute to locate the barges. They sat unguarded and alone.

Everything had gone according to plan so far.

NINETEEN

I entered Landing Bay One, which was dark as death and silent.

The night-for-day lenses in my visor lit the scene well enough. The landing-bay floor was enormous and packed tight with seven transports. Parked with their rear hatches open, the heavy birds sat so close together that their stubby wings interlocked like a cog. I had to walk along the outer wall of the landing bay to get to my ride; the space between the ships was too tight.

The men in my company had already boarded the transports. I expected to find them swarming the deck like ants at a picnic; but there was no room on the deck, so they huddled in the kettles, readying for war. If I listened in over the inter-Link, I would hear some of the men muttering final prayers and others swapping jokes, the more profane the better. Some men faced death in quiet meditation; some tried to hide their fear from everyone, especially themselves.

A few of the boys gave in to the dangerous temptation of rechecking their weapons. Marines clean and load their weapons the day before the mission, when they are calm. There's always a temptation to distract yourself by stripping and cleaning your piece on the way to battle, but nervous men tend to speck up. Guns that worked perfectly sometimes jammed when stripped and assembled right before battle. Equipment that was safely packed sometimes fell out of your go-pack if you tried to reorganize on the way to the battlefield.

The spy ship was still a few minutes from the barges but closing in quickly when I entered the lead transport. The sailor coordinating the mission gave the signal, and our pilot sealed the rear hatch and prepared to launch.

A sled towed the transport through the flight tube, past

disabled atmospheric locks. We did not launch when we reached the end of the runway. Our transports weren't cloaked. Once they launched, the Unifieds would spot them, and the countdown would begin. Instead of leaving our transports lined up on the deck, Flight Control lined us up in the tube. As each bird left the ship, the next one would follow on her tail.

Along with a company of Marines, our transport carried a team of three sailors. Once we secured the barge, it would fall upon these men to pilot her out. I hoped they were up to the challenge. We had no intel about what we might find inside the barges. For all we knew, they worked off brain waves or fart commands.

As I waited in the kettle, a Marine approached me and saluted. He said, "General Harris, sir, the other transports are in place." My visor read his identity from a chip in his visor and labeled him Major Hunter Ritz.

I returned his salute. "Ritz," I said. "Didn't you serve on Terraneau?"

"Yes, sir. From the beginning, sir," he said. "I went down with you and Hollingsworth when you liberated the planet."

He couldn't see through the visor of my helmet, but a smile worked its way across my lips. Not many men had survived that battle. "And now you're a company commander?" I asked.

"Yes, sir," he said.

I was glad to have a battle-tested Marine in my ranks, a man who would not lose control if things headed south.

"I'm going up to the cockpit," I said.

"Aye, sir," Ritz said.

Heading into this battle, he was all spit and polish, but I remembered Ritz on Terraneau. He stumbled into a dormitory filled with orphaned girls and referred to it as a harem. Spit and polish were the last fluids on his mind that day.

Those were the same girls Ava had taught in her classes. They were all dust now. Everyone remaining on Terraneau was dust.

The sea of men parted for me as I crossed the kettle. I climbed the ladder, walked the tight catwalk, and entered the cockpit.

My pilot was Lieutenant Christian Nobles, the Marine I

had adopted as my private pilot. He wore combat armor. Once all the transports were docked, he would join in the fight. On missions like this, every man joined in the fighting ... everyone but the sailors we brought to fly the barges. Marines are interchangeable parts. Flight crews are not.

We traded salutes, and I sat in the copilot's chair. I sighed, and said, "Once more into the breach."

Nobles said, "I saved your seat for you, sir; but I wasn't sure you were coming. I thought maybe you forgot about me."

Maybe Nobles thought I was invincible. He never complained when I dragged him into deadly situations. If he thought my invincibility would protect him as well, he'd never looked at my record and had no idea how many friends had died around me. If he'd known, he might not have been so confident.

Some pilots sit as still as statues while they wait to take off; Lieutenant Nobles was a tinkerer. As we waited for the outer hatch to open, he fiddled with the instrumentation around his seat. He checked dials and flipped switches. I tried to ignore him as he pulled out his M27, but ultimately asked, "When was the last time you stripped and oiled your piece?"

"Yesterday, sir," he said.

"Can you think of any reason why you would have botched the job?"

"No, sir," he said.

"Is there any reason why anyone would have specked with your weapon?"

"No, sir."

"Have you dropped it in mud since you stripped it?"

"No, sir."

"Were you drunk when you assembled it?"

"No, sir."

"Then leave it alone," I said.

"Aye, sir. Yes, sir."

Nobles sat back in his chair and crossed his arms. A few seconds passed, and pretty soon, he was testing the controls again.

I received a message over my commandLink. "General, we are almost in place, sir. Fifty miles and closing."

Outside the cruiser, the space around Mars was silent. Inside our transport, amber lights flashed and Klaxons tolled. In

the last moment before we launched, the ship went silent. The
outer hatch slid open, revealing a galaxy of stars and darkness. With a tap of our thrusters, Nobles lifted the transport
off the sled and we glided into space.

By this time, we had circled Mars and come around to the
side facing the sun. A dust-colored planet glowed below us,
and I saw Mars Spaceport, a white-and-gray plateau that
looked too large to be man-made. It formed a plain across a
small corner of the planet's surface.

And above the spaceport, moored in five razor-straight
rows, were the barges we had come to collect. They did not
look like ships. They looked like floating boxes.

"Listen up," I said over the interLink, opening a channel
that every man on every transport would hear, both sailors
and Marines. "This is General Wayson Harris. I am person-
ally overseeing this operation. You've all been briefed. You
know your objectives.

"You know your assignments. Shoot anyone who gets in
your way on this op. With all of the planets we need to evacuate, every one of these barges is worth millions of lives. We
can't afford to lose a single barge." Even as I said it, I wondered how many other missions of mercy had begun with
similar instructions—*kill anyone who crosses your path.*

"We don't have time for mistakes or mercy on this one," I
said, and with that, I signed off.

No long motivational speech, no threats or cussing. Maybe
I was getting soft.

It might have been that no one was guarding the barges, or it
might have been that we caught them napping. The big ships remained stationary, silent, and dark as we sidled up beside them.

Seeing the mammoth barges from a lowly transport, I felt
like a flea approaching a dog . . . no, an elephant. We had just
come out of a cruiser that ferried twenty-one transports
crammed into three overcrowded landing bays. With a little
creative packing, we could have fit a thousand transports inside one these behemoths.

The barge did not have landing bays. It was designed for
quick evacuations; and the slow act of towing transports in
and out through launch tubes and atmospheric locks did not fit
the mode. The hulls of the barges were dotted with landing

pads, hard points with magnetic clamps and retractable entry-ways. These ships did not have weapons or shields. They were leviathans, giant whales traveling the galaxy, defenseless against attack.

The first four transports to leave the spy ship had to fly double duty. While the rest of the transports docked, they would return to the cruiser for a second set of Marines, who they would deliver to a second barge. The transports themselves were meaningless. Even if everything went according to plan, we would lose them when we broadcasted out. They would fall from the clamps along the hulls of the barges like flakes of dead skin.

Our transports touched down on the landing pads, and the entryways automatically extended. They attached to the rear hatches of our transports, creating a seal. I reminded myself that entering the barges would, in theory, be no more difficult than entering a grocery store.

Time was of the essence. I left the cockpit, breezed across the short catwalk, and slid down the ladder. As lieutenants and sergeants organized the platoons, I made my way to the hatch.

The muffled bang and thud of the struts touching down sounded through walls, and the metal floor bounced and settled under our feet.

There we stood, in the dark metal can that was our military transport, our ranks organized into fire teams, squads, and platoons, our M27s ready in case of resistance.

My heart pounding hard and steady, my combat reflex already begun, I stood at the front of my company, like a private on point duty, my finger already over the trigger of my gun as I watched the doors of the transport slowly grind open.

Cross this line, and the Unifieds will never let you rest, I told myself. The Unified Authority had declared this war, not I; but by stealing their barges, we would take this conflict to a fiery new level. They would come after us. They would hunt us. If we took these barges, the population of Earth would be trapped on a targeted planet. They had already decided to leave every man, woman, and child on every one of our planets to die; now they would see how it felt to be alone with their fate. Bastards.

Since the barge had hundreds of landing pads along its hull, there was no way a skeleton security patrol could have guarded every entrance, so it was no surprise when the hatch opened to an empty tube.

From that point on, I would no longer speak to the entire team on an open frequency. A designated coordinator would take control of the mission. The platoon leaders called the shots with their men.

We charged down the entryway—two platoons, each with its own commanding and executive officers. I led the way. We were one hundred men entering a ship designed to ferry 250,000 people at a time.

The entryway was a hall wide enough for ten men walking side by side. As I ran ahead, the shifting field of gravity played with my balance. The floor was a gravitational field that twisted along the outside wall like the thread of a screw. What had been the ceiling when I entered the tube became the floor twenty feet in. To the men behind me, it must have looked like I was running upside down. When I reached the exit, the orientation of the entryway floor matched the deck of the barge.

Though I had seen the barges during the evacuation of Olympus Kri, I had never set foot on one. The grand size of it took me aback. Maybe it would look smaller crowded with people; but seeing the long, empty deck overwhelmed my senses. It looked like an unfinished spaceport. The floors were flat and wide and open. The glint of naked aluminum girders accented the ceiling. The walls were so far away that they seemed to press themselves into a distant horizon. The frame supporting the deck above us was so low that I could reach up and touch it. Had Freeman come on this mission, he might have bumped his head every few steps.

Dozens of spiraling stairwells twisted up from the floor like giant corkscrews. There was no furniture.

Since I had assigned myself to point position, Major Ritz expected me to report. He asked, "General, do you see anyone?"

"Either they're hiding in the heads or this deck is secure," I said. "Head" was Marine-speak for bathroom.

"Aye, sir, I'll send a couple of men to flush out the head."

I started to laugh at the man's juvenile pun, then realized

that he had made the pun inadvertently. "You do that. We don't want anyone sneaking out from behind the toilets."

"Aye, sir."

Then I said, "Tell your men to stay alert. If there's anybody on this bird, they're going to hit us as we go up the stairs. That's how I would do it. The stairs or the cockpit."

"Stairs and cockpit, aye, sir," said Ritz.

A couple of men split off to check the toilets, the rest of us started toward the stairs. That was when the shooting began.

Ritz divided his men into platoons, then he broke the platoons into squads, allowing him to cover eight sets of stairs at one time. The spiral stairwells were a natural bottleneck. Even worse, they were a bottleneck with a blind spot. Anyone climbing the stairs would be defenseless as he passed through the ceiling and entered the floor above.

The stairs were wide enough for three men to climb at a time, but we stuck to procedure, offering up a point man who peered from the top of the stairs into the next deck as a vulnerable gopher climbing out of its hole.

We sent men up eight flights of stairs, and every single one came rolling back down with blood leaking from large holes in his helmet. The men guarding this bird used guns with bullets. That was good. It meant they were wearing standard armor. If they'd been wearing shielded armor, they would have fired fléchettes that left little pinprick holes.

On any other mission, we would have lobbed grenades up the stairs. We would have hit them with grenades, then come running in on the heels of the explosions to mop up any survivors. We couldn't do that on this mission, though. We needed the barge in working condition. Even a low-yield grenade might cause the walls to buckle in this enclosed environment.

As Major Ritz pulled his men back, I sprinted aft, away from the action. As wide as the barge was, built to carry ten thousand passengers on each of its twenty-five decks, there were hundreds of sets of stairs. They'd need an entire battalion to cover every set of stairs on a bird this big.

I sprinted a couple of hundred yards to reach the far side of the deck and climbed the last set of stairs. I crept up quietly, paused just below the ceiling, my finger on the trigger of my M27. I peered up from the top of the stairs and saw a wide-open floor. I spotted the unfriendlies, but they were a long way away and very distracted at the moment. They did not notice as I continued up the stairs to the next deck.

I called Ritz once I was safely stashed one floor above the disputed deck. "Do you read me?" I asked.

"General."

"Got any flash grenades?" I asked as I crept across the empty deck. I lay on the floor and stared down a stairwell at the attackers. They were not dressed in armor. I got the feeling they were maintenance, deck sweepers, and latrine wipers; but I could not get a count of their numbers.

"Yes, sir."

"Lob a couple up the stairs, then give me a few seconds to clear out the debris," I said.

Flash grenades did not make a violent percussion. They might burn the floor, but they would not blow holes in walls or change the air pressure.

"Are you up there?" asked Ritz.

Borrowing a tactic from Freeman, I answered the question by ignoring it. Instead, I told him, "Make sure your grenadiers know which pills to throw; we can't afford to damage the ship."

"Yes, sir."

"And Ritz, make sure your men don't shoot me when they come up the stairs. I'm the only one wearing combat armor."

"Aye, sir," said Ritz.

I activated the tint shields to protect my eyes as I lay still and waited. Two, maybe three, seconds passed, and the explosions began, brilliant flashes that changed the atmosphere from brightly lit to blinding. I only saw a trace of the flash through the tint shields. The glare evaporated quickly, and I switched back to tactical vision as I leaped down the stairs.

The two nearest men to me lay squirming on the floor. I shot one. The other climbed to his feet, leaving his gun on the floor. He was blind, but he tried to run just the same. I capped him in the back. I didn't worry about the morality of shooting a blind, unarmed janitor in the back. Morality was a game played by college professors.

A few yards away, two men staggered along the floor. Both men carried guns, but neither man had his gun up to shoot.

One guy held his right hand over his eyes like a kid promising not to peek. I shot them.

Short bursts of gunfire rang through the cabin.

Ritz's men secured the ship quickly, and we rushed our pilots to the cockpit. We did not bother checking the engine for booby traps. The Unifieds would not do anything to endanger the barges. They couldn't. In a few short weeks, they would need the birds as much as we did.

The other barges were commandeered without taking casualties. We were the only team that encountered resistance.

CHAPTER
TWENTY

Stealing the barges went smoothly. Getting away did not.

As I entered the cockpit, I heard our pilot say, "What the hell do you mean they're off-line? No one shuts their reactors down."

The nuclear reactors were made to run without interruption. The only time you shut onboard reactors down was for engine maintenance or to retire the ship. With the Avatari making their way across the galaxy, the Unified Authority could not retire the barges.

The answer came from a squawk box. "It's not the reactors. We can't engage the engines."

"Why would they take their engines off-line?" asked the pilot, now sounding nervous.

"Maybe it's a security measure," the engineer said over the squawk box.

The pilot turned to me, and said, "We've got a problem, sir. The engines aren't responding."

I wanted to ask the bastard what he expected me to do about it, but I kept my mouth shut.

Like the rest of the ship, the cockpit was crude—not much more than a two-man booth with windows instead of walls. This bird did not have a wheel or a stick, just large touch screens for the pilot and navigator.

"There must be a security code. See if you can override it." the pilot shouted into the console.

"How the speck am I supposed to do that?"

I had to remind myself that these were not real officers. They were enlisted men who had received minimal training when they were bootstrapped to officer country.

"Find the docking computer and disengage it," the pilot shouted.

"If this specker has a docking computer, it's going to be in the cockpit."

"He's probably right," said the navigator.

The pilot played with his computer, then mumbled, "Specking hell. I found it."

Now that he knew what to do, the pilot mumbled, "Disengaging docking buoys," the floor trembled, and the barge hummed to life.

Then we pulled away from the buoy, and the barge went completely dark. There wasn't any warning. One moment we were moving, and the next moment, the lights went out and the power shut off.

"What the speck just happened?" the pilot asked. I was not sure if he spoke to himself, to me, or to his engineers.

A moment later, the mission coordinator sent a message from the spy ship informing me that the power had died on all twenty-five barges. I stepped to the window of the cockpit and looked out at the row of darkened ships beside us.

Off in the distance, five anomalies appeared like small explosions—the Unifieds had broadcasted ships in to intercept us. They were tens of thousands of miles away, but the term "thousands of miles" loses its meaning when discussing ships capable of traveling thirty-nine million miles in an hour.

Using the commandLink in my visor, I told the mission coordinator, "We have a serious problem here. Have your engineers hacked into the broadcast station?"

That was the beauty of having a spy ship in your fleet. Somewhere out there, a team of engineers sat on an invisible cruiser as they broke into Unified Authority transportation computers.

Figuring that the security signal stopping our barges must be coming from the broadcast station, I said, "The Unifieds must have remote access to our controls."

"I am aware of the situation," said the coordinating officer. He sounded so damned cool. What did he care about the approaching ships? He was safe in an invisible ship.

"Are you also aware that half the damned U.A. Navy just broadcasted in to stop us?" I wasn't scared. Hell, I was in the middle of a combat reflex; fear would have felt good at the moment. Frustration, on the other hand . . .

"They won't attack, General. The Unifieds need those

barges." The bastard threw my arguments for launching this mission back in my face.

I looked out the cockpit and into space. The U.A. ships had already closed the gap and were hovering less than a hundred miles away. I could not see the ships themselves, just the gold-colored glow of their shields. The Unified Authority had placed their ships between us and the broadcast station. We were trapped.

"They have us cornered," I told the officer.

"I have the situation under control," he said.

Outside our barge, the Unified Authority continued to close in on us. Now I could see the shapes of their ships. They were long and narrow, shaped like daggers. They slowly inched toward us, circling the area like sharks smelling blood, evaluating the situation.

Our barges sat defenseless. We sat defenseless. They would not attack us with their cannons and fighters, but we weren't going anywhere with our engines down and our power off.

"You better do something," I said.

"Not yet," he said.

"What the speck are you waiting for?" I asked, the beginnings of desperation sounding in my voice as I watched the U.A. ships wade toward us. I felt helpless. I felt vulnerable; but I did not feel afraid. I did not like the idea of being shot, but I feared failure more than dying. Pathetic as it sounds, I only cared about completing my specking mission.

"General, you do realize that the Unifieds may be listening in on our conversation," the officer said.

The Unifieds had sent five ships to stop us, five capital ships. I could see them clearly. I could see the sharp tips of their bows and the flares from their engines. Only a few miles away, they drifted toward us, circling in for the kill. One of the ships lowered its shields and a line of transports drifted out from each of its landing bays.

The same lack of precautions that had enabled us to enter this barge would now work against us. In another five minutes, those transports would attach themselves to our barge.

The coordinating officer's next comment came over the interLink on a frequency that every man on the mission would hear. He said, "Engage tint shields." I obeyed, but I did not understand.

"Shit," said my pilot, as he pointed out into space. He was not looking at the advancing Unified Authority transports or the battleships.

Behind the battleships, the Mars broadcast station flared into overdrive, its power glowing as bright as a star. It was closer to the Unified ships than I had imagined and moving in fast with threads of lightning flashing across its dish.

I did not know how they accomplished it, but somehow our hackers had freed the station from its orbit and sent it flying in our direction. In another moment, its anomaly would destroy the Unified Authority's self-broadcasting ships. Ships with built-in broadcast engines need to avoid broadcast stations because exposure to an externally generated anomaly overloads their broadcast generators. The anomaly destroyed the U.A. transports as well.

And then the juice from the broadcast station engulfed the barges. I saw the lightning through my tint shields, jagged, dancing slabs of white fire that wrapped around the cockpit, then vanished. When I lowered my tint shields and looked out into space, we were orbiting Gobi.

Moments later, the spy ship materialized. I leaned against the cockpit wall and let out my breath. Using my commandLink, I asked, "Did we get any of their ships?"

Admiral Jolly answered. He said, "We got all of them, General." He sounded ecstatic. "We destroyed two self-broadcasting destroyers and three self-broadcasting battleships."

Jolly paused for a breath or maybe to let me get in a word. When I did not say anything, he added, "I don't know how many battleships they have left, but I bet they don't have any to spare."

We did not have any reliable intelligence about the U.A. Fleet, but it had to be small. The Enlisted Man's Navy had taken a big chunk out of their Navy when they fought us at Terraneau at the start of our rebellion, and they'd not had a chance to rebuild.

"No," I agreed. "Sooner or later, they're going to run out of ships."

TWENTY-ONE

Earthdate: November 22, A.D. 2517
Location: Open Space
Galactic Position: Outside Solar System A-361
Astronomic Location: Bode's Galaxy

With the lights dimmed, Yamashiro and a few of his officers studied every detail as the holographic image played over the conference table. It showed the destruction of the *Kyoto*. For some reason, the satellite monitoring the *Kyoto* had captured the destruction more clearly than the satellites covering the other ships, not that it made much of a difference. Whatever happened to the three battleships had happened in an instant.

Yamashiro's analysts had searched the transmission for lasers, particle beams, and other rays. Nothing. They found no distortions around the ship in the moments before the attack. There were no signs of missiles, rockets, or enemy ships.

Yamashiro paused the feed. The analysts had added a red arrow to the display to mark the mass that they claimed was the wreckage of the ship. The arrow pointed at an unidentifiable wad of material that looked like a glob of soft wax. Measurements appeared along the bottom of the image. The unidentifiable wad was 336 feet long and 56 feet wide. The measurements were about one-tenth the size of the battleship the wad had supposedly replaced. Intelligence analysts said that properly compressed, the *Kyoto* could fit into an even smaller space.

Admiral Yamashiro spoke in a low, slow voice as he said, "This is all that is left of the ship."

The other officers remained silent for several seconds.

Captain Takahashi broke the silence. "That cannot be," he said. "It happened so fast."

Yamashiro had made the same comment when the analysts showed him the image.

Takahashi rose from his chair and leaned over the conference table until his nose almost poked into the ethereal image. He stared at the thing that had once been a battleship, then moved around the table, studying it from different angles. "It's too small to be the *Kyoto*."

Yamashiro said, "You need to read Hara's report. He explains it." Lieutenant Tatsu Hara, a computer-simulations specialist and intelligence officer, ran the *Sakura*'s Pachinko parlors, bars, and casinos. Every sailor on the ship knew him. In Japan, the *Yakuza* had always run the Pachinko parlors and casinos. The *Yakuza* ran the fleet's casinos and Pachinko parlors as well. Tatsu Hara was a gangster.

"Hara says that the right amount of heat applied inside the hull, maybe ten thousand degrees, would cause a battleship to melt and implode."

Takahashi continued studying the display. "Ten thousand degrees inside the ship? How do you heat the inside of the ship? It's not possible."

Before the Avatari invasion and the Mogat Wars, when his daughter Yoko had first brought a boy named Takahashi Hironobu home, Yamashiro had found the boy impressive. He was studying finance at a good university. Yamashiro approved of the boy's life's goals, though he would not have admitted as much to his daughter. When Takahashi graduated, he took a job as a stockbroker . . . a salesman.

Still a salesman, Yamashiro thought to himself.

Master Chief Corey Oliver showed no emotion as he watched the feed. Sitting beside him, Chief Petty Officer Brad Warren followed his lead. When the feed finished, Oliver asked, "May I have permission to speak candidly, Admiral?"

"Speak," said Yamashiro, giving his son-in-law, Captain Takahashi, a glare. Takahashi did not demonstrate the same martial intelligence as the SEALs. Though he knew it was based on an old prejudice, Yamashiro could not shake off feelings that Takahashi was more of an administrator than an officer.

"I don't see how this changes anything," said the master chief.

"You lost three-quarters of your men. You had twelve thousand SEALs, now you have three thousand. I commanded a fleet, now I have one ship, and you have only three thousand SEALs."

"Three thousand men . . . twelve thousand men, we never had enough men to capture a planet," said Oliver. "This was a suicide mission from the start. At least it was for us. I still have enough men to accomplish my objectives."

"What are your objectives?" asked Takahashi.

"The SEALs came to make sure the aliens never attack Earth again," said Oliver.

"Can you do that with three thousand men?" asked Yamashiro.

"We could do it with three hundred men, sir. We just couldn't do it with conventional tactics."

"Master Chief, we came here to protect Earth, not to commit suicide," said Takahashi.

"With all due respect, Captain, we can't protect Earth and ourselves at the same time," said Corey Oliver.

Listening to the SEAL fascinated Yamashiro. He was a clone. He had the face of a monster, no, a demon . . . The nickname *kage no yasha* ran through the admiral's mind, and he dismissed it. Yamashiro gazed at the clone with the oversized bald head. The SEAL's gray skin reminded him of a cadaver lying in a morgue. For the first time, Yamashiro looked past the low, bony brow and saw only admirable qualities.

The SEAL spread his hands on the conference table, and Yamashiro studied his long fingers with their sharp, clawlike tips. They looked like human fingers somehow merged with an eagle's talons.

Senior Chief Warren sat silently beside Oliver. Except for their uniforms, the two SEAL clones looked exactly alike. Yamashiro wondered if they thought alike as well.

"I am not privy to your orders, Admiral, but they can't possibly have included capturing the planet," said Oliver.

"Ships are not used for capturing planets," said Yamashiro, spouting dogma he'd read since becoming an officer.

"Neither are SEALs. We're the fifth column," said Oliver. "The SEALs are the men hiding inside the Trojan horse. We creep inside the walls and open the gate for an invading force. We don't take the town ourselves, that falls to the Marines."

"There are no Marines," said Takahashi. "Not on this mission."

Yamashiro turned to glare at Takahashi. Just for a moment, he felt ashamed of the boy. The admiral's gaze strayed to Senior Chief Warren, sitting silently, allowing his superior to speak as the lone voice. He admired Warren. He admired Oliver. Then he thought about his son-in-law, who had left his wife and children to fly this mission. Yamashiro recognized Takahashi's sacrifices, and his irritation eased.

"What do you suggest, Master Chief?" asked Yamashiro.

Takahashi spoke before the SEAL could reply. He said, "Admiral, we have lost three-fourths of our fleet. We no longer have the firepower we need to carry out our mission. We must return to Earth. We must report that we have located the aliens and request a larger fleet and more troops. As the master chief has suggested, we should have our SEALs open the way, then send in Marines."

Oliver did not speak. Yamashiro asked a second time, "What do you think we should do, Master Chief?"

Oliver paused to consider his words, and said, "Maybe we should return to Earth."

"We should return?" Yamashiro repeated.

"We should return and report what we have found. If we attack now and we fail, everything we have learned will be lost. If the Linear Committee sends another fleet after us, that fleet will be forced to begin the search all over again unless you report our findings.

"We should return to Earth, but not for Marines. We need to make our report, then launch our attack. We're not here to defeat this enemy—we need to destroy them."

Yamashiro listened to the SEAL explain his case and realized something about himself. He didn't want to go back to Earth, not empty-handed. Forced to choose between carrying out a Kamikaze mission and returning to Earth for more ships, he preferred the Kamikaze mission.

Maybe my flagship should have been the Onoda, he thought, reminding himself about the war hero for whom the ship was named.

* * *

After the meeting ended, Master Chief Oliver remained standing beside the conference table as Takahashi escaped like an alley cat running from a fight. He waited for Admiral Yamashiro to finish speaking to his assistant, then he asked, "Admiral, sir, this SEAL wishes permission to speak?"

"What is it, Master Chief?" barked Yamashiro.

"We fired weapons at two moons, is that correct?" asked Oliver. "We fired infiltration pods at the moons?"

"That is correct," the admiral answered in a voice calculated to convey mild irritation.

"As I understand it, only one of the moons was destroyed. Is that correct?"

"What is your point, Master Chief?"

"One of the moons had an atmosphere, the other did not," said Oliver.

"Do you want to see the video feed?" asked Yamashiro.

"No, sir," said Oliver. "Admiral, it seems like the aliens' technology only works when there is an atmosphere present. There was no atmosphere on the smaller moon, and the aliens were not able to prevent our attack. The large moon had an atmosphere, and the aliens destroyed our pods."

Caught off guard by the theory, Yamashiro asked, "What about the battleships?" He figured out the answer to the question even as he asked it.

"Our battleships have atmospheres, sir," said the SEAL.

"Yes, they do," thought Yamashiro, remembering that the intelligence report stated that the heat was internal.

"Admiral, that might also explain why the aliens did not attack our transports," said Oliver. "The pilots purge the oxygen out of our transports."

TWENTY-TWO

Location: Gobi
Galactic Position: Perseus Arm
Astronomic Location: Milky Way

The last census reported the population of Gobi at nearly one million, but that was before the Avatari invaded the planet. At the time of the evacuation, slightly less than a half million people resided on Gobi, most of them living in concentrated clusters. We only needed two barges to evacuate the planet.

We could not have designed an easier scenario for an evacuation—a mostly uninhabited planet with a few centralized population sites, an impoverished people who abandoned their homes and belongings without complaining, an underdeveloped world with empty skies. Few of the civilians owned anything as fancy as private planes, so the navigation lanes remained clear. We'd need to deal with rich people who wanted to fly their own yachts on wealthier planets; but anyone who could afford a yacht would have sailed away from Gobi long ago.

While I was off hijacking barges, Admiral Jolly sent a clutch of senior officers to oversee the evacuation. By the time I arrived on the scene, they had nearly completed their work.

I flew to Morrowtown, the largest city on the planet, population fifty-three thousand. Not much of a city.

One of Jolly's officers, a Captain James Holman, ran the operation with ruthless efficiency. He lifted the people out first, allowing them no more luggage than a change of clothes. That part of the lift took approximately eight hours. Once he had the people out, he sent teams of scavengers to look for food, medical supplies, and other essentials. Holman had thought of something I had overlooked. Before the month was out, we would have millions of refugees to house and to feed. We would need more than food and water. When they became sick, they would look to us for medicine, clothing, soap, shelter, bedding, building supplies, everything.

I did not wear my armor on this excursion. Having spent the first three months of my career on Gobi, I knew I would miss the temperature-controlled bodysuit; but I was more concerned about privacy.

Gobi was wall-to-wall desert, with no oceans, no lakes, and no moisture in its air. Wet spots started forming under my arms and around my collar the moment I stepped out of my transport. By the time I reached my ride, drops of sweat rolled along my spine.

Morrowtown was a two- and three-story burg composed of sandstone-colored buildings. Its streets were dirty and empty; the capital had faded into a ghost town.

Admiral Jolly flew in from the Perseus Arm to accompany me during my inspection. He must have mistaken me for a real officer. He saluted.

"We have three hours until things start heating up," I told Jolly. My information came from Freeman, who had remained on the *Bolivar*. He and I had just finished chatting with the late Arthur Breeze. "We need everyone off the planet by 18:00."

"Where did you get that information?" asked Jolly.

"Anonymous tip," I said.

"You want to share your source?" asked Jolly.

"No, Admiral, I don't," I said.

Before I left Gobi, I would relieve Jolly of command. He was weak and pondering, the kind of commander you indulge during good times but cannot afford during bad. One way or another, he had to go.

"I told Holman not to leave until he packs every iota of food and medical supplies on the planet," Jolly said.

"He's got three hours," I said.

"That sounds suspiciously like an order," said Jolly.

"Not at all, Admiral. I'm not the one calling the shots. In three hours, the atmosphere will ignite, and everything on the planet will burn. The food will burn. The men looking for the food will burn. The Avatari are the ones controlling the clock."

Jolly nodded, then eyed me carefully. He still looked angry. I pretended not to notice.

Using an old farm truck commandeered by his men, Admiral Jolly and I began our inspection. The truck's engine growled so loudly I thought it might give birth. The suspension bounced like it was made of trampoline springs. Jolly and I sat in the back. A master chief petty officer played chauffeur. With the dirty deed I had in mind, I would have preferred a loyal Marine for a driver.

We passed dozens of abandoned vehicles parked along the streets. People had left their hopes and possessions behind. I couldn't judge their hopes, but their possessions had been pretty meager.

I noticed something interesting. The doors of the houses were closed, and many people left their cars parked and locked as if the occupants expected to return home to them. As we passed one building, a dog watched us from behind a window.

I saw sailors and Marines entering buildings and loading supplies on to trucks. When we drove past grocery stores, restaurants, and offices, we found lines of men carrying out supplies by the crate. Driving by a hospital, we passed pallets loaded with cartons marked MEDICAL SUPPLIES.

We drove around a corner and I saw something so out of place that I shouted "Stop!" When the master chief hit the brakes, I climbed out to take a closer look.

It was a double-long freight truck, a real blue whale compared to the small, antiquated vehicles you normally saw in Morrowtown. The truck had jackknifed, its enormous cargo trailer had slid out of control and crashed into the side of a building. As I walked around the front of the cab, I saw that the hood had crumpled during the collision. A steady stream of smoke rose from the engine.

"What happened here?" Jolly asked as he came up beside me, the master chief petty officer following behind him.

The streets seemed empty around us. Dry wind whistled through the buildings, and the sound of a flag's flapping echoed on the breeze.

Looking over the scene, I wondered how recently the attack had occurred. A string of bullet holes decorated the driver's side door.

I had a particle-beam pistol tucked in my belt. It wasn't much of a weapon at long range, but at least I came armed. Admiral Jolly, who had come empty-handed, saw the bullet holes and turned a ghostly white.

"We need to get MPs out here," he said. He sounded out of breath, probably from fear. The watery folds of his second and third chins wobbled as he spoke, and sweat poured over his forehead and cheeks.

"Shh," I said.

"We need help," he said.

A dead sailor lay sprawled on the hood of the truck. He was covered with blood. He'd been shot in the head, and that had no doubt killed him; but he'd also flown through the windshield. Shards of glass poked through his cheeks and his hair and his eyes.

By the way the driver sat slumped against the steering wheel, I could tell that he had not had time to reach for his gun, assuming he had one. One of his hands was still on the wheel.

"Damn," I said. We were evacuating one of our own planets, and we still lost men.

Jolly looked over my shoulder, and asked, "Do you think they're dead?"

They ain't happy, I thought; but what I said was, "The question is how long they've been dead."

Like Admiral Jolly, our driver had come unarmed. It wouldn't have mattered if he had brought a gun; the looters shot him before he could have used it. One moment he was standing behind Jolly, staring up into the eyes of the dead sailor hanging through the broken windshield, the next moment his head exploded and blood gushed from his shoulders and chest. The first shot hit him in the head, splattering his skull and brains onto the truck. The next two shots hit him in the back, leaving exit wounds wide enough for me to stick my hand through.

With Jolly crowding me the way he was, I hadn't noticed a door opening across the street. Five men had emerged. They spotted us, and opened fire. I pushed the admiral out of my way, dived to the ground, and returned fire.

Jolly stood screaming, his hands waving in the air, and the pack instinctively knew he posed no danger. Three of them toted boxes, while two carried guns; but as the shooting began, the three with the boxes tossed the goods aside and produced M27s. Military-issue M27s, the kind that could only be obtained by spilling blood.

Bullets flew wide and high, but nothing came close to hitting me. These boys had big guns and lots of bullets, but they could not shoot for shit when they had to worry about targets shooting back at them. Their bullets hit the back of the truck and the wall of the building behind me. I don't know if they spotted Admiral Jolly as he crab-walked to a Dumpster.

Not worrying about ammunition, the looters advanced toward me, ripping the cab of the truck apart with their bullets long after I had dropped flat on the ground.

Aiming my pistol between the truck's two front tires, I hit the first man in the leg. The glittering green beam struck his shin, blowing it apart. The shreds of the man's dark pants caught on fire as meat, blood, bone, and muscle exploded into a fine mist in the air.

He tried to step on the leg and fell, then he started shrieking as he rolled on the ground. I could have shot the bastard to put him out of his misery, but I didn't. I was in full combat reflex, and my thoughts followed the cold logic of the battlefield. The man no longer posed a threat, and his suffering meant nothing to me.

These men liked shooting unarmed sailors and men they caught unawares, but they weren't prepared for me to return fire. As they stood gaping at their injured friend, I rolled out from under the truck and shot one in the face.

Being shot with a particle beam is nothing like being shot with a bullet. There is no kick, no force of physics that sends you flying backward as the slug tears a tunnel through your body. The ray from a particle-beam pistol hits with no more force than the beam from a flashlight.

The man I had shot dropped where he stood, his hands twitching as his head, neck, and collar evaporated into a blood-colored fog.

One of the remaining looters tried to hold his ground, pointing his gun in my general vicinity and spraying unaimed bullets into a wall. The other two cut and ran.

I nailed the shooter first, hitting him in the right shoulder. He screamed and fell down thrashing, an inch of arm bone poking out of shredded flesh. I hit the first of the two runners in the ass as he dashed up the street. If he'd had another second, he would have reached a corner to hide; but the particle beam blew his legs from under him. He fell face-first to the ground. I left him there, knowing he'd bleed to death in another minute.

The last of the looters ran like a gazelle, his long legs pumping as he screamed and pleaded. Still not looking back, he pitched his rifle over his shoulder and continued running and screaming.

Me, I had turned into a mass of instincts, reflexes, and anger. The Liberator gland had flooded my body with enough adrenaline and testosterone to bring back the dead. I could have picked this last guy off, but ripping him apart with my bare hands seemed like a more satisfactory solution.

Unlike this poor bastard's M27, my tiny particle-beam pistol had not slowed me as I ran. I was in better shape than him, too. He had a head start; but he also had a gut, and I gained ground on him quickly.

Pumping his legs and arms as fast as he could, he risked a quick look back over his shoulder and saw me coming. He tried to run faster, but he had nothing in reserve. He stumbled, righted himself, and lost more ground as we tore across empty streets.

I was breathing hard but not panting as I came up on him. His wheezing breaths sounded painful, and his hair and neck were covered with sweat. So were mine. We were on Gobi, the galaxy's biggest desert. Still running, I reached out, grabbed the bastard by the collar, and pulled back as hard as I could. His feet went forward, his head fell back, and he landed square on his ass.

"Don't shoot! Please, for God's sake, don't shoot!"

Fat old Admiral Jolly came waddling out of his hiding hole issuing orders as if I were a private. "Kill that man!" he yelled. "Shoot him."

Still holding the looter by the back of his collar, I twisted his neck so that he rolled on his stomach with his face pressed into the ground. "Any last words?" I asked.

"I didn't do it. I didn't shoot at you. It wasn't me! It was Todd. The whole thing was Todd's idea." I had a knee in his back, and I crushed his face into the street. His words sounded muffled.

"Kill him!" Jolly shouted.

"Todd's idea . . . Todd's idea. Oh God, don't shoot me. I didn't know he was going to kill anybody," the guy sobbed.

"Look, we got all kinds of stuff." The stupid bastard wanted to bribe me. He told me that he had already found millions of dollars' worth of stuff, and that he would find more.

I was too busy calculating the odds to listen.

"I promise I'll give you half of everything . . . no all of it. All of it! I'm good for it."

In my mind, looters were the lowest of the bottom-feeders, lower even than natural-born officers. I believed in the policy of shooting looters on sight. The policy made sense. In this case, though, I made an exception.

My instinct, of course, was to kill, but giving in to that instinct would have been dangerous. I was in combat-reflex mode. The more violent I became, the more hormone ran through my veins.

"Sounds like you've got the golden goose," I said.

I took some of my weight off the guy's back; and, still whimpering, he placed his hands over his head to protect himself.

"Maybe I should let you go," I said.

"We can be partners. Don't shoot me." His whining gave me a headache.

"How do I know you aren't going to keep it all?" I asked.

"I'll bring it. I promise. We can split it fifty-fifty!"

So now we were back to fifty-fifty, I thought. "I don't trust you," I said, pressing his face into the ground.

"I swear! I swear!"

Jolly shouted, "Kill him, Harris. That's an order." He hadn't figured me out yet. He would in a moment.

"Don't kill me. Please don't kill me."

"How do I know I can trust you?" I repeated.

"Ask anyone. I'm honest. I'm good for it."

"I'd ask your friends, but they're all dead. Everyone else is gone," I growled. Good thing the looter could not see the smile on my face. I was playing with him and having fun.

I gave his face one last shove into the street, then I stood and let him up. I said, "We meet right here day after tomorrow. If you're not here with enough swag to fill a transport, you're a dead man. You hear me?"

"Yeah, yeah! You're going to be a rich man!" he said.

"I can still shoot you. Tomorrow, next week . . . You got that?"

"You won't be sorry. You won't. You're going to be rich."

"Get out of here," I said.

The bastard tried to shake my hand. If he'd been the one with the gun, he would have shot me in the back and not thought twice about it. But I had the gun, so he assured me that I was going to be a wealthy man, then he walked five paces away and sprinted around a corner.

"Why did you let him go?" asked Admiral Jolly.

"Didn't you hear? He's going to make me rich," I said.

"You're never going to see him again," said Jolly.

"Damn straight I'm not going to see him again. Why the speck do you think we evacuated this planet? In three hours, this city is going to be dust, and that bastard is going to be dust along with it," I said. I caught a brief glimpse of the looter scurrying away like a rodent. That summed him up, just another rodent.

Jolly was indignant. He screamed, "I told you to kill him. I ordered you to kill him! You disobeyed a direct order." His face flushed with anger, he waved his hands like he wanted to fly. He became even more flustered when I ignored his rant and walked past him.

"Yeah," I said as I knelt and picked up the M27 to examine it. "We need to talk about that. Admiral, I am relieving you of command."

"You're what?" asked Jolly.

"I'm relieving you of command. These are dire times, Admiral, and you're not fit for command."

"I'm what?" asked Jolly.

"Not fit for command," I repeated. "I am telling you to step down."

"To what?"

"To retire," I said. "Go set up a villa by the beach. Go spend time with your grandkids." He didn't have any grandchildren, of course. He was a clone, and we clones were as sterile as boiling alcohol. You could probably kill germs with the "sperm" we produced.

"Who the hell do you think you are speaking to?" he screamed.

"Admiral Steven R. Jolly, Enlisted Man's Navy, retired," I said.

"And who do you think will take my place?"

"Probably Admiral Liotta . . . maybe Wallace. I haven't decided."

"Do you honestly believe Warhawk Wallace is fit for command?"

"Nope," I admitted. "It really doesn't matter. If Wallace isn't any better than you, I'll retire him."

Jolly shook his head, laughed, and said, "You can't do this," so I shot him with the M27. When I reported his death, I'd say that the looter had done it. This wasn't the first time I had killed a superior officer; and, judging by the men lined up to replace Steven Jolly, it wouldn't be the last time, either.

As the last of our transports left the planet, I received a message from Captain James Holman inviting me to the *Bolivar*'s observation deck.

I had never met Holman in person, but I liked the way he evacuated Gobi. As I had already rifled through one-third of my top leadership prospects, I made a mental note to watch Holman as a possible alternative once I ran out of one-stars.

I went to the observation deck, and there was Holman, who might have been the oddest-looking clone in history. When I first saw him, I even mistook him for a natural-born.

Holman dyed his hair. Older clones were known to dye their hair blond; but Holman, a man in his early thirties, had dyed his hair a coppery version of fire-engine red. He also had a beard. I had seen clones with whiskers, but a beard . . . Like his hair, the beard was that same unnatural color of red.

It was a short beard, trimmed to follow the curve of his jaw. He shaved the beard so that it fell short of his lower lip. The top of his beard followed the curve of his lips to create a well-trimmed look.

"Hello," said Holman in a deep, throaty voice that did not sound clonelike. He had been sitting, watching the planet through a viewport, but he stood and saluted as I entered the deck.

I returned the salute, and said, "You put together a good operation."

"Not good enough," he said. "I understand there were looters."

"You can bring a horse to water," I said.

"But they shot Admiral Jolly. This is a blow to the Enlisted Man's Empire."

I gave him a sly smile, and said, "Not as much a blow as you might think. I understand he planned to retire right after the evacuation."

"He never told me," said Holman. He sounded suspicious.

"Yes, well, Admiral Jolly kept his plans pretty quiet."

With that, we sat and we waited. Death arrived on Gobi six hours late. This had happened before. The virtual ghost of Arthur Breeze tended to err on the safe side with his predictions.

At 03:17 S.T.C. time, the Avatari ignited the Tachyon D particles they had pumped into the atmosphere, and the temperature instantaneously spiked to nine thousand degrees.

Unable to see the destruction through the viewport, Holman and I switched to a computer display. The first thing we saw was the destruction of Gobi Station. Several of the smaller structures around the base exploded. The base itself, a tall spindlelike building armed with cannons and radars and landing pads, seemed untouched by the heat for twenty seconds. Laser cannons exploded, launchpads melted, but the base remained erect.

The heat continued for precisely eighty-three seconds. During that time, the sand around Gobi Station turned orange and melted into a shallow ocean of glass. Outcroppings of rock exploded.

The superheating of the planet caused the atmosphere to rise in its own convection. As it rose, the atmospheric pressure lifted with it, and Gobi Station burst like a balloon. The inner framework remained, but the outer walls blew off the building, leaving the inner structure to wilt in the extreme heat.

When the eighty-three-second attack ended, the atmosphere cooled and fell back into place, crushing the remains of Gobi Station into a twisted pile of girders.

I thought about the looter I had allowed to escape. He'd probably died in the first second of the attack. One moment he'd have been looking at whatever swag he'd accumulated, and the next moment, he was dust.

At least he'd died happy, after all; he'd outwitted a dumb Marine.

TWENTY-THREE

Earthdate: November 23, A.D. 2517
Location: New Copenhagen
Galactic Position: Orion Arm
Astronomic Location: Milky Way

The Japanese Fleet had begun its mission in 2514, right after the aliens were turned back on New Copenhagen. At the time they embarked, it looked like the war for the Milky Way had ended and the Unified Authority had won.

Yamashiro Yoshi recognized the decrepit state of the Unified Authority and saw it as dangerous. The Unified Authority was an empire in collapse. One more attack, be it from renegades like the Morgan Atkins Believers or aliens, and the empire would fall—it was teetering that close to the edge; but an empire teetering on the brink of extinction is also an empire on alert. Fearing that the U.A. Navy might start shooting before the crew of the *Sakura* could identify themselves, Yamashiro decided it would be safer to begin the journey to Earth by stopping by its nearest populated neighbor—New Copenhagen. He would go to the secondary planet first, identify himself and his ship, then continue on to Earth.

The *Sakura* broadcasted in ten million miles off New Copenhagen. The moment the ship cleared the anomaly, Captain Takahashi ordered his engineers to start recharging the broadcast generator . . . a preventive measure.

Takahashi, Yamashiro, and Commander Suzuki Hideki stood around the map table staring into a three-dimensional holographic map looking for signs of ships patrolling the area. They saw no movement, but their radar found several wrecks orbiting the planet. They tried to signal the planet but received no response.

"Perhaps they have abandoned the planet," suggested Commander Suzuki.

Yamashiro grunted his agreement. "Maybe so," he said. "As I understand it, the cities were destroyed during the war with the aliens."

"Should we proceed to Earth?" asked Takahashi.

"No," said Yamashiro. "Send down a transport. There may yet be people on this planet."

"If there are people on New Copenhagen, then they are hiding. We've tried to signal them on every frequency, military and civilian," said Takahashi. "They should have a robot transponder on this planet at the very least."

"New Copenhagen was the Unified Authority's final colony. The Linear Committee would not abandon its final colony without a fight," said Yamashiro. "If they have abandoned the planet, I want to know why." And then he said the words he wished did not need saying, "We may be defending a people who are already extinct."

He gave his son-in-law a sympathetic gaze as he said this, but Takahashi looked away. *She is my daughter as well as your wife. Your children are my grandchildren. We would share in the loss,* he thought.

"Admiral, do you think the aliens have attacked Earth?" asked Suzuki. The conversation did not weigh as heavily on the commander as it did on Yamashiro and Takahashi. He was a bachelor.

Takahashi answered. "It's been three years since we have had contact with Earth. Any one of a million fates may have befallen it during our absence. History may have left us behind. Perhaps the known laws of time do not apply in Bode's Galaxy. By our clock, we have been absent for three years, but one thousand centuries may have passed on Earth."

"Do you really think that is possible?" asked Suzuki.

"Possible? Anything is possible," said Yamashiro. Then he spoke in a hollow whisper as he added, "Perhaps we only saw the first wave of a more massive assault before we set off for their galaxy."

Time passed as the *Sakura* approached New Copenhagen.

The mood on the bridge remained grim. "Admiral, do you want to send SEALs to search the planet?" asked Suzuki.

"Our transports will cover more territory from the sky," said Yamashiro.

"Satellites are even faster," said Takahashi.

Yamashiro began to brush off the suggestion as cowardice, then realized that what Takahashi had said was true. "Ah, satellites, they would be faster still."

The transport deployed three satellites and returned to the ship. Fearing the worst, Yamashiro had the satellite feed sent directly to him. He sat alone in his office, reviewing a live video that confirmed the worst of his fears.

When the Joint Chiefs had briefed him about his mission, they told Yamashiro that the aliens destroyed cities and left them in ruins. He had seen footage of soldiers and Marines fighting battles in forests. General Alexander Smith, the head of the Joint Chiefs, complained that the aliens had "knocked us back to the Stone Age."

The New Copenhagen Yamashiro saw in the video feed was not in the Stone Age; it looked like a planet that would not support life. Where there had once been forests on this planet, the trees had all burned away leaving fields of charred stumps and scorched earth. Yamashiro searched for leaves, moss, ferns, grass, and animals. He found no signs of life, not even around the rivers and lakes.

He studied the ruined landscape for fifteen minutes, then he shut his eyes and pressed his fingers against his eyelids. He thought about the *Onoda*, the *Kyoto*, and the *Yamato*, reasoning that any weapon that could scald an entire planet could certainly melt a battleship into a lump of clay. Trying to repress the fear and anger he felt, he returned to the video feed and was hypnotized by the devastation.

The feed showed a city in which few buildings stood. He saw the frame of a skyscraper. The glass and skin of the building had fallen away from the frame. He saw an old-fashioned brick tower that leaned as if it had melted. The tower reminded him of an ice sculpture left in the sun.

Scanning the remains of the city, Yamashiro did not see flagpoles, steel roofs, glass, or bridges. The ground sparkled like broken crystals. The deserts he saw might once have been pasturelands. Where there once had been deserts and beaches, the sand had melted into glass.

Yamashiro winced when the feed identified Valhalla, the capital city of New Copenhagen. A few buildings still stood in downtown Valhalla, but most had been crushed. The streets had melted. The remaining cars, mostly melted hulks without paint, tires, or windows, sat mired in the street, sunk down to their axles.

They escaped the frying pan only to perish by fire, thought Yamashiro. In this war, the first wave was invasion. The second wave was death by fire. *There can be no question about my duty now,* Yamashiro decided. He and his crew would return to Bode's Galaxy. They would repay death with death.

Should we go to Earth? he asked himself. Few of his sailors knew that they had returned to their home galaxy. Yamashiro decided to show the video feed to Takahashi and the master chief of the SEALs. They would decide together whether or not they should return to Earth.

That was Yamashiro's strategy before the attack. After the attack, he changed his mind.

Three ships broadcasted into New Copenhagen space less than one million miles from the *Sakura*. The ships glowed. Captain Takahashi had never seen ships that glowed like these ships, and the *Sakura*'s sensors could not identify them.

The ships were long and narrow. The only naval ships Takahashi had ever seen were wide and wedge-shaped.

"Can you hail them?" asked Takahashi.

His communications officer said, "No."

His helmsman reported that the ships were closing in at thirty-nine million miles per hour. The fastest Unified Authority ships Takahashi had ever seen had a maximum speed of thirty million miles per hour.

With the ships only one minute away, Takahashi gave the order to broadcast out, and the *Sakura* returned to Bode's Galaxy.

CHAPTER
TWENTY-FOUR

Location: Gobi
Galactic Position: Perseus Arm
Astronomic Location: Milky Way

The Unified Authority sent a spy ship into space near Gobi. The ship dropped a communications satellite and broadcasted out. The satellite carried a video feed that the Unifieds wanted us to see . . . a warning. It showed the fleet of ships we had patrolling Magus, a planet in the Sagittarius Arm.

On the screen, the ships and the planet are plainly visible. A pair of mile-wide discs, the Magus broadcast station, floats in a distant corner of the screen. The station blends into the vastness of space though an occasional flare in its electrical field gives its position away.

Made up of ships from the Sagittarius Inner and Central Fleets, the fleet patrolling Magus includes one fighter carrier, seven battleships, and a fringe of destroyers, cruisers, and frigates. The ships sit in a loose cluster, the smaller ships toward the edge and the fighter carrier in the center.

The first two anomalies appear between the ships and the broadcast station. They look like budding flowers made out of electricity. Unified Authority battleships emerge from the anomalies.

The shields protecting the U.A. ships glow the color of a fading sun. The hulls of the ships are sharp and sleek, they seem to slice through space as they approach the patrol.

Our carrier launches her fighters. Our battleships fire torpedoes and particle beams. Our destroyers fall into place, flanking the intruders, allowing our ships to hit the enemy from every angle. In past battles, the Unified Authority's new shield technology has been strong but not impenetrable. Hit it with a sufficient amount of strength, and it will break down. In a prolonged fight, our fleet has more than enough torpedoes to break through the shields.

A third U.A. battleship broadcasts in on the other side of our fleet, between our ships and the planet. The enemy approaches our ships like wolves attacking a flock. They are predators, unafraid, ready to kill.

If our ships had broken formation and run, some of them would have made it to the safety of the broadcast zone. The U.A. ships are self-broadcasting, they cannot follow ours into the broadcast zone without being destroyed.

With his fighters launched, however, the captain of the carrier cannot cut and run, so our battleships slowly shift into position, forming a border around the carrier.

The Unifieds have a new toy that they want us to see—upgraded torpedoes.

As the U.A. ships muscle their way into our formation, they fire torpedoes at our battleships. Instead of stressing the shields, these new torpedoes obliterate them. They strike the clear, electric panes that form our ships' shields and explode in a glittering flash of red and yellow and gray. The shields light up like glass reflecting bright sunlight, then they vanish.

Admiral Liotta, the newly appointed commander and chief of the Enlisted Man's Empire, froze the video as a torpedo struck the forward shield of the fighter carrier. He let the feed run for another second, froze it, then pointed to the antennae that projected the shields. "Do you see what's happening here? Right here. Look at the antennae. Did you see how they caught fire and exploded. Did you see that? These new torpedoes make our shields overcharge.

"Now look at this. See here, on the shields."

Fire smoldered where the torpedo had struck the shield of a battleship. It wasn't a flaming fire, not the kind of fire that gets extinguished by the vacuum of space. This looked like phosphorous, as if the chemical had somehow attached itself to the shield and fed on itself.

"One hit. One hit. All they needed was one specking torpedo to knock out our shields," he said. "There's no telling what other damage it did inside the ship."

He started the video feed rolling again, this time closing in on one of the Unified Authority battleships as it attacked.

The U.A. ship fires a second torpedo, striking our unshielded carrier just below the bridge. The armor gives way immediately. Flames burst out of the ruptured hull and disappear. As the disintegration spreads along the hull, armored tiles break off like scales, and the ship seems to decompose before us.

Admiral Liotta stopped the feed. "It appears they are using two kinds of torpedoes, one for shields and one for ships." He replayed the attack, this time without pausing for explanations.

Shaped like a knife, the Unified Authority's new battleships have torpedo arrays on either side of their hulls. The ship charges in, hitting multiple targets, leaving them moldering in her wake. A destroyer, two cruisers, and a battleship, are demolished with two shots as the U.A. battleship streaks toward our fighter carrier.

Hoping to stop the inevitable, our fighters swarm the enemy battleship. Fast and small, they are well suited for attacking battleships, baffling their guns and torpedoes with agile maneuvers; but they are too weak to damage the U.A. ship. Their cannons and rockets peck at the shields, causing no damage. They are like bees attempting to defend their hive from a bear. No, it's even worse. They are like minnows attacking a shark.

With our fighters pecking uselessly at her shields, the first of the U.A. battleships fires a torpedo at the fighter carrier. The forward shield lights up. It shimmers and erases as a second torpedo strikes the carrier across her bow.

The front of the carrier caves in on itself, coughing up huge sprays of debris and fire. Bodies fly out in the eruption, men who died the instant the torpedo hit the ship and men who died when they entered the vacuum of space.

The U.A. ship fires one final torpedo, which erases any chance of survivors. When that last torpedo strikes, it breaks the fighter carrier in half.

*   *   *

Seen in real time, the demolition looked even more brutal than it did in slow motion. The Unifieds knew they only needed two shots to destroy our ships. The first shot was the jab. The second shot was the fatal blow.

We all sat in silence for several seconds after the feed ended. "Damn," I whispered quietly so that no one else would hear me. *Why should we even try to defend ourselves?* I thought. If the Unifieds attacked those ships to send us a message, the message they were sending was, "Give up all hope."

"We did not lose every ship in that encounter. After they destroyed the fighter carrier, the Unifieds allowed our remaining ships to escape," said Liotta.

"What were the damages?" asked Admiral Wallace. "How many specking ships did we lose?"

Liotta looked at his notes, and said, "Nine ships. Seven fighters."

"Only seven fighters?" I asked.

"We're in contact with the other fighters. As soon as we are sure the coast is clear, we'll send a carrier out to retrieve them."

"Admiral, who shot the video?" I asked.

"Unknown," said Liotta. "We should assume the Unifieds sent a spy ship to record the battle."

"The sons of bitches sent a spy ship to record a specking massacre," said Wallace. "What a nightmare. What a specking nightmare."

"Well?" asked Liotta. "Any suggestions?"

"It seems obvious," said Captain Holman, who had been the late Admiral Jolly's right-hand man. Holman and I were still orbiting Gobi, still in the Perseus Arm. Liotta and Wallace appeared through the magic of a confabulator.

"What's obvious?" asked Liotta, shooting Holman an icy glare. He did not like having a captain at a summit for admirals; and he especially disliked having that captain participate as if he'd been invited to speak.

Holman looked around the table to see if anyone had seen whatever he had seen. If he was looking for support, he had wasted his time. Not finding any backers, he turned to Admiral Liotta, and said, "We don't need to fight them, they're not trying to take our planets from us. They want their barges back; but they can't fire at the barges because they need them as much as we do. You with me so far?"

He was exactly right. The Unifieds wouldn't waste time trying to conquer colonies they knew were going to be burned. All they wanted was the barges, and they could not take the barges by force.

Holman was a straight shooter. The admirals might not have appreciated his candor, but I did.

"So they want their barges back, so what?" asked Wallace.

"Don't you get it, sir? They can't just take the barges," said Holman.

"What do you mean they can't take the barges? We can't defend our ships against those torpedoes," said Liotta.

Holman said, "Admiral, they can't use those torpedoes on the barges. They need the barges as much as we do. If they break the barges, everybody dies.

"Even if they board the barges, where are they going to take them?"

"They'll specking take them back to Earth," said Wallace.

"How?" asked Holman. "Those barges don't have broad-cast engines. They would need our broadcast stations to take the barges back to Earth."

"Shit," said Wallace.

"You're right," said Liotta. "They can't take the barges without our help. They'd need us to surrender so they can use the broadcast network."

"That's why they're trying to scare us," Holman said, start-ing to sound more confident. "That's why they're using the killer torpedoes. They're trying to scare us into submission. They want us to surrender the barges and the broadcast net-work without a fight."

"Assuming you're right," said Liotta, "what does that get us?"

There he goes, I thought, *Curtis "the Snake" Liotta living up to his dismal reputation.* Holman had seen things the rest of us had missed, now Liotta wanted to make sure the young captain did not get credit for it. I liked Holman. He was an officer I could follow into war.

Holman did not take the bait. He leaned forward in his chair, stared at Admiral Liotta's holographic image through the window, and said, "We don't need to fight. They won't attack our ships if they don't get anything for their trouble. They want us to stand and fight because they know they won't lose. If we run and take the barges with us, they can't come after us if we enter a broadcast zone."

"That's your strategy?" asked Liotta. He laughed. "That's your observation? You think we should just run away." He turned to Admiral Wallace, and said, "I'm sorry. I shouldn't have let a . . ."

Holman interrupted Liotta. He asked, "Do you have a better idea?"

"Captain, I think you'd better . . ."

Holman interrupted Liotta a second time. He said, "Admiral, if we keep our ships close enough to our broadcast zones, the Unifieds won't be able to attack them."

No longer willing to tolerate Holman's insubordination, Liotta slammed a fist on the table. Watching him, I realized that he was no more real to me than Sweetwater or Breeze. Sure, he was actually alive, but what I saw was a holographic hand striking a holographic table. I watched the scene in silence, wondering how long I should wait before relieving Admiral Curtis Liotta of his useless command.

Admiral Wallace cleared his throat, and said, "I'm not sure that a goddamned specking mass retreat counts as a strategy, Admiral; but the kid's got a point."

"What point?" shouted Liotta. "What is his point?" He sounded frustrated. His holographic image stood, paced along its side of the table.

"If we keep our ships just outside the broadcast zones and run when the Unifieds arrive, they won't be able to hit us."

"That's a coward's way of running a navy," sneered Liotta.

"But it will work," said Wallace.

"How about you, Harris? You're the big, hairy-chested fighting machine. How do you feel about ducking for cover every time we see the Unifieds?"

"Works for me," I said. "I think it's an ingenious strategy."

"An ingenious strategy," repeated Liotta. "Well, if we're going to employ the captain's *ingenious strategy* from here on out, let's just hope the Unifieds don't turn up while we're evacuating Bangalore."

Bangalore was the next planet slated by the Avatari for execution. We had already begun evacuating it.

"I'll tell you what," Liotta continued. "We'll leave a hell of a lot of people to fry if we run away at Bangalore." He sat back down and rubbed his eyes, then pressed his hands together as if saying a prayer. "God, I hope they do not attack us at Bangalore."

I wondered if his rantings were the result of theatrics or fatigue? He seemed sincere.

Holman said, "If it comes to a choice between evacuating Bangalore or evacuating all of our other planets, we'll need to abandon Bangalore, Admiral."

Liotta turned to look at me. His eyes were bloodshot, and dark bags circled their bottoms. He asked, "Do you think the Unifieds know that Bangalore is next?"

"They know," I said. They got their information from the same source we got ours—from the virtual ghosts of the late, great scientists William Sweetwater and Arthur Breeze.

TWENTY-FIVE

Earthdate: November 24, A.D. 2517
Location: Bangalore
Galactic Position: Norma Arm
Astronomic Location: Milky Way

What took a couple of hours on Gobi had already taken an entire day on Bangalore, and the end was not in sight.

Admiral Liotta tried to write off the clusterspeck as a question of population. Gobi had a population of under five hundred thousand. Bangalore had eight million residents. It took two barges to evacuate Gobi. If we filled all twenty-five barges to capacity on the first round, we'd still need to send some of them for a second pass.

And it wasn't just a question of loading the people onto the barges. Once we loaded them on, we carted them to Providence Kri, where we had to transport them down to the planet. Off-loading passengers went more quickly than loading them, but not quickly enough.

Once we airlifted the people off the planet, assuming we were able to airlift all of them, we'd still need time to search for food and supplies. We might have been able to evacuate the people and the supplies had Liotta's team not cataclysmically botched the opening hours of the operation.

Liotta's officers were afraid to go down to the planet. They had heard that Bangalore was going to go up in smoke, so they sent seaman and petty officers to run the show in case the Avatari attacked before they were supposed to attack. So battalions of seaman and petty officers went down to the planet and did the heavy lifting, while Liotta's chickenhearted senior officers tried to run the show from orbiting battleships. The arrangement did not work well.

The junior officers running the evacuation were used to taking orders, not giving them. Trying to run things from their Mount Olympus above the clouds, the officers in charge were too removed from the operation to adjust the logistics. Five hours into the operation, the wheels were so badly specked that only one million people had been lifted off the planet, and the officers in charge admitted they would not be able to airlift all of the remaining seven million. By the time I reached Bangalore, searching for food and medicine had become a pipe dream.

Despite all of his bluster at the summit, Admiral Liotta was an idiot who surrounded himself with idiots. It's a popular form of camouflage that many officers use. Hoping to hide their ineptitude behind the greater stupidity of others, morons surround themselves with other morons. There's an old saying that, "In the valley of the blind, the one-eyed man shall be king." In officer country, men with two eyes and two testicles are hard to come by.

Seven hours into the evacuation, Admiral Liotta flew to Bangalore to run the show himself. He began his salvage operation by sending thousands of officers down to the planet and telling them that he would not allow them back on their ships until the evacuation was complete.

Score one point for "Curtis the Snake."

The ground operation progressed slowly, with sailors and Marines herding entire towns into spaceports and makeshift way stations. Transports ran on tight schedules. Loading and unloading times were cut in half, and the pace of the rescue picked up. Sadly, no one realized that they needed to stage the evacuation in waves. The clusterspeck that once slowed operations on the ground simply shifted to a clusterspeck that tied up operations on the barges.

I traveled down to Bangalore to inspect the evacuation and crack a few skulls. As we left the *Bolivar*, I saw six barges hovering in a group just above the atmosphere, looking like a neighborhood of warehouses. Lights flashed along their hulls, directing the lines of transports to open landing pads.

Except for my shuttle, the only ships approaching the planet were transports. Thousands of them climbed in and out of the atmosphere, forming a Y-axis traffic jam that would take hours to untangle. Had the barges been able to fly down to the planet, we could have finished the evacuation in one-tenth the time; but they were big bulky boxes without wings, designed to float weightless in space, free of the forces of friction and gravity.

Off in the distance, a huge fleet of warships loitered just outside the local broadcast zone like clown fish swimming beside an anemone. If the U.A. attacked, our ships would dart into the sanctuary of the zone, where self-broadcasting ships could not follow.

And if the Unifieds went after the barges . . . We'd rigged them with bombs. We were prepared to blow ourselves up one barge at a time until the Unified Authority realized that if we had to die, we'd die happy in the knowledge that we were dragging our natural-born creators down with us.

I started the trip to Bangalore in the luxurious main cabin of my personal command shuttle—a remnant from happier days. A minute after we cleared the *Bolivar*, I entered the cramped cockpit. My pilot, Lieutenant Nobles, and I had developed a friendship; I felt an obligation to go chat with him.

"Do you think they're out there?" Nobles asked as I entered.

"Who? The Unifieds? They've got eyes out there. You can count on it," I said.

Somewhere out there, a U.A. spy ship would be watching, recording our every move. They recorded the destruction of New Olympus and Terraneau. Why stop there? They probably recorded our evacuations and evaluated what worked and what failed. They'd have an evacuation of their own soon enough. If they got started right away, they could probably even build a new fleet of barges by the time the Avatari arrived; but they would not do that. We had stolen their property. The bastards wanted it back.

As we neared the atmosphere, a flash appeared in the distance as one of the barges entered the broadcast zone, ferrying another quarter of a million people to temporary shelters on Providence Kri.

We could not continue storing people on Providence Kri forever. The clock was ticking on that planet as well. We'd eventually need to pull everybody off that rock, too. The logistics of evacuating Providence Kri would be staggering, tens of millions of people.

Five hundred thousand evacuees from Gobi, eight million from Bangalore—the numbers added up quickly. Sooner or later, we'd be hauling fifty million refugees. What would we do at that point?

The Avatari were rolling through the galaxy, and we were trying to keep ahead of the storm instead of working our way around it. Sooner or later, we would need to start settling one of the planets that the aliens had already incinerated. If we moved refugees anywhere else, we would need to move them again.

"What do you think the Unifieds will do when the aliens reach Earth?" Nobles asked. "Think they'll ask us for help?"

"They might," I said. "I think they'd rather kill us and take their barges back. If they can't, they'll probably ask for help."

"Yeah, well, if Tobias Andropov asks me for a ride, I'll tell him to kiss my ass," said Nobles. Andropov was the senior member of the Linear Committee, making him the most powerful politician in a mortally wounded republic.

We entered the atmosphere, the shuttle's sleek profile piercing the bubble with very little resistance. When transports fly down to planets, they batter their way into the atmosphere with all of the grace of a hammer hitting glass. My shuttle pierced it like a needle.

"I heard they wanted to set up undersea cities," said Nobles.

Before becoming a Unified Authority signee, the French government had launched an undersea mining and colonization program called the Cousteau Oceanic Exploration program. They hoped to form an alliance that would rival the U.A.'s space-exploration alliance, but only Tahiti signed on.

"I heard that, too," I said.

"Think they can go deep enough?" Nobles asked.

"Depth isn't the problem." Forty feet down would be deep enough. The French built a city called Mariana that was three miles down. It only held five thousand people. I said, "Size is the problem. Their undersea cities are too specking small."

"That's funny," said Nobles. "Now they know how it feels."

The shuttle handled atmospheric travel like a jet, channeling air currents to turn and rise and dive. Nobles slowed us to a sluggish three hundred miles per hour as we dropped toward the clouds. It was night, moonlight made the clouds gray, and the ocean below us was black. Wherever I looked, I saw transports muscling their way through the sky, looking no more aerodynamic than bumblebees, and exceptionally clumsy at that.

Nobles whistled, and said, "Man, we really specked them over when we stole their barges."

"They specked themselves," I said, remembering how the Unified Authority had forced the clone military into rebellion.

A twisted peel of clouds veiled my view of the city below. Pockets of lights sparkled in the darkness on the ground. *Evacuation centers,* I thought.

A few minutes passed, and we flew over the city. We slowed as we approached a sports stadium that had been converted into a spaceport. Three transports rose from its rim, dozens more sat side by side on its open field. The lines of people packed around them looked like grains of sand.

The entire scene was awash with light. Bright lights showered down around the rim of the stadium, orange-tinted lights mapped the parking lot, and a long, slow-moving line of headlights traced the street leading into stadium.

Just a few moments later, we passed a bubble of light that resolved itself into a shopping mall, its enormous parking lot converted into a landing strip. A sea of people covered the parking area.

We flew to the Bangalore pangalactic spaceport, the hub of the evacuation. Transports, which have skids instead of wheels, can land in tight spaces and on tiny platforms in sports stadiums and shopping centers. My shuttle had wheels. We needed a runway.

The control tower cleared us, and Nobles set us down. It happened that fast. Three officers met us as we left the shuttle. As I left the shuttle, I inhaled a jolt of ozone. Some of our transport pilots were flying with their shields up. The shields generated ozone. With so many transports flying in and out of the atmosphere, I wondered what kind of pollution problems the ozone might create. Whatever problems it created, they would not last long.

The officers had a sedan waiting on the runway. They hustled me into my seat, and we drove into the city.

In the minutes it took me to get through Gandhi Spaceport, I saw two, maybe three, hundred passengers charging toward a transport made to carry one hundred people. The stampede left bloody bodies in its wake.

We passed roads clogged with panicked refugees and a city with masses who looked ready to riot. "Slow down," I told the driver, as we passed a corner on which armed soldiers manning a chest-high barricade tried to hold back a crowd.

"Stop the car," I said.

I climbed out of the car. The people looked terrified, so did the officers who had come to organize the evacuation.

"A hundred at a time," I mumbled.

"What was that?" asked one of the officers.

"Nothing," I said. "Just thinking out loud." Evacuating a planet with eight million people in transports that were only capable of carrying one hundred refugees at a time seemed incredibly inefficient. It took ten thousand transports to move one million people, and it would take eighty thousand to empty this planet. Eighty thousand liftoffs . . . Eighty thousand dockings . . .

The officers drove me to an Air Force base, where a small knot of Marines came out to greet me. We traded salutes and pleasantries. Admiral Liotta had placed my Marines in charge of looking for food and dealing with looters. Armed troops carrying M27s patrolled the streets. Looters would not be offered evacuation. The Marines had orders to shoot them on sight.

"How is the evacuation going?" I asked one of the Marines.

"It's a mess, sir," said the colonel in charge. "I don't know who came up with these evacuation plans, but we're finding looters on every street. It's a mess."

A Marine captain said, "General, these people are scared. We're herding them like cattle, and they're scared of us. They're even more scared we're going to leave them behind."

"I can take you to see what we're dealing with if you want, General," the colonel offered.

I shook my head and turned to one of Liotta's officers. "Will we get them all out?" I asked.

"It's going to be close, sir," he said.

"How about supplies?" I asked. "Do we have enough time to gather supplies?"

"We already gathered 'em. We've had teams out all day. We have the food and the medicine. All we need now is transports to lift the supplies out."

"Where are the supplies?" I asked.

"Stacked up and ready at the spaceport."

"Outstanding," I said. "So the supplies we need will be in neat stacks when they burn to dust."

"But, sir . . ." Liotta's officer started to explain himself, then thought better of it and fell silent.

"Where is Admiral Liotta?" I asked the officer.

"I'm not sure, sir. He might be at Gandhi."

"Back at the spaceport?" I asked. "Well that's excellent. Let's go find him. You can show me the supplies when we get there."

I'd lost track of Ray Freeman since the last time we'd contacted Sweetwater. I ran into him as we left the Air Force base. He stood outside the gate looking more tired and old than I had ever seen him, his dark skin blending into the shadows as he waited for my car to clear the gate.

I told the driver to wait for me and climbed out of the car. I walked on the loose gravel along the side of the road and approached Freeman. I asked, "What are you doing here?"

"You listed me as a civilian advisor," he said. "I came here to advise."

"Looks like these guys need all the advice they can get," I said.

"We don't have enough time to get everyone off the planet," Freeman agreed.

"Yeah, I know. I think it's time I relieved the officer in charge," I said. "I hear he's at the spaceport."

"You mean Liotta?" asked Freeman.

"That's the man," I said.

"He's left the planet," said Freeman.

"Know where he went?"

Freeman said, "I can find him for you."

I smiled, and said, "Ray Freeman, welcome to the Praetorian Guard."

* * *

When we returned to the spaceport, I noticed things that had eluded my attention when I first arrived. I asked the commanding officer to take me on a tour. He pointed out the crates and pallets along the runways. I saw trucks loaded with supplies waiting by the hangars.

Five hangars, each the size of a college auditorium, stood in a row behind the airfield. The doors of the first four hangars hung open, revealing stacks of supplies that seemed to overflow from within their walls. I asked one of my guides about the fifth hangar.

He answered, "That's the crematorium, sir."

"The crematorium?" I asked.

"A civilian came through . . . a big man. He was a black man, bald and built like a mountain. He had orders identifying him as a civilian advisor."

One thing about Freeman, he always left a lasting impression.

"He took a jeep into town. When he came back, he had a busful of prisoners," said the officer. "He identified most of them as gangsters, but a few of them were fleet officers as well.

"He said he caught the gangsters bribing their way onto a transport."

"And the officers?" I asked.

"They accepted the bribes."

Freeman had probably spotted some civilian driving a truck up to a transport and gone in to investigate. He'd come to Bangalore hoping to save lives, but Ray Freeman did not mind killing people who got in the way of salvation.

"He left the prisoners in the bus and parked the bus in the hangar. That's why we call it the crematorium. He left them there to burn."

I looked at the hangar and smiled. A private crematorium for gangsters and crooked officers . . . it had a certain ring to it.

TWENTY-SIX

I got the feeling Admiral Liotta suspected me of having something to do with Admiral Jolly's untimely demise. Liotta conducted his business via the confabulator, holding daily summits and refusing to grant me a face-to-face interview. I did not understand the Navy way. In the Marines, we treated our subordinates like missiles, we told them what to do and launched them in the right direction, knowing that destruction would follow. In the Navy, the officers seemed so damn political.

Once again finding myself in a war room, speaking through a confabulator, I missed the halcyon days of summits with Gary Warshaw. Back when he ruled the Enlisted Man's Empire, he held summits in which all the top brass met behind closed doors.

At least I was not alone in the conference room. Captain Morris Dempsey, the officer Liotta placed in charge of evacuating Bangalore sat to my left. Captain Jim Holman, the redheaded clone, sat to my right. Dempsey looked stressed. Holman looked like a man who didn't have a care in the world.

"What is the status of the evacuation?" asked Liotta.

Dempsey said, "It's in progress, sir." Then he quietly muttered, "Whatever happened to briefing and debriefing, and leaving me to do my job in between?"

"Is it running according to schedule?"

Dempsey fielded the question. He said, "We fell behind schedule at the start, sir, but things are looking up now."

Holman, who was pretending to take notes, lazily wrote "Bullshit" on his notepad.

"Glad to hear it," said Admiral Liotta. He sounded enthusiastic about the news. By that time, I had come to realize that Liotta was both a coward and entirely inept.

Admiral Wallace seemed surprised by the report. Using Liotta's undermining tactics, he asked, "Will you be able to rescue the entire population?"

"Yes, sir, Admiral," said Dempsey.

"Really," said Wallace. "Every man, woman, and child?"

"Yes, sir. We almost certainly will."

His expression serious and intent, Holman made obscene gestures with his hand under the table. Since he managed to keep his shoulders steady, the admirals had no clue. Dempsey saw it, though. His eyes turned to daggers.

"Well done, Dempsey," said Liotta, giving Wallace a crooked smile.

"How about supplies?" asked Wallace.

Momentarily distracted by Holman, Dempsey could not prevent his insecurity peeking from behind the façade. "I . . . I need to get back to you on that one, Admiral. I'm not certain where we stand, sir," he said.

Under the table, Holman's hand stopped in midmotion and returned meekly to his lap.

Liotta sighed, and asked, "So are you telling me, Captain, that we are evacuating millions of people but we will not have food to feed them? Is that what you are telling me? Why the hell should we evacuate them? If they're going to die either way, we might as well leave them to burn on Bangalore, Captain. That way they will die faster." As Liotta's rant built into a scream, a ton of blood must have pumped into his head. His face turned the bright red of oxygenated blood. It looked like he had a fever.

I had the feeling that Liotta did not feel as concerned about the supplies as he pretended. Wallace had just shown him up, and that affected Liotta deeply. He shouted, "Start pulling supplies, Dempsey. Do not leave Bangalore with an ounce less than one million tons of supplies. That is an order."

Dempsey said, "Sir, zero hour is at 08:00." That was three hours away.

"Son of a bitch," muttered Liotta. He wasn't calling the captain a son of a bitch, he was referring to the situation. "Then you had better come up with something fast. Don't even try leaving that planet without the supplies, or I'll leave your ass there to burn."

It was a pathetic threat made by a cowardly leader. Even with the supplies waiting in the hangars, we lacked the manpower and space needed to load one million tons of supplies onto transports in a three-hour stretch.

Dempsey took a moment to compose his thoughts. He breathed in deeply, held it, exhaled. His shoulders hunched, and his back drooped. He said, "Yes, sir. I will do my best, sir."

Holman had returned to taking notes. He wrote "Pucker Up Slut" on his notepad.

"Don't do your best," said Liotta. "I've already seen your best. Your best is what got us into this situation." He sounded so smug, so sanctimonious. The admiral had dumped a nearly impossible task on a useless lackey; and now that the lackey showed he was not up to the job, Liotta wanted to dodge any blame.

I decided to take some of the heat off Dempsey's shoulders. I asked, "Admiral, what is happening with the rest of our fleet?"

"Nothing important," said Liotta.

"That's funny, I heard the Unifieds attacked our ships in the Cygnus and Perseus Arms," I said. "Maybe it's just me, but that sounds important."

On Holman's pad I saw:

Hair Ass
Wall Ass
Curt Ass

He tilted the notepad for me to see, stifling a smile. Next time I attended one of these meetings, I'd make him leave the notepad outside.

"We kicked their asses," said Wallace.

Still playing with his notepad, Holman wrote "Truth" and "Bullshit," with a little box beside each choice. He placed a check mark under "Bullshit."

"Is that so?" I asked. "I heard the Unifieds kicked our asses."

"Specking lies," said Wallace.

Holman ticked a second check under "Bullshit."

"Did we lose any ships?" I asked. I knew the answer. We'd

lost fifteen ships, including five battleships and a fighter carrier.

"Well, yes. We took losses."

A tick under "Truth."

"Did we destroy any of their ships?" I asked.

"Damn straight we did. We destroyed three of their ships."

Holman placed a check in the middle of the pad, halfway between "Truth" and "Bullshit."

Somebody needs to teach Wallace the difference between winning and losing, I thought to myself. He seemed to believe that winning a fight meant losing more ships.

I changed the subject. "Admiral, we have eighteen more planets to evacuate," I said. "We're in trouble on Bangalore, but that will just be the start of our problems if we can't find a permanent place to relocate evacuees."

"How about Earth?" asked Admiral Wallace.

"Be serious," said Admiral Liotta.

"I'm being serious," said Wallace.

"So am I," said Admiral Liotta. "Now shut the speck up."

Maybe I had emboldened Wallace by calling his bluff, or maybe he sensed Liotta's fear. Either way, he did not back down as Liotta had expected. He said, "Admiral, we buy ourselves a reprieve by taking the Unifieds out of the equation. They have food to spare, space to spare, and their planet is the last one on the aliens' agenda."

"We don't have time for this, Admiral," said Liotta. "Right now we need to concentrate on getting people off Bangalore."

"You want to know about Bangalore; I'll tell you about specking Bangalore," said Wallace. "A lot of people are going to die on that goddamned rock. We are not going to pull any specking supplies in time. Your shit-for-brains evacuation plan failed, and now we're wasting our specking time trying to play catch-up. That's what is happening on Bangalore, Admiral."

"Wallace, you are out of line," growled Liotta.

I did not like Wallace, and I hated myself for agreeing with him; but he was right. He sat there calm and self-satisfied, the skeletal remains of a man, so skinny and pale and covered with scars that he looked near death.

Rattled, angry, and trying to regain control of a meeting that seemed to have left him behind, Admiral Liotta turned to me, and asked, "Do we know which planet is next? Please, for God's sake, don't say it's Solomon."

But, of course, it was Solomon.

"How did you know it was Solomon?" I asked.

"We had five ships patrolling Solomon," said Liotta. "As of two hours ago, we lost contact with them."

They must have been under Wallace's command. He squirmed in his chair as Liotta delivered this information. Wallace wiped sweat from his forehead and loosened his collar but remained absolutely silent.

Five more ships, I thought. "Why didn't they broadcast out?" I asked.

"That's the problem with Solomon, the broadcast station is too far from the planet," said Liotta. "It's the same setup as Earth with the Mars broadcast station, depending on where the planet is in its orbit, the trip can take ten hours."

Liotta let that sink in, then he said something chilling. "I've put a lot of thought into this one, Harris. We're not going to evacuate Solomon. It's not worth the risk."

"What do you mean by 'not going to evacuate'?" I asked.

"I mean that we are not going to sacrifice ships and men on a mission that cannot possibly succeed," Liotta said. "Harris, the Solomon broadcast station is currently sixty-three million miles from Solomon. It would take two hours to cover that space in our fastest ships. Those barges don't even fly five million an hour. It would take them a full day just to fly to the planet and back.

"If you think we're having trouble getting people off Bangalore, just try figuring out the logistics for Solomon," Liotta said, sounding totally at peace with his decision.

"So you are not even going to warn them?"

"What could we accomplish by warning them?"

"They can find caves and tunnels and basements. They can go underground," I said.

"That's not what would happen," said Admiral Liotta. "If you tell those people that their planet is going to explode, you get riots and chaos. Some people might survive . . ."

"There are seven million people on Solomon," Wallace announced in a cold, cold voice. "You make the call, Harris. Maybe we should lift the kids from the planet, that's the humanitarian move, yes? We rescue the children, then transfer them across the galaxy as a shipload of orphans.

"Of course we could take the pragmatic approach . . . save the scientists, the politicians, the people with something to contribute. Or we could be practical. We can save everyone on one of the continents, maybe even an entire hemisphere."

"Get specked," I snarled, though I knew the son of a bitch was right. He was also an asshole. He had come to the right decision but I doubted he had made that decision out of a sense of duty or propriety. Liotta and Wallace were bastards first and officers afterward. They would abandon the people on Solomon because it was easy to abandon them, not because it was necessary. That was my take.

Having made the tough call, neither Liotta nor Wallace showed interest in debating their decision. For once they were in agreement.

"We need to warn those people, we owe them that much," I said.

"You warned Terraneau," Wallace pointed out. "How did it work out?"

"Solomon is a lost cause, General," said Admiral Liotta. "It's time you accept that."

Maybe he was right, but I specialized in lost causes.

TWENTY-SEVEN

Earthdate: November 25, A.D. 2517
Location: Solar System A-361
Galactic Position: Solar System A-361
Astronomic Location: Bode's Galaxy

It was as if every man on the bridge had forgotten to breathe.

Takahashi felt it. Looking over at Yamashiro, he saw that his father-in-law felt it, too.

Reentering the solar system felt like climbing into an open grave. They were tempting fate. The aliens had destroyed three battleships in this solar system, melting them from the inside out.

"I've located the transports, sir," said the communications officer.

That was a relief. Takahashi had half-expected to find the melted shells of the two transports floating lost in space. "Tell the pilots we are on our way," he said.

The *Sakura* had reentered the minefield, and every sailor knew it. No one spoke unless there was an official reason. Takahashi had never seen a bridge so quiet for so long.

"I want the broadcast engines charged and ready," he told Suzuki. He spoke in a whisper though he had no idea why. It was as if he suspected that the aliens might be eavesdropping on them.

"Yes, sir. It's already begun."

The *Sakura* did not have room for two more transports in her landing bays. Takahashi planned to create room for the stealth birds by jettisoning two standard-issue transports. He needed stealth transports for an experiment.

When the aliens had destroyed the *Onoda* and her sister

ships, they did not attack the transports. Maybe the aliens could not see through the transports' stealth shields. To test the theory, Takahashi planned to purge the oxygen from a stealth transport and send her out as a drone. If he could sneak stealth transports past the aliens, maybe he could send them to their planet for an old-fashioned bombing run. Maybe.

Moments after entering the solar system, Takahashi learned that the mission would fail.

His chief navigator approached the table where he stood with Admiral Yamashiro and Commander Suzuki. All three men turned to look at him, but the navigator spoke directly to the captain.

"Captain, sir, the aliens have placed an ion shield around their planet," said the navigator.

He pointed to a display showing a planet that looked like a ball bearing. Instead of clouds and continents, the planet's surface appeared to be sheathed in a white gold sleeve.

"Thank you, Lieutenant. That will be all," Takahashi said. He tried to appear unconcerned even as he felt his heart sinking.

"Yes, sir," said the navigator. He saluted, turned, and walked back to his post.

Deafening silence followed.

Takahashi looked back at the image of the planet, a gleaming white gold ball surrounded by the luxuriant darkness of space. It looked like a gem, or possibly the eye of a demon. It looked both beautiful and evil.

"They've sleeved themselves," said Yamashiro. "Just like they sleeved Shin Nippon."

Frustrated beyond words, Takahashi looked down and shook his head. He felt a momentary urge to shout, but he swallowed down his emotion, just as he had swallowed down every other emotion over the last three years of his life. "The dice never break our way," he said.

"Captain, sir, we still need to rescue those pilots," said Suzuki.

"Rescue our pilots and fire our bombs," Takahashi told Commander Suzuki. "We proceed with our mission as we planned it."

He looked to his father-in-law for approval. Grim-faced as ever, Yamashiro met his gaze and gave him a single nod.

* * *

When the Japanese Fleet had first left for Bode's Galaxy, Yamashiro considered the SEALs expendable, maybe even disposable. He also believed he could locate the aliens and destroy their planet without needing the SEALs' services. After seeing three of his battleships destroyed, the admiral no longer held either belief.

Sitting in his stateroom, the lights dimmed so low he could not read from paper, he rubbed his temples, stared into a dark corner, and thought about the honored dead. He pictured Captain Miyamoto Genyo, whom he had come to regard as the last of the Samurai. Yamashiro had admired Miyamoto more than any man he had ever known. He revered Miyamoto above even his own father. When the aliens had destroyed the *Onoda*, they destroyed a portion of Yamashiro's soul. With the burning of the *Onoda*, much of Yamashiro's strength melted as well. He had leaned on Miyamoto's resolve throughout the mission.

Yamashiro believed he was different than other men. Other men joked about having angels and devils on their shoulders; his voices came from fear and aggression. An angel and a devil would have been easier to deal with. The devil might have been persuasive, but you always knew it was lying to you. Unable to ignore fear or aggression, Yamashiro found himself performing a balancing act. Sometimes, despite instincts telling him to wait, he needed to pull the trigger and finish the job. Sometimes it went the other way.

Now that Miyamoto was gone, Yamashiro Yoshi had to divine his own philosophy of war. Under Miyamoto's tutelage, the admiral had come to equate honor with death in battle. Now, having seen three battleships melt, he'd come to realize that there was no honor in a pointless death. He was not afraid of dying in battle, doing his duty even when it might cost him his life. Having a chance to succeed, that changed the landscape of Yamashiro's mortality. He did not mind dying during the invasion of the alien home world. Dying during the destruction of an abandoned base on a forgotten moon, though, that was pointless.

Yamashiro did not mind laying down his life invading the Avatari. By extension, he would willingly ask every man and woman under his command to make the same sacrifice . . . if they had a chance of accomplishing their mission.

If death took on meaning in battle, Yamashiro realized he had dishonored the noble dead by assigning every dangerous detail to the SEALs. He admired the SEALs. He respected their courage. He would not deny the SEALs their chance to die with honor; nor would he deny his sailors that opportunity, men and women alike.

The flashing light on Yamashiro's communications console interrupted the darkness and his thoughts alike. He knew who was calling and why, his assistant had already warned him. Though he did not feel like having the discussion at that time, Yamashiro answered the call.

"Moshi Moshi," he said.

"Admiral."

"What do you need, Captain?"

"The master chief of the SEALs came to see me."

"So I understand."

"He says he has men who have been trained to pilot a transport."

"Yes. He left a similar message with my assistant."

"He offered to have his men fly a mission to A-361-B." Takahashi sounded excited, like he had made a great discovery and expected Yamashiro to applaud. He waited for Yamashiro to say something, but the admiral did not respond.

"Admiral, we don't need to risk our men," said Takahashi.

"Hiro," Yamashiro said in a cheerless whisper, "the SEALs are our men."

Takahashi did not argue the point.

"Tell Master Chief Oliver that his offer is appreciated, but that on this mission, I would prefer to send Japanese."

Yamashiro knew that the SEAL would misinterpret this response. He would mistake it for prejudice, but that was okay. In his dealings with Illych and Oliver, he had seen how well the SEAL clones dealt with prejudice. The worse he treated them, the more happily they seemed to respond. Yamashiro did not think they would cope with his concern for their well-being quite so easily.

CHAPTER

TWENTY-EIGHT

Location: Solar System A-361-B
Galactic Position: Solar System A-361
Astronomic Location: Bode's Galaxy

Before the destruction of the *Onoda*, the *Kyoto*, and the *Yamato*, Yamashiro considered the Kamikaze farewell an appropriate tribute. On this day, he did not see the two transports off as they left for A-361-B. The time for ceremony had passed.

A few friends came to see the crews as they boarded their ships. The crews entered the launch area and noticed the deck more empty than usual. The only sailors they saw were a couple of mechanics bending over the open engine compartment of a transport. When the pilot looked in their direction, the mechanics turned away.

"We're flying a mission, right?" one of the technicians asked the pilot of the lead transport.

"Last I heard," said the pilot.

"What relief. For a moment I thought maybe we had leprosy."

The open hatch at the rear of the transport reminded the pilot of a mausoleum. He took one last breath before putting on his helmet, held the air in his lungs, then sighed as it escaped through his lips.

He placed his helmet over his head, and the technicians followed his example. They walked up the ramp and into the kettle, no one speaking. An even dozen stealth infiltration pods lay on the deck of the kettle, strapped along the wall, their polished tops reflecting the light from the technicians' helmets.

"The SEALs call them caskets," one of the techs told the pilot.

"Yes, I've heard that," said the pilot. He felt hollow inside. He felt scared. This was the part of the mission that worried him most, thinking he might reveal the fear he so wanted to hide. The pilot believed he would have better control once his transport left the *Sakura*; but at present, he doubted his own courage.

It was not the pilot's first mission. He'd flown Illych and his team to A-361-F, the fatal mission. He'd observed their Kamikaze farewell and remembered thinking the ceremony was a waste of time as he watched the SEALs board his transport.

"Secure the cargo," he told the technicians as he climbed the ladder to the cockpit.

The pilot walked the narrow catwalk between the ladder and the cockpit, a man facing the destiny he could no longer escape. He walked slowly, his head down, arms dangling by his sides. In his heart, he hoped that Admiral Yamashiro would call off the mission; but he knew that would not happen. Now that the hatch was sealed, and he had entered his cockpit, the pilot found the resolve that would enable him to carry out his duty.

"Flight Control, this is Transport 1," he began, and he went through the launch steps as if they were the five stages of death. He contacted the pilot of the second transport to make sure his ship was ready.

Flying at its top speed of thirty million miles per hour, the *Sakura* ferried the transport to a delivery point approximately three million miles off A-361-B. That would leave the transports with a long, slow flight; but that was how it had to be. If they launched too close to A-361-B, the aliens would surely spot the *Sakura*.

When he received the message that the ship had arrived, the pilot purged the air out of the kettle and launched.

Calling from the kettle of the transport, one of the technicians asked the pilot, "If the aliens made the air in the *Onoda* nine thousand degrees, what's going to stop them from igniting the air in our helmets?"

"Probably it's not enough air," said the pilot. "They have ignored our helmets so far."

"They had better targets last time," said the technician.

"No one forced you to take this mission," the pilot pointed out.

It was true. Per Admiral Yamashiro's orders, none of the crew had been required to accept this mission. Before assigning pilots and technicians, Captain Takahashi asked them if they believed they could carry out their duty. They all said they could.

"Are you kidding? This is my ticket to the Yasukuni Shrine *before the SEALs fill it up*," said the technician, sounding almost serious. The Yasukuni Shrine was a Shinto temple in old Japan that served as a designated resting place for the spirits of soldiers and heroes. Tradition had it that the spirits of the Kamikaze went to Yasukuni.

When the Japanese Fleet had begun this mission, only a handful of crew members had heard of Yasukuni. Now every man and woman in the fleet knew about the shrine. Not many sailors claimed to believe the stories, but no one made jokes about the shrine the way they used to.

"This is not a Kamikaze mission," said the pilot. "Yamashiro would have given a farewell if it were."

"He should have given us a farewell," said the technician.

"You should tell him that when we return," said the pilot.

Both transports crews were made up of lieutenants. Captain Takahashi had decided that this mission was too important for enlisted men and too likely to fail to dump in the lap of a senior officer.

It's going to be a long mission, thought the pilot. He had six million miles to travel in a transport with a top speed of two hundred thousand miles per hour.

CHAPTER
TWENTY-NINE

Location: Solomon
Galactic Position: Norma Arm
Astronomic Location: Milky Way

Liotta pulled the *Bolivar* out from under my feet. He left strict orders with all of his ships' captains that they were forbidden to fly their ships to Solomon.

As long as I traveled in ships belonging to the Enlisted Man's Fleet, Solomon would remain out of reach. So I chose a ship that did not belong to the fleet. I took the spy ship. I captured it. As far as I was concerned, it belonged to the Wayson Harris Fleet, a growing armada that now included one shuttle, eight transports, and one scuffed-up Unified Authority cruiser complete with stealth shield and broadcast engine.

Technically speaking, my crew was AWOL; but I was the highest-ranking officer in the fleet and the head of the new Praetorian Guard. I'd pardon the infraction. It was a small crew. I hoped no one would notice.

"Admiral Liotta's going to shit himself when he finds out we took this ship," said Captain Holman, the corners of his mouth twitching as he held back a smile.

"You're not thinking of backing out?" I asked.

"Not a chance. I just get a kick out of the idea of Liotta shitting himself."

I liked Jim Holman. He was casual. He was relaxed. He was also easy to recognize with that red hair and beard.

We could have broadcasted in within a hundred thousand miles of Solomon, but Holman brought us in beside the Solomon broadcast station—a satellite that had fallen out of orbit and been left to drift as the planet it once circled traveled around its sun.

He did not reveal his flight plan to me until after the broadcast. "Why exactly are we taking the scenic route?" I asked.

"Broadcasting in beside a working broadcast station provides good camouflage," he said. "If the Unifieds are out there, they'll detect the anomaly but they won't see our ship. They'll think debris floated into the broadcast zone."

"Clever," I said.

"Basic tactics," Holman said.

I doubted Curtis Liotta knew about it.

"Besides, I'm not supposed to be here. If Admiral Liotta knew I came with you, he'd throw me in the brig."

"I appreciate the ride. I just wondered why we took the longer route."

Holman was right, Liotta would have court-martialed Holman if he had known about the mission. "Why are you here?" I asked.

"Do you want the long answer or the short one?" asked Holman.

"Might as well give me the long answer, we've got time to kill," I muttered.

Holman laughed. "I have a personal stake in this trip. I'm transporting contraband."

"You're smuggling contraband to a planet that's about to get scorched?" I asked.

"It's not really contraband, and I'm not smuggling it . . . and it's not going to the planet exactly. General, I think you are going to like this." He left the ship's tiny bridge and motioned for me to follow him. "Let's make a quick inspection of the forward cargo bay," he said.

I thought maybe Holman had brought a stash of booze for the ride. Though it would have taken a barrel of hooch to get me drunk, a stiff drink sounded good; and Holman absolutely struck me as the kind of officer who might enjoy an occasional libation while crossing long stretches of open space.

"I wish I could take credit for this," he said as he led me down the hall. "Scott Mars came up with the idea."

Lieutenant Mars again, I thought. What if I had left him on Terraneau? We would not have been able to reach the barges had he and his men not repaired this spy ship. We would not have been able to escape with the barges if his men had not hacked into the Mars broadcast station. And now he had some new surprise. I wondered if it would be as good.

We passed a couple of sailors as we went down the stairs to the second deck. They saluted Holman, and he addressed them by name. He'd handpicked the crew for this mission, choosing loyal men who would think straight in battle . . . men who weren't afraid to take unauthorized leave for a good cause.

"You came to save lives," Holman said, still sounding casual and friendly. Judging by his tone, you might have thought he'd invited me for beers after a round of golf. "I'm here to end some."

"When did you take up with Scott Mars?" I asked.

"When you made me captain of this ship."

Most of the lights were still out on the second deck, but Mars's engineers had restored the heat and air. Maybe it was good that the lights were out; that way, I did not have to see the patches in the walls.

Rather than rewiring the old lights, the engineers had placed temporary domes along the walls at twenty-foot increments. The domes glowed softly, producing enough light for us to see the doors along the corridor.

"You know, General, I have to admit, I was surprised when you put Admiral Jolly in charge. He was a joke as an officer."

"Yeah," I agreed. "He was a mistake."

"And 'Curtis the Snake' is more of a politician than an officer," said Holman. He was out of line saying this. He was way out of line; but we were flying an unauthorized mission in a stolen ship. I decided I could overlook the impropriety.

"From what I understand, Liotta is considering an early retirement," I said.

Holman stopped walking, and asked, "No kidding? Early retirement, just like Admiral Jolly? Do you think he'll be killed by looters as well?" The man was smart. He'd figured out what happened to Jolly. At least, he had his suspicions.

Holman started walking again. "Listen, here's why you shouldn't have put Liotta in charge. He's not going to run into looters. If he thinks he's due for an early retirement, he's going to hide someplace safe, where no one can touch him."

"You don't have much respect for the man," I said.

"Not much," he said. "He'd have been a good senator if he wasn't a clone."

"You mean for the Unifieds."

"Yeah, a good man for Unified Authority politics."

We entered a cargo hold at the bow of the ship. Like the corridor outside, the room was dark. Most of the light in the hold came from the low glow of dials along a far wall. Three sailors saluted as we entered. Holman returned their salutes, and they went back to work.

The light, by the way, was not the pale white that shone from the domes in the hall. In one part of the room, the light glowed red. In the other, the light glowed blue. This was a cargo hold. It should have sat empty except for crates and supplies. As my eyes adjusted to the dim lumens, I saw equipment built into the walls and deck.

"This is why I volunteered for this mission," Holman said. "What do you think?"

"You didn't volunteer. I asked you," I said.

"Okay, this is why I agreed to come. That's kind of like volunteering. So what do you think?"

"I don't know what I'm looking at," I said.

"It's a torpedo room."

"Mars built a torpedo room in a spy ship?" The ship was small and relatively harmless, designed for flying stealth missions and gathering information, not fighting battles.

Having torpedoes made sense on one level, though. With its stealth generator going, the cruiser flew virtually invisible. We'd be able to catch our targets unawares.

"Those skinny things are torpedo tubes?" I asked. "They look more like peashooters."

Holman called one of the sailors over, and said, "Senior Chief, can you show General Harris the pills."

"Aye, aye, sir," the sailor said. It's not hard to read how sailors feel about their commanding officers. This guy not only respected Holman, he also liked him. I could see it in the way he responded. The senior chief petty officer spun around and headed toward the twin chrome-and-iron tubes.

"You're right about the tubes, they're small," Holman said, a hint of pride in his voice. "Standard tubes have a thirty-two-inch bore. These tubes have an eight-inch bore."

"You're firing quarter-sized torpedoes?" I asked, fighting the urge to laugh.

"Don't blame me, I didn't design them," Holman said.

"This was Mars's idea?" *Maybe he's lost his touch,* I thought.

"He didn't make the torpedoes; he just installed the tubes. Oh, and he told me where to find the torpedoes."

Nestled in the nearest tube, as snug as a bullet in the chamber of a gun, sat a three-foot-long torpedo with red lights etched along its shaft. The glow from the torpedo was the lurid color of blood oranges, and the lights along the tube matched the color precisely.

The tube beside it held a torpedo that glowed ice blue. The senior chief removed the torpedo from the blue tube and brought it to me so that I could have a closer look.

He cradled the ice blue "pill" as he carried it. Small or not, this baby would certainly kill everyone in the cargo bay if it exploded.

As I inspected the torpedo, I realized that it wasn't marked with blue lights; the glow came from the inside. The outside of the torpedo was made of some kind of thick polymer through which the inner core shone. The dark areas along that shaft were labels of some sort.

"What is this?" I asked.

"These are *the* torpedoes," Holman said. He even laughed as he said it.

He watched me, expectation showing in his expression. When I did not pick up on it, he rolled his eyes, and said, "We salvaged them from the battleships."

"What battleships?" I asked.

"You know, Mars . . ." He waited.

"Lieutenant Mars?" I asked.

Holman smiled, and said, "The planet Mars."

And then I understood. I understood everything in a flash that left me dizzy. It was like waking up from a midday nap. We had destroyed several U.A. battleships when we stole the barges. Those battleships might well have been loaded with *the* torpedoes—the torpedoes that could destroy our ships with a single shot.

"These are the killer torpedoes?" I asked.

"The very ones," said Holman. "If we've got it right, the

blue ones dissolve shields. We call them 'shield-busters.' The red ones pack the punch."

"How can you tell?"

"The red ones are nuclear-tipped."

I looked back at the red torpedo, still snug in its tube, and shivered. I hated nukes. You can have your rats, your sharks, your snakes, and your space aliens. Nothing scared me nearly as much as nuclear weapons.

"How many of these things did you recover?"

"Thirty-six of each," he said.

"Thirty-six," I said. "That could be enough to finish off their entire fleet. Last I heard, they didn't have thirty-six capital ships left in their navy."

An invisible ship armed with shield-buster torpedoes. The Unifieds would not know danger was near until it was too late for them to protect themselves.

The Unifieds had just destroyed the small fleet we had patrolling the space around Solomon. They almost certainly had ships waiting in the area in case we sent a rescue party. With these torpedoes, we could turn the tables on them. I asked, "Have you run a test fire?" I did not think the cruiser would survive a misfire.

"Like I said, that's why we're here. That's why I volunteered for this mission," Holman said. "I'm here to test the new weapons system."

Jim Holman wasn't the only person who had *volunteered* for the mission. Ray Freeman had come as well.

Since Holman did not allow civilians on his bridge, Freeman waited for me in the third landing bay. I found him in a transport, sitting by himself in the unlit cockpit. Like any trained sniper, he was immune to boredom.

"Did you hear about the torpedoes?" I asked as I sat down in the copilot's seat.

Freeman looked up but did not respond right away. Finally he said, "This is a spy ship. It doesn't carry torpedoes."

"This one does," I said, and I told him all about the modifications and the *pills*.

"Is that why we broadcasted in so far from the planet?" Freeman asked.

"Holman says he did that for camouflage. He broadcasted in near the broadcast zone so the Unifieds would mistake our anomaly for debris."

Freeman simply nodded. "What happens if we run into U.A. ships?"

"It sounds like he's thought of everything," I said. "If it comes to a battle with one-hit-kill torpedoes, the invisible ship wins."

"What if Solomon is like Terraneau?" asked Freeman. "What if they won't listen to us?"

"Terraneau was a neutral planet. Solomon is part of the Enlisted Man's Empire," I said. "There was no reasoning with Doctorow; he saw us as an enemy." Doctorow was the late Right Reverend Colonel Ellery Doctorow, a pacifist dictator who had defected from the Unified Authority Army and declared himself president of Terraneau.

"Would you have believed a clone and a mercenary if they told you to evacuate your planet?" Freeman asked.

I shrugged my shoulders, and said, "We'll do what we can."

Freeman said, "It's in God's hands after that." He wasn't being flip. If there was a gene that gave people their sense of humor, Ray Freeman did not have it. His father had been a Neo-Baptist minister; and more and more, Ray's religious roots were finding their way back into his thinking.

"Yeah, God's hands," I said. Ray could take his place among the specking saints if he chose. I did not want any part of it.

"You don't believe in God," Freeman said. "You used to."

"I used to believe that God was a metaphor for government," I said. "Now I'm a heretic. I don't believe in governments."

"And God?" asked Freeman.

"If there's a God, why did He create the Avatari? Why is He letting them kill entire populations?"

Freeman didn't answer.

"I find it pretty specking hard to believe that there's a God out there who loves everybody, but He sends them to Hell if they don't believe in Him," I said.

"Maybe He doesn't send them to Hell," Freeman said. "Maybe He's just like us, running from one planet to the next, trying to save as many people as He can from a disaster that's already occurred."

"How about clones?" I asked. "Do you think He tries to save clones?"

According to every major religion, clones did not have souls and therefore had no place in Heaven.

We were on a spaceship manned by clones, flying through enemy territory on a mission to save natural-borns. According to religious authority, the people who wanted to sink us had souls, and so did the people we wanted to save; but we were the saviors here, and, according to every major religion, we were soulless.

"I don't believe in souls," said Freeman.

"You don't believe in souls?" I asked.

"I don't know if there is a life after this one; but if there is, I think that everyone gets a part of it. You're a walking, breathing man, Harris. That makes you just like everybody else."

But Freeman was wrong, I wasn't like everybody else. I was sterile. All clones were sterile. I might walk and breathe, but much of my thinking was the direct result of neural programming that my designers had hardwired into my brain.

"So is God the reason you're here?" I asked. "Is God the reason you're risking your life?"

Freeman shook his head but said nothing. The man was a sphinx.

CHAPTER
THIRTY

The wreckage of the E.M.N. ships floated still and silent above Solomon's radiant atmosphere. Seeing the dark outlines of our ruined ships, I wondered how much the people on the planet understood. So close to the atmosphere, the space battle would have been visible through civilian telescopes and traffic radars. Some of the explosions might have been visible to the naked eye.

Could the people have known that the battle signaled their planet's demise? Did they know that the bad guys had won and that the darkened carcasses above their planet were ships that had come to protect them?

"Ah, damn, they got our ships," Holman said, as we approached the wreckage.

"Mystery solved," I said.

I sat on the bridge, an invited guest of Captain Holman. Freeman waited for me on the transport, two decks below. Once we knew the coast was clear, I would join Freeman, and we'd fly down to the planet.

Holman had his crew on full alert. Our shields were up, our stealth generator was on, and the first round of torpedoes was loaded into the tubes.

We slowed to a near crawl as we circled the remains of the ships. I had grown numb to this morbid form of sightseeing. I no longer thought about the people who had died on the ships or the terror of their last moments. We cruised by slowly like mourners passing an open casket, and we stared in silence.

The first wreck we passed was a frigate, a small ship designed to block fighter attacks. I identified the frigate by her size. The Unified Authority's killer torpedoes had smashed every other recognizable feature from the hull. The moth-shaped frame had exploded into three separate sections still connected by a few shreds of metal. The nose of the ship was a jagged twist. No light shone from its remains, not even the flicker of electricity.

"These ships came from the Perseus Outer Fleet," Holman said. He stood trancelike, staring at the scene. "I served in that fleet."

Behind the frigate, the other ships assigned to the patrol looked equally demolished. They showed in silhouette only, dark and dead, silent forms floating over the sunlit sphere of Solomon.

"Captain Holman, I've located two U.A. battleships," called one of the bridge officers.

"We should introduce ourselves," said Holman.

Naval battles. As the ship goes, so does every man aboard her. During ground battles, Marines can conceal themselves or fight their way out of danger. One Marine can turn the course of an entire battle. It doesn't work that way on a ship. I had my share of phobias—nukes and naval battles were at the top of my list.

"You okay, General Harris? You look a little pale," said Holman.

I didn't answer. Better to let him wonder if I was nervous than to let him hear it in my voice.

Moving slowly, we came around, circling the wreckage so that we were between the dead ships and the planet. We were so small. As we passed the ruins of a battleship, I realized that there was more than enough room for us to park on one of her busted wings.

A few moments passed, then I spotted them, two small shapes glowing like phosphorescent sea creatures as they came around the planet. It was always possible that they had spotted us. Our ship was a spy ship and had the finest stealth technology that the Unifieds had developed, but it used Unified Authority technology. Could they really have been so stupid as to create stealth generators without also developing a technology for seeing through the cloak?

The U.A. ships showed no signs of detecting us. They held their ground as we approached them.

"Captain, there's a third ship about eighty thousand miles away, halfway around the planet."

"Good to know," said Holman.

Holman turned to me, his face beaming as he asked, "General, do you care which ship we sink first?"

"It's your show," I said. *Like shooting fish in a barrel,* I thought. With the stealth generator hiding us from detection, they would not be able to find us or protect themselves. Perhaps they would even think the first ship had suffered a malfunction. It would never occur to the arrogant bastards that a crew of lowly clones would use their ship and their torpedoes against them.

If we hit the second ship before they realized that an enemy had attacked, the third ship would try to flee the scene. Our spy ship was small, invisible, and fast, a predatory bird with a deadly strike. If we moved quickly, we might even hit the third ship before she engaged her broadcast engine.

"Fire blue *pill*," Holman said.

"Blue torpedo away."

"Fire red *pill*," said Holman, spacing the torpedoes no more than three seconds apart.

"Red torpedo away, sir."

"Now bring us around."

Holman was a good officer, a careful officer. Firing the torpedoes would give away our position. By giving the order to "bring us around," he was telling his helmsman to find a new place for us to hide.

We attacked that first ship from a few hundred miles out. It took the torpedoes a couple of seconds to cover the distance.

The moments passed slowly. Every man on the bridge stared at the viewport. My breath had caught in my throat.

The first torpedo struck, splashing a wave of electricity that arced along the shields—a gush of blue-white light flashed and vanished along the glowing golden sheen of the enemy ship's shields. But the shields remained along the U.A. ship like a translucent skin.

Three seconds later, the red torpedo struck—a brilliant light that popped and vanished leaving the ship untouched.

"Fire another blue," Holman barked.

"Aye, aye. Torpedo away."

"Fire another after that. Helm, steer us below the target."

The silence. The tension. The moment. I had no idea what

was happening in the cargo hold/torpedo room; but on the bridge, the only people not sitting in stone silence were the officer steering the ship and Holman, who was telling him where to go.

I traced the small blue dots on the tactical display, then turned to the viewport in time to see the torpedoes hit their mark one right after another. The first pill struck, creating a flash that splashed across the shield. Before the first flash disappeared, the second torpedo renewed it. This time the blinding bright light engulfed the entire ship. Then the third torpedo struck. The torpedoes were powerful, no doubt; but so were the new shields on those ships. The torpedoes did damage, but they weren't battering their shields as thoroughly as they had battered ours.

The tint shields spread, leaving the viewport as dark as a mirror in a room with no light, its shiny surface reflecting light from the bridge, but the viewport itself was opaque.

Holman shouted to his helmsman, "Hard about. Put us on top of them."

Our torpedoes might or might not have destroyed the U.A. ship; either way she wasn't moving. We could no longer see the scene on the viewport, the tint shields were too thick. The circle marking that ship on the tactical display remained as still as an island.

Our attack must have caught the other two ships unawares. All three ships remained perfectly still for half a minute then the navigator shouted, "Captain, two of the ships are approaching fast."

While the ship we had hit remained listless, her mates circled the area, randomly firing lasers into pockets of space as they groped in the darkness to find us.

"What do you know; they can't see through their own stealth technology," Holman said.

"Did you think they might be able to?" I asked.

"They still might. They might also have a code that shuts down our generator."

"To prevent someone from turning their own technology against them," I suggested.

"Exactly right," Holman said. "Right now, they're looking for a needle in a haystack and hoping they'll get lucky."

"But they won't?" I asked. Naval battles made me nervous. Sitting on a tiny ship hiding from two enormous ships had me on the verge of panic.

"They'd need to get very lucky. We're a moving target, and we're invisible. We'll be safe as long as we don't do anything that gives away our position."

"What would give away our position?" I asked.

Holman met my gaze, paused, and said, "Launching a transport would give us away." Then he turned from me, and said into his communications console, "Fire a red at the crippled ship."

"Torpedo away, sir."

"Fire another one." Speaking in a cold calm voice, he said, "Fire another."

"Aye, aye."

"Helm, down and away."

The tactical showed the U.A. battleships as shapes, not ships. The circles representing the live ships had been moving like the hands of a clock, circumscribing a circular pattern, firing lasers while sniffing for targets. Once we launched the torpedoes, both ships streaked in our direction.

The dot representing our ship scurried to safety as the first of our red torpedoes struck the target ship, then the second.

Moments passed, and the tint shields evaporated from the viewport. At first, I could not tell what I was looking at. The helmsman clapped his hands, and said, "Hell yeah!" Then everyone on the bridge cheered. The final torpedoes had penetrated the crippled ship's shields.

The Unified Authority battleship sat battered and lifeless but not destroyed. She would not fly anytime soon. We would need to fire another torpedo to deal the fatal blow, but her shields were down. She had twists and cracks along her dagger-shaped hull. Lights still blazed throughout the ship, but the new torpedoes had ruptured the hull, not broken it.

Holman looked at me, and said, "We could finish her."

"She looks done," I said, not sure if the instinct that led me to say this had more to do with mercy or self-preservation. "After this point, it's not combat, it's murder."

"That's what they did to our ships," Holman said.

"Yeah. They're murderers."

He turned to his helmsman, and said, "Power up the broadcast engine. We're going home."

"What about Solomon?" I asked.

"General, there are still two more battleships out there. They're on high alert. They will destroy us and the transport if we try to launch."

He was right. So were Liotta and Wallace. They'd been right all along. Seven million people would die on Solomon. We could not evacuate the planet. If we tried to warn the people, there'd be riots and chaos. Warning the people to go underground might save lives but not many. Most of the lucky few who found shelter underground would be sealed in once the heat melted the ground above them.

"We need to send a warning," I said, though in my heart I had already abandoned the mission.

"Those U.A. ships can trace our signals," said Holman.

I tried to convince myself that it was for the best. We could never have saved more than a small fraction of the population. By leaving them in ignorance, we would allow the people of Solomon to live their last few hours in peace.

They would not know they'd been incinerated until God told them what had happened. It wasn't a bad way to go, I suppose; but I didn't feel good about letting it happen.

THIRTY-ONE

On the surface, Freeman appeared to take the news about leaving Solomon with cold indifference. I told him about the Unified Authority ships and the battle, and he listened in silence. His expression remained impassive, as slack as a death mask. His eyes, though. His eyes bored through me.

If you could see into a man's soul through his eyes, I thought I glimpsed the fires of Hell deep within Freeman. His skin was dark as wet stone. His head was bald and scarred. He'd abandoned a religious home for a life of battlefields and gunfights; now death followed him like a shadow as he returned to his roots.

"I asked Holman about warning them," I said.

"The Unifieds would track the signal," Freeman answered, speaking mechanically. "Even if they got the message, we wouldn't save many people," he said, parroting Curtis Liotta's words. He paused, stared straight ahead the way blind men stare straight ahead, then he said, "Dust to dust."

We stood together in the kettle of the transport, a large metal cavern with steel-girder ribs along its iron walls. Freeman wore his custom-made battle armor with his helmet off. I had come in my Charlie service uniform.

At six-foot-three, I was the tallest clone in the Enlisted Man's Empire. Freeman stood nine inches taller than I and might well have packed twice my weight. He was big and strong and deadly, a fierce man who'd spent most of his life caring about no one but himself. He'd become a murderous messiah, a man on a quest.

I did not know the Bible from front to back, but I remembered a few words here and there. Six of those words came back to me. I said, "Let the dead bury the dead."

The words woke Freeman from his stupor. He glared at

me, and growled, "What is that supposed to mean?" That was the first time I'd ever heard rage in his voice.

"It means that we can kill ourselves trying to warn people who cannot be saved, but we cannot save them. It means that I would rather get caught by a sniper's bullet than be stood in front of a firing squad. They will spend their last hours humping girlfriends, fishing, reading, going to the specking ballet . . . doing whatever it is they like to do. I'd rather go that way than spend my last hours panicking about death."

As I said this, I thought about mothers holding their children. What does a mother do when she learns that all of her children will die at the end of the day? Does she tuck them into bed and tell them a story? Does she give them candy for their final meal? Does she think about her own death? Having never had a mother, I imagined each of them as superhuman, a cross between a saint, a martyr, and a drill sergeant.

I had no concept of what it meant to lose family. Freeman did. His father, a Neo-Baptist minister, died defending his colony. The Avatari had burned Freeman's last relations when they attacked New Copenhagen. I was haunted by my imagination. He was haunted by his memories.

Sounding like Admiral Liotta and hating myself for it, I said, "Solomon was a lost cause."

Freeman, big as he was, standing there so still and silent, reminded me of a spider on a web in some abandoned archway. I was a weakling, and he was a spider, and we lived in a universe that was crumbling around us. He spun webs, and I made plans, but we were feeble. Neither his webs nor my plans mattered in the end.

There is nothing I hate more than the feeling of helplessness, I told myself; but it was not the truth. I hated the Unified Authority more than I hated feeling helpless; and I hated the Avatari more than anything else.

THIRTY-TWO

Earthdate: November 26, A.D. 2517
Location: Planet A-361-B
Galactic Position: Solar System A-361
Astronomic Location: Bode's Galaxy

Under normal circumstances, the pilot of the first transport was a talkative man. So were the two technicians. But flying a mission they all expected to result in their deaths, they had lost interest in chatting.

From one million miles out, planet A-361-B looked like a very small moon. Each hour brought them two hundred thousand miles closer to their destination, and from their current position, the pilot could see that the planet was the color of platinum rather than the dull white of a moon.

He sat alone in the cockpit. They did not need to spend these hours flying to A-361-B; the S.I.P.s could have traveled to the planet in one-one-hundredth the time. The pilot thought about mentioning that fact to his crew, then decided against it. What if the aliens tracked the S.I.P.s to their transport? This way, maybe they could buy themselves a few additional hours to live.

His orders were to fire the pods from just outside the ion curtain. Yamashiro's orders made it clear that firing the pods from a million miles away wasn't an option, however much it was a temptation.

In his heart, though, the pilot knew it didn't matter. Nothing would penetrate the tachyon shell. It disassembled waves. Sound and light dissolved into it. The S.I.P.s would hit the outer side of the sleeved atmosphere and explode. Maybe the ion curtain would suck the energy out of them, then repulse them.

The few times the pilot peered out of the cockpit, he found his technicians sitting along opposite ends of the same kettle wall. They could have been talking over the interLink, but he doubted they were.

The pilot made no effort to control the flight. He'd switched the computers to autopilot and spent the time slumped in his seat, reviewing his life. He thought about his failures and successes, remembered his parents, relived the pain of his young wife's death, and wondered what life might have been like had she had lived. He had no children.

From five thousand miles away, planet A-361-B filled the cockpit's windshield. He realized that he didn't see the planet, just the "sleeve" that had closed around its atmosphere. From the outside, it looked like a solid layer, like someone had dipped the planet in white gold.

"We're here," the pilot told the technicians. "We're almost in position. Let's make this quick."

He did not want to die, though having accepted that his death was imminent, it did not scare him as it had back when he began the flight. Since leaving the *Sakura*, he had gone through all the steps. Denial and anger came first but ended almost after takeoff. The bargaining stage did not last long because he had some measure of control over his fate. If the pilot turned the transport around, he would survive the mission and live as a coward. A man of duty, he preferred death over a life of shame . . . and maybe a short life at that. He'd seen what had happened to the *Onoda*, the *Kyoto*, and the *Yamato*.

The pilot did not believe in God, and the idea of an afterlife trapped in the Yasukuni Shrine held no fascination for him. Now, as he spun the transport so that the rear hatch faced the planet, depression and acceptance glided along parallel tracks in his head.

The pilot did not hesitate as he worked the controls. Maybe the aliens could target the oxygen in his armor, or maybe they would target the air in his lungs and sear him from the inside out. It no longer mattered. All that mattered was the mission, and the pilot would give his life and the lives of his technicians to see it through.

He switched off the controls for what he believed would be

the very last time and walked out of the cockpit. In the kettle, the technicians had already loaded the S.I.P.s into the launching device but had not yet pulled the device into position. As the pilot watched from the catwalk, one of the techs hit the button to open the hatch.

Here it comes, thought the pilot. He was sure that it would be the moment, and he braced himself. A soft tremor ran through the belly of the transport as the thick iron doors slowly ground into place.

Standing on his perch above the kettle, the pilot could not see the ramp. His curiosity got the better of him, and he slid down the ladder. He had not turned off the gravity inside the transport, just notched it down to about one-third gravity level on Earth.

He touched down lightly on the metal deck, turned, and saw the far end of the ship. The rear hatch framed the view of A-361-B glinting like a giant shining sphere of molten silver. As the pilot watched, the technicians pulled the launching device along a rail that ran down the ramp. The device reached from the floor to the ceiling. It looked like a miniature Ferris wheel, with coffins instead of seats. When it locked into place at the bottom of the ramp, blocking his view of the planet, the pilot went even closer. In the distance, he could see the second transport still drifting into position, its rear hatch open.

From initiation to completion, the firing process took five seconds. Once the launching device was in place, a technician pressed a button, and the device fired the S.I.P.s into space. Knowing there was no point in trying to escape, the crew stood in place and watched.

They could not see the infiltration pods. Powered by field-resonance engines, the pods traveled the five thousand miles to the planet in a fraction of a second. Nothing happened. The S.I.P.s did not explode. The air in their rebreathers did not heat up to thousands of degrees.

They stood there, at the edge of the transport, staring out at the planet, realizing that nothing had or would happen. They would return to the *Sakura* having failed their mission and survived. The technicians slid the launching device back in place, and the pilot began the long flight back.

CHAPTER THIRTY-THREE

Location: Open Space
Galactic Position: Outside Solar System A-361
Astronomic Location: Bode's Galaxy

"We cannot go back to Earth. There's no going back if the Unified Authority is at war. They'll shoot us down before we can identify ourselves," said Yamashiro.

Where have they gone? he asked himself. Miyamoto Genyo, the modern-day Samurai, had always sat to Yamashiro's left. With the *Onoda* destroyed, Miyamoto's seat remained vacant. Takahashi sat to his right; but the chair beside him, which once belonged to Captain Takeda Gunpei of the *Yamato*, sat empty. At the far end of the table, an empty chair marked the space once occupied by Yokoi Shigeru, the late captain of the late *Kyoto*.

Commander Suzuki now sat at the table. This had once been a room for admirals and captains; now it had space for commanders and enlisted men—Master Chief Corey Oliver sat at the table.

Yamashiro harbored no prejudice against clones. He did not care about the master chief's synthetic conception. His rank was another story. Oliver was a master chief petty officer, an enlisted man; and that, by definition, placed him below real officers.

So there they sat, the admiral of a one-ship fleet, the captain of that ship sitting with his second-in-command, and an enlisted clone. *I should invite Lieutenant Hara,* Yamashiro thought. *He could come representing the underworld element.*

"We cannot destroy the enemy, and we cannot return to Earth," said Takahashi. "It sounds like we have run out of options?"

Yamashiro turned to study the SEAL. *He knows what I am going to say,* he thought. *Somehow, the* kage no yasha *knows what I am going to say.*

"No. We can still destroy the enemy," he said, and he was not surprised when Oliver gave him a slight nod.

"How can we do that?" asked Takahashi. "We fired our most powerful weapon at their shield, and it failed. If infiltration pods can't break through, nothing can."

"I intend to detonate the pods from inside the layer," said Yamashiro. "We will broadcast this ship into the atmosphere . . ."

"They'll melt us like they melted the *Onoda,*" said Takahashi.

"They won't," grunted Yamashiro, his expression cold. "If we broadcast the *Sakura* inside their atmosphere, they will not be able to incinerate us without incinerating themselves."

"Broadcast inside the sleeve?" asked Takahashi. "That would not be possible. Nothing gets through the sleeve."

"We would not broadcast through it. We would materialize inside it," Yamashiro barked. Then his voice softened, as he said, "We are honor-bound to succeed. This is the only way that we can."

Takahashi did not believe he had heard his father-in-law correctly. Stunned, he reviewed the sentence in his head. Finally, he said, "Admiral, we won't be able to fly our ship once we are inside. The sleeve grounded the U.A. Air Force during the battle for Copenhagen. The fighter pilots weren't able to fly higher than a thousand feet before their jets stopped working. The same thing will happen to us. Our computers . . . our electrical systems, our defenses . . . We'll be just as vulnerable as those fighters were, with less room to maneuver."

Yamashiro responded with a smile so sour that his son-in-law looked away. He said, "No, Hironobu, we won't need to worry about that. We won't live long enough for it to be a factor."

THIRTY-FOUR

Earthdate: November 27, A.D. 2517

"The information we are going to discuss is classified," Yamashiro grunted the words. He had received the information twenty-four hours ago but postponed the briefing until he had time to compose his thoughts.

Yamashiro did not hold the briefing in the conference room just off the bridge, the place he normally conducted business. The conference room was secure, but secure was not secure enough, not when the discussion involved the destruction of the *Sakura* and her crew. He held the briefing in the small office attached to his billet.

Starting the moment the briefing ended, he would never again allow himself to speak kindly in public. When asked questions, he would grunt single-word answers. When he wanted work done, he would bark his commands. He could reveal no weakness and no indecision. Kindness and civility could be mistaken for weakness, so he would keep his eyes hard and his expression flat.

Yamashiro presided over the briefing, but it was Lieutenant Tatsu Hara's show. As the intelligence officer who ran the computer simulations, Hara supplied the critical information.

Though every person on the *Sakura* knew Hara, Yamashiro began the meeting by introducing him, then he sat down.

Tatsu Hara was young, and tall, and skinny, a man in his early twenties with the moon-shaped face of a sixteen-year-old. His hair was regulation length, short at the back and off the ears; but his inch-long locks had been pressed into tight curls and bleached brown and blond. He lived on the edge of regulations, brantoos—a tattooing process that involved burning the skin, then tinting the scar—of lotus flowers, *Kanji* characters, women, and demons covered his arms and neck. He wore dark glasses and, as he stood, paused one second to remove them before opening his mouth, then placed the shades in the pocket of his blouse. The man was an officer but also a gangster. The brantoos, the hair, and the shades were the tokens of the *Yakuza*.

Hara ran the Pachinko parlors and the bars aboard the ship, but he performed his MOS (Military Occupational Specialty) well. He was a gifted computer tech; and his side operations contributed to crew morale. Had he been asked what he thought of Lieutenant Tatsu Hara, Yamashiro would have described him as an asset to the mission.

Lieutenant Hara briefly explained his responsibilities as a computer-simulations specialist in intelligence, then spent a few minutes explaining the simulations process. Commander Suzuki, who had been a lawyer before the Mogat Wars, thought the man talked like an expert witness in a court case.

Hara carried an antiquated clipboard computer. His computer established a wireless connection with the computer in the Intelligence division. Without giving any explanation, Hara ran the video feed of a battleship, probably the *Kyoto*, imploding. The holographic image appeared in the space above Yamashiro's desk, cropped tight to display every detail of the destruction.

"Lieutenant, we've all seen this feed," said Takahashi.

"Maybe you have not seen this particular simulation, sir," said Hara. Traditional in his mannerisms, Hara did not want to contradict a superior officer. Yamashiro and Takahashi understood him perfectly. As he had just used it, the word "maybe" was for decoration. What he really meant was, *This is a simulation, not the video feed you have seen.*

Hara slowed the feed so that the attack occurred over a period of nearly two minutes. As the initial hit began, the hull of the ship expanded ever so slightly. Hara pressed a button on his computer, and the outer hull of the ship faded, revealing its inner workings. "I only finished running this simulation an hour ago."

Believing that he had been shown up by a subordinate officer, Takahashi turned red around the ears.

The SEAL sat unmoved. As far as Hara could tell, the SEAL paid no attention to anything and anyone in the room as he focused all of his attention on the computer simulation.

The simulation showed the destruction inside the ship. Screens and panels exploded, tables and cabinets and engines caught fire, floors and bulkheads melted. Before the entire cataclysm could erupt, however, the outer skin of the ship turned to liquid, smothering everything inside it.

"This is a simulation of what happens to a battleship when the air inside it heats up to ten thousand degrees," said Hara. He tapped the screen of his clipboard computer. This time the simulation of the inside of the ship appeared side by side with the feed of the outside of the ship. In the simulated ship, the air glowed red to signal the beginning of the attack.

"You can see that the details match up," said Hara. He froze the display, pointed to several areas, and said, "If you look here, the heat causes the air and metal inside the ship to expand."

"What about the crew?" asked Yamashiro. "Were they alive at this point?"

"I did not include the effects on humans in this simulation," said Hara.

"What is your best guess, Lieutenant?"

"Maybe they did not live this long. They probably died in less than a second," said Hara. Then he followed by apologetically adding, "This is just a guess."

Yamashiro nodded, then he muttered something mostly to himself, but he said it loud enough for everyone to hear. He said, "Death comes quickly in Bode's Galaxy."

Hara paused, waiting for Yamashiro to tell him to continue. When the admiral did not say anything, he waited a few seconds and continued on his own. He finished the demonstration, showing how the ship first expanded from the heat, then air escaped through her melting walls without the cold of space lowering the heat inside her hull. With her frame melting, the battleship quickly collapsed in on herself and became a bubbling liquid cloud before being cooled by the vacuum of space.

Hara said, "We experimented with dozens of variables. This simulation came the closest to what we saw during the attack on the *Kyoto*. It's not a perfect match, but it comes close."

Takahashi said, "Your simulation does not explain what they used to attack the ships."

"No, sir. We don't know how they delivered the heat to the ship," said Hara.

"Oh, so, that is still unknown," said Takahashi.

"Yes, sir," said Hara.

Hara noted the way that the SEAL continued to study the frozen image of the destroyed ship. The SEAL did not join in the discussion.

SEALs made Hara nervous. He tried to ignore the clone, but his eyes kept trailing back toward him.

Hara was not the only *Yakuza* on the ship. He had fifteen men in his organization. There had been more. Three had stolen drugs from the infirmary and tried to sell them. One had beaten a female sailor. All four men had disappeared. Hara believed that the SEALs killed them.

Hiding a body on a ship might be hard, but you could always dump it into space. When he looked into the cold, dark eyes of the SEAL, eyes hidden in shadows under that bony ridge of brow, Hara saw the eyes of a man for whom murder came easily.

Hara tapped the screen of his computer, and a new image appeared above the desk—the image of a wasted city.

"Is this a simulation?" asked Takahashi.

"No, Captain. This is a video feed from a satellite," said Hara. "This is what we found when we arrived at New Copenhagen."

The image showed burned buildings and streets lined with buildings that had been both charred and smashed. It showed a burned forest in which the remaining trees looked like giant pins stood on end. The feed showed a desert in which the sand had melted to glass. Hara explained some of the details.

The SEAL finally spoke. He asked, "Lieutenant, are you saying that the aliens attacked the ships and the planet with the same weapon?"

Hara answered in an indifferent tone. After all, killer clone or human, the SEAL was still an enlisted man. He said, "That seems rather obvious, Master Chief."

Hara called the SEAL by rank to remind him of his place. Deep in his heart, he hated the SEAL. In Japanese society, the *Yakuza* and the police enjoyed a mostly peaceful coexistence. The SEALs were not Japanese, and Hara resented their intrusion.

"How is that possible?" asked Yamashiro.

Now that he was dealing with authority, Hara took a mental step back. He said, "Sir, we have no idea what kind of weapon they have used, but it generates a lot of heat within an atmosphere. I used my computer to simulate the destruction on New Copenhagen, and it is in keeping with what happened to our ships."

"Show us the simulation, Lieutenant," said Yamashiro.

Hara shook his head, and said, "I apologize, sir, but I did not create an animated model."

"What does that mean?" asked Yamashiro.

"The simulation predicted what might happen to a planet if you raised its temperature to ten thousand degrees without generating a visual display," said Hara.

"What would happen?" asked Yamashiro. He seemed to become more intense by the second.

"You would incinerate plants; melt streets; melt anything made of plastic, steel, or glass; evaporate streams." He ran the video feed of New Copenhagen, then stopped it on an image of a broken skyscraper.

"This building is broken down to its base. It appears to have been crushed. In my computer simulation, the high temperatures caused the planet's atmosphere to rise like a hot-air balloon. Buildings that survived the heat were smashed when the temperature returned to normal, and the atmosphere fell back into place."

"Would it be possible for someone to survive on that planet?" Yamashiro asked in Japanese.

"Survive?" Hara sounded incredulous. "Admiral, these temperatures . . ."

"No. Not during the attack, now. If we placed people on New Copenhagen, would they survive?" Yamashiro asked the question in Japanese, glancing over at the SEAL, who did not appear to be listening.

"There are no plants to generate oxygen. I'm not sure if

you could plant crops in this soil. The temperatures may have burned the nutrients out of the soil. That's just a guess.

"You probably would not have to worry about germs," Hara said, thinking to himself that as far as he could tell, the planet had been sterilized. He added, "This is not my area of expertise, sir."

Continuing to speak in Japanese, Yamashiro said, "Yes. Yes. I know. Lieutenant, we no longer have the luxury of sticking to our specialties. I would not be the admiral of a one-ship fleet if we did."

"Yes, sir," said Hara.

"In your opinion, Lieutenant, could a colony survive on that planet?"

Hara thought for several seconds. He ran a hand along his jaw, closed his eyes, muttered to himself, then shook his head. "I don't know, sir."

"What about a breathable atmosphere?" asked Yamashiro.

"I have no way of knowing, sir."

His frustration showing, Yamashiro growled, "What would be your best guess?"

"Sir, your opinion would be as good as mine."

"What do you know?" asked Yamashiro.

Hara said, "The radiation levels on the planet are manageable. My simulation predicted no rise in radiation."

Yamashiro nodded, and said, "From what you are not telling me, it appears that a colony might stand a chance of survival."

"Yes, sir. It might."

THIRTY-FIVE

Life on the *Sakura* was divided into three shifts. Most of the crew worked eight-hour shifts; they had eight hours to eat, drink, clean their billets, and relax; and they had eight hours to sleep.

Lieutenant Tatsu Hara lived by his own schedule. He put in his full eight-hour work detail, sometimes extending his shifts to twelve when needed. A man of infinite energy, Hara only slept three to four hours per day. He spent the rest of his time running his businesses.

The *Sakura* had a "love hotel." It was not a brothel. Hara and the other *Yakuza* had originally planned to convert it into one, but sailors who tried to push drugs or prostitution disappeared along with their enterprises. Now the hotel simply rented rooms by the hour, and Hara did not get a cut.

He still ran the hotel. Knowing who reserved the rooms and knowing which officers slept with which women brought Hara more power than profit. A less patient man might have abandoned the hotel, but Hara did not measure success by money alone.

He and the fifteen remaining *Yakuza* made plenty of money from the casino, the Pachinko parlors, the dance club, and the five bars that they ran. They would have preferred to own these businesses, but operating them was profitable enough.

Hara sat in the back of his most profitable bar thinking about the future. Unlike the officers' clubs, this bar was dark and quiet, a romantic place only a few doors from the hourly hotel. Soft music played over the speakers, hanging in the air like the scent of perfume. The door opened, and in the light from the hall, he saw the silhouette of a short man with a bald head.

The SEALs did not walk like other men; they glided with

the sinewy grace of a cat on the prowl. He was alone. No woman. No friends. He walked into the bar, selected a small open table, and sat facing Hara.

Wearing dark glasses that did not block out light but did hide his eyes, Hara continued to watch the SEAL and the clone stared back at him. A second passed, and Hara walked over to the table. He said, "Master Chief, I'm surprised to see you here."

Oliver smiled, rose to his feet though he did not salute, and said, "Lieutenant, I hope I am welcome here."

"It's an open bar, Master Chief," said Hara. "Men, women, officers, enlisted men, it's open to everyone."

"Even clones?" asked Oliver.

"Are you waiting for a date?" Hara asked, though he knew the answer. The SEALs did not fraternize. He sometimes wondered if they had sex with each other though he doubted it. They were saints. They were demons. They were the *kage no yasha*.

"No," said Oliver.

"Mind if I join you?" asked Hara.

The SEAL waved to the table, and they both took their seats. Though he prided himself on knowing everything that happened on the *Sakura*, Hara did not know what decisions Yamashiro had made after he left the briefing that afternoon.

Hara signaled to the waitress and ordered two glasses of single-malt Scotch, speaking in Japanese. Then he turned to the SEAL. Still speaking in Japanese, he asked, "Do you want yours on ice?"

When the SEAL pretended not to understand him, Hara said, "I know you speak Japanese."

Oliver smiled at the waitress, and said, *"Mizu de ii desu."*

She bowed, thanked him in Japanese, and went to get the drinks.

"Water?" asked Hara.

"I'm not much of a drinker," said Oliver.

"When did you learn to speak Japanese?" asked Hara.

"After we left Earth," Oliver said. "How did you know I could speak?"

"I watch more carefully than Admiral Yamashiro or Captain Takahashi."

"You watch me more closely?"

"I watch everything more closely."

The waitress returned. She gave Hara a five-finger tumbler with Scotch over ice. She gave Oliver a glass of water. She was a pretty girl with long hair and a dark complexion. Before leaving, she smiled at Oliver and nodded at Hara.

Oliver touched the water to his lips. He might have taken a small sip, Hara could not tell.

"You aren't thirsty," Hara observed. "Then why did you come to a bar?"

"Why do you think?"

"How did you know where to find me?"

"I'm like you, Lieutenant. I'm watchful," said Oliver. His right hand sat on the table, the sharp fingers curled back, the knuckle of his forefinger knocking against the glass of water.

Hara was again reminded how much he disliked the SEALs. There was an order to Japanese society, a rhythm between authority and corruption. The SEALs disrupted it. Deciding to test the clone's manners, Hara said, "We don't see the *kage no yasha* in our bars very often."

If he took offense, Oliver did not show it. He smiled briefly, and said, "Yes, we shadow demons prefer to remain in our lair."

"You know that term as well," Hara said, sounding both impressed and disappointed. "I was looking forward to translating it for you."

"Sorry to disappoint you."

Hara noticed that there was something different in the SEAL's demeanor, and it made him nervous. Under most circumstances, the SEALs had an almost embarrassed air about them, as if they were ashamed to be seen. But Oliver was sitting in the open, his banter as comfortable as if he were family.

"What did you want to discuss, Master Chief?" Hara asked as he fumbled to slip the thumb of his left hand into the sleeve of his shirt. Hidden in the cuff, he had a panic button. By pressing it, he sent a distress signal to the other *Yakuza*.

"I came to let you in on a secret," said Oliver. "Would you like to know what we talked about after you left the meeting?"

"As a matter of fact, I am curious about that," Hara said.

Oliver spoke in a soft voice, a voice so calm and even that Hara had to lean over the table to hear him. The SEAL's gaze fixed on Hara's eyes.

In the past, the SEALs did not meet other officers' gazes. *There's something different about him,* Hara thought again. *Something threatening.* He rolled his thumb over the panic button again.

"But, Master Chief, isn't that restricted information?" asked Hara.

Oliver did not respond to the question.

Hara watched as the door of the bar opened. With his back to that door, Oliver did not see the two brantooed sailors enter the bar. His eyes hidden behind dark glasses, Hara watched the men as they quietly slipped into a nearby booth.

"We're heading back to New Copenhagen. Yamashiro wants to start a colony."

"On New Copenhagen? That cinder of a planet might sustain life, but it would not be a life worth living," said Hara.

"No one is calling it the Garden of Eden," said Oliver.

"What about the ship they saw, the one that chased us away? What will he do if that ship returns?"

"We hit it with our best weapon," Oliver said. "We have plenty of stealth infiltration pods."

"You do realize that that was a Unified Authority ship. Does Yamashiro really want to fire on a U.A. ship?"

"We could always broadcast to Earth and ask the Unified Authority if the ship belongs to them," said Oliver.

A man and a woman entered the bar. Hara did not care about the couple, but he was glad to see that there were three men with brantooed necks and dark glasses waiting outside the door, along with the two who had entered the bar. For the first time since the conversation began, the lieutenant allowed his thumb to drop from the panic button.

"I don't understand why we are returning to the Orion Arm at all," said Hara. "We have not completed our mission. Is the old man admitting defeat?"

"We still have a way of getting around the ion curtain," said Oliver. "You're a betting man. I'll wager you've run a simulation of it."

"Broadcasting the *Sakura* into their atmosphere? I've run the simulation. The ship won't survive long. It's suicide."

"Good thing we're leaving all nonessential personnel on New Copenhagen."

"Where they will starve to death if they don't suffocate first."

"Where they will have a chance of surviving."

"Why are you telling me this?" asked Hara. He gazed over the clone's shoulder at the *Yakuza* who had entered the bar. Hara had as unreadable a poker face as any man on the ship, but his eyes would have given him away had it not been for the shades.

"I am here to let you know that you will not be joining the colony," said Oliver.

He sounded so relaxed. *He thinks he's in control,* Hara thought. *If only he could see the men sitting behind him.*

"Did Yamashiro send you?" asked Hara.

"No, I came on my own."

"And I see that you came alone," said Hara.

"I hoped we could keep this between us."

"A gentleman's agreement?" asked Hara.

"Something like that."

"You want me to go down with the ship?" Hara asked.

"Consider it *seppuku* if you like."

"You are not a pilot or a weapons technician, doesn't that make you 'nonessential personnel'? Do you plan on committing *seppuku* as well?" Hara could feel his heart racing. He could feel the sweat running down the outside of his chest and along his back. He was in control of the situation, and the SEAL still rattled him.

Calm as ever, Oliver said, "I'm staying on the ship."

"You can commit suicide if you want. Why should I?"

"Because there will not be room for serpents in the Garden of Eden," said Oliver. "The colony won't have room for gambling or prostitution or vice lords. There won't be time for gangsters or secret organizations."

Hara nodded to the men behind Oliver. Watching his men rise to their feet and walk to the table, Hara felt a wave of relief wash over him. He laughed, an explosive mirth-filled bray. "You think I'm a gangster?"

"I think you are one of the losers," said Oliver.

"'The losers'?" asked Hara. Seeing his men standing behind Oliver, he felt giddy. Taking this man, this inscrutable SEAL, had been so easy.

"*Ya Ku Za*. Eight-nine-three, I believe it refers to a losing hand in cards," said Oliver.

"Very good," said Hara. "You have a good grasp of Japanese."

One of the men laid a hand on Oliver's shoulder and pressed the tip of his butterfly knife into the SEAL's back. Corey Oliver did not flinch. He did not move. His eyes remained fixed on Hara's.

"You have decided that I should die with the ship, and I have decided that you do not have the right to make that decision," said Hara, adding, "If you go out quietly, we won't need to eliminate witnesses."

No more words passed between Hara and Oliver. While his men escorted the clone out of the bar, Hara returned to his table at the back. He felt no regret about what would happen to the SEAL. When you worked both sides of the law, the occasional murder was a survival mechanism. He did not have time to think about Oliver; he needed to make plans for New Copenhagen.

The SEAL had been correct, the name, *Yakuza*, did refer to a losing hand in cards. In Hara's mind, it was the losing hand that made the *Yakuza* the winners. In his mind, the *Yakuza* were not the ones who held the cards, they were the ones who dealt them.

Hara's feeling of triumph turned cold when he saw the next two men who entered the bar . . . a pair of SEALs.

With four of his men surrounding the SEAL and his knife pressed into the clone's back, Ricky Oshiro should have felt confident. They moved silently down an empty service hall in a pack surrounding the SEAL. Two men led the way. If MPs or witnesses entered the hall, the men in the lead would scare them away. Oshiro and another man flanked the SEAL. The man bringing up the rear lagged ten feet behind the pack. He carried an S9 pistol in his hand. If the SEAL made a move, he would shoot to kill.

They turned into a service hall that led behind the mess area. Their footsteps echoed off the walls as they marched past the galley area.

The man in the rear was the first to go.

The two men leading the pack turned a corner. Oshiro and the SEAL followed. And that was it. The last man never appeared. When Oshiro looked back to see what had happened, the SEAL broke his arm at the elbow and wrist. The reversal happened so quickly that Oshiro did not notice anything until he felt the pain and his knife had clattered to the floor. As the SEAL went for his next target, he shattered Oshiro's leg with a kick to the side of the knee.

The *Yakuza* were tough men, dangerous by nature and experienced fighters; but the SEAL was a demon by design. As Oshiro cradled his broken wrist, the SEAL slid his talonlike fingers across the neck of the man on his right, puncturing skin and tissue, then tearing out tubes. The man gasped and collapsed, uttering only a whisper. The sheet of blood that sprayed from the wound stained his shirt, the wall, and the floor around him. He died holding a hand to the wound as blood bubbled out between his fingers.

The men in the front did not respond quickly enough to save themselves. The SEAL swept an ankle from under the man on the right, breaking the joint and leaving him hobbled. With a cry of pain, he fell to the floor.

Only one uninjured opponent remained. The man did not run. He had a gun, but he knew he could not draw it fast enough to save himself. He kicked at the SEAL, but the clone ducked, spun, and moved away. The man chased, his arms guarding his face, his fists clenched tight.

As the SEAL came in range, Oshiro tried to kick him, but the SEAL dodged the kick, dropped to one leg, and struck the inside of Oshiro's injured knee with a back-fist. With his right elbow and left knee broken, Oshiro fought back the pain as he rolled toward the knife he had dropped. The SEAL leaped over his shoulder and drove the heel of his foot into the wounded *Yakuza*'s neck, killing him.

The uninjured *Yakuza* lunged at the SEAL, an aggressive mistake that ended the fight. Using his fingers like a knife, the SEAL drove his fingers into the man's gut. Blood jetted out of the wound, but the SEAL had not finished. He slashed the man across his left biceps, then along his throat. The cut across the arm was disabling. The holes in his stomach and neck drained the man's life in a matter of seconds.

The last of the *Yakuza* lay helpless on the floor. He did not have a gun, and the knife was too far away for him to reach it. He tried to drag himself to safety, but Oliver slid silently behind him, grabbed his head, and snapped his neck.

Only when the fighting had ended did the three SEALs behind the corner emerge with the body of the fifth *Yakuza*, the gunman. "Not exactly a textbook assault," Senior Chief Warren said in the condescending tone of a teacher correcting an errant pupil.

"I just eliminated four men," said Oliver.

"Yes, and it wouldn't have been much louder if you had attacked them with a set of kettledrums and a bugle," said Warren.

The other SEALs set to work without a word. They loaded the bodies onto a cart, which they rolled to the same waste-disposal unit that the *Yakuza* would have used to incinerate Oliver. While Oliver and Warren mopped the floor and cleaned the walls, the bodies of the gangsters burned to ash.

In less than three minutes, the SEALs cleaned the service hall and disposed of the bodies. They prided themselves on efficiency.

THIRTY-SIX

Earthdate: November 28, A.D. 2517

"Fifteen of my men are missing," said Admiral Yamashiro. "What do you know about the disappearances, Master Chief?"

The master chief stood at attention, his eyes straight ahead, his chest out, his arms at his side. "Nothing, sir," said Oliver. It was a lie, and he knew that Yamashiro could see through it; but lying was within the parameters of his mission. Before leaving Earth, the SEALs had received special orders.

"You know nothing about it?" asked Yamashiro. He stood and stared angrily into Oliver's eyes, looking for any sign of nervousness, then he walked around the SEAL. "I think you and your men have been poaching."

"Poaching, sir?" asked Oliver.

"Hunting without permission," growled Yamashiro.

Oliver did not respond.

Captain Takahashi, who sat in a corner of the office watching the interrogation, silently shifted in his chair.

"I will not tolerate vigilantism on my ship," Yamashiro grunted. He did not raise his voice.

"'Vigilantism,' sir?" asked Oliver. "Was somebody breaking the law?"

"The missing men are all *Yakuza*."

"Permission to speak, sir?"

"Speak," said Yamashiro.

"What are *Yakuza*?" asked Oliver.

Yamashiro looked to Takahashi for help. The captain said, "Gangsters."

"Lieutenant Tatsu Hara is missing," said Yamashiro.

"Hara?" asked Oliver.

"The intelligence officer who spoke at the briefing yesterday."

"The man with all the brantoos?" asked Oliver.

"Yes."

"And the curled hair?"

Yamashiro glowered.

"And the dark glasses?"

This time, Yamashiro did not respond at all.

"Was he a gangster?" asked Oliver.

"You were seen in the *Shin Roppongi* bar last night," said Yamashiro.

"Me, sir?"

"You were seen."

"What makes you think it was me?" asked Oliver. "With all due respect, sir, there are three thousand Navy SEALs on this ship, and we all look alike."

Yamashiro growled, and Takahashi giggled. Yamashiro whirled around to face his son-in-law, and snarled, "Do you think this is funny?"

Takahashi fought back a laugh, and said, "Yes, sir. I do."

"I see no humor . . ."

"Admiral, when we left Earth, you were given orders that you have not shared with the rest of the crew. What makes you so sure Master Chief Oliver is not following special orders as well?"

"Is that the case, Master Chief?" growled Yamashiro.

Oliver, his gaze still straight ahead, said, "This sailor has received no special orders, sir." He hated lying; but he preferred it to disobeying orders.

"But you would not be able to tell me if Admiral Brocius gave you a direct order, would you?" Yamashiro asked, then he turned back to Takahashi, and asked, "What kind of orders?"

"Orders to enforce Unified Authority regulations," said Takahashi. "Orders to do whatever he sees necessary to ensure we accomplish our mission."

"This is not a Unified Authority ship," Yamashiro grumbled.

"But the SEALs are on loan from the U.A. Navy."

"Admiral Brocius is the only officer who would have authority to issue those orders," said Yamashiro. He turned to Oliver, and yelled, "Did you meet with Admiral Brocius? Tell me."

"It could have come from the Linear Committee," Takahashi said. "It might be an executive order."

"Do you think the orders included assassinating members of my crew?"

"Naturally," said Takahashi. "They may include assassinating you if necessary."

Yamashiro sighed, and said, "Maybe so. At ease, Master Chief." He walked behind his desk. Before he sat down, he asked, "Do you believe I have shown good judgment as a commander, Master Chief?"

"Yes, sir," said Oliver.

"We did not need those men, I suppose. Hara was a useful officer," said Yamashiro, then he muttered the words, "bootleggers and extortionists."

The admiral sat down and asked the SEAL to sit as well. Only when Oliver was seated did Yamashiro begin speaking. He asked, "Master Chief, what do you know about colonizing planets?" There was a notepad on Yamashiro's desk. He picked up the stylus and focused his attention on the small screen.

"They didn't cover colonization in special operations, sir," said Oliver. "I do have men who specialized in survival training."

"Survival training?" asked Yamashiro.

"Supplementing limited resources by living off the land, locating and purifying sources of water . . . building shelter . . . camouflage. Some of it could be useful."

"We may need them for protection as well," said Takahashi.

Yamashiro grunted his agreement, and said, "Master Chief, as you know, we're sending all nonessential personnel down to the planet. We will not need your SEALs to complete our mission. I want to leave them with the colony."

"Yes, sir. I've thought about that, sir, and I believe that would be a mistake, sir."

Yamashiro looked up from the notepad for a moment, his eyes on Oliver; but the SEAL did not meet his gaze. "You think I am making a mistake? Just yesterday you recommended sending all nonessential personnel to New Copenhagen."

"Yes, sir."

"Have you changed your mind?"

"Not entirely, sir. I still believe we should establish a colony. I have had second thoughts about the size of the colony."

"Everyone left aboard this ship will die," said Yamashiro. "A-361-B will be a Kamikaze mission."

"Yes, sir," said the master chief. "Sir, resources are going to be scarce on New Copenhagen. It may take years before the colony becomes self-sufficient. I'm concerned about overpopulating the colony."

Yamashiro placed the stylus back on the notepad, and said, "Who do you think we should leave on the colony?"

"Not me or my men, sir. I believe we have nothing to contribute to a colony."

"Master Chief, once we program the broadcast coordinates into the broadcast computer, we can fly that mission with a skeleton crew," said Takahashi. "We won't need you on this mission."

"What would we contribute to the colony? If the objective is to preserve life . . . to continue humanity, Admiral, we're clones. We're sterile.

"One hundred of my men have been trained in basic survival tactics. They may be useful. They can serve as peacekeepers, they know how to build shelters and purify water. They can contribute. The colony will need farmers, not saboteurs. They didn't teach us farming in SEAL training. We don't belong in your colony."

Yamashiro sighed and rubbed his eyes. Takahashi made a whistling noise that sounded like a bomb dropping, and said, "You're a cheerful fellow."

"Do your men agree with your assessment?" asked Yamashiro.

"To a man," said Oliver.

Yamashiro let a moment pass before asking, "What do you suggest we do?"

"Leave our survival specialists on New Copenhagen."

"And you think I should take the rest of you to A-361-B?" asked Yamashiro.

"Yes, sir," said Oliver.

"You don't want to live?" asked Takahashi.

"Sir, we were created to help ensure the survival of the human species. We want to do what we were created to do, sir," said Oliver. "You will not need us in your colony, Admiral. Life in your colony does not fit our mission."

A smile flickered across Yamashiro's lips and vanished while his eyes remained cold and hard. His irises were such a dark shade of brown that they appeared to be black.

"In my colony? It may not have occurred to you, Master Chief, but you are not the only man in this fleet who is willing to go down with this ship. I have no intention of hiding on a planet while my ship is destroyed."

"You mean my ship," said Takahashi. "I command the ship; you command the fleet."

"Which is down to one ship," snapped Yamashiro. "Captain, the *Sakura* is my fleet."

"With all due respect, Admiral, there is no fleet," said Oliver. "There will be a colony, and it will need a governor. You will be needed on New Copenhagen. Any part you would play during the destruction of A-361-B would be insignificant. Your leadership in the colony, on the other hand . . ."

Yamashiro would not have looked more stunned and angered if the SEAL had spit on him. His jaw clenched tight, his eyes narrowed to angry slits, and he said, "I am more than seventy years old. Do not deny an old man the opportunity to die with dignity."

Takahashi stood and walked over to his father-in-law. He placed a hand on the old man's shoulder, and said, "You are a miserable excuse for a fleet commander. You were a fantastic governor and a masterful politician, but I never liked the way you ran the fleet."

Yamashiro's shoulder tightened, then sagged. For a brief moment, it looked like he might take a swing at Takahashi, then the strength leaked out of his body. When he looked up, his eyes were moist. He asked, "Was it my fault? Was it my fault that we lost the other ships?"

At some point Takahashi had blamed Yamashiro for their losses. He had sided with the warlike Miyamoto instead of listening to his other captains. Now, though, Takahashi realized the weight of command and forgave. "No," said Takahashi. "It was nobody's fault."

Oliver added, "The colony will need a government and laws. It will need a leader, someone who can tell the people not to eat more food than they can grow even though they are hungry."

"That is not me," said Yamashiro.

"That can only be you," said Takahashi.

"What about you?" asked Yamashiro, desperation rising in his voice.

"You were the governor of a planet, I am the captain of this ship, both of our futures have been decided for us. You will lead the colony, and I will protect it."

"And die a hero," whispered Yamashiro.

"Sometimes it is easier to die for your beliefs than to live for them," said Takahashi. "I think my job will be easier than yours."

THIRTY-SEVEN

Earthdate: November 29, A.D. 2517
Location: New Copenhagen
Galactic Position: Orion Arm
Astronomic Location: Milky Way

Thirty-five stealth infiltration pods hovered in space, ten thousand miles away from the *Sakura* forming a loose blockade around the ship. The technicians controlling the pods kept their field-resonance engines fully charged and on the brink of overcharging. They were like grenades, keys pulled and ready to throw.

Theoretically, the enemy ships only needed to venture within five thousand miles of one of the pods for the trap to work. When your bombs explode with enough force to shatter small planets, marksmanship is not really an issue.

Within an hour of the *Sakura* drifting into place above New Copenhagen, three ships streaked into view. They glowed a brilliant orange gold in the darkness of space, like fireflies flying in formation. They might have been broadcasted in millions of miles away or they might have been lying in wait. *Sakura* security never detected their anomalies.

Three anomalies appeared behind the first ships, signaling the arrival of three more ships. Another trio of ships appeared on the opposite side of the *Sakura*.

Watching the nine ships advance, Yamashiro said, "First wave, support wave, third wave to flank, cutting off retreat . . . Those must be Unified Authority ships, they are using the same tactics they used against the Mogats.

"Who are they at war with? Why attack us?"

"Are they responding to our signal?" asked Takahashi.

"No, sir."

"Keep trying," said Takahashi.

Another few seconds passed, and he asked, "They're still not responding?"

"No, sir."

"Are they in range of the pods?" asked Takahashi.

"Almost, sir. They're flying very slowly. They've dropped down under one thousand miles per hour."

"Maybe they want us to escape," Yamashiro said. He had already begun the transformation from military leader back to statesman.

"Still no response?" asked Takahashi, now getting nervous. Knowing that destroying the ships could start a war between the Unified Authority and New Copenhagen, Takahashi wanted to avoid bloodshed.

"The first three ships are in range of the pods," said the weapons officer.

"Still no response?" Takahashi asked one last time.

"Captain, we need to . . ." Yamashiro did not get the chance to finish his sentence.

Takahashi knew his job. He took a deep breath, and said, "Fire the nearest pod." He spoke in English. It was his bridge now; ceremony and tradition had never interested him. He and his crew spoke Japanese, but they spoke English more fluently.

To the naked eye, it looked like nothing happened. If there was a flash from the explosion, it was so small that nothing showed on the monitors. There was no visible shock wave, no wall of debris. An uninformed observer might have thought that the three glowing ships had simply malfunctioned.

What struck Takahashi was not the destruction of three ships with a single weapon but the completeness of their demise. Torpedoes left holes. Sometimes, they set off chain reactions. Sometimes, small parts of the hull broke off.

That was not what happened to these ships. In the invisible wake of the explosion, the three glowing ships slid sideways like boats caught by a powerful wave. Their bows continued to face toward the *Sakura* as they skittered to the side and began shedding parts. Their shields disappeared, and the armor fell from their hulls in flakes, revealing skeletons of twisted girders. Because they were in space, and there was nothing to stop them, the U.A. ships continued sliding sideways until the *Sakura*'s telemetry could no longer track them.

For a moment, the universe seemed to freeze.

This wasn't a naval battle. It was like crushing an insect, thought Takahashi.

"The other ships are leaving, sir."

On his tactical display, Takahashi watched six glowing ships disappear into anomalies.

Admiral Yamashiro and Captain Takahashi stood in the control tower of one of the landing bays. Below them, lines of sailors, both men and women, marched onto transports. They wore uniforms and carried duffel bags. They moved slowly onto the transports, heads down, steps short. "It's like watching prisoners on their way to a firing squad," said Yamashiro. "They think they are the ones who are going to die."

Takahashi asked, "Is living easier than dying?"

Yamashiro said, "Your crew would mutiny if they knew what you planned. You, Hironobu, you are the brave one. You know where you are going and what you need to do."

"My mission will end three minutes after it begins. There's no need for bravery," said Takahashi. He did not look at his father-in-law as he said this. He stared away, watching the lines of sailors boarding the transports. *Lifeboats,* he thought. *These men and women will escape my sinking ship.*

For the first time in three years, Yamashiro smiled at his son-in-law. Speaking in Japanese, he said, "You cannot convince me that flying a Kamikaze mission over an alien planet is the act of a coward."

There is much you do not know, thought Takahashi. Takahashi Hironobu, who could not return to his wife on Earth and was about to lose his ship, took comfort in the thought of a quick death.

For the first time in his short life, Senior Chief Jeff Harmer raised his voice as he asked, "Me? Why do I have to go?"

In his five short years of existence—other military clones were raised in orphanages, but the SEALs "crawled out of the tube" with the bodies and minds of twenty-one-year-old men—Corey Oliver had never seen a SEAL show such insubordination.

They convened in a small room, the ten senior chiefs sitting in a single row of chairs, all looking exactly alike. Each man was short, five feet and two inches tall, with a charcoal-colored tint to his skin and a bald head. *We really do look like shadow demons,* thought Oliver.

"Are you refusing to follow a direct command?" he asked. Just two weeks earlier, he had been a senior chief petty officer as well. Now he was a master chief, the commander of the SEALs, but he was no older or more experienced than the ten remaining senior chiefs. He had not performed his duties better than they had. In his mind, the selection process had been arbitrary, not by merit.

Looking sorry for his outburst, Harmer lowered his eyes, and said, "No, Master Chief." Judging by his posture, he might even have called the master chief, "sir," but that would not have been appropriate. The SEALs were enlisted men, they did not refer to each other as, "sir."

"It's just, Master Chief . . . Why are you assigning me this duty?" asked Harmer.

Oliver smiled, but he did not respond in a soft voice. "What is your MOS, Senior Chief?" he asked.

"Special Reconnaissance," Harmer said, sounding like a child caught in a lie.

"And your training included?" asked Oliver.

"Survival tactics."

"And?"

"Geographical assessment."

"And?"

"And assault planning and damage assessment."

"You have an appropriate skill set, so you go," Oliver said. "You and a company of SEALs will work as survival specialists, policemen, and drill sergeants. Once a sustainable living situation is achieved, you will train the colonists in defensive tactics."

"Nursemaids," said Harmer.

"Protectors," said Oliver, his voice every bit as grim as the words he said. "You will report to your transport in thirty minutes, Harmer. Go prep your men."

Harmer nodded. He did not salute. Enlisted men did not salute each other. He rose to his feet and walked out of the room without saying a word.

"I'll tell you what," said Oliver, "if any of you are having second thoughts about returning to A-361-B, Harmer will switch places with you. Any takers?" Oliver looked over the nine remaining senior chiefs. "No one?"

No one raised a hand. No one spoke. They sat in their chairs, staring up at Oliver, the ugliest men the master chief had ever seen.

Do you want to die? Oliver silently asked his men in his head. *Do I?* He could not answer for his men; but for himself, the answer was, "No." He had no desire to die, nor did life as a colonist appeal to him. If everything went right, if the crops grew, and they found enough oxygen and water, Harmer and his men would serve as policemen and soldiers until they were too old to matter; then they would go on for years, eating food meant for reproducing humans, outcasts, weak and alone among a tribe of people who cared for them only because they felt indebted. The thought made Oliver cringe.

He could not imagine a worse fate. In truth, Corey Oliver, a man with no ambitions, hated command. For some reason the fates had not only condemned him to replace Illych but to order men to their deaths.

"Captain Takahashi tells me he can fly this ship with 120 men," said Oliver. Warren started to ask a question, and Oliver put up a hand to stop him. He added, "That's just what it takes to keep this ship flying. It takes an additional two hundred men to keep things running in a battle situation. That's 320 trained sailors.

"For this mission, he's got a thousand sailors and us. Admiral Yamashiro is taking most of the bridge crew with him to New Copenhagen. We're taking the old and the sick sailors with us."

"Are any women coming with us?" asked Senior Chief Billings.

Oliver stopped speaking, glared at the man, and asked, "What's the matter, Billings? You hoping for a first fling before you die?"

The other clones laughed.

"No. No women. No young men, either. The average age on this boat just jumped from twenty-nine to thirty-six," said Oliver.

"Are you factoring us in those statistics?" asked Senior Chief Warren.

Was this part of their programming? Oliver wondered. Some of Illych's Kamikaze team had acted the same way before they left on their mission. They made jokes as they boarded the transport. Even normally somber SEALs kidded each other before their final missions.

Not all of them, though. Oliver remembered that Illych did not join in the banter. Just as Oliver now felt the weight of command, Illych must have felt it at the end. His men were going to die, and Illych would have felt the weight of their lives on his shoulders, just as it was Oliver's turn to feel that weight.

Oliver smiled, looked at his notepad, and said, "I factored you animals in as twenty-six-year-olds. Factoring you in as five-year-olds, the average age drops to twenty-five."

He looked around the room, meeting his men's eyes and searching their faces for fear, and Oliver realized they could relax only if he relaxed with them. They would go. They would fight, and they would die, and they would never complain; but he saw that he could give them strength if he would just relax and joke with them. He said, "You should have seen what happened to the average IQ on the ship when I factored you animals in. We cut it in half."

The senior chiefs laughed, their morale restored.

THIRTY-EIGHT

Earthdate: December 1, A.D. 2517

Transferring twenty-two hundred colonists—one thousand women, eleven hundred men, and one hundred SEAL clones—to New Copenhagen took an hour. Stripping the *Sakura* and shipping supplies down to the planet took two days.

Every morsel of food, be it frozen, dehydrated, powdered, extruded, or fresh, was sent to the planet. Power generators were removed from the ship and sent down to the planet, leaving entire decks without electricity. Weapons, everything that wasn't built into the *Sakura*'s hull, were sent down, including fifteen low-gravity tanks that consumed such massive amounts of fuel that the colonists would never operate them— they would be torn apart and used for scrap metal; their engines were too inefficient for anything else. Beds, portable storage facilities, and furniture were sent down. So were cooking and eating utensils. Engineers even scavenged metal and wiring from the wall panels and floors.

Yamashiro stayed aboard the *Sakura*, overseeing the operation as men stripped the ship of nonessential items to send down with nonessential personnel. By the time they finished, the medical bay was empty, the team having pillaged light fixtures, wiring, and electrical panels as well as medicines, furniture, equipment, and flooring.

The entire third deck had been stripped down to its iron girders. Once the location of living quarters, rec rooms, Pachinko parlors, bars, and galleys, it now sat dark and empty. Eviscerated. Yamashiro and Takahashi quietly observed the carnage as the admiral made his final inspection of the ship.

* * *

"Admiral on deck!"

The crew, about eighty men and fifty SEALs, stood to salute Yamashiro. He returned their salute.

As they entered, Takahashi said something about his new bridge crew being ready. Yamashiro scanned the area, taking in the desks, the booths, the computers, the table at which he had spent the last three years looking at tactical displays and reading three-dimensional maps. He would not miss the bridge of the *Sakura*, not in the least.

Yamashiro nodded to sailors and returned their salutes. He shook a few men's hands even though he wanted to leave. He felt old, even ancient. His head hurt, and he needed a nap. *All these men will die saving me and the colony,* he thought, and the weight of the thought pushed down on him.

Yamashiro no longer saw himself as an admiral. The bridge had become a foreign land to him, one that he needed to escape. He thanked the men nearest the hatch and left, a silent Takahashi at his side. As they stepped through the door, Yamashiro whispered, "How much do they know?"

"The SEALs know everything," said Takahashi.

"And the sailors?"

"They know we are going to broadcast into the atmosphere and that it will be dangerous," Takahashi said.

The hall was empty.

When it sailed into the Orion Arm, the *Sakura* had carried six thousand hands. Now it had thirty-eight hundred, most of them SEALs, who seldom ventured onto the upper decks.

"Are you going to tell them?"

Takahashi looked back to make sure no one had left the bridge behind them, then asked, "What should I tell them? It's not a mission, it's a death sentence. If I tell them what we're really going to do . . ."

"Would you blame them?" asked Yamashiro.

"I can't fight my crew and the aliens at the same time," said Takahashi.

The hall was long and dim and silent. Half of the light fixtures had been stripped from the ceiling. They passed a row of dormant elevators, their bulky metal doors removed. The doors and the cables would not be used for their intended purposes by the colony. They would be melted down.

You will go down to your grave with a heavy conscience, thought Yamashiro, but he did not say it. Instead, he simply said, "I do not envy you, Hironobu, you carry too much weight on your shoulders."

They continued down the hall until they reached the stairs.

"I won't carry that weight for long," said Takahashi. "No more than three minutes once we are under way."

They reached the crowded corridors of the bottom deck. With their compound stripped empty and most of the crew off the ship, the SEALs milled about in the halls.

Yamashiro looked up and down the hall. In the muted light, the SEALs looked more like shadows than people. Groups of SEALs stood in dark corners speaking quietly among themselves. When they recognized the admiral, they snapped to attention.

Seeing them in their lines, as unmoving as statues, Yamashiro remembered the words *kage no yasha* and dismissed them quickly.

"Admiral, sir, Master Chief Oliver was looking for you," said one of the SEALs.

"I would like to speak with him," said Yamashiro.

The SEAL, a lowly petty officer third class, saluted and walked off in search of the master chief. In his dark suit, with his dark skin, the clone disappeared into his surroundings as he hurried down the hall. A moment later, two shadows appeared in the distance.

Both men stopped and saluted.

Takahashi and Yamashiro returned the salute, then Yamashiro said, "Master Chief, I wish you . . . success."

"It's been an honor, sir," said Oliver.

Yamashiro took a deep breath, held it in his lungs for seconds, then slowly released the air. He searched the hallway, taking in every detail. This was the last time any of these sights would be seen by surviving eyes. *From this moment on, everything that happens on this ship will be a secret that the dead will take with them.*

Yamashiro wanted to say something. He wanted to tell the SEAL how much he admired his courage. He wanted to thank all of these men; but his throat and tongue felt swollen, and he found himself struggling to breathe.

"Admiral, may I make one last request on behalf of my men?" asked Oliver.

"Anything," said Yamashiro.

"Sir, the men and I were wondering . . ."

As Oliver spoke, the hatch behind him opened and light spilled out. Looking over the SEAL's shoulder, Yamashiro saw thousands of men standing at attention in rows. The master chief stopped speaking, and Yamashiro stepped around him to look in the doorway.

Wearing dress uniforms, the SEALs all faced a dais upon which ten men waited at attention. On that dais stood a barrel, and on that barrel sat a ceramic bottle of sake and a line of thimble-sized cups.

"Sir, if you would give us a proper send-off," said Master Chief Oliver.

Yamashiro Yoshi bowed to the SEAL clone and marched into the room without saying a word. He had already transmogrified from an officer into a politician; but now he struggled against the tide of his instincts and forced himself to behave like an admiral. He scowled at the men as he stalked past them, neither smiling nor showing his pain.

And so the retired admiral climbed the steps of the dais, took his place behind the barrel, and, barking out orders in Japanese, told the ten senior chiefs and the master chief to step forward. He poured sake into the twelve *ochoko* and stood at attention as the men met his gaze. At his order, the men took their cups, and he took his. He toasted them; and then, at his order, they drank their wine, and replaced the cups on the barrel. The SEALs saluted him.

Yamashiro, standing at attention, extended his return salute as he looked up and down the rows of men. Struggling to hide his emotions, he dismissed the senior chiefs. Then he turned to the master chief, and said, "I must return to the colony."

Oliver saluted one last time, and Yamashiro left the *Sakura*.

Yamashiro Yoshi felt overwhelmed by emotion. He walked quickly to the landing bay and wasted no time entering the transport that would take him to New Copenhagen. At the base of the ramp, he turned to his son-in-law.

Takahashi stood erect and saluted. His shoulders trembled, and Yamashiro knew the younger man was scared. He did not return the salute; instead, he embraced Takahashi Hironobu, the husband of his daughter, Yoko. "You're a fine officer, Hiro," he said. "I wish my daughter could see the man she has married."

Yamashiro stepped onto the ramp, returned the salute, and forced himself to enter the transport without looking back.

THIRTY-NINE

Captain Takahashi Hironobu watched as the sled pulled the transport toward the first atmospheric lock. Low and squat, with tiny wings that looked like an engineering afterthought, the transport rolled past the blast doors and stopped to wait as the lock closed behind it. The metal blast doors closed slowly, taking fifteen seconds to slide into place.

How will they remember us? Takahashi asked himself. *When their batteries run dry and their generators break and the technology that launched them does not survive to the next generation, will they believe in space travel or write us off as a myth? Will they see us as martyrs or saviors? Will the parents of some future generation teach their children that gods placed them on this planet and promised to return?*

Takahashi thought about his wife and how much he missed her. He missed the children, too, of course. If the Morgan Atkins Believers had never declared their civil war, and the aliens had not invaded the galaxy, the Takahashi family would have remained on Ezer Kri. He would have grown old watching his children mature into adults and start families of their own.

If the Broadcast Network had not been destroyed, he could contact them. Even from New Copenhagen, light-years away, he could have told his wife that he loved her and seen how his children had grown. He wanted to see his family again, just once before he died; but Earth was at war again, and he could not approach the planet without risking everything.

Takahashi was not alone in the landing bay. SEALs and a handful of technicians had come to prepare infiltration pods for the attack. He watched as one Japanese technician and three SEALs carried a pod to a computer station. A SEAL attached a line from the computer to the S.I.P. as the tech typed on the screen.

Takahashi approached the technician, and asked, "Ensign, how many pods do we have?"

The man grunted without looking back to see who had asked the question. He casually looked up from his work, then snapped to attention. Fear showing on his face, he saluted.

Takahashi returned the salute and repeated his question, "How many pods are left?"

"Sir, I have not checked the inventory, sir," said the technician.

Doing a credible imitation of his father-in-law, Takahashi growled, "Go check."

The man saluted and ran.

Be polite, Takahashi reminded himself. *This man will die in a few minutes preserving the colony.*

Takahashi wondered if the man would mutiny if he knew the turn that his life was about to take. The captain had complete confidence in the SEALs, though. They knew what was coming.

The captain returned their salutes, studied their faces, then grunted, "As you were."

The SEALs quietly went back to preparing the S.I.P.s. The bombs. They were preparing the very bombs that would end their lives. They were digging their own graves.

"Captain Takahashi, sir, we have 1,118 pods, sir," the ensign said as he returned.

Ten of these should be enough to destroy a planet. We might be able to collapse a star with twenty of them, he thought. "Prepare one hundred pods," he told the ensign. "I want them in place and charged within the next five minutes."

"Yes, sir," the man said. He saluted again and relayed the order to the other teams. There was something strange in the way the ensign spoke. Maybe it was an odd note in the voice, maybe it was the frightened look in his eyes.

That was when Takahashi realized that, like the SEALs, his crewmen knew that they were about to die. On some level, they knew. They might not have known the mechanics of their fate, but they knew how the mission would end.

The pods look like coffins, Takahashi thought as he watched SEALs wheeling S.I.P.s into the bay. He had never seen one up close, but now he saw that they looked like coffins, oblong, man-sized, loaf-shaped boxes with rounded corners and convex surfaces on all sides. They were black with a dull gloss sheen. And they had no visible engines, no rockets, no thrust chambers or manifolds. Whatever propelled them was concealed inside their smooth shells.

In the darkened landing bay, with a few lights shining in the ceiling and the low glow of the computer stations, Takahashi stood fascinated by the coffin-shaped bombs and the demonlike men preparing them. He thought, *It will all be over soon. Just another few minutes, and it will all be over.*

On his notepad he had a picture of Yoko, his wife. He stared at her and took courage in the thought that this mission might well protect her. He also knew that the only way he would ever see her again was in death.

Leaving the bay, Takahashi paused to take one last look along the darkened deck. He saw men who looked like demons scurrying on an errand of mercy and murder, working as silently as shadows.

The main hall of the lower deck was dark and mostly empty. Once Admiral Yamashiro had given them their ceremonial farewell, the SEALs disappeared into the woodwork. Hundreds of them must have reported to the *Sakura*'s four landing bays.

It took Takahashi longer to reach the bridge than usual. He found curiosities everywhere he looked. In the dim light, his sailors looked like ghosts. They floated up and down the corridors, haunting the decks that still had lights and walls and flooring.

He found the top deck crowded with sailors. Most of the men did not recognize him until he stood among them. They moped along the hall, whispering among themselves. All discipline seemed to have drained out of them. When he stepped close enough for them to see him clearly, they stood nearly at attention and saluted.

The bridge, though, was different. Here the mood remained businesslike. Takahashi entered the bridge, and Suzuki circled toward him like a bird of prey.

"Are we ready to launch?" asked Takahashi.

"We just heard from the landing bay, sir. The infiltration pods are charged."

"Good. And our broadcast engines?"

"Ready, sir."

"Where do you have us broadcasting in?" asked Takahashi. It came so easily now. He was talking about his own death, but he might have been talking about visiting old friends back home.

Suzuki stepped closer so that no one would hear what he said next. "I programmed the computer to broadcast us into the center of the planet."

Takahashi thought about that. "Interesting plan, Commander, but it leaves no margin for error."

"What could go wrong?" asked Suzuki.

Takahashi smiled, and said, "Something will go wrong. Something always goes wrong."

"Yes, sir. Would you prefer to enter above one of their cities?" He had the coordinates. Their spy satellites had mapped the entire planet before the Avatari sleeved the planet.

"Someplace flat and low," said Takahashi. "Even if everything goes according to plan, we will still need to avoid their tachyon shield."

CHAPTER
FORTY

Location: Planet A-361-B
Galactic Position: Solar System A-361
Astronomic Location: Bode's Galaxy

The anomaly shattered the cold, bright sky at the edge of the city. One thousand feet in the air, the inside of the tachyon layer formed a perfectly smooth ceiling above the planet, a silver-white surface as bright as a sun shining through the gauze of clouds. Like the other ships of her make, the *Sakura* had a black hull that offered reasonable camouflage in space but stood in stark relief against the bright sky.

Not designed to fly among such atmospheric abstractions as wind currents and convections, the battleship fumbled in the air. Inside the bridge, navigators struggled to stabilize the big ship in the air, using boosters engineered for course correction in space. The ship jumped and dropped like a fledgling bird struggling to fly.

With his ship bouncing five stories at a time, Takahashi found it almost impossible to think, and his survival instincts took control of his brain. Even though he had come on this mission planning to die, fear and panic now filled his mind. Had he not been in his chair when the ship broadcasted into the atmosphere, he would have hit the ceiling above his head. To his left and right, men and clones who had been standing, now lay on the floor, some writhing in pain, some unconscious.

Holding on to workstations and walls to lock himself in place, Commander Suzuki fought his way to the navigation station. An experienced navigator, he squirmed behind the console and took control of the ship. Seconds passed. Tremors still rocked the *Sakura*, but Suzuki stabilized the ship.

Takahashi rose partway out of his chair. His mind cleared. "Landing bay . . . Landing bay . . ." he yelled into the communications console.

No one responded.

Takahashi tried to climb out of his chair, but his legs were weak. The acid-and-sawdust smell of vomit filled the bridge. Takahashi ran a hand across his forehead. When he looked at the hand, fresh bright blood covered his fingers and palm.

The door to the bridge opened, and in staggered Master Chief Oliver. He looked at Takahashi and asked, "Why hasn't it happened?"

Takahashi put up a hand, waited a moment, then spit out blood and two teeth.

Corey Oliver had short legs, but he could run three four-minute miles without a break. Now he sprinted down the hall, trying to keep his balance as the deck rose and dropped beneath his feet.

Oliver had already shifted his mind into combat mode. Thoughts took second place to reflexes and autonomic judgment. A sailor lay on the ground in the fetal position, his arms across his stomach. Oliver leaped over the man, landed, and kept running without looking back. Another sailor stood leaning against a wall for support, a stream of blood pouring from the gashes along his left eye and cheek. He reached a hand out to Oliver, who spun to dodge him and just kept running.

The ship fell and bounced. It was a big bounce. Oliver held a hand above his head as the floor dropped from beneath him. His wrist and elbow slammed into the ceiling. The SEAL knew how to land on hard surfaces; bending his knees, balancing perfectly, he rose to his feet and ran to the stairs, already aware that he had dislocated his shoulder. Cradling his right arm with his left, the clone stumbled to the stairs, then jumped whole flights in his rush to reach the landing bays. He landed hard, bounded face-first into the bulkhead, turned, and jumped the next flight. A wounded sailor tried to stop him. Oliver pushed the sailor aside and found his way to the bottom deck. The lights had gone out. The deck was so dark that he would have needed lights had it not been for the genetic enhancements in his eyes.

The air smelled of fire, sweat, excrement, and blood. Men had died. Oliver saw bodies. With the panels removed from the ceiling and the walls, men had flown into girders and piping in the turbulence.

Oliver opened the first landing bay and hit the "panic" button on the communications panel. When he saw the destruction, his breath caught in his throat.

Showers of sparks shot out of holes in the walls. Bodies and equipment lay scattered like garbage along the floor. Two launching devices had fallen over, the "caskets" they held now scattered among the bodies on the floor.

Aware that he might be entering a room filled with radiation, Oliver ran to one of the S.I.P.s. The stealth vehicle did not have gauges or timers on its smooth outer shell, and the dark matte finish revealed no secrets.

"Bridge," said Oliver. He waited a moment, then asked, "Captain, can you hear me? I'm in the landing bay."

"What is the situation?" asked Takahashi.

"It looks like a tornado just blew through here," Oliver said, then added, "maybe an earthquake."

"What about the pods?" asked Takahashi.

"I can't tell. It looks bad, the computer stations were smashed."

"What about the other bays?" asked Takahashi. He started to say something else, then signed off.

Oliver did not check the bodies. He did not have time to care for wounded men who were already marked for death.

There was nothing he could do in this landing bay. Whatever had happened to the pods, Oliver could not diagnose or fix the problem without a working computer station, and the stations in this bay had been smashed.

Having been designed for deep-space travel, the *Sakura* was not aerodynamic. Unlike airships, she could not glide. If her thrusters faltered, she would drop.

Captain Takahashi felt helpless as he watched Suzuki, his second-in-command, typing maneuvers on the navigation keyboard. Battleships like the *Sakura* were controlled with computers instead of sticks and throttles. Buttons lit up on the panel, and Suzuki pressed or ignored them. Alarms blared, lights flashed, warning signals went off, and the ship stuttered.

"We can't hover like this for long. She's not made for this!" said Suzuki.

Staring into screens and not looking back, Suzuki yelled, "We're down to one-third of our fuel." Unlike the ship's main engines, the *Sakura*'s thrusters used fuel made from liquid oxygen.

Takahashi listened but did not answer. He knew that fuel meant for course corrections would not keep a ship in the air for long. The continuous booster stream needed to keep the big battleship afloat would drain their already three-year-old fuel supply.

"The engines are too hot. They're going to melt!" yelled Suzuki. "We can't do this."

Takahashi looked through a tactical display to the glare-filled sky outside. "Take us to the shoreline," he said.

Suzuki did not argue. He said, "Aye, sir," and began working the computers.

Maybe we should land the ship, Takahashi thought; but he could not give that order. The *Sakura* was made for deep-space travel, away from gravity. She did not have the wheels or skids needed for landings. When she needed repairs, the *Sakura* floated into a deep-space dry dock. The only gravity she was designed to withstand was the gravitational force of an orbit.

The second landing bay had been stripped for the colony. Oliver found an empty chamber, vast and black. No lights shone in the void, not even over the emergency exit. With his genetically enhanced eyes, he could see that the floor was bare. No equipment. No bodies.

Other SEALs came to help. Some were injured. One man had broken his right arm, a nub of bone stuck out of his forearm. He carried a flashlight in his left hand. Seeing this, Oliver wanted to send him away; but with his dislocated shoulder, Oliver needed as much help as he could get.

"You, with the flashlight, over here," Oliver barked at the injured SEAL. The man came to join him. "Follow me."

Oliver led the pack to the third landing bay. There they

found the same kind of damage that the master chief had seen in the first bay. Oliver also saw something else. Hitting the communications button, he said, "Bridge," waited a moment, then said, "I'm entering the third bay."

"The pods?" asked Takahashi.

"I'm just entering."

"We're running out of time, Master Chief," said Takahashi.

"Yes, sir," said Oliver.

Nearly one hundred SEALs entered the bay behind him, some bleeding badly.

"The only easy day was yesterday," muttered the man with the broken right arm and the flashlight. It was a proverb often repeated by SEALs.

Oliver heard the words and nodded, then told the SEAL to check the computer stations.

The SEAL stumbled off to look at the toppled stations. A moment later he returned, and said, "The computer stations are broken."

"Did you hear that, sir?" asked Oliver.

"I heard," said Takahashi.

Despite the calm in Takahashi's voice, Oliver read his desperation.

"What happened down there?" asked Takahashi.

"They weren't expecting a rough ride, so they didn't secure the launch devices. I don't know how we could have secured them anyway. They're made to fit in transports."

Senior Chief Warren entered the bay and pushed his way through to Oliver. He asked, "What can I do?"

"Take some men and get me a launcher and twelve caskets," Oliver told him.

"What are you doing with caskets?" asked Takahashi.

"That's SEAL-speak, sir. *Caskets* are infiltration pods," Oliver explained. "I was speaking to one of my men."

"What is the condition of the pods?" asked Takahashi. "Why haven't they exploded?"

"It's just a hunch, sir, but I'd say the broadcast disrupted the charging process," said Oliver.

"That doesn't make sense," snapped Takahashi. "Those pods have been through thousands of broadcasts."

"Not when they were charged, sir," said Oliver. As he spoke, Oliver surveyed the wreckage. One moment everything looked hopeless, then he saw a transport and the solution occurred to him in a flash.

"I need seven minutes," Oliver said as he stared at the bulky old transport.

"Seven minutes? We may not last one minute," shouted Takahashi.

"I need seven minutes, sir," Oliver repeated.

"It only takes three minutes to charge up the pods, and I'm not sure we can last three minutes."

"It will take you seven minutes to charge your broadcast engine. Captain, I think you and your men are going to survive this mission," Oliver said.

"Survive? What are you talking about? How are we going to do that?" asked Takahashi.

As he walked through the shadows to have a closer look at the transport, the *Sakura* sputtered, bounced up, then dropped so quickly that Oliver felt his feet leave the floor.

"What do you mean we're almost out of fuel? Use the reserves. There have got to be reserves." Torn between two conversations, both urgent, Takahashi sounded distracted. He yelled, "Master Chief, we aren't going to be around in seven minutes."

FORTY-ONE

After that last shake, Oliver understood what had happened to the men and machines in the landing bays. On the bridge, the furniture was attached to the floor. The ceiling was low. When the ship bounced, sailors who did not brace themselves got bounced. On the big bounces, they hit their heads and shoulders on the ceiling, then landed hard on the floor.

In the docking bays, there was nothing to stop a man from bouncing twenty-five feet in the air. The ceiling was twenty-five feet up and there was nothing on the deck to secure the men to the floor.

The *Sakura* took another hard knock. Men and machinery flipped in the air. Already broken, the launchers crashed, shattered, and bent. Stealth infiltration pods dropped on bodies and slid. Oliver was thrown ten feet in the air and landed badly, trying to catch himself with his dislocated arm as he tumbled.

But the transport did not move.

The transport did not move. It was clamped into a launch sled.

The rear hatch of the transport hung open, a gaping maw in the dim light of the bay. Oliver looked back and saw two teams of SEALs wheeling in pods and equipment. He signaled for them to follow him, then trotted into the transport.

Fortune smiled upon him in the grimmest of ways. As he started up the ramp, he spotted a launch device and computer station in the darkness of the kettle. No glow rose from the computer screen, and no lights winked along the side of the launch device, but the transport had obviously been powered down, and Oliver thought that the odds were pretty good that both mechanisms still worked perfectly.

The *Sakura* hit what might have been a small pocket of

turbulence. The deck of the transport dropped out from beneath Oliver. It was a small bounce. He landed on his feet, rolling his right ankle. If he somehow survived another hour, the sprain would hurt; but he knew that he would not live long enough to feel it. For now, he could still walk. The joint did not seize; it simply felt stiff.

He looked at the pod-launching equipment. Both the computer and the launch device had not moved. Bolted into tracks that ran across the floor and ceiling of the transport, the launcher remained fixed.

Oliver crossed the kettle. He struggled as he climbed the ladder one-handed. When he reached the top, he flopped onto the catwalk. Ignoring the pain in his dislocated shoulder, he stood and entered the cockpit.

Like many of the SEALs, Corey Oliver had received flight training for transports. Hoping the bird had not been abandoned because of mechanical problems, Oliver climbed behind the stick and powered up the controls. The board lit up without a hitch.

He would fly the transport and launch the S.I.P.s himself. It was a one-man job. Only one man would die. The *Sakura* and her crew would live.

Looking at the tactical screen, Takahashi saw a city that showed no signs of life. Buildings both round and square, some metal, some mirrored, stood in straight-edged rows. He saw bridges and streets. Part of the city was covered with waterways that looked both narrow and deep; but he did not see boats, cars, flying vehicles, or pedestrians.

"Sir, maybe they've evacuated the city," said one of the weapons officers.

"Maybe they're in emergency shelters," said Suzuki.

Given the view in the tactical screen, either man might have been right; but to Takahashi, the city looked abandoned. There would have been cars along the roads if the population had hidden in shelters. There would have been debris. The city looked like it had been stripped bare by time.

Most of the buildings were a few hundred feet high, but some stood a couple of thousand, vanishing into the perfectly flat dome of shining energy.

"Captain, we can't navigate around these buildings. The *Sakura* doesn't handle like a fighter, she's too big," said Commander Suzuki. They'd already bumped hard as they tried to maneuver around one of the buildings.

Just beyond the city was the shoreline. Takahashi said, "Take us over open water, Commander."

As the captain of the *Sakura*, Takahashi Hironobu would not let her die until she had completed her mission. If they could just hold on for a few minutes more, she might not need to die at all. "What's our fuel status?"

"We're out," said Suzuki.

"We're still flying," said Takahashi.

"We should have gone down three minutes ago," said Suzuki.

"Just keep us up," said Takahashi.

He looked at the timer by the tactical display. Five more minutes. He did not know what was keeping the *Sakura* in the air. He did not know the source of the miracle, but he hoped it would last. A few more minutes, and the broadcast engine would be charged. Then they could launch the transport and broadcast to safety.

A three-dimensional holographic map showed in the air above the captain's table. The map showed the cityscape along with a representation of the *Sakura* flying above it.

Takahashi walked to the chart table for a closer look. He bent so close over the scrolling holographic city that he could see through the translucent landscape. *It's not a city, it's an artifact,* he thought to himself.

He remembered a conversation from before everything went wrong, a briefing Admiral Yamashiro had held with his four captains. Seen from thousands of light-years away, some of the stars in Bode's Galaxy appeared dormant. They'd been dead for hundreds of thousands of years. The aliens must have mined them all those millennia ago.

The occupants of this planet had probably killed off their nearest neighbors first. Who knew if they had even seen resistance, let alone retaliation. If they had, how long had it been since enemies had knocked on their door?

"Captain, I found our route." Suzuki's voice woke the captain from his musings. Suzuki sounded excited. He said, "I'm going to need to clear a path. May I engage weapons?"

Takahashi laughed. "We came here to destroy the planet." *Maybe there is no one left here to destroy,* Takahashi thought. *What if they died fifty thousand years ago, and all that remains are the machines they created?*

"Captain, there's something out there," said the weapons officer.

"Where?" asked Takahashi.

"I'm changing course! I'm changing course," yelled Suzuki.

The holographic map showed the outer fringe of the city followed by an endless plain of pristine, cerulean sea.

"There's nothing on the display," said Takahashi, his heart pounding, his breath short. He looked at the timer. They had three minutes and twenty seconds to go. Just another two hundred seconds!

FORTY-TWO

"The caskets are loaded," said Senior Chief Warren.

"Okay, get out of here. Every man off the transport, I need to launch this bird." Oliver checked the instrumentation. Everything was ready. "Get the atmospheric locks opened."

"I've never worked a control tower before," said Warren.

Oliver rolled his eyes, and asked, "How hard can it be? It's automated." If he'd been a swearing man, if the ability to use profanity had not been programmed out of him, the master chief would have unleashed a string of expletives.

"You should take somebody with you . . . just in case," said Warren. "How are you going to pilot a transport? You have a badly sprained ankle and a broken arm."

"It's not broken."

"It ain't whole," said Warren.

"Good thing I'm not flying far," said Oliver.

"You need a copilot, somebody to help launch the caskets."

"Senior Chief, you are wasting valuable time. Now get to the control tower and get the locks open!"

Though it was not proper protocol to salute another enlisted man, Senior Chief Warren saluted Oliver and left the cockpit. Oliver didn't see the salute. He'd already turned back to his controls and powered up the engines.

He looked at his watch. The S.I.P.s were overcharged. With a simple computer command, he could make them explode. It would take the *Sakura*'s broadcast generator another minute and a half to finish charging.

Ninety seconds, thought Oliver. *If I can hold out for ninety seconds, they can escape.*

Oliver's dislocated shoulder hurt, but he ignored the pain. The injury rendered his arm useless for climbing and lifting, but he only needed one arm to fly the transport.

Warren and his men solved the riddles of the control tower quickly. Even before Oliver managed to check the power to his booster rockets, the sled beneath his transport came to life, pulling the bird forward toward the first of the atmospheric locks. Up ahead, the heavy metal door slid open.

Thank you, Senior Chief Warren, Oliver thought. *You deserve to survive.* He smiled and nodded, then said it again, out loud, "You deserve to live."

"There's nothing on the tactical," said Takahashi.

"Fifteen miles and closing," said the weapons officer. "It's moving slowly. It's shadowing us."

"It looks like it's moving into our path," said Commander Suzuki. "It's advancing slowly, like it's stalking us."

There were dozens of sailors on the bridge, but everyone else had become silent.

"I need a visual," said Takahashi. His frustration quickened into desperation. There was something out there, possibly sent to destroy his ship; and he could not see the threat. He felt like he was drowning, like someone was holding his head underwater. "What is it? Where is it, Commander?"

Maybe the tachyon sleeve was distorting their readings. The sensors and computers inside the ship could only map the area around the ship. Suzuki and the weapons officer had located the threat using old-fashioned radar, but the data did not show on Takahashi's holographic display.

Takahashi chewed on the knuckle of his right thumb as he thought. He weighed his options. The broadcast engine needed another minute to charge. So much could happen in a minute. The aliens could fire weapons. The world could explode.

"Turn us around," he said. "Take us back over the city. We don't want to fight."

"Aye, aye, sir," said Suzuki.

Takahashi looked around the bridge. It was the only choice he could make. Perhaps the aliens would think twice before engaging a battleship over their city.

"It's coming after us," said the weapons officer.

Takahashi hit the communications panel. "Landing Bay Three," he said. "Oliver, are you launching?"

"This is Senior Chief Warren. The transport is passing the second lock, Captain. The outer door is opening. It's out!"

"Shields up!" yelled Takahashi. With the transport safely away, he could raise his shields. *We need to engage them,* Takahashi thought. *We need to buy Oliver time.*

When the threat appeared on his holographic map, he saw it was not a ship or a fleet, but a swarm. It looked like a cloud of fine lines. He tried to get a clearer picture, but his computer would not cooperate. All it showed him was a cloud of tiny lines. If the hologram was right, the alien defenders flew ships no bigger than a pencil.

"They're robotic," shouted one of the sailors. "I'm detecting a signal."

"Block it!" yelled Takahashi. "Disrupt the signal!"

He turned to his weapons officers, and shouted, "Lasers! Torpedoes, fire everything we've got!"

The enemy drones looked small and weak on the holographic display, but they moved quickly. Even before the lasers fired, the swarm scattered. "Clear a path. We need to break through!" shouted Takahashi.

The *Sakura*'s lasers obliterated drones by the hundreds, but that barely thinned the swarm. Torpedoes cleared pockets, not paths; and the pockets filled with new drones almost immediately. The *Sakura*'s weapons were designed for ship-sized enemies, not swarms of tiny ones.

The drones did not return fire. They formed a cloud in which the individual units moved independently, like a swarm of mosquitoes. Seeing that his ship was now surrounded by short-range weapons, Takahashi realized that the end was near. He had come all this way only to find out he was unprepared.

One of the drones neared the ship. From a mile off the *Sakura*'s bow, the drone fired a single bolt of light that seared through the shields and punctured the hull. There were no casualties and no explosions, but the wound was fatal. With a breach in the hull, the *Sakura* could not broadcast.

Takahashi heard the report and looked back at the map in time to see the swarm close around his ship.

Corey Oliver left his transport on autopilot. He stepped onto the ladder that led into the kettle, climbed down two rungs, then dropped the rest of the way. He would give the *Sakura* a minute to launch, then he would fire the five S.I.P.s he had loaded in the launch device. They were overcharged and ready.

The hatch stood open at the rear of the transport. Oliver went to the computer station and looked at the timer, then peered back at the sky through the open hatch. The *Sakura* should have broadcasted already, but he could see her hovering slowly over the city. Smoke rose from her bow, but the master chief decided to give her another moment. As he watched, the battleship fell from the sky. He sighed, inwardly apologized to the men he had hoped would escape, and fired the pods at the planet below.

FORTY-THREE

Earthdate: December 2, A.D. 2517
Location: Nebraska Kri
Galactic Position: Perseus Arm
Astronomic Location: Milky Way

Michael Khumalo, probably the greatest military philosopher of the modern era, said, "Give a fool a rope, and he will hang himself. Give that fool an Army, and he will hang his nation."

Truer words were never spoken.

With its population of somewhere between three and four million people, Nebraska Kri should have been an easy evacuation. A farming planet with several centralized population centers but no large cities, the planet was a logistical dream. All Admiral Liotta needed to do was escort the barges to the planet, park them above the major townships, and arrange a semiefficient shuttle service.

Too timid to risk a confrontation with the Unified Authority, Liotta only flew three of the twenty-five barges to Nebraska Kri at a time. He kept the barges in a tight cluster near the broadcast station. Instead of a short trip in and out of the atmosphere, the transports were forced to travel halfway across the planet, turning a twenty-minute hop into an hour-long journey.

Because he only had a few million refugees to rescue, Liotta would get all the people off the planet all right; but Nebraska Kri was a galactic breadbasket. This was a planet with three million people that produced food enough to feed a hundred million people for an entire year. Most of that food sat crated and ready to load; but thanks to Liotta's incompetence, all of that food would end up as ash when the Avatari scorched the planet.

By that time, botched civilian airlifts had become a joke around the officer corps. In private, some of the officers referred to them as *ejacuations* instead of "evacuations." Captain Dempsey, for instance, told me, "You just wait until Admiral Liotta gets started on Nebraska Kri. It's going to be a premature *ejacuation*."

When I pointed out that the *evacuation* of Bangalore, an operation Dempsey ran, had not gone so smoothly, he said, "Don't you blame me; I followed Admiral Liotta's orders to a T. It wasn't my fault that the *ejacuation* went so slowly that no one could tell that we came."

"You were the officer on the ground. You should have found some way to speed it up," I said. I pointed out that Admiral Jolly got everybody off Gobi.

"No, sir, General. That wasn't Jolly. It was Jim Holman got those folks off Gobi. If it had been up to Jolly, no one would have *gotten off* at all."

When I reported that conversation to Holman, he took it in stride, shrugging his shoulders, and saying, "I guess that's why Admiral Jolly kept me in a subordinate position."

Sitting in a one-on-one virtual debriefing with the soon-to-retire Admiral Liotta, I allowed my mind to wander as he bragged about botched evacuations and battles in which our casualties had been way too high. When he boasted, "We lifted nearly every person off Bangalore, and we will have rescued the entire population of Nebraska Kri. Not a bad record," I wondered whether he was trying to con me or himself.

"What about the U.A. attacks?" I asked.

"I am happy to report that we have held them off," Liotta said with a cocky smile that dared anyone to prove him wrong. I think he already knew I had lost patience with him, and he now exuded the petulance of an emancipated child.

"As I understand it, we have lost fifteen more ships since beginning this rescue operation," I said. "It sounds like the Unifieds have stepped up their attacks."

"Yes, there have been more attacks."

"Do we know what set them off?" I asked.

"I'll ask my pal Andropov next time he calls," Liotta said.

"So, to sum it up, we have lost fifteen ships, and we are not going to get enough supplies off Nebraska Kri to feed the people we are rescuing, but you are pleased with how things are going," I said.

I knew I was being unfair, but I didn't care. This was high comedy. I was talking to a naïve mountain climber who sprays himself with shark repellent and brags about never being bit.

"Fifteen ships," he said. "That's not a lot of ships. Our fleet is a thousand times larger than theirs. We can crush them anytime that we choose."

Coward that he was, Liotta refused to come anywhere near me. Since I had returned to the Perseus Arm to inspect the evacuation at Nebraska Kri, he remained in the Cygnus Arm, circling Providence Kri, fifty thousand light-years away.

"Anytime we choose, Admiral?" I asked. "I choose now. Let's put together an attack plan. I want to put those bastards out of business before we lose another boat."

"It's not that easy, General. Invasions need careful planning. How are you going to deal with the broadcast problem? Once we get our ships there, we won't be able to bring them back. The Unifieds aren't going to sit back while we hack into their station again."

"Admiral, right now we are losing two wars at once. The aliens have us on the run, and the Unifieds are picking off our ships," I said. "At least one of those situations must be fixed."

Deciding that he outranked me, Liotta went on the offensive. He said, "General Harris, Intel intercepted a distress signal from the Norma Arm. Know anything about it?"

"Not offhand," I said.

Liotta continued to push. "Someone destroyed a U.A. battleship near Solomon. Do you know anything about that?"

"Sure. I was there."

"You were given orders to stay away from Solomon, General."

Like you have the balls or the authority to give me orders, I thought as I said, "I am aware of that, sir."

"Were you anywhere near New Copenhagen?" asked Liotta.

"No, sir," I said.

"Three Unified Authority ships were destroyed near New Copenhagen."

"No shit?" I asked. "That's great."

"Did you have anything to do with it?" asked Liotta.

"I wish I had," I said. "Do we know who did it?"

"I am asking you," said Liotta.

"I wish I knew, I'd give him a cigar," I admitted. *I might even promote him to emperor,* I told myself.

Liotta shook his head. He said, "I'm going to give you the benefit of the doubt, Harris. You admitted going to Solomon, so I am going to assume you're telling the truth about New Copenhagen."

Don't do me any favors, I thought. What I said was, "I'm leaving for Terraneau in a few hours. We need a permanent home for our refugees. They can't stay on Providence Kri."

"And you think Terraneau is the place?" he asked.

"It's got oceans and lakes. There's a reasonable amount of oxygen in the atmosphere."

"I thought all the plants were destroyed," said Liotta. "That's what happened on Bangalore."

"Not in the deep water," I said. "Seaweed and algae are good oxygen producers." I would not have known that on my own, of course. I was channeling the wisdom of the late Arthur Sweetwater. The disembodied circuits of Sweetwater and Breeze suggested I take a closer look at Terraneau.

Liotta asked, "What about Olympus Kri? That planet had oceans and lakes."

"It's in the Orion Arm," I said. "It's too close to Earth." He should have known that.

I said, "Admiral Liotta, I think you might be in over your head commanding the Enlisted Man's Navy."

"What?" he snapped.

"I don't think you are fit to command the Enlisted Man's Navy."

"Who the hell do you think you are, Harris!"

"I think you should step down," I said.

Liotta smiled. He said, "I bet you do. Is that what you told Jolly, too, that 'he should step down'?"

"Admiral Jolly was killed by a looter," I said.

"I am not giving up my command," Liotta said. He paused, smiled, and added, "Don't look so smug, Harris. If I were you, I'd watch my back."

Before leaving the conference room, I contacted Ray Freeman. I started the conversation by asking, "Ray, have you ever wondered who made the decision to abandon Solomon?"

"You did," he said in that low, dark voice that made me think of storm clouds.

I said, "I didn't have any choice. We needed more ships. We needed a fleet and barges. Admiral Liotta made the decision to abandon the planet. I wanted to send barges and an armada, but Admiral Liotta overrode my suggestions."

"Why are you telling me this?" asked Freeman.

"I just tried to relieve him of command. He doesn't want to step down."

Freeman did not respond.

I said, "In case you're interested, he's touring Providence Kri at the moment. I guess he feels safe there."

Silence. Freeman broke the connection about ten seconds later. Five hours after that, I received news that Admiral Curtis Liotta had been shot while visiting the planet. The sniper vanished without a trace.

Apparently the late Admiral Curtis Liotta had called Admiral Wallace sometime before his demise. Wallace did not tell me what they discussed; but when I asked him about taking command, he had decided to retire from the Navy instead.

FORTY-FOUR

I never asked Freeman about Liotta's death. He'd become something of a shadow of his former self, spending most of his time alone. We were back on the *Bolivar*, Holman's ship. Freeman, who had never been much of a talker, spent most of his time on the observation deck, sitting alone.

Something about him had changed; I could see it in his eyes. Freeman's gaze had always had this menacing intensity. Looking into those eyes used to remind me of staring down the muzzle of a double-barreled shotgun. He didn't just look at the world around him; he seemed to X-ray it, peel it apart with his stare, and coerce it into revealing secrets.

As I thought about it, I'd seldom seen Ray Freeman verbally threatening victims. He didn't need to make threats; his eyes did it for him. Not anymore. Only a week had passed since we left Solomon; but in that time, much of the menace had evaporated from his gaze.

Now he looked tired, worn down by the universe and ready to call it quits. Freeman was a giant, a killer for hire, and an outcast; but what I saw when I stepped onto the observation deck was a man who needed a rest. Once, Freeman fell asleep where he sat. He looked like a man who might not ever wake up.

On this day, he had the deck to himself and did not turn to look at me as I entered. He sat staring out into space or possibly at his own reflection in the glass. I couldn't tell.

"Is Wallace any better than Liotta?" Freeman asked, still not looking in my direction.

"He's decided to resign his commission," I said.

"Smart choice. From what I heard, he was even more of an asshole than Liotta. You would have sent me to retire him by the end of the week," Freeman said.

Freeman did not use profanity very often. He seldom did anything that exposed his emotions.

"I'm going to ask Jim Holman to take over," I said.

Freeman did not exactly smile, but the muscles around his mouth relaxed slightly. He said, "Holman? Good man."

"Ray, what's bothering you?" I asked.

He did not answer.

I knew the answer. Since learning that his sister and nephew had died on New Copenhagen, Freeman thought about nothing but saving lives. He'd become obsessed with rescuing the masses, not caring what sins he might commit along the way. He'd developed a messiah complex and would have happily laid down his life saving the people on Solomon; instead, he'd had to turn his back on them, and he couldn't live with it.

"I have some recon I need to run," I said.

No response. Did he blame me for Solomon . . . for what would happen on Solomon? The attack had not happened yet and probably would not happen for another few hours.

No, he didn't blame me. If he'd thought it was my fault, he probably would have killed me along with Liotta. Freeman did not hesitate when it came to killing. At least the old Ray Freeman didn't.

This Freeman-shaped cadaver took in my words and said nothing. His silences used to scare me; now they had a moping quality about them.

"Look, the Unifieds are watching everything we do. They want their barges back and they're going to keep harassing our ships until we run out of Navy."

Freeman just sat there, staring at me, his face devoid of emotion. Did he agree or disagree? Did he care?

"We can't keep sending people to Providence Kri. I want to start relocating refugees to Terraneau, but I can't do that until I know it has a breathable atmosphere."

"You want me to take you to Terraneau?" he asked.

"No," I said.

"No?" he asked.

"No. I want to send Sweetwater and Breeze to Terraneau."

Anyone else might have pointed out that they only existed in a Unified Authority computer, a sharper wit might have offered to upload a map of the planet for them; but Freeman shrugged his shoulders, and asked, "How do you plan to get them there?"

"We'll work out the details later," I said. "Just get them on the two-way."

He nodded.

"Within the hour," I added. I was pushing him, testing him, seeing if he would put me in my place.

The old Freeman did not take orders from me or anybody. Tell him what to do, and he decided for himself if he wanted to do it. This new Freeman reminded me of a whale: huge, powerful, and docile. He spent a second considering what I said and agreed.

CHAPTER
FORTY-FIVE

I returned to the bridge to have a word with Holman.

The bridge of the *Bolivar* bristled with activity. Holman stood at the hub with Tom Mackay, who was captain of the ship. Holman and Mackay had the same face and build, but I could tell them apart. Mackay kept his hair its natural brown. Holman's dye job was starting to fade, but his hair and beard still had that copper-colored tint.

As I approached, Holman spun, saw me, and smiled. "General, I was just going to send someone to find you. Are we going to Terraneau?" he asked.

I tried to maintain a casual expression. I wanted to give off a relaxed vibe. "Captain Holman, how much do you know about ancient Rome?" I asked.

"I know about the Praetorian Guard," he said.

"Really? Are you a fan of the classical age?" I asked.

"Not until recently," he said. "Am I looking down the barrel of a promotion?"

"A big one," I said.

"Does Admiral Wallace know?"

"He won't stand in your way."

"Is he standing at all?" Holman asked.

Apparently news of the other "demotions" had gotten around. Maybe that was for the best. I didn't want officer candidates running scared, but I needed them to step out of the way once they proved unfit for command.

I gave an obtuse response. "What do you mean by 'standing'?"

"Did you kill Wallace?"

"I haven't killed anybody," I said.

"What about Admiral Jolly?"

"Shot by a looter," I said. "That was on Gobi. You saw the report."

"And Admiral Liotta?"

"I was as surprised as anybody."

Holman's voice dropped a note when he asked, "Is Wallace dead?"

"He's alive and planning his retirement."

"Isn't he next in line?" asked Holman.

"He was, but he didn't feel up to running the show. Frankly, I think that was an excellent decision."

"And now you're placing me in charge?" Holman asked. He wanted the promotion; I could see it in his smile.

"I think you're the man for the job," I said.

"What if it doesn't work out?"

"I'm sure it will work out. I have every confidence in you."

"Did you have every confidence in Admiral Jolly?"

"He was a formality. I was obligated to give him a shot because of his seniority."

"You killed him."

"Not me. It was the looter."

"The looter you did not capture. The one you left on Gobi to die?" asked Holman. "Was Liotta killed by a looter?"

"I don't know. I wasn't there," I said. "Do you accept your new post?"

"Are you going to kill me if I screw up?"

"You'll do fine," I said.

"What if I run into trouble?"

"I need a commander. Are you in or out?"

"I'm in," he said.

"Glad to hear it. You couldn't have taken this post at a better time. We're about to launch a sensitive operation."

I really was glad he'd accepted. The three previous candidates were little more than stuffed suits with unearned stars. Holman was different. He'd shown judgment, talent, and initiative.

"I hate to start off on the wrong foot, General, but moving refugees to Terraneau is a bad idea. General Hill will see it coming," he said. General George "Nickel" Hill was the head of the Joint Chiefs. "He knows our situation.

"He'll expect us to move refugees someplace with large bodies of water, that means Terraneau or Olympus Kri."

"Those are the planets with the best chance of sustaining life," I said.

"What about New Copenhagen? It has oceans?" asked Holman.

I remembered something the late Curtis Liotta had mentioned, something about an attack on three Unified Authority ships. If they were patrolling the area, entering it would be a bad idea. It sounded like something happened there, someone had rolled through with enough firepower to sink three U.A. ships. It must have been the Avatari using some new weapon. No one else had that kind of firepower.

"I've put some thought into this," I told Holman. "I think we can draw their navy away."

"How do you suggest we draw them away?"

"By invading Earth," I said. "It's time we went on the attack."

Both Sweetwater and Breeze took the call. They had the lab to themselves.

"You want us to send a team to Terraneau to survey the planet? That could present a problem," said Sweetwater. He looked tired. His face, which generally had a ruddy complexion, now had a grayish pallor. The bags under his eyes had darkened so that they looked like bruises. "We could probably get away with running remote tests from a satellite, but a certain Mr. Andropov is going to ask questions if we send an explorer."

The dwarf was right, but I did not see any other options. "What can you get from your satellites?"

"We won't be able to determine sustainability," Sweetwater admitted. "We'd need soil samples for that. We can certainly determine oxygen and radiation levels. You probably already have those."

"We need to know about drinking water and farms," I said.

"You will need filtration equipment for potable water," said Sweetwater. "The ash in the atmosphere is a pollutant. The lakes are contaminated, but they're not especially toxic."

"We have enough food to last six months. After that, the colonists will starve if they can't raise their own food," I said.

Sweetwater shook his head. "We'd suggest taking them to Earth, but we'll need to evacuate Earth soon."

"You can worry about that next month; right now, let's talk about Terraneau," I said.

"There is no way to test the water without landing a team," said Breeze.

"Even if we authorized the work, we'd never persuade the U.A. Academy to land a team out there," Sweetwater said, still referring to himself as "we." "Andropov doesn't trust us. The Linear Committee just sent a team of auditors to check our work."

"That's a problem," I said.

"You have a spy ship, maybe you could gather samples," Breeze suggested.

I shook my head. "The Unifieds would spot our transports."

Breeze, tall and skinny and alien in appearance with bug-eyed glasses, stared into the camera as I spoke, desperation showing in his magnified eyes.

"If they don't trust you, they may be listening in on us now," said Freeman.

"Not on our side, they aren't," Sweetwater said. "We devised a secure communications console."

How does that work? I wondered. William Sweetwater, the virtual person, could only build a virtual communications console using virtual parts provided to him by the Unified Authority. One way or another, this communication had to loop through real hardware. Outside his virtual satellite station, Sweetwater would have no control.

"We could send explorers to all of the planets," said Breeze.

"What?" asked Sweetwater.

"They might suspect something if we tested sustainability on Terraneau, but what if we sent teams to New Copenhagen, Olympus Kri, Gobi, Solomon, Nebraska Kri, and Bangalore."

Funny thing. When Breeze mentioned Solomon, a shock ran through me. I became dizzy and fell back in my chair.

"Solomon is a confirmed kill?" I asked, though I should have known.

Sweetwater stared into the camera, no emotion on his face, and said, "That is affirmative."

I did not ask about survivors, I knew the answer.

"We can say we are running tests on all seven planets,"

said Breeze. "We can tell them we need to start searching for a suitable place." He meant a suitable place for the population of Earth.

I played with the idea in my head, looking at it from every direction to see if I could poke holes in it. The idea held water. "They haven't started searching?" I asked.

"We think they have," said Sweetwater, "but they haven't informed us about their progress."

"How will they react if you suggest a survey?" I asked.

Sweetwater considered the idea for several seconds. The plan was not without its risks. If Tobias Andropov already suspected Sweetwater and Breeze of collusion, he might see the tests as absolute proof.

Sweetwater sat on his tall stool, staring into the camera. One moment his face flushed with anger. He might have been more worried about his own arguable existence than the millions of lives spread out across our last remaining worlds. Then he smiled, and said, "Brilliant. Even an idiot like Andropov will recognize the importance of creating an evacuation plan."

FORTY-SIX

Location: Sol System
Galactic Position: Orion Arm
Astronomic Location: Milky Way

We were running reconnaissance. For the mission, we took the spy ship.

I asked Don Cutter to captain the ship. He had time on his hands. Mars and his Corps of Engineers had not even begun working on the *Churchill*; and, now that Holman was running the Navy, he did not have time to play chauffeur.

If we'd broadcasted in behind Jupiter or Saturn, we might have come in undetected; but Jupiter was four hundred million miles from Earth and Saturn was eight hundred million miles away. Even flying balls-out, at thirty-nine million miles per hour, it would have taken twenty hours to cover that distance, and we did not have a day to spare.

We broadcasted in behind Mars, knowing that the Unifieds had figured out that trick. They might detect our entrance, but that did not necessarily translate into their tracking our route. The moment we entered the Sol System, Cutter engaged the stealth generator, and our spy ship became invisible . . . we hoped.

In the old moon-shot and satellite days, navigators planned trajectories that curved around the sun as they plotted routes from Earth to Mars. Back in that day, spaceships traveled only twenty-four thousand miles in an hour. At fifteen hundred times that speed, we took a more direct approach, pausing to add the occasional curve to make our route less predictable.

I stood on the bridge beside Captain Cutter, staring out the viewport. I'd known this man for only a month, but we had the familiarity of the battlefield. We'd faced death together. In military circles, that made us family.

"Do you think they've figured out a way of peeking through our cloak?" I asked.

"They probably don't even know we have a stealth cruiser," said Cutter.

I thought about the day Holman and I had attacked their Solomon patrol, and said, "I think they've figured that out."

Cutter looked at me, and said, "General, has anybody ever mentioned that you're a pessimistic man? You go through life a lot happier if you're an optimist."

"I'm not pessimistic," I said, though I knew he was right. I hadn't always been a pessimist. How had I changed? Was it fatigue? Was I worn-out from fighting wars on two fronts? Maybe it was the drugs? For the last few weeks, I'd been taking stimulants so I could work around the clock. The medics warned me that the drugs could have side effects—rollercoaster emotions, the sensation of feeling hyperalert, paranoia. Light hurt my eyes. Sounds made me jumpy. Looking around the little bridge of the spy ship, I felt closed in.

"Do they have ships out there?" I asked.

Sounding more calm than he reasonably should have, Cutter said, "Dozens of them. They're searching everywhere, but they can't see us. We came to look at their fleet, right? You wanted a peek at their forces; here they are."

I nodded.

"So let's look," he said as he led me to his tactical display. The holographic display showed a chunk of space that included Earth and its moon. A rainbow of different-colored threads, each as thin as a strand of a spider's web, traced the paths of ships as they circled the planet in search of the intruder. The scene fit Cutter's description precisely. The Unifieds were everywhere. We had kicked the hornets' nest.

Cutter pointed to the legend at the bottom. Red lines marked courses traveled by the new generation fighter carriers. There were only two of them. Gold threads marked the paths of three new generation battleships. The computer tracked five Perseus-class battleships and three Perseus-class carriers. Even throwing in cruisers, dreadnaughts, destroyers, and frigates, the Unifieds only had fifty-eight capital ships.

"Ah, look, here comes the cavalry," Cutter said. He did not sound worried.

The tactical display marked broadcast anomalies with Xs. Seven of them appeared. Three of them dissolved into the red lines that marked new generation fighter carriers. The other four resolved into the gold of new generation battleships.

The U.A. ships concentrated their search on an area close to Earth. Hidden by a stealth shield, we watched the U.A. ships from a half million miles away. They never came near us.

Clearly, Cutter enjoyed spying on the enemy with impunity. He laughed when ships searched in the wrong direction, tracing their flight paths with his finger and making lame jokes.

"Sixty-five ships? Do you think that's all they have?" I asked.

"They'd have a lot more if you hadn't stranded them at Olympus Kri," said Cutter.

We spent another half hour watching their movements. No new ships appeared on the scene though a few ships broadcasted out. "Do you have what you need?" Cutter asked. He almost never addressed me as "sir." From anyone else I might have taken that as a sign of disrespect but not from him.

"How close can we get to Earth without their spotting us?" I asked.

"They're already on alert," Cutter said, a crooked smile forming across his lips. In the time that we had been standing by the tactical display, the multicolored threads representing the various ships had knitted themselves into a fabric. "We'd be taking a risk."

"How big a risk?" I asked.

"Those ships are traveling at thousands of miles per hour," he said, pressing a button to expand the ledger. Now it showed single-line readouts on every ship. The battleships and destroyers traveled at a uniform fifty thousand miles per hour.

"The fighter carriers aren't moving," I said.

"They're preparing to launch attack wings," Cutter said.

"But they don't know where we are."

"That's the standard procedure when you're dealing with an invisible threat. In another minute, they will start firing particle charges."

I stared down at the display. With their fighters launched, the Unifieds expanded their net. They had started out between the Earth and its moon; now they had spread their search beyond it.

"Particle charges?" I repeated. I thought about the rickety hull of the ship, with its many patches. "Could we withstand a direct hit?"

"Easily. They don't use particle charges to destroy enemies; they use the charges to locate them."

Though I did not keep current with Navy weaponry, I knew what he meant. The charges exploded in bursts of energy-seeking ionized particles that attached themselves to energy fields like the electricity in our shields. In the vacuum of space, those particles would travel thousands of miles, while techs aboard the U.A. ships traced their movements.

"What if we lowered our shields?" I asked.

"How do you feel about radiation poisoning?"

I smiled, and said, "I'm not committing suicide until I can take the Unified Authority down with me."

CHAPTER
FORTY-SEVEN

Who do you trust in a time of war?

I once had a lieutenant named Thomer with a debilitating drug addiction. He used to sit through staff meetings in a near-catatonic state staring at walls, never speaking unless he was spoken to. Against my better judgment, I kept him in place during a big showdown with the Unified Authority Marines. He fought brilliantly and saved lives.

The first time I had met Ray Freeman, I wrote him off as a thug. Now I considered him my closest friend. I needed more friends.

Freeman and I sat in an empty transport. On a ship as small as the cruiser, the transports were the only place you could go to be alone. Freeman sat in the pilot's chair. "Have you reached Sweetwater and Breeze?" I asked as I sat down in the copilot's chair.

"I'm here," said Breeze. Freeman must have routed the signal to the transport's communications system. We had an audio signal, but the video was off.

"Is Dr. Sweetwater there as well?" I asked, as we only had an audio connection. I heard him through the communications console.

"It's just me this time. William is checking the results from the survivability survey," he said.

Freeman sat silent, staring straight ahead through the windshield. He looked big and strong and vanquished, like an evil giant in a fairy tale who has been tricked but not yet killed.

"General, do you remember William's mentioning the auditors that the Linear Committee has sent to oversee our work? He is leading them on quite a wild-goose chase. I think he has them counting the number of stars in the Galactic Eye."

I thought he was joking; there were billions of stars in the Eye. When I laughed, he asked, "Why are you laughing?"

"He's really making them count stars?" I asked. "Aren't there billions of stars in the Galactic Eye?"

"Seventy-eight billion in the section he has given them," Breeze said.

"They can't count seventy-eight billion stars. It would take a lifetime."

Freeman sat beside me, either not listening to us or not caring what we said. He stared out the window, his face impassive.

"No one is going to count that many stars," I said.

"He told them it was an accounting irregularity," Breeze said.

"An accounting error in the stars?" It didn't make sense.

"He found a glitch in their programming," Breeze said.

That caught Freeman's attention. He stared at the communications console, and I saw the old intensity in his eyes.

"What do you mean?" I asked.

"How long have we been dead?" Breeze asked.

I did not answer.

"Am I a brain scan? Is this a simulation of the Arthur Clarke Wheel?"

"What are you talking about?" I asked, desperate, scrambling to take control of the conversation.

"Sweetwater loaded a list of stars and locations into an accounting ledger and gave it to those men. They didn't even bother looking at the number of entries. They didn't care that there were billions of entries. Men get overwhelmed when you hand them a ledger with seventy-eight billion entries. Computer programs begin counting without checking the volume of the work."

"They're government number crunchers," I said. "They probably get paid by the line."

"Seventy-eight billion lines?" Breeze asked. "William built a randomizing engine into the database. Every time they complete one billion lines, the engine shuffles the data and reinserts it back into the file."

"They probably think they hit the jackpot."

Beside me, Freeman looked up from the console and shook his head in warning. Real or not, we needed the scientists' help. Their work could determine the future of mankind; and if Breeze shut down, Sweetwater would follow.

"Whoever programmed this simulation didn't understand the physics of the Arthur Clarke Wheel," Breeze said. "It uses centripetal force to create gravity instead of a generator."

"What are you talking about?" I asked.

"I visited the control room last night. It has a gravity generator."

"Maybe it's there for backup," I said. "Maybe it's there in case something goes wrong with the rotation."

"It's cosmetic," said Breeze. "I turned it off, and nothing happened." I heard an odd tone in his voice that might have been irritation or anger.

Freeman remained mute. He ran the show during assassinations and invasions, but this was a delicate matter. He left it up to me.

"Maybe the people who built the Wheel built the switch in as a joke," I said. "You said it yourself, the Wheel generates its own gravity."

"When did I die?" asked Breeze. "When," not "if."

I did not answer.

"How did I die?" he asked. He sounded so reasonable. I heard no panic in his voice. No hysteria.

"You died on New Copenhagen," I said.

Still absolutely silent, Freeman gave me the slightest nod. He approved. I had risked everything. Hearing that he was dead, the ghost of Arthur Breeze could shut down, and he could very well take Sweetwater with him; but Freeman wanted him to know the truth.

"I died in the mines, didn't I?"

"Yes," I said.

"And William? He died, too?"

"He died taking the bomb into the mines."

Breeze sighed. I imagined him taking off his glasses and smearing the dandruff and grease on the lenses as he tried to wipe them away. Maybe the Unifieds did too good a job programming his emotions. He must have felt hollow at that moment, the moment in which he learned that he was not human. I'd been through that.

"I remember the day I learned that I was synthetic," I said.

"I never liked that term, 'synthetic,'" Breeze said. "General, you have a heart beating in your chest. It's not made out of plastic. You have a brain and hands and lungs that hold air. None of those organs are synthetic. You're not *like* a human, you *are* a human.

"I suppose I am, too," Breeze said. He sounded dazed. He sounded like a young soldier coming off the battlefield for the first time, alive and questioning his own existence.

"Are you okay?" I asked.

He grunted as if he had just hurt himself.

"What are you doing?" I asked.

"I just pricked my finger," he said.

"What?"

"I pricked my finger with a dissection pin," he said. "The pain was exactly as I always remembered it." This was a tall, dried-up old man. He had spent his life in science labs. He did not handle pain well. His real, violent death must have been excruciating while it lasted.

"Why did you do that?" I asked.

"I wanted to see my blood. I bleed like a living creature. You've seen me, General. Do I look like a real man through human eyes?"

Homely as ever, I thought as I said, "Exactly like you looked the day you went into those caves."

"They did a better job simulating my blood than they did simulating the space station," Breeze said. "It's perfect."

I answered, "You are a perfect virtual model of the man I knew on New Copenhagen."

The heads of every major religion could only find one topic on which they all agreed—cloning. They said clones did not have souls and, therefore, were less than humans. They might have been right, too; but as I spoke to the ghost of Arthur Breeze, I realized the computer program that brought him back to life had perfectly captured his soul.

"But I am stuck in this machine," he said.

"Your universe is as vast as mine," I said. "You can visit simulations of every known world."

"How about a world in which I would really exist?" he asked.

I did not answer.

"When Andropov figures out we're helping you, he'll unplug us. I suppose that wouldn't be as bad as dying."

The real Arthur Breeze had been ripped apart by giant spiders.

I did not say anything.

"Thank you for being honest," he said. "You and Raymond, you were always truthful with us. You always were." His voice seemed to shrink as he spoke. "What did you do when you found out you were a clone?"

"I went to a bar with my sergeant. We drank three glasses of Sagittarian Crash and got so drunk we nearly died."

"Did it help?"

"The next morning, I felt like someone had stabbed a knife into my skull, that wasn't helpful. I was still a clone, getting drunk didn't change that. It softened the blow. It got me through that first night."

"Maybe I need to do that," he said. "We've got an excellent bar on the Wheel."

"Don't hit it too hard, we need you sober. They made you so you puke and piss and fall down when you get drunk. The original you didn't handle liquor so well, and the virtual you won't handle it any better," I said.

"I doubt they will allow me to die in an intoxicated stupor."

Still sounding battle-weary, Breeze said, "There's enough air to start a colony on Terraneau, but you're going to need an oxygen generator until you establish a significant plant population. Farming is going to be a problem. The surface soil is ruined. Your colonists are going to need to dig three feet down to find soil that can sustain life."

"But it can be done?" I asked.

"I am always amazed by the things human beings achieve when their backs are against a wall, General."

Was he talking about our colonists or the men who programmed him? Was he talking to them or me?

"We ran soil and atmosphere samples on an area near Norristown. Planetwide, the radiation levels are stable and acceptable. The air quality is low but tolerable. I recommend wearing rebreathers until you get oxygen generators in place. I've also checked for tachyon residue. There is no trace of Tachyon D on Terraneau." Breeze was all business as he said this. Then his tone lightened as he added, "Now, if you'll excuse me, General, I am going to go drink myself into a coma."

With that he signed off.

Ray Freeman smiled. He even laughed. It wasn't much of a laugh, just a quick "Huh" that sounded a little like the noise some Marines make when they are doing sit-ups.

"Maybe I shouldn't have told him," I mumbled to myself.

Freeman shook his head, and said, "I would have shot you if you'd lied."

FORTY-EIGHT

Location: Providence Kri
Galactic Position: Cygnus Arm
Astronomic Location: Milky Way

During their stints as commander in chief, Steven Jolly and Curtis Liotta had given orders, but they never really took charge. They were apprehensive leaders, too fainthearted to issue orders and face the consequences. Once Jim Holman ascended to admiral, he took charge.

Watching him conduct this meeting, I realized just how much I liked Holman's style. There was nothing imperial in his demeanor. He cared about his men, but he also made the tough decisions when he needed to. Seeing him speak, I realized that the empire was finally in capable hands now that its highest-ranking officers were out of the way.

Holman began his command by calling his captains together. He did not use a confabulator for the meeting. This was no remote conference with people popping in from all over the galaxy. Nor was it a lavish summit for fleet commanders only.

The captains of every destroyer, dreadnaught, battleship, and carrier sat in the audience. So did every regiment commander from the Marines. I sat beside the commanders of the thirteen fleets on the dais, watching them try to look comfortable though they had no idea why Holman had called the assembly.

Most of the commanders I had known during my career took charge slowly, giving their officers time to gossip and spread rumors. Given the opportunity, fear will work its way through fleets like a virus, infecting every sailor and Marine. Holman did not wait for that to happen. Now that he ran the show, he took charge.

Before the rumors spread, he called his men together. He did not mince words. Instead of starting with standard-issue apologies and promises, he began the meeting by saying, "Let me explain the situation. We have evacuated the populations of Gobi, Bangalore, and Nebraska Kri to Providence Kri. In all, there are now twenty million people on Providence Kri. We now need to move them off the planet.

"From what we can tell, the aliens will burn Providence Kri sometime within the next eight days. That gives us eight days to move twenty million refugees and gather as many supplies as we can."

There were fourteen of us sitting on the dais—thirteen fleet commanders and me. We sat in simple chairs with straight backs and hard seats. Holman stood at a podium about twenty feet in front of us, wearing the proud white dress uniform of the Unified Authority Navy. (It had only been a year since we had declared independence, and new uniforms were not a priority.) Mostly, from where I sat, he was a silhouette. The bright lights in the ceiling above the audience pointed back on him, their crystal white glare both blinding and bleaching. For us at the back of the dais, the gallery below the stage and the lights was a sea of black, as silent as it was dark.

"It's not just a question of evacuating Providence Kri. New Carillon, Uchtdorf, and St. Augustine will all be burned within the next seven days. The next week will be a nonstop rescue operation." Here Holman laid his cards out on the table, spelling out the size and scope of the operation so that every man in the room could understand. "By this time next week, we will have transported thirty-two million people to a new planet. Know this, gentlemen. Anyone we miss will die."

The officers respected Holman. They did not whisper among themselves as he spoke.

"Our only chance of survival is to establish a colony on a planet that the aliens have already attacked. I'm not going to lie to you. It's not going to be easy. Scientists have run tests on the air, water, and soil. The air is breathable but thin. We will take oxygen generators. The water is polluted, but not so badly polluted that it cannot be filtered. We will need to dig a few feet down to plant crops. These are obstacles we can overcome."

A soft rumble rose from the audience. Holman ignored it. He stood behind the podium, short and slender, with the glare of the lights making his red hair and beard look like they were on fire. He might have been a clone, but he was an instantly recognizable one.

He told the audience, "We are going to colonize Terraneau."

That shut everybody down. They all knew the planet. Terraneau had been the capital of the Scutum-Crux Arm, the outermost arm of the Milky Way. We had all been raised to judge places by their position relative to Earth. Terraneau was just about as far as you could get from Earth without leaving the galaxy.

"As many of you know, the Unified Authority patrols that area. Our barges will be vulnerable." Holman stood silent for several seconds. When he began speaking again, he changed his train of thought.

"The Navy has asked a lot of you over the last month, and you have delivered. Now I'm going to ask even more of you than ever. Some of you will be asked to make the ultimate sacrifice. In order for this plan to work, we will need to draw the U.A. Fleet away from Providence Kri and Terraneau. That means opening a front that will draw the Unified Authority's forces away. We are going to invade Earth."

Down in the darkness, a single voice shouted, "Hell, yeah!" The entire room went silent for a moment, then burst into laughter and applause. Holman made no attempt to stop the applause. He let it run its course.

"We've run a recon mission to evaluate the Unified Authority's military strength. We sent a spy ship into Earth space and found fewer than sixty capital ships patrolling the lanes. They detected our anomaly, and seven more ships broadcasted in. As far as we can tell, that is their entire fleet, sixty-five capital ships.

"It is entirely possible they have a few additional ships in reserve. They may have as many as eighty ships, but we have seen most of what they have."

A possibility of eighty ships . . . Fifteen hundred men sat in the audience, each representing a capital ship in the Enlisted Man's Navy. We had seventy-seven fighter carriers and

229 battleships. Maybe they sank our ships when they caught our stragglers, but they would never survive an all-out assault. Their ships would not last long outnumbered seventy-seven to one. Our numbers would be overwhelming . . . at least they would be overwhelming in space.

"We're going to send a ground force as well as a naval attack," Holman said. "Crippling their navy will not be enough for us to achieve our objectives. We need to uproot the Unified Authority government and all. We need to occupy Earth."

Everyone in the room knew what that meant—we would send our Marines to fight their soldiers and Marines. At last count, we had three million fighting men. We'd have the numbers and the superior firepower. They'd have shielded armor that would neutralize our firepower and render our numerical advantage meaningless.

Forty-five minutes, I reminded myself. The batteries that powered their shields would only last forty-five minutes. If we survived the first hour . . . If . . .

"Win or lose, there will be no returning from Earth. The Unified Authority has a temporary broadcast station near Mars. We believe they will destroy the station at the first sign of an invasion. Before I assign men to the invasion, I am going to ask for volunteers."

The enthusiasm vanished. No one spoke as the electricity drained from the air.

"We're going to reserve one-third of our fleet to escort our barges, the rest of you will be assigned to the invasion. Any captain who wishes to enlist his ship in the invasion, please stand."

The blinding lights rolled from Holman and down to the audience. My eyes were tired from the glare, and the drug-induced drumming in my head made it difficult to concentrate; but when the lights shone on the gallery, it looked like every man was on his feet.

FORTY-NINE

The meeting ended much the way it had begun. Holman got the ball rolling by summing up a bad situation. He finished by thanking his officers for their courage, then reminded them that our struggles would extend long beyond the combat.

"Once we establish our colony on Terraneau, every day will bring new battles. We will need to fight to plant crops, then keep those crops alive. Finding water will be a struggle. So will establishing a new nation.

"Those of us invading Earth will be tasked with governing a hostile planet. You will guard the planet until the aliens attack, then, if you survive, you will face the same day-to-day challenges that we will face on Terraneau.

"We are going to divide our forces, and neither side will ever know if the other side survived. Earth will be removed from our broadcast grid. The only way we will know if the invasion of Earth succeeded is if it fails, and the Unified Authority attacks us."

As he closed the meeting, Holman said, "I came here hoping for a few volunteers. Nearly all of you have volunteered. Because of your bravery, I must decide which of you will escort our barges to Terraneau. Those of you I assign to Terraneau will have the easier job."

He should have known these men would volunteer for the harder duty once he leveled with them. I'd wager that none of them had ever seen an admiral willingly level with his men. With one quick speech, Holman had raised himself from admiral to messiah.

Besides, their neural programming included the drive to volunteer. They would pick the harder job, and they would fight; but that didn't mean they would like it. I knew, because I didn't like it. Holman had originally asked me to ride the barges, and I refused. I was going to face the Earth Fleet. If I survived, I would face the aliens. If I survived again, I would colonize a scorched planet. I volunteered for the hard fight. I hated myself for doing it.

Earth was due for a baking, and Holman would not send the barges back to Earth once he'd landed everyone on Terraneau. He couldn't; without a working broadcast station, the Sol System would become a dead end. No one and nothing he sent to Earth would ever return, including his Fleet and his Marines.

With eight hours to go before I left for Earth, I flew to Hightower—a city left desolate after the first Avatari invasion, now densely populated with refugees from other planets and the clone servicemen who rescued them. Ava was there, somewhere.

In the past, I could always find her. She was a celebrity, a movie star, and always the prettiest woman in town. Men learned where she lived for the same reason that true believers memorize the locations of religious shrines. Before the Avatari had reduced the planet to ashes, Ava-fascination had spread like a virus on Terraneau. Ask any woman in Norristown if she'd ever seen Ava, and she would tell you where Ava lived, her place of employment, and the latest gossip.

I flew down to Providence Kri, believing I would find a similar situation in Hightower. As I left the spaceport, I asked a civilian security guard if he knew where I could find Ava Gardner. An older man with salt-and-pepper hair and sixty pounds of extra gut, the guard grinned at me, said, "In my dreams," and walked away.

The spaceport was all but abandoned. Military transports flew in and out of the city, but Holman had not yet begun the evacuation. I walked long, empty halls, brightly lit and large enough to accommodate thousands of people at a time. In another few hours, refugees would fill the halls beyond capacity. I'd seen too many evacuations over the last few years. Given a choice between a battlefield or a mass evacuation, I would take the battlefield every time.

When I reached the terminal lobby, I saw that work had already begun to stage the evacuation. Marines in Charlie service uniforms, complete with MP armbands, were lining up guardrails and assembling checkpoints and help stations.

They saw my uniform and snapped to attention. A major, a clone well into his fifties, stepped out to meet me.

"General, sir, no one notified us that you were coming," he said as he saluted.

I returned the salute, and said, "Yes, I'm a bit surprised myself."

"Are you here to oversee our preparation?"

"No, Major, I'm here looking for Ava Gardner."

He must have mistaken the comment for sarcasm. He turned pale and stiffened. Sputtering, he said, "Um, I . . . sir."

"At ease, Major," I said. I began to feel annoyed. I hated unearned shows of respect. Having stars on my collar did not make me a better man. Steven Jolly and Curtis Liotta both had stars, and they died buffoons.

"Yes, sir," he said, though he remained rigid.

Behind him, the other Marines still stood at attention, watching us carefully and not sure what to do.

"This is not an inspection, so just relax," I said. "Get your men back to work." Knowing the scene that lay ahead, I gave in to a sympathetic impulse, and said, "And, Major, I am here looking for an old friend."

"Yes, sir," he said, but still he stood there, a sputtering old waxwork, an old man whose career should probably have ended many years ago.

"Is there something else?" I asked.

"Yes, sir," he said. "Did you want a car, sir? I can arrange for a car."

"Good thought," I said. "A car would be helpful." The major's version of a car would come complete with a driver, hopefully someone who knew his way around town.

"Sir, if you can give me your friend's name, I'll run it through the computer," he added nervously.

"Ava Gardner," I said. "Her name is Ava Gardner."

"Like the actress?" he asked.

I smiled, and said, "Like the actress."

He doesn't know she's here, I thought. Back in Norristown, every man, woman, and child in town knew about Ava. Granted, Hightower had a transient population, the city had sat empty until we populated it with refugees; but this clone didn't even know Ava was on the planet.

"Yes, sir. Give me a moment, sir, I'll get you an address and arrange for a vehicle." He saluted, I saluted, and he trotted off, leaving me in a lobby filled with Marines still standing at attention.

"As you were," I growled at the men. They went back to work.

The military is filled with ass-wipe officers who try to link themselves to higher brass at every opportunity. If this major was of that persuasion, he would return with some lame excuse why he should escort me. I started to suspect that the doddering old boy would do just that, and I felt my temper rising. When he returned, he saluted, told me the car was waiting outside the terminal, and returned to work with his troops.

"What's your name?" I called back to him.

"Perry, sir. Major Andrew Perry. Is there a problem?"

"No, Perry. No problem," I said.

"What year did you attend the Academy?" I knew he had not attended Annapolis, but that was not the point. He was a clone, and not a Liberator. I did not want to kill the old boy, and asking him about orphanages might cause him to figure out he was synthetic. It could trigger a death reflex.

"I didn't attend the Academy, sir. I grew up in an orphanage and got field-promoted when we started the empire."

"In an orphanage?" I repeated. "I grew up in UAO 553," I said. UAO stood for Unified Authority Orphanage. There had been hundreds of orphanages, clone farms churning out young conscripts whose highest aspiration was to become a sergeant.

"Three-O-Nine, sir," he said; but his focus was not on me; he kept stealing glances at his men. He did not want to gab, he wanted to work.

I saluted, grunted "Carry on," and walked to the street. *Perry,* I thought. With a last name, a rank, and an orphanage number, I should be able to track him down. I planned to take most of the E.M.N.'s Marines with me to Earth in a few hours, but I would leave Perry behind. Holman would need the old boy more than I would—a man who cared about mission more than career. Traveling with Holman, the major might even survive.

As for me, I did not expect to survive the day. That our ships would destroy the Earth Fleet, I had no doubt. We'd take casualties, but we'd control the solar system. We would come with more fighter carriers than the Unified Authority had ships. They'd hurt us; but based on size alone, our fleet would smother theirs.

Once we landed on Earth, though . . . We would outnumber them on Earth just like we did in space; but on Earth the numbers would not matter. "Specking shielded armor," I muttered quietly enough that I hoped no one would notice.

"General," the driver said as he snapped to attention. He was a Marine sergeant who looked to be about my age, a man reaching thirty. He opened the door of the sedan, and I climbed in.

"Do you know where we're going?" I asked as he sat behind the wheel.

"Yes, sir," he said, and off we went. *Perry,* I reminded myself. *Orphanage 309.*

I'd found the abandoned neighborhoods on Bangalore and Gobi depressing. As we drove through Hightower, I saw something worse. We drove past parks and playgrounds filled with people. We passed kids playing football in a street.

The evacuation would begin in two hours; but for now, these people were happy, naïve, and enjoying life. *They were already refugees,* I reminded myself. They had only been in Hightower for a couple of weeks at most. Here they lived in an overcrowded city with parks and buildings. In another few hours, they would be herded like sheep and taken to a planet with charred soil and ash in the air. Some would fall into deep depressions that would last for the rest of their lives. Some of these people would commit suicide, and others would starve. The survivors would fantasize about dying under blue skies and being buried in green fields. Would any of them ever really live again?

I imagined a park on Solomon with families playing and young couples kissing and old couples holding hands. In my mind's eye, I saw the sky turn the orange-red color of live coals. I imagined the trees and grass bursting into flames; but I could not bring myself to see what happened to the people. Try as I might, I could no longer see them.

Strange as it sounds, I saw the people of Solomon as the lucky ones. I could not see how life in a colony on a cinder in deep space would be worth living. Freeman was wrong. We weren't saviors rushing from one planet to the next to prevent disasters; we were the recruiters for Hell, packing up the dead and crating them off to an inferno.

My driver stopped beside a large apartment building with an arched awning over its doorway and abandoned storefronts. He opened my door, stood at attention, and waited for me.

I climbed out of the car.

Still standing at attention, he said, "She's in apartment 8201, sir. I can run up and get her for you if you prefer."

"No," I said, distracted by my thoughts. "No, that won't be necessary." I stared up the side of the building thinking, *Eighty-two-O-one, the eighty-second floor.* How many people lived in a building of this size? How many people could it house? In another few hours they would have no shelter and a limited supply of food. The air would be thin, the water bitter with the taste of ash.

We did the people of Solomon a favor when we left them behind, I thought. *They knew less than a second of discomfort as death knocked on their door.*

These people had a fight ahead of them. They would scratch hard earth to plant seeds that might or might not grow. What stories would their descendants tell?

"Wait for me in the car. This shouldn't take long," I said.

Maybe God is just like us, running from planet to planet, trying to save people from the disaster He knows is going to happen. Freeman's words echoed in my head. I shook my head, and whispered, "Bullshit."

The doors to the building were not locked, and the security booth in the lobby sat empty. This may once have been a luxury high-rise, but the building now housed the poor and rich alike. I noted the handprints on the walls and the mud stains on the carpet.

The elevator panel had buttons for 120 floors. Ava did not live in a penthouse apartment. I wondered if such things still mattered to her.

I pressed the button marked 82, the elevator doors slid

shut, and I listened to the whir of air as the car turboed up eighty-two floors. The doors slid open a moment later.

The hall was dark. An unlit chandelier hung from the ceiling, unlit lamps leaned out of the walls like round shadows. I heard muffled conversations as I passed doors. In former times, the building must have been a showpiece. The doors were nearly soundproof. I heard voices as I passed some of the apartments. They sounded like the ghosts of earlier occupants.

Where do you go when you die? I asked myself. *Every major religion agrees,* I reminded myself. *Clones turn to dust.* I wasn't afraid, just resigned.

They said that clones could not have souls . . . "they" being the top dogs of just about every major religion. They said you could clone genes, but there was no DNA in the soul. So far as they were concerned, I would simply cease to exist when I died. Maybe that was for the best. I never much cared for the whole God thing anyway.

Eighty-two-O-one was a corner apartment with a shiny brass address plate. I knocked on the door, not sure why I had come or what I would say. I did not think that I loved Ava anymore. She had moved on, and so had I. I had no good reason for coming to say good-bye; but still. I knocked a second time. When she did not answer, I knocked a third time. I waited another minute, then gave it one last try.

The door opened an inch. There was a pause in which I heard her sigh, then Ava opened the door to me. She stood in a sheer white robe that might have been made of silk or satin. The sleeves ended at her elbows, and the hem was down to her knees. "Wayson?" she asked, then she reached out like a child just learning to walk and wrapped her arms around me.

She held me. She did not kiss me, but she hugged me and pressed her face into the hollow between my chest and shoulder.

It was the middle of the afternoon. When I saw her in the robe, I thought maybe I had walked in on her and a lover; but that was not the case. It was late in the day and she was alone, the shades on her windows drawn against the sunlight. Her apartment smelled of dirty clothes and inactivity.

My eyes had adjusted to the darkness in the halls, so I saw the room around me clearly. There was furniture in the room, probably left behind by the original occupants. She had a couch and matching chairs, lamps, tables, bookshelves, and a thick oval carpet.

"Can I turn on the lights?" I asked.

"We don't have electricity," she said. "They hooked a generator to the lift. It's the only thing that works on this floor."

"Can I open the blinds?"

"I wish you wouldn't," she muttered.

I did it anyway.

She had aged a decade in the days since I had last seen her. She had changed in ways that time alone cannot accomplish. You sometimes see a fleshy softness in the faces of the depressed. It had happened to Ava, almost as if the muscles in her cheeks had atrophied. The Hollywood goddess who viewed the world with an ironic smile seemed more like a forgotten dream than a recent memory. She still had the same olivine green eyes, but the lids had grown thicker, giving her the look of exhaustion.

And she had lost weight. Her face had been a perfect oval broken only by the cleft in her chin. Now her face was long, and her cheeks looked sunken. I did not need to ask what happened, I knew. I had gone through it as a young Marine. Maybe I was still going through it.

"Do you ever get out?" I asked.

"Get out for what?" she asked.

"For food?"

"I have my rations."

"To talk to people?"

"What would we talk about?"

"To breathe fresh air?"

"If I want fresh air, I can open a window."

I looked at the windows, and said, "They're fixed in place. They don't open."

"Oh," she said.

"They must have power going to the air-conditioning," I said. "You'd suffocate if they didn't."

She turned and walked toward her bedroom. I followed.

Ava sat on the bed and her robe fell open all the way up her thigh, not that she noticed. Her hair hung lank and tangled. The air in her bedroom was even more musty than the air in her living room.

"Are you hungry? I can fix you some food. I still have most of this week's rations."

"I've eaten," I said.

"Well, that's all right then."

She no longer looked like a movie star. Walking down the street like this, she would no longer turn heads; even so, she was an attractive woman. She sat on the bed, staring ahead, not looking at me but not ignoring me, either. I stood beside her.

"Do you want to talk about it?" I asked.

"About what?"

Neither of us said anything for several seconds.

Finally, she looked at me, and said, "I had two hundred girls in one of my classes." The way she said it was so plain and matter-of-fact. She did not cry, nor did tears form in her eyes. She'd probably cried herself dry days ago.

I realized that I liked her more than ever now that her Hollywood sheen had vanished. The tough, the polished, the beautiful Ava that filled movie screens no longer existed. Given the chance, I thought I might just fall in love with the empty shell that she had left behind. This was a woman scarred by death, a woman who knew my world.

"We're going to evacuate Providence Kri," I said. That was classified information, but this new Ava did not strike me as a security risk.

"Where are we going?"

I did not want to tell her about Terraneau, not while she was still in the grieving process. "They're going to try to resurrect one of the planets that have already been burned."

"Terraneau?" she asked.

"No," I said, but she saw through me.

"Liar," she said. "I can't go back."

"You can't stay here," I said.

"It's as good a place as any," she said.

"The aliens will be here by the end of the week. If you stay here, you'll die."

She thought about that, and asked, "Are you going to Terraneau?"

"No," I said.

I thought I saw the ghost of her old sardonic smile. "Then

you came here to say good-bye. You always come to say good-bye. Have you noticed that, Harris? You and I, we say good-bye to each other more than anything else."

I did not know what it was about this woman that stirred my heart. I wanted to hold her and to kiss her, and I felt an urge to do more. She was empty and I was lonely and we could never again satisfy each other; but for the first time since I had met Ava Gardner, I knew that I loved her.

"I love you," I said.

She ignored me. She asked, "If you are not going to Terraneau, where are you going?"

"Earth," I said. Using the now-familiar line, I added, "It's a one-way ticket."

"I don't suppose it's a social call."

"No. Not a social call," I said.

Ava listened and nodded, but she did not speak.

Time passed.

"I love you," I said.

"You don't know love," she said. "You know war. You know death. You don't know love."

Maybe she's right, I thought. Whatever I felt for Ava at that moment, it matched up with the way I expected love to feel.

If I left her alone, she would stay in the apartment and die when the Avatari attacked the planet. I could have begged her to leave, and maybe she would have considered it. I could have sent Major Perry to collect her. He could take her by force. He could drag her to a transport and cart her off to Terraneau, but he couldn't put the life back into her.

I bent down, stroked her hair, kissed her on the forehead, and whispered, "This is our final good-bye."

Her eyes met mine, and she said two words. "Thank you."

I wanted to say good-bye to Scott Mars before I left for Earth. Hearing he was aboard the *Mandela*, one of the handful of fighter carriers headed to Terraneau, I flew out to visit the ship.

"The Corps of Engineers is down in the fighter bay," the officer in charge told me when I entered the landing bay.

"What the hell are they doing down there?" I grumbled.

"They're engineers. They're probably fixing up the fighters, sir," said the officer.

"They aren't mechanics, they're engineers," I said. "Engineers don't fix fighters, they design them."

"Good point, sir," the officer said, a diplomatic way of telling me to speck off.

Still wondering why the head of the Corps of Engineers was inspecting fighters, I hiked down to the hangar. The place was enormous—a double-tall deck teeming with techs and mechanics. Like most warships, the *Mandela* had a hot-bunk rotation with three shifts, but that rotation collapsed as the empire prepared for evacuation and war. All three shifts had reported for work, and Mars and his engineers had come to join them. Dressed in red jumpsuits, the mechanics and technicians looked like ants crowded around the fighters.

I found Mars stooped under the wing of a fighter inspecting who knew what. I stood waiting for him to notice me, but he didn't. After more than a minute, I finally asked, "Did Holman bust you down to fighter maintenance?"

Mars spun to face me, still holding a laser probe in his left hand as he saluted me with his right. "I wish to God he had," said the perennially positive, born-again clone. "I'll take Tomcats and Phantoms over Stone Age farming."

"You're not excited about Terraneau?"

"Building tent cities and digging latrines . . . It may be my calling; but no, I'm not excited about it."

"It won't be totally primitive; you'll still have tractors and cranes," I said.

"We're riding Space Age technology into an Iron Age existence," he said.

"You can build churches, too," I said, trying to appeal to his religious side.

That brought a smile. He said, "Wanna see the surprise we planned in case we run into resistance?" Mars fixed me with a distinctly un-Christian grin and nodded toward the undercarriage of the Tomcat.

I squatted and edged my way under the wing, but I did not see anything other than the standard laser array and rockets. "What am I looking at?" I asked.

"We added a hard point for torpedoes," Mars said. "Their torpedoes, the shield-busters. They know we have 'em, but they won't think our fighters are packing them."

I liked the idea. Somewhere down inside me, my confidence grew. A weapon like that could turn the tide of the war.

Mars ran his fingers along the wires at the back of a torpedo tube, then he shined a light into the seam at the top to inspect the joint. He reached for the lid to the electrical panel, paused, then opened it.

"Not sure it will work?" I asked.

"It's going to work perfectly."

"Then why are you opening it?"

He said, "Because I am here and it's there and that's what engineers do," a hint of self-mockery in his voice.

I patted the fuselage of the fighter the way a man might pat his horse, and asked, "How many of these are we taking?"

An engineer lit a laser torch under the wing of a nearby Tomcat. Mars shaded his eyes from the glare. He squinted toward me, and said, "None."

"What?"

"They're all going to Terraneau."

"What the hell are you going to use them for on Terraneau?" I asked. "You're setting up a colony. We're the ones going into battle."

"It wasn't my idea—Holman's orders."

"Holman?" Hearing who gave the orders, I felt like I'd been kicked in the gut.

The blue-white light of the laser welder flashed and flickered along the hull of the fighter. It lit one side of Mars's face. The acrid tang of melting metal filled the air.

"He says we need them for insurance in case the Unifieds get around you," said Mars. "Harris, don't worry. You're going to outnumber the Earth Fleet a hundred to one."

I once saw a man pour a bag with fifty goldfish into a tank with five piranhas. There were ten goldfish for each of the predators, but they lasted less than a minute. Each time a piranha snapped at a goldfish, it left behind nothing more than orange-gold scales and the tips of the fins.

Was the empty knot in my chest formed by frustration or disappointment? "Those fighters could save a lot of lives during an invasion," I said. I was also thinking, *If they hit us fast enough, we won't even get the chance to land our troops.*

When Navy ships go to battle, the Marines inside of them sit helplessly as they wait for their turn to fight.

"General, what you really need to do is appeal to a higher power," Mars said.

"I know, Holman's orders."

"No, there's a higher authority than Jim Holman . . . God helps those who ask for help. You need to pray."

A rush of anger ran through my brain. *You pray, and I'll take the Tomcats with the shield-busters,* I thought. Mars and I had been through a lot together. I considered him a friend, and I did not have many friends, so I kept that to myself.

"I've never had much luck with prayer," I said. I didn't mind Freeman's sermons because he had more questions than doctrine. For Freeman, God was a concept that had recently started to make sense. Scott Mars, on the other hand, bought into Christianity with all of its hooks, lines, and sinkers.

He accepted all its voodoo. He believed that a virgin gave birth to a man who walked on water when he wasn't changing it into wine. Mars believed in blind men seeing and burning bushes. Make up a story about a dead man rising from his grave, and Lieutenant Mars would praise God and declare it a miracle.

Freeman tried to extract the truth from the mythology. Mars swallowed it all in one great gulp of faith.

He followed me out from under the wing of the Tomcat, and asked, "Have you ever actually prayed?"

Not sure how I would react if he offered to pray with me, I admitted that I had never actually dropped to my knees.

He smiled, and said, "Whoever came up with that thing about there not being any atheists in the trenches never met you, Harris. I'll pray for you."

"While you're asking God to spare my synthetic soul, would you mind asking Him to do something about U.A.'s specking shielded armor? That's the miracle I'd pray for . . . if I ever prayed."

Mars smiled, and said, "God works in ineffable ways."

I said, "So do broadcast stations. If, by some miracle, we find a working broadcast station when we get to Earth, maybe I'll see you again."

Lieutenant Mars saluted, and said, "Wouldn't that be a miracle."

FIFTY-ONE

Location: Sol System
Galactic Position: Orion Arm
Astronomic Location: Milky Way

We loaded men and guns onto the transports as pilots boarded their fighters. In another minute, our ships would enter the broadcast system, and the invasion would begin. We'd emptied every corner of the Enlisted Man's Empire. Every working ship would either escort barges or join the invasion.

One thousand two hundred thirty-six ships now prepared to enter Earth space. We had sixty-eight fighter carriers and two hundred battleships. We had Tomcats, Phantoms, and Harriers by the hundreds. Our landing force included one thousand helicopter gunships and nearly ten thousand transports, which we would use to deploy our three million Marines.

We had an overwhelming force. Why did I not feel confident?

When Freeman came to see me, he wore his armor and carried his go-pack. He had a sniper rifle, an M27, laser and particle-beam weapons, and grenades. Strong, smart, and a masterful assassin, he could pulverize men with his fists or snipe at them from two miles away. He knew how to set charges and hack into computer systems. Having Freeman on our side was reason enough to feel positive. Ray Freeman could tip battles and win wars.

"I ran into Scott Mars. He says he's going to pray for us," I said.

Freeman certainly heard me, but he did not respond. He stepped into my billet, a seven-foot giant as wide around the chest as a wheelbarrow, with ebony skin and scars on his scalp. The improbably wide sleeves of his armor hid the muscles in his arms.

"I told him to keep his prayers and give us fighters with U.A. torpedoes."

Freeman asked, "You go to tell him good-bye?"

"Something like that," I said.

Freeman placed his little two-way communicator on my desk. "We need to warn Sweetwater and Breeze about the invasion."

"Warn them? Ray, they aren't people. They're software. It's like kissing your bunk good-bye. You might have had some good times together, but that doesn't make it human."

That sounds a lot like the crap that natural-borns say about clones, I thought to myself. I said, "Let's give them a call."

Freeman placed the communicator on the desk for me to handle the security codes. I felt the weight of his eyes on my neck and the weight of my words on my conscience.

Living, breathing men would die today. I might die. I had somehow convinced myself that I did not have time to worry about virtual people. I was an asshole. William Sweetwater and Arthur Breeze deserved better. If the Unifieds suspected that the scientists had helped us, they would pull the plug on them. Alive or not, they would cease to exist for having helped us . . . having helped me.

I muttered, "Next you're going to want me to tuck them in bed," but it was just for show. Like Freeman, I'd come to think of the scientists as human.

"Hello, Harris. Has your invasion begun?"

The screen did not show an odd pairing of scientists in a lab, it showed a man sitting at an oak desk in a richly furnished office. Instead of Sweetwater's gravelly voice or Breeze's low whisper, this man had deep resonance and polish. He had the voice of a politician.

Tobias Andropov, the youngest member of the Linear Committee, sat alone at his desk. He looked into the camera, smirked, and let his head bob in a way that made him seem all the more arrogant.

I felt my gut bounce, and my lips involuntarily formed the word, "speck." Other than that, I sat in silence.

The camera was aimed at my head and shoulders. Trying

to move as little as possible, I reached for my communications console with my right hand. Keeping my eyes on Freeman's little two-way, on Andropov, I fumbled with the console. If I hit the right buttons, Holman and his aides could listen in.

Trying to act more sure of myself than I felt, I smiled, and said, "I must have the wrong number."

"We knew they were spying for you. We've been watching all along, Harris. You had to know we could see everything they did; we programmed them. We programmed their environment. We had access to their thoughts. Hell, Harris, we didn't need cameras or bugs to listen in on them; everything they did took place on our computers."

"Then why did you let them help us?" I asked.

Andropov laughed. "Let them help you? The synthetic brain . . . Sometimes I think we should have given you clones bigger brains.

"We didn't let them help you. We let you help us. We wanted you to evacuate those planets."

"Bullshit," I said.

Andropov shrugged his shoulders, and said, "Think what you want."

"We stole your barges."

"Yes you did, and make no mistake, we will take them back."

"You attacked our fleet."

"A ship here or there, mostly fighter carriers. Strategic hits. We wanted to weaken you. We were playing with you, testing your abilities. I must say, your Navy was always pathetic."

"We have enough ships to . . ."

Andropov shook his head. "You still don't understand. Harris, it doesn't matter how many ships you send here; they're as good as dead.

"You gave us a scare with that device that you used off New Copenhagen; but it won't work this time, not unless you plan on destroying the planet." He paused to smirk.

"New Copenhagen?" I muttered. *He must mean Solomon,* I thought. *He's talking about the torpedoes Holman fired.* Maybe the test had gone better than we thought.

Andropov turned away from the camera, but he continued speaking. He said, "Ah, I see your fleet has arrived. Sixty-eight carriers. Two hundred battleships." He nodded, turned to face me, and said, "Very impressive."

Even as he said this, the Klaxons began their howling call to stations.

No longer able to stop myself, I looked down at the communications console and saw that I had not succeeded at powering it up. Holman had not heard a word of the conversation, not that it would have mattered. The gears of the invasion were already in motion.

Looking back at Freeman's two-way, I said, "Just so you know, it's personal between us. I'm coming for you."

He nodded, and said, "Don't you have a transport to catch?"

I did not know if I signed off or he did. My hand was on the two-way, but I did not remember killing the power. I reached for the communications console, signaled the bridge, and spoke to Captain Cutter. I said, "Better kill the engines. I think they're expecting us."

FIFTY-TWO

We searched the space lanes and found only a few U.A. ships. The Unifieds had six Perseus-class ships in the area. These were older ships, the same make as our ships. They didn't pose any threat at all.

The Unifieds might have had spy ships watching us; but just as Andropov had said, their fleet had gone.

I sat in a conference room with Cutter. We had an audio link to all the top officers in the fleet. Cutter repeated everything I had told him, then said, "I'm open to suggestions."

Several officers mumbled indistinct answers, but no one spoke up.

Cutter looked at me and shook his head. "It's hard to know what to do when you don't know what you're up against."

We were just off the bridge of the *Alexander*, a recently refurbished ship that still seemed only partially ready for battle. The engines worked fine. As far as I could tell, the shields worked right. Maybe it was just my nerves.

"If he has some kind of superweapon, why doesn't he fire it?" asked one of the disembodied voices.

"Could be short-range," said another.

"Or proximity-based," said another. "They could have laid mines. If he salted the space lanes, he'll need to keep his ships out of the area."

"He knows we're not going anywhere," I said, "not unless he hands over the keys to the Mars broadcast station."

Cutter interrupted me. "The station is gone. There's no trace of it."

"They must have destroyed it," I said.

"I don't think so. There would still be wreckage unless they towed it away," said Cutter.

"So we're stuck here," I muttered. "What are they doing?"

Cutter said, "You know, he could be bluffing. It's always possible that we caught the bastard with his pants down, and he's trying to stall the attack until his fleet returns."

"If it returns," I said.

Several people asked, "What?"

"Holman stole the shield-buster torpedoes from the ships we destroyed when we took the barges," I said. "Andropov thinks we have them. The bastard's in for a surprise if he sends his fleet to Terraneau. Holman's still got them."

"Holman's battleships are carrying shield-busters?" asked Cutter.

I said, "Not his battleships, his fighters," and I told him about my meeting with Mars. I went over it quickly, leaving out the shit about Mars praying for our salvation.

Cutter listened carefully and smiled. "Brilliant strategy. He's letting the Unifieds go after the nest when they should be chasing the hornets."

"He still only has three carriers," said one of the ships' captains.

"That's why it works," Cutter said in a voice so bright you would have thought we'd already won the war. "The Unifieds will go after the carriers first. They'll home right in on them. Once they do, Holman will slip his fighters right past them. He's going to hit the bastards in the gut, and they won't know where it came from."

"They'll figure it out before he finishes off their ships," I said.

"Those fighters are going to give Holman the element of surprise, and they'll be hard to track. The Unifieds won't know which fighters have shield-busters and which ones have lasers," said Cutter. "One thing about Holman—he always thought ahead of the curve."

"That doesn't help us," said one of the captains.

I disagreed. Every ship Holman sank in the Scutum-Crux Arm was another ship that would not return to Earth. If he sank enough of them, we might be able to take the Sol System uncontested . . . except that still left the question about Andropov's superweapon.

Cutter sat silent while the voices on the communications console debated scenarios and outcomes. I sensed uncertainty as I listened to them.

One officer suggested we approach slowly and prepare to retreat. Another wanted to send two battleships to probe their defenses, then regroup. It sounded intelligent.

Cutter responded quickly, interrupting the man. He said, "No. We go in hard and fast, and present a moving target. Whatever they have, it's got to be a surface-to-space weapon. They might have cannons, but it's probably rockets. It's almost sure to be rockets . . . a lot of rockets. That's why they haven't rebuilt their Navy, they've been allocating their resources to a rocket defense. We need to go in fast, land our Marines, and get the speck out of there."

That ended the debate.

Cutter finished by saying, "God help us if I called this wrong."

Lieutenant Mars couldn't have said it better.

I told Freeman about the meeting, and he said, "Missiles, not rockets."

"How do you know that?" I asked.

"They recently built three high-security missile bases around Washington, D.C."

"There must be more," I said.

"Just those three."

"Why would they build all of them in Washington?" I asked.

Freeman glared at me. "This is the Unified Authority."

"Yeah. The whole damned planet belongs to the Unified Authority," I said.

"Where are you planning to attack?" asked Freeman.

"The capital," I said.

He was right. They were right. It did not matter where else we attacked, the war would be decided on the eastern seaboard of the former United States. In their minds, no other target was worth invading. It was the only target in my mind as well. The Unified Authority would remain in place so long as Washington, D.C., remained.

"Damn it," I said.

Freeman watched me silently.

"How dangerous?" I asked.

"They're big bases. They have millions of missiles," he said.

"So we're screwed," I said.

"I can shut them down."

He was a skilled saboteur. I asked, "Do you have a way to hack into their system?"

He shook his head. "I wouldn't even try; the security is too solid."

"Do you know how to break into the bases?" I asked.

He shook his head.

I thought he'd probably come up with something elegant, some imaginative loophole. I was wrong. He said, "I bought warehouses near each of the missile bases and filled them with bombs."

I had to laugh. "You said you weren't sure which side you were going to take," I pointed out.

Freeman looked down at me, blinked once, and asked, "Do you want me to tell you about the bombs I set up next to your bases?"

CHAPTER
FIFTY-THREE

After speaking with Freeman, I spent fifteen minutes throwing together a strategy for establishing a beachhead, then I told Cutter to launch the invasion.

I boarded a transport and sat in the cockpit, in the copilot's seat. Beside me, Lieutenant Christian Nobles ran the controls. "Sir, do you know what we're up against?" he asked, as the sled dragged our transport through the first set of locks.

"You're going to have plenty to deal with on the way down," I said. "The Unifieds have a new missile defense."

"What about the Earth Fleet? What did they do with their fleet?" Nobles asked.

"We don't know. If I had to guess, I'd say the bastards sent it to intercept the barges at Terraneau." I did not mention my conversation with Tobias Andropov. Nobles had not returned to Earth for most of a decade. Tobias Andropov had risen to power during Nobles's absence, and I doubted that the name would have meant anything to him. The sled began dragging our transport into the launch tubes.

"It sounds like the Unifieds are in the shit," Nobles said.

"What do you mean?" I asked.

"We captured the Golan Dry Docks, right? That left them high and dry without anyplace to build new ships. We don't have anyone who can design ships. They don't have anyplace to build them. Either way, you end up stranded once you run out of ships. I bet that's why they're using a missile defense."

I silently stewed over Nobles's words as we entered the second atmospheric lock and the huge metal door closed behind us, sealing off the rest of the carrier as the outer hatch opened, revealing space. We left the artificial-gravity field. Nobles gave the thrusters a slight kick, and the transport coasted out to space.

We were at the head of an enormous armada, flying toward Earth at several million miles per hour. In space, where there is no friction to slow you down, a slow-flying bird like a military transport can travel a million miles per hour riding on the inertia of the ship from which it launched.

The first wave of fighters led the way, and we followed, an enormous swarm of transports. Ahead of us, I saw the sun, the Earth, and its moon. The engines of our Tomcats looked like tiny sparks. They traveled ahead of us, looking like a field of amber-colored stars. Above them, a few capital ships cleared the way.

At that point, the transport pilots used their thrusters to slow their ships as the invasion fleet left us behind. The change in speed played havoc with the gravity inside the transports. I felt a wave of nausea roll over me as the artificially generated gravity that rooted me to the floor did a tug-of-war with the genuine gravity that pulled me forward.

As the gravity from our deceleration stabilized, I put on my helmet and used the commandLink to speak to Ray Freeman. We did not fly down to Earth on the same transport.

"Ray, you there?"

"Yeah."

"How long will it take you to destroy the bases?" I asked.

"Depends how far I need to travel."

"We're going to try and come in as close to Washington, D.C., as possible," I said. "If we run into resistance, you may have a trek."

That was when the shelling began. Far ahead of us, so distant that the explosions looked like light shining through hundreds of pinholes, U.A. missiles lashed out at our capital ships.

"Harris," Cutter called. His voice came on a direct line over the interLink and on the communications console.

"Harris, here," I said.

"We found their missiles," Cutter shouted. He probably did not mean to shout, but the man must have been drowning in adrenaline. His voice rang in my ears. "We're losing ships. Damn, we're losing ships."

Cutter had planned the pass correctly. Our big ships streaked by at several million miles per hour, traveling so fast that the missiles could not lock in on individual targets.

Cutter mumbled something, then said, "We lost twenty-seven ships." Having seen the extent of the damage, he sounded more stressed than panicked.

Twenty-seven ships did not sound like a lot. I said, "They only nicked you. This could end early."

Cutter put the damage into perspective. "We lost twenty-seven ships passing four hundred thousand miles outside of Earth's atmosphere at three million miles per hour. You'll be entering the atmosphere at two thousand miles per hour."

"We're going to get nailed," I said.

He did not respond.

"Warn your men," I told Cutter. "They deserve to know what they're up against."

Cutter signed off and changed frequencies. A moment later, speaking on an open line that every fighter and transport pilot would hear, he made his report.

"This is Captain Donald Cutter of the E.M.N. *Alexander.*

"The Unified Authority is using nuclear-tipped missiles to defend its space. The Unifieds' defense strategy involves flooding our path with these missiles. We can minimize the damage using defensive tactics, but we expect to take casualties.

"This mission will succeed or fail based on our ability to land our transports in strategic locations. That places a heavy burden on you fighter pilots. We are asking you to give this everything you've got. We need you to escort our transports to Earth. Do not return to the fleet until the Marines have landed.

"Good luck to you," he said, and signed off.

If every transport landed, we would start our invasion with three hundred thousand Marines. That would be the first of four waves—three thousand transports, each carrying one hundred troops and equipment. The second wave would have fewer troops and bigger guns, two hundred thousand men plus tanks and artillery.

Maybe five hundred miles ahead of us, our fighter escort entered into the storm. These were small, agile ships, able to execute tight maneuvers and armed with decoy buoys, sonic shields that could detonate warheads and missiles. They had ghosting technology designed to scramble enemy targeting systems with false readings. They dropped phosphorous-burning target drones that distracted heat-seeking missiles and sent them off course.

Our defensive tactics were designed for dogfights in mostly empty skies. The wing escorting our transports included thousands of fighters wedged too tightly together to maneuver. The shields on our fighters would offer little protection against nuclear-tipped missiles. With our pilots flying so close together, fooling a missile into missing one fighter might well send it into another.

Missiles began to burst in flashes that, from our transports, looked no bigger than the flame of a candle, but those explosions burned bright in the darkness.

Off to the side, Earth revolved as smooth and round as a child's dream. The sun shone down on the far side of the hemisphere, lighting the nearest edge of Europe and farthest shore of the Atlantic. And directly ahead of us, men in Harriers, Tomcats, and Phantoms did something that will forever color the way I think of fighter pilots. With missiles slamming into them from every side, they slowed their speed.

Had they bashed their way through at full speed, the vast majority of those fighters would have survived the attack. They would have left us behind, and the Unifieds would have renewed their attack on our unescorted transports. I doubt a single one of our slow-flying birds would have survived.

The fighters throttled back to a crawl. We caught up to them so gradually, I might not have noticed had it not been for Nobles. He muttered, "Specking hell, they're almost at a dead stop."

"What?" I asked.

"Thirty seconds, sir, and we'll be in missile range."

Then I saw it. We had nearly caught up to the fighters as they weaved around each other and waited for us. With the Earth turning peacefully in the background, I saw a Phantom take a direct hit. The missile struck it just behind the cockpit. The missile hit it "in the gills," in the pilots' vernacular.

The missile exploded outside the shields—an electrical layer that showed like a flat plane of glass, then vanished as the force of the blast tore, shredded, and melted the fighter all at the same time. Pieces of wing, and nose, and fuselage spun into space, scattering like buckshot from a shotgun.

A few hundred yards away, a Phantom banked, looped, and nose-dived toward Earth, then pulled into a corkscrew as it led multiple rockets away from our transports. I did not have a clear view of the fighter when the first of the missiles hit, I just saw the flare of the explosion.

Then we entered the pack and found ourselves as much a target as the fighters that protected us. Fighters darted in and out of view. The debris of broken fighters floated around us; and in the distance, Earth was ten or maybe twenty times the size of a full harvest moon.

I did not see the missile that shot toward our bow, but I caught a glimpse of the particle beam that disabled it and I saw the fighter that fired the beam as she passed. The fighter streaked by so quickly, I could not tell if she was a Tomcat, a Harrier, or a Phantom.

Nobles said, "That was close."

I said, "That fighter almost hit us."

Nobles said, "The missile came closer."

Until he mentioned the missile, I had not understood. "Can you tell how many transports we've lost?" I asked. We were at the front of the wave. I had no idea what had happened behind us.

"Seventy-five so far," he said. "The fighters are taking it worse than us. They're down a few hundred."

I barely heard what Nobles said about the fighters because I was already trying to raise Freeman on the interLink.

"Ray. Ray, are you there?" If we lost Freeman, the mission was over.

"Here," he said.

"We're losing transports," I said.

Just ahead of us, three fighters formed a small wing to clear our path. They stayed in a tight formation for a minute or two, firing lasers and particle beams into the glowing atmosphere ahead of us.

A missile hit the fighter on the right. It happened so fast I did not see where it hit or if the bird survived. One moment there were three ships, then the tinting over in our windshield darkened. When the tint cleared, there were two fighters instead of three.

"Just making sure you're okay," I said.

Freeman didn't answer.

"Better brace yourself," Nobles said. "We're coming in hard."

Before I could react, we slammed into the edge of Earth's atmosphere and glanced off, only to strike it again and break through. The impact of the entry slung me back in my seat, my arms flying to the sides, my head snapped back. The force of the drop held me pinned in my chair. I struggled to sit up, to breathe, to see through the windshield.

Our fighter escort did not lead us down to the planet. We dived through bright mist and empty sky with no ships leading our way. The sky around us was crisscrossed with slowly evaporating vapor trails.

The Unifieds would not fire their nuclear-tipped missiles at us now that we had entered the atmosphere, the radiation would have come back to fry them. As we flew through the paper white sky, thick beams of silver-red light slashed the air around us.

"Lasers," Nobles mumbled. He said it dismissively. We could survive a direct hit from a laser. He studied his scopes for a moment, and said, "Whatever is left of us has already entered the atmosphere. The fighters are headed back to the fleet."

"How many transports do we have?" I asked.

Nobles hesitated, swallowed, said, "Two hundred sixty-five."

"What the speck do we do now?" I asked. That left us with twenty-six thousand men plus change. We weren't going to conquer Washington with twenty-six thousand men.

"We'd better land. Sooner or later, those lasers are going to wear down our shields," Nobles said. Either a particle beam or possibly a short-range missile hit us. I thought it might have been a particle beam by the way we dropped. A hundred feet . . . a thousand feet . . . One moment we were flying straight ahead and the next falling straight down.

We had reached the eastern seaboard of the territory once called the United States. This was the seat of power, the capital of the Unified Authority. The ground below us was trussed with roads and highways. We skirted cities and traversed forests as we traveled up the coast at three times the speed of sound.

It was a clear day. We might have been ten miles out of Washington, D.C., the city skyline rose out of the tree-covered landscape up ahead. Until that moment, the Unifieds had only fired ground weapons at us, and I finally understood why. They were herding us, guiding us toward the capital itself and Joint Base Anacostia-Bolling, the largest military air base on Earth.

I shouted, "Put us down."

"We're in the middle of nowhere," Nobles said. Then he saw fighters on his radar and the flashing amber warning light.

Nobles was a good pilot and a smart man. He knew we had a better chance of surviving a crash landing than an aerial assault. We had powerful shields but no weapons and limited maneuverability.

Nobles set off Klaxons to alert the Marines in the kettle about the upcoming crash. He hit the radio, and shouted, "Incoming fighters! Drop where you are! Drop where you are!"

We nose-dived toward the forest. Our shields obliterated the bare branches of trees that had shed their leaves for the winter. We skipped across the tops of the trees as Nobles cut our speed from thousands of miles per hour to hundreds. He righted our attitude, and our momentum hurled us forward. As I watched Nobles steering us into trees, I realized he was using them to slow us.

The shields held. Nothing hit the ship itself, but we spun and bumped and tilted and bounced, working our way down the last thirty feet. And then we touched down as delicately as a ballerina completing a grand jeté, and the world around us was silent.

FIFTY-FOUR

Location: Earth
Galactic Position: Orion Arm
Astronomic Location: Milky Way

Back on Terraneau, Lieutenant Mars and his engineers tested the batteries in the Unified Authority's new shielded armor and discovered that the batteries stored enough energy to power the armor for forty-five minutes. Their power usage spiked whenever anything hit the shields. If we hit them with a continuous laser stream or enough bullets, we could cut that battery life to a few minutes.

The only weapons their Marines could use while wearing the armor were the built-in fléchette guns that ran along the outsides of their sleeves—decidedly short-range weapons, accurate to one hundred yards.

The original plan was to cut off any outside support by surrounding Washington, D.C., then tightening the noose around the city's neck as our reinforcements arrived.

They, of course, would retaliate by sending out soldiers in shielded armor; but we had that all figured out. With our M27s, we could hit the defenders from outside their range. We would drain their shields; and, once we depleted the batteries in their shields, we would annihilate them.

It was a good plan, and it probably would have worked had I had three hundred thousand troops. Instead, I had twenty-six thousand men, and we were cut off. We'd lost 90 percent of our birds on the way down, and there would be no reinforcements as long as the missile defenses remained operational.

Both Freeman and I survived. Most of the transports in the front of the pack made it through. That was because the fighters that cleared our way took the brunt of the attack. As long as Freeman was alive, there was still hope we might shut down the missiles.

"Everyone out! Regroup. Regroup!" I shouted over the interLink. I used a frequency for company commanders. The Unifieds would come looking for us shortly, and they'd have artillery. They would not have any trouble locating our transports; we'd practically crushed the forest when we crash-landed. As we did not have enough men to guard them, we'd need to leave the transports behind.

Our only hope was to hide in the forest, where we might be able to escape the Unifieds' fighters. It wasn't much of a hope. Once the fighters failed, the Unifieds would send slow-moving, low-flying helicopter gunships to flush us out. First they'd send gunships, then they'd send in tanks and Marines. We needed to move.

"Freeman, where are you?" I asked on a direct Link.

"I'm on my way," he said.

"Do you want me to send a team with you?" I asked.

He didn't answer. It was a stupid question. Sometimes a lone man can accomplish feats that an army could not. Working by himself, Freeman could hijack a car and infiltrate Washington unseen. Every person he added to his entourage made him that much more visible; and in this game, visibility was death.

"Is there any chance the Unifieds found your buildings?" I asked. Maybe I was losing faith.

The enemy had better armor, artillery, air support, and more men; but we were Marines. We organized and spread out under the cover of the trees as the first of the U.A. fighters arrived overhead.

The fighters didn't worry me . . . much. Fighters were made for fighting each other, not ground forces. They worked best when they moved fast. We had drone planes and rockets. Those fighters would need to slow down to a vulnerable speed to attack us. If they did, we would give them something to think about.

Fighting back against Unified Authority gunships and troops would be another story. We needed to evacuate the forest before the Unified's ground forces arrived. We wouldn't stand a chance against tanks and shielded armies fighting here in the trees; but we might find safety in the eye of the storm.

"We need to get to the city," I called out to the troops.

The first explosion was of the benevolent variety, at least it was benevolent toward us. A few miles east of us some charges went off. Though he did not call it in, I suspected Ray Freeman had set something off. Looking up through the trees in the direction of the blast, I saw a column of white smoke rise into the air. White smoke, clean smoke, the kind of smoke you get from charges.

In this case, Freeman had hit a communications tower to try to buy us some time. I heard the pop of cables snapping and the yawn of metal bending. The tower fell through trees as it collapsed. I heard the sounds, but they meant nothing to me until we crossed over a ridge and found the tower lying twisted in a bed of broken branches.

"What is that?" asked one of my captains.

"A relay tower," I said. Losing the tower would not cripple U.A. communications in the area; it might not even slow them down.

The trees around us were spindly but tall, most of their trunks no more than four inches across. They had silver-gray bark. Looking up through the trees, I saw a nickel-colored sky with high-flying clouds. A crow flew across my path, or maybe a raven. It looked like a fast-flying shadow against the sky.

Fighters streaked overhead. First we heard the growl as they approached, then the screech as they slammed past us, and finally the bang as the noise of their engines followed. They flew at supersonic speeds crossing the woods in a matter of seconds. Beneath the trees we walked ten-minute miles, hoping that our slow speed would make us harder to follow.

Then came the dull *thudthudthudthudthud* that I did not want to hear. Gunships approached. Looking around, I saw several men spin and fire distortion canisters into the air. The canisters burst in a cloud of shimmering silver glitter that vanished somewhere between the tops of the trees and the increasingly cloudy sky.

Those canisters would not harm the gunships, but they would wreak havoc on their radar, sonar, and infrared tracking systems. They filled the air with invisible filaments that gave sonar false readings and choked out radar and other tracking technologies.

Negotiating my way through grayscale landscape, I felt abandoned by the God in whom I did not believe and the fleet in which I did. The trees were gray, and the sky was silver; sunlight showed like platinum streaks casting shadows on the muddy ground. No help was coming, and we could not defeat the enemy. The best we could hope for was to lengthen the fight as we waited to die.

With their tracking systems hobbled, the men flying the gunships circled over the tops of the trees, hoping to establish visual contact. The gunships had thick, powerful armor. They were flying tanks armed with rockets, chain guns, and excellent tracking equipment, which my men had now blinded.

Trying to force us into the open, the gunships fired rockets into the trees. One ship loomed over us like a shark following prey. When we came to a clearing, the gunship spun into position and sprayed bullets into a company of men.

The chain guns were large and powerful. The bullets stabbed through my men and their armor. Blood sprayed out of the holes as men stumbled and fell. The gunship fired a rocket that hit the base of a tree, sending five men tumbling through the air. They landed as corpses; arms, legs, and armor blown away from their bodies.

One of my grenadiers scored a hit with a rocket-propelled grenade, but the handheld rocket didn't dent the gun bird. More of my grenadiers joined in the fight.

It was like hitting bulletproof glass with a baseball. Hit it enough times, and the glass will weaken and break. I had thousands of grenadiers on the ground. Once enough of them fired rockets, the gunship slowly came apart, tumbling into the trees, then crashing to the ground in a fiery wad of smoke and metal.

My visor displayed each Marine's name above his helmet. They were faceless to me, but not nameless. When I looked at the dead men lying in the clearing, their armor broken and their blood seeping into the ground, I almost gave up. I felt tired and weak and unfit to lead a division of men faced with a challenge that might be too big for the entire corps.

We continued our trot toward the outskirts of D.C. The gun birds shadowed us; but having lost a member of their flock, they did not attack. Fighters still flew far overhead. The air above us seemed to echo with the sounds of their engines.

We came to a break in the trees and stopped. A six-lane highway ran the gap like a border between two nations. The Unified Authority's tanks, trucks, and troops had not yet arrived, but a swarm of gunships hovered over the road like vultures waiting for a carcass.

I knew this area. If we followed the highway, we would end up on Capitol Hill, but it was a twenty-mile march. We were farther west of the city than I had hoped.

While I waited for my men to regroup, a colonel came and asked me if I had any ideas.

"Two," I said. First, I pointed to the gunships waiting for us to cross the highway, and said, "We need to take care of them.

"Then we head east. There's a spaceport a few miles east of here. If we can make it to the spaceport, that will be the place where we make our stand."

"Do you think we should make a stand?" the colonel asked.

"Colonel, the Unified Authority has cut us off from the fleet. We have twenty-six thousand men armed with M27s. We are too small to invade Washington and too big to hide in the woods. At the moment, I cannot think of a better alternative. How about you?"

"Aye, sir. I'll send my grenadiers bird hunting. Let's see what they can bring down," he said with a salute.

"That sounds like a fine idea, Colonel. Carry on."

FIFTY-FIVE

The colonel relayed the order to shoot down the gunships. Several companies sent grenadiers to join in the attack. Three minutes later, a fusillade of rocket-propelled grenades came streaming out of the trees. Most of the choppers skated away untouched. Three gunships left trails of thick smoke in their wake. Two went down.

The unharmed gunships lifted above the trees, spun, and returned fire. Hovering in the air like wasps around a nest, they launched rockets and fired chain guns. Flames and smoke boiled out from the forest, trees bounced in the air before toppling onto the highway.

"Everyone out of there!" I yelled.

"Hey, General, watch this," a self-assured-sounding voice said over the interLink. My visor identified the cocky phantom as Major Hunter Ritz. I knew the name, but I did not have time to register it.

The enterprising bastard fired a mortar into the air. It shot out from the trees, leaving a perfectly arced steam trail in its wake. Mortars were big, stupid weapons that were meant for demolishing buildings and landscapes. No one in his right mind would use a mortar to hit a flying target no matter how slow-moving . . . only the gunships weren't moving.

One thing about mortars, you could modify their shells. You could attach a radioactive charge, or a nuclear warhead, or a gas canister. In this case, Ritz had added a warhead that emitted an electromagnetic pulse.

The gunships hovered over the highway like cats watching over a mousehole. When the mortar shell reached the apex of its arc in the center of the flock of gun birds, it dropped a dozen yards, and burst. There was a double flash. First, there was the white and black you get with your basic explosion.

Next came a burst of something that looked like steam. It filled the sky and vanished.

The force of the first explosion sent the gunships skittering into each other. They slid through the air. A few rotor blades collided. Before the collisions could result in real damage, the pulse struck, sending the birds into hibernation. Shields would have protected the gunships from that pulse; but these birds carried heavy armor instead of shields.

The Unifieds had twenty, maybe twenty-five, gunships in that flock. Ritz knocked them all down with a single shot.

"Nice shot, Colonel," I told Ritz on an open frequency that every man on the planet could listen in on.

"I'm a major, sir," he said.

"Not anymore," I said.

Ritz's trick might have slowed them down, but the Unifieds were still herding us, still driving toward the location of their choice. They had more gunships, and their fighters still streaked over the trees. They could end the fight from the air if they wanted, but apparently they didn't.

They're still using us for military exercises, I thought. That strategy had backfired on them before, when we established our empire. It could backfire again.

We crossed the road and waded back into the woods. It was late in the afternoon, and the winter sky was darkening. The low-hanging layer of gray clouds turned to charcoal as the sun went down, then the trees looked like shadows.

Traveling through the dark woods, we needed to rely on night-for-day vision. Our lenses would show the world in blue-white monochrome, ignoring shadows and indirect sources of light. We could not, for instance, see the glow of shielded armor once we switched to night-for-day vision. We could not see ten yards ahead without it.

I issued an order to my company commanders. "Team leaders, automatic riflemen, and grenadiers, switch to night-for-day vision. Riflemen stay with tactical lenses. Fall to the rear of your fire teams. Aim your Viridians on the man in front of you and stay close in behind."

Viridian lasers were the laser aiming devices we attached to our guns. They housed both a thin green laser beam used for aiming and a flashlight.

Darkness came quickly. A suffocating stillness filled the woods. There might have been owls in the trees, but I did not hear them. There might have been a breeze, but I did not hear the rustling of branches. In the solitude of my helmet, I was alone.

The U.A. fighters ran a flyby. First the woods were silent, then they rang with the roar of engines. Those pilots knew our location and just how to hit us. A few of the men ahead of me stopped to stare into the sky.

"They could kill us if they wanted to," commented one of my majors.

I did not answer. If I confirmed his theory, his fear would spread like a virus through my troops; and I did not like lying to my officers. Better to ignore my men than to scare them or lie.

We first spotted the glow of shielded armor at 19:00. The golden light looked ghostly as it weaved through the trees at improbable speeds. The units stayed far away. We heard their engines, saw the pale, golden glow, and knew the Jackals were behind us. They wanted us to know they were there, the bastards. They were pushing us forward, guiding us to their trap. Fighters forcing us to stay on the path, Jackals hurrying us along, we were cattle headed to the slaughterhouse.

Jackals were upgraded jeeps with powerful engines and armored turrets. I'd used them in battle, but I'd never seen Jackals with shields.

"Ritz, you hear those Jackals back there?" I asked on a direct Link.

"Hard to miss 'em," he said.

"Think you could hit one with a rocket?" I asked.

"Shouldn't be much of a problem," he said.

"Do you think you can hit one and get away alive?"

"Wouldn't do it any other way."

"Take three grenadiers. Have them cover your ass in case it comes after you," I said.

"Aye, sir," he said.

Every man in armor had access to the interLink; but I was the only officer in the field with the commandLink. I could look through any man's visor, see the world as he saw it. Using optical commands, I created a window that let me look through Ritz's helmet. I saw his world as he dropped back from our ranks, hiding behind trees, darting behind bushes.

He did not carry a mortar for this job, just a handheld RPG, a foot-long silver tube that he held in his right hand. He stuck to the shadows. I could hear his breathing over the audio. If we made it through this mission, I would have a word with him about his conditioning. He was breathing heavily, like a man who had just run two miles instead of a couple of hundred feet.

He scurried to a mound of leaves and logs, slid in behind it, and switched to his tactical view. Dark forest surrounded him.

"You guys back there?" he asked as he went back to night-for-day vision.

"Yes, sir."

"Right behind you."

"Just making sure," Ritz told them.

He took one last scan of the landscape, then darted to a spot where three spindly trees grew out of the rotted trunk of a long-dead oak. He switched his visor back to night-for-day and spotted a Jackal a few hundred yards away and closing the distance.

His breathing slowed. "Yeah, I see you, specker," he said to himself. "Yeah, that's right, you just bring your fat ass this way. I got a present for you." He switched his visor to tactical.

Seeing the world through the unenhanced tactical view, Ritz was surrounded by darkness. Looking through his visor using my commandLink, I could make out the trees he used for cover, but I saw them only as textures in the blackness. He held out the RPG. I could not see the tube, just the shape of his arm.

In the distance, the Jackal sped through the forest, dodging obstacles. It juked around trees and skipped over ditches, disappearing briefly behind a hill, then emerging not more than twenty yards from Ritz. He could have hopped out of his hiding hole and popped it. Instead, he waited, letting the vehicle approach.

"That's right, darlin'. A little closer. A little specking closer."

The kid was patient. The best Marines are patient.

He didn't move. The Jackal came within thirty feet of him, dashed right past, and went by unmolested. It streaked away, offering him a clear shot at its tailpipe and turret.

Ritz stepped out from behind his blind and fired.

"Next time watch your ass, boys!" he yelled as he switched to night-for-day vision and sprinted for safety. He was screaming. He was whooping. He ran without breathing, then struggled for air, never looking back to see what his grenade had done. He jumped over a fallen log, cut to the left behind a clump of trees, and yelled, "Hell yeah!" as he scrambled up a small rise.

The Marines he took with him fired RPGs that sailed past him. Ritz did not turn to see what they were shooting at.

"Let's get the speck out of here!" he screamed to his backup.

"What the speck does it take to kill that specking whore-humper?" asked one of the men.

"More than you're packing," Ritz said. He huffed and puffed as he ran, wheezing with each step.

The sound of high-caliber machine guns tore through the forest. A tree off to Ritz's left splintered and split. He muttered, "Are you trying to shoot me in the back, you bastards?" He spun and fired another RPG without aiming. It hit a tree or a rock and exploded. Ritz turned and continued running into the woods.

The Jackal darted ahead of him, skidding around trees without coming to a stop. Fire flashed from the machine gun in the turret. He should have dived for cover, but Ritz fired another RPG instead, hitting the Jackal above the rear tires. Had it not been for the shields, the Jackal would have exploded. Even with the shields, the percussion of Ritz's grenade knocked the Jackal for a loop. It spun like a dog chasing its own tail, slid down a rise, and disappeared into the shadows.

"That's two up your ass," Ritz screamed as he panted. Then, more quietly, he added, "I got more where that came from."

He stumbled up a rise. As he ran down the other side, he was surrounded by Marines. He had rejoined us.

"General," he said over the interLink, fighting to breathe, "General Harris."

"Colonel," I said. I did not want him to know I'd been spying on him, so I asked, "Were you able to locate a Jackal?"

"Yes, sir," he said as he panted. "I took two men with me. We hit it three or four times."

"Did you destroy it?"

"We couldn't get past the shields," he said.

"Good to know," I said. "Thank you, Colonel."

Their fighters could have annihilated us. We could not penetrate the shields on their light-armored vehicles. They were using us to test their equipment, and all that remained to be tested was their troops.

FIFTY-SIX

We'd been on the ground for nearly four hours when we reached the municipal spaceport. We came out from the trees, and there it was—a chain-link-wrapped clearing that ran as far as I could see. It sat as flat as a pond and as wide as the plains.

The twenty-foot fence that ran its length posed no challenge. When one of my officers asked if I thought it was electrified, I answered, "Doesn't matter."

I pulled the particle-beam pistol from my belt, and shouted, "Stand clear" as I fired at the nearest post. The emerald green beam did not heat or burn the metal post, the beam disrupted it, leaving molten splinters in its place. I aimed at the chain link. It tore like a spiderweb.

Beyond the fence, the spaceport was a patchwork of shadows. The ground was black and smooth like a lake on a dark, still night. No light shone in the windows of the terminal building, but the reflection of the moonlight showed on the glass.

"They're specking with us, aren't they, sir?" Ritz asked.

"Colonel," I said, "they are playing with us the way a misguided feline plays with a rabid mouse. They have no idea what we have in store for them." I wanted to sound confident, but probably sounded deluded.

I switched frequencies, and said, "Ray, we're just about at the end of the line here."

Freeman said, "I was wondering when you'd call."

"Where are you?" I asked.

"I've set two of the detonators."

"They never found them?" I asked. When Freeman didn't answer, I mumbled the answer for him, "Apparently not." Then I said, "I hope you get to the third one fast, the bastards have us bottled in a spaceport."

Freeman said, "Shouldn't be long."

"Let me know," I said.

"You'll be the second person to know," Freeman said, and he signed off. He meant that he would signal Don Cutter first.

The Unifieds had chosen a battlefield designed around our defense. We had long-range weapons, M27s, snipers, and grenadiers with rockets; but we needed cover. Their short-range weapons would not work until they reached the spaceport, a man-made butte in the middle of an asphalt desert. The spaceport was a massive building surrounded by runways, open fields, and parking lots. In that building, we'd have cover.

They would not switch on their shields until they strolled within range of our snipers. The Unifieds knew how long their batteries lasted. The power would spike every time we hit the shields. If we hit them with a steady stream of bullets, the armor might wear out in eight minutes; but that required continuous attack.

If we stalled their charge . . . if we could keep them from entering the spaceport for forty-five minutes, their armor would run out of power. The fléchette guns on their armor were great short-range weapons; but once the batteries ran out on their shields, the enemy would be as vulnerable as us.

So many variables. Could we slow them down? What would they do if we took control of the battle? Would they send in tanks and fighters? And then there was Freeman—the man was always a wild card. If he managed to shut down the missile defense . . . how long would Cutter need to send in reinforcements?

We crossed the runway. Three-foot-tall posts with lanterns rose like cattails out of the tarmac, but the lights remained out. Dressed in dark green armor, my men looked like shadows in the night. They crossed the ground in fire teams and formations, guns ready, moving quickly and covering their flanks.

If the Unifieds caught us crossing the runway, we'd have no place to hide and absolutely no cover. They would have mowed us down. We were twenty thousand men, out in the open, with no place to hide; but the cocky bastards did not want to squander the opportunity to test their soldiers. They wanted to give their ground troops live targets and hand-to-hand combat experience. They would let us reach the building and dig ourselves in. What did it matter to them?

The second and third stories of the terminal had walls made of thick glass. Those were the passenger areas. The Unifieds did not squander taxpayer dollars on the ground floor, the service area used by luggage handlers and mechanics. That floor had cement walls and metal doors.

The first of my Marines entered the terminal building. A fire team opened a side door and tossed in a flash grenade. The phosphorous light blazed like a flash of silver-white, like a sheet of lightning that did not fade for nearly a minute.

I watched as teams scrambled into the building. Silver-white glare lit up the windows as teams reached the second floor. The building was empty. Not a shot was fired.

"We've entered the building, sir, and we have not encountered enemy resistance," one of my colonels reported. "A bit too easy if you ask me."

Another genius of the officer corps, I thought. "Yes, it's almost like they wanted us to take the building," I said in a mechanical voice.

I surveyed the building from the runway. "Break the windows," I said. "Riflemen and automatic riflemen on the second floor. Grenadiers on the third. Snipers on the roof."

I'd done all of this before, and I knew how it would work. You can only slow an enemy who has something to fear. Our bullets would not hurt these men. The blasts from our rockets might knock them over, but they would resume their attack unhurt. They had nothing to fear, and they would cross the runway in five minutes flat.

That would leave them with forty minutes to sweep the terminal building. Under normal circumstances, capturing a building the size of a spaceport could take days; but that was against an enemy who could injure your men. Again, with that damned shielded armor, the Unifieds could throw cautionary procedures to the wind. They could storm up the stairs and run through the halls. Tactical maneuvers be damned, they could walk right into our fire.

Glass shattered above my head as I reached the building. A blizzard of shards and slivers poured down and shattered behind me. I didn't worry about getting cut, my armor would protect me from falling glass. Fléchettes were another story.

The ground level of the terminal building was little more than a garage, a cavernous empty space with an oil-stained cement floor. A fleet of electric carts sat in a line along one of the walls. I saw conveyor belts for moving luggage, security posts, and a bumper crop of stairwells and service elevators.

Climbing to the next level was like entering a different world. The second floor looked like a shopping mall. It had carpeted hallways, storefronts, restaurants, and seating areas with padded benches and rows of chairs. I didn't know if there was power in the building or if my men had left the lights off. During combat, you usually want your environs darker than your enemies'. Darkness offers its own brand of camouflage.

Looking around the lobby, I saw sergeants running their squads. If I had listened in on their frequencies, I would have heard platoon leaders and company commanders screaming themselves hoarse. Everything they said would be "specking this" and "specking that," and they'd call everyone "bastard," friend and foe alike.

I generally thrived on those sounds . . . the shouting, the cursing, the intensity; but on this night, I preferred the solitude of my helmet. I felt the weight of the entire galaxy upon me. Today, every death and injury would color my conscience. I had led these men into this disaster. If we lost, I would have their deaths on my head. If we won, I would likely preside over the deaths of everyone on Earth.

How did I get myself in these situations? By recommending the invasion? I did not regret making that recommendation though I wished the Unifieds had not anticipated our every step. Maybe we would all die. Maybe a few of us would survive. It didn't matter, not really. The only action that mattered would take place on Terraneau.

After all my big talk about antisyntheticism, maybe I was the ultimate bigot. I had brought thousands of clones to Earth, with millions more in reserve. Why was I sacrificing them?

Had I bought into the whole "expendability" argument? I asked myself the question, and I hated the answer.

At least we were killing natural-borns as well as saving them. The thought of taking a few hundred natural-borns down almost made up for my mistakes. We'd give them an evening to remember. We would not go down without a . . .

"Harris, the missile bases are down."

"You did it?" I asked.

I walked to the window and saw the red glow in the sky. It wasn't bright, and it did not appear and disappear like an atomic explosion. Whatever Freeman had set off, it filled the sky with a burned orange glow that lit the bottoms of the clouds.

Beside me, thousands of men lay on their guts or knelt beside window casings, their guns pointing out into the night.

"Have you reached Cutter?" I asked.

"He's on his way with the second wave," said Freeman.

I smiled, but the smile was bitter. How far away had he taken the fleet? A million miles? Ten million miles?

No one paid attention to me as I inspected our ranks, and I knew why. On the far end of the runway, an eerie golden glow shone from between the trees.

FIFTY-SEVEN

Even using the telescopic lenses in my visor, I could not get a clear view of the bastards. I only saw the glow of their shields emanating from the edge of the woods. They were testing their armor, getting ready to strike.

A few minutes passed, and the ghost light vanished on the far end of the runway. I watched them through my telescopic lenses, saw how they slowly moved in, keeping a wary eye out for ambushes. Our snipers could not hit them that far away, but our mortars and RPGs sure as hell could. The moment our shells started rumbling, the glow of their shields came back on.

It took us ten minutes to cross the runway. Wearing shield armor, knowing that the clock would run out if the battle lasted forty-five minutes, the Unifieds rushed ahead.

As they surged toward us, a soft ruffle of thunder rolled through the air, and it began to snow. At first the flakes were tiny, like salt crystals falling from the sky. Then the gates of an unseen dam spread wide, and coin-sized flakes tumbled out of the clouds. A strong wind picked up and drove the snow as it fluttered to the ground. Partially blinded by the snowstorm, the U.A. Marines slowed their charge.

The snow and wind played havoc on our mortars. Shells seemed to fly wild. It didn't matter. They had their shields going, and we needed to conserve ammo.

Hoping to get a better look at the enemy, I found a stairwell and raced up the four flights that led to the roof. The door was hanging open on a quiet scene under low clouds. Wearing armor, I could not feel the wind; but I saw the angle of the falling snow. A powerful wind was blowing.

I could have taken a temperature reading with the gear in my visor, but I did not bother. Whatever it was, it must have been cold. The snow had already started to pile up. A quarter-inch layer of it already covered the roof. On the runway, the tarmac looked gray instead of black.

"General," a major said when he turned and saw me. He snapped to attention and saluted. His men remained as they were; this was a battle situation.

I pointed to one of the snipers and asked to see his rifle. The major retrieved it for me.

How long will it take them? I asked myself, thinking of Cutter and the fleet, not the U.A. Marines. Our ships could cross a million miles in a couple of minutes, but launching transports and fighters would add time.

I lifted the rifle and peered through the scope. Nine-tenths of a mile away, men in armor lit the edge of the runway as they poured out from between trees and ran onto the tarmac. I could hit them from that distance. Most of my snipers could hit a target from a mile away, but we could not afford to waste ammunition. At that point, our high-powered rifles were no more effective than a swarm of mosquitoes.

As I watched through the scope, the flood of men in glowing armor continued to flow out from behind the trees. They came from every direction, completely closing us in. Confident their armor could protect them, they jogged toward us. By that time, only the blizzard conditions stood between us and them.

Looking for a clean shot through all of the snow, I aimed the rifle at one Marine's head and pulled the trigger. The rifle bucked in my hand. It did not have much of a kick. Three seconds passed. My aim was off, the scope was calibrated for another shooter. My bullet missed the target and struck the man behind him. There was a flash where the bullet hit, just over his right cheek.

I handed the rifle back to its owner. The other snipers waited for me to give the order to fire. The snow would not help their accuracy; but at seven hundred yards and firing at a slow-rushing tide, the bullets would hit enemy Marines.

Using a channel that only the snipers would hear, I said, "Fire."

Along the roof, the muzzles of the guns flashed and went dark. The boys spent more time aiming than I would have liked, waiting ten and sometimes twenty seconds between shots.

"When the Unifieds get within one hundred yards, bring your boys in," I told the major.

"Should I take them down to the third floor?" he asked.

"No, just bring them in from the ledges. We'll leave them up on the roof for now."

"Aye, sir," he said.

At one hundred yards, M27s and RPGs are nearly as accurate as sniper rifles. Once the Unifieds reached that point, we'd need to dig in and prepare to fight at close range.

By that time, a thick layer of snow had begun to crunch under my boots. I slid in it as I walked back to the stairs. When I stepped in the open doorway, I kicked the jam to get the snow off my boots.

Cutter's voice came over the interLink. "Harris, where are you?"

"We're holding a spaceport just outside Washington, D.C.," I said. "The bastards have us surrounded."

"Just hold on," Cutter said. "We're almost ready to launch."

Almost ready to launch. Almost ready to launch. The words made my insides knot like a kick to the crotch.

"Thanks," I said in a voice that was distracted and weak. *We're specked,* I thought. Maybe the second wave would win the ground war. *No, it will be Ray Freeman and his hidden bombs who win the war, if we win it.*

As for me, I liked the idea of going down swinging. I didn't feel hope, but I did feel a sense of excitement. I ran down the stairs and took my place by the grenadiers on the second floor.

The Unifieds were four hundred yards away, too far away to return fire with their fléchettes. Along with my snipers, my grenadiers began firing rockets and grenades, squeezing off shots, then tossing old tubes out the window and grabbing the next. Below us, the runway looked like a moonscape. It was white from the snow and pockmarked with craters from our rockets, grenades, and even a few mortars. And crossing that moonscape, slowed more by the damage to the tarmac than the rockets themselves, the Unified Authority Marines tightened their ranks as they approached the building.

There were more of them than there were of us. I couldn't count them, wouldn't even have tried, but I estimated them at fifty thousand strong.

"Harris, I'm almost at the spaceport," Freeman said.

"Go away," I said.

"I can . . ."

"You wouldn't happen to have a nuke that knows the difference between clones and natural-borns?" I asked.

He didn't answer.

"Ray, there's nothing you can do here." I thought for a moment. "Ray, can you hack into their shields?"

"What?" Freeman asked.

"The shields. The shielded armor. Do you think there's some way you can hack into it with a computer?"

"No," he said. "How many are you up against?"

"I'm guessing fifty thousand."

"And you?"

"Not even half that many."

They were closing in. In another few minutes, the Unifieds would enter the building. They would pour into the vacant bottom floor of the terminal. They would charge up the stairs, and we would be in range of their fléchettes—depleted uranium needles coated with neurotoxin. Once they entered the building, the slaughter would begin.

It was while I stood by that broken-out window that my combat reflex began. Calm washed over me as testosterone and adrenaline flooded my bloodstream, and my anxiousness disappeared. I heard the music of the battle in my head. The men around me seemed to move in slow motion. They aimed their weapons, fired shots that did not matter, and held their line against an unstoppable enemy that had not yet begun to fire back.

Using the telescoping lenses in my visor, I took a closer look at the Unifieds. Some stumbled as they ran through the snow. They were natural-borns. Their genes were not selected for battle, they did not have our abilities. Some sprinted, some trotted, some had already run out of breath. A few stared back in my direction as they ran. Snow fell on them, and their shields vaporized it. Steam rose from the spots where their shielded boots kicked through the snow.

As I watched, a rocket struck one of the U.A. Marines in the chest, exploding in a flash of fire, steam, and shrapnel. That rocket was designed to fell small buildings and turn tanks upside down. Had he not been in shielded armor, it would have left the man nothing more than a splash of blood on broken concrete. Instead, the blast slammed him to the ground. He hit hard, bounced ten feet in the air, and fell limp into the snow. The fall hurt him, and he rose to his feet like a dazed fighter, stumbling, weak in the knees. He limped as he took a few steps, then he fell to the ground. The bastard had landed badly and hurt his leg. That was the most we could hope for, to make them trip.

They were closing in, twenty-five yards from the terminal building and closing fast. Some paused to fire fléchettes at us. They ran, pointed arms in our direction as if saluting us, and fired darts that mostly hit the ceiling above our heads. A man a few feet from me was hit. He dropped his gun, reached for his neck, and fell to the ground, where he convulsed for several seconds before dying. A thin and steady stream of blood leaked from the hole in his armor.

If we had a bomb, something big but not nuclear, we could set it off once the Unifieds entered the building, I thought to myself. That was how I had beaten them before. I lured the Unifieds into an underground garage, then blew it up as my men exited through the back door.

If we demolished this building, we would die, too. I did not mind that idea. Was the combat reflex influencing my thinking? At least we would take two of theirs for every man we lost.

Outside, the front edge of the Unifieds had almost reached the building. They were close enough to hit us with their fléchettes, and the fusillade had begun. A steady stream of uranium needles flew in through the crashed-out window, forcing us to our knees. I crawled over the jagged glass fringe that remained in the window casing, climbed to one knee, and fired my M27 down at their heads. Fléchettes zinged past me, like wasps chasing prey, but I held my ground and fired, and I ignored everything around me.

"Harris, get out of there," somebody screamed over the interLink. The name Ritz showed. I did not recognize the name. The part of my brain that recognized people and names had closed down for the evening.

A fléchette brushed across the side of my helmet. I roared in anger and squeezed the trigger of my gun. Men came from my left and my right. The bastards grabbed me and hauled me back away from the window. I screamed and struggled. I would have shot them, but they piled on top of me and held me down.

Somebody pulled my helmet off my head. Still trying to free my arms, I looked up and growled like an animal. "Get off me. Get off me! I'll kill you all," I screamed.

Somewhere in the distance, there were muffled explosions. Flames coughed out of open doorways. Clouds of smoke and dust billowed in from the stairwells. Men had tossed bombs or grenades down the stairs. I did not care. All I cared about was killing, I needed to kill, and these crazy bastards were holding me down. I wanted to kill them. Once I killed them, I would go after the enemy. The calm and the music of battle had left me, they faded from my mind like a drug evaporating from the brain of an addict, and all that they left behind was the need for more.

I fought. I struggled to get loose. A man in combat armor slapped me across the face, his hardened armor glove slamming my cheekbone like a hammer. I was a rabid dog. I turned, stared at him, silently dared him to do that again.

They might have been speaking to each other, but they used the interLink. My helmet was gone. I could not hear them as I snarled and fought to free myself.

Until that moment, I still held my M27 in a hand that was buried under a pile of Marines. I felt the stock slipping from my fingers. I felt desperate, crazed, like a man held underwater. *God, not my gun; I need it to breathe!*

A part of my brain watched the struggle like an innocent bystander witnessing a mugging. In one of my mind's many eyes, I could see that I had turned into an animal. I could see myself clearly, and I hated what I saw. *Stop it. Stop it, stop it, stop it!* I thought to myself.

But that part of my brain was a distant satellite. The rest of my consciousness had shut down entirely. All that remained was anger and instinct. I needed to free myself and to kill, I needed to kill more fiercely than a man held underwater needs to breathe. Life, death, right, wrong, nothing mattered except killing, feeling the hormone in my brain, the missing song of battle.

With the gun out of my hand, I managed to pull my right shoulder free of the men who had piled on top of it. The man in the armor slapped me across the face a second time. If he'd lived another minute, he might even have hit me again, but the doors to the stairs slammed open and men in glowing armor invaded our world.

Not even trying to understand the events around me, I watched as fragments of plaster chipped from the ceiling and walls. Men fell to the floor. The men who had wrestled me down now tried to pull me away. I flailed. I kicked. I got one arm free and slammed my fist into one of my attackers. I hit the front of his helmet. His head jerked back, but I did not even put a crack in his visor.

More men dropped. Some fell in spasms. Some fell still, their blood leaking from pin-sized holes in their armor. I brushed men off my other arm, kicked wildly, and I was free.

My desperation slackened. The part of me that still had intelligence told me to put on my helmet. I lay on my stomach, propelling myself along the ground by faking convulsions. With the Unifieds just entering the floor, I rolled to my side so I could slip my helmet back over my head without being seen. Once I had my helmet secured, I wrapped my hand around the stock of my M27, it might have been my M27, and I played dead. I lay in a pile of dead Marines. I saw the men sprawled on the floor around me and realized they'd died trying to save me.

I played possum, a paisley piece in a collage of dead bodies—one that the Unified Authority might never find. Natural-borns ran past the bodies without sparing a second glance. Knowing that anyone they shot would die, they did not worry about the wounded.

Sensibility slowly set in. I was not entirely in control. I felt some semblance of thought coming back to my brain.

"Ritz. You there?" I asked. I felt ashamed of myself; but I did not have time for embarrassment. There would be a time to apologize, but it would come after the battle. For now, I had shown enough weakness already.

"Harris?" I heard doubt, maybe even fear.

"Did you send men to save me?" I asked.

He answered my question with one of his own. "Where are you?"

"What do you have in the way of explosives?" I asked. I was about to suggest demolishing ourselves and the building. My Liberator programming would not allow me to detonate the bomb myself, but I thought maybe I could give the order. Then something caught my attention and I forgot about bombs.

FIFTY-EIGHT

I lay on the ground, doing my best imitation of a corpse, albeit one that had fallen with a gun still in his grip. My arms stretched past my head, my finger still on the trigger. Thanks to my armor, I could breathe and still look no more alive than the dead men around me. An intelligent Marine might notice the lack of blood leaking from my armor, but there was plenty of blood on the ground around me. About twenty U.A. Marines had already walked past without giving me a second glance.

The glow of their shielded armor had died. The batteries must have run out, though I had no idea what could have caused it.

The Unifieds walked through the dead, stepping over bodies, ready to fire fléchettes into anything that moved. These were the men on point, the sacrificial lambs . . . the canaries in the air vents.

"Ritz, listen to me. I think their armor is running out of juice."

"What?" he asked.

"The batteries in their armor are running out of power." I shifted ever so slowly, gradually rolling to one side, allowing my left arm to loll in place while shifting the M27 in my right hand so that I could aim it. "Their shields are out."

No one noticed. I was just another corpse, just another piece of trash on the floor. As I fumbled to free an RPG from my belt, I watched the door to the stairwell. A never-ending parade of men in flickering armor strode through the opening.

Working blind, I managed to snag a grenade from my belt. I twisted it in my hand. An RPG would have worked better, but the grenade would do. I would use it to create a distraction; and then, in the confusion, I would escape.

One of the Unifieds meandered past me, then stopped. He just stood there, sightseeing in the empty spaceport, I supposed, no more than ten feet from me. His armor winked on and off before it went out entirely. He looked in my direction, and I froze. After a moment he took a step toward me. If he inspected me more closely, he might notice that I was holding a grenade in my left hand and an M27 in my right, and that I had no holes in my armor and no blood oozing from my helmet. In fact, I did not look especially corpselike, not that this shit-for-brains natural-born would have noticed.

"Ritz, where are you?" With my helmet over my head, I could talk, and the bastards around me would not hear my voice or see my mouth move.

"I'm on the third floor," he said.

"What's the situation?"

"They haven't sent anyone up here."

"Yeah, they're still securing this floor," I said.

"I can get you out of there, General. I can . . ."

I hissed, "Shut up and listen." It was harsh. I was still in the tail end of combat reflex, my every instinct was to kill. Ritz, the Unifieds, civilians, at that point it didn't matter. The violence welling up in my brain no longer cared about sides or alliances.

"There's going to be some trouble down here," I said. "Let's see how they fight without their shields."

The U.A. bastard hovering around me walked over for a closer look. Would he notice the way I rested my finger over the trigger of my M27? If he did, it would be the last thing he saw before God welcomed him to Heaven.

The bastard moved slowly, like I was some kind of museum exhibit. He twisted his head to see me from different angles, bending far enough forward that he should have seen the ping-pong-ball-sized grenade cribbed in the fingers of my left hand. I mean, what kind of corpse cradles a grenade in his hand? If I saw a body like that, I'd pump a couple rounds into the head to make sure it never came back to life; but this idiot stared at me for a few seconds. When I did not move, he walked away.

I made my move. With a subtle flick of my wrist, I half rolled/half tossed the grenade, hoping it would reach the nearest set of stairs. It came up short. Instead of rolling into an open doorway about thirty feet away, the grenade skittered to a stop beside a dead Marine.

I did not know whether or not the upgraded Unified Authority armor would protect its occupants from the blast, but my armor sure as speck would not. A second before the blast made milk shakes of everyone it touched, I sprang to my feet, shot the Unified bastard who'd been hovering around me in the face, and sprinted for the nearest corner.

Several Unifieds saw my miraculous rise from the dead and fired at me with their stupid fléchette guns; but I'd caught them napping and put space between us. They didn't worry me. When it came to aiming accurately and firing fast, give me a good old-fashioned pistol or an M27 with a short stock any day. I did not return their fire. I sprinted for a corner, then I dived over a row of chairs and slid to safety behind the wall as the blast of the grenade shook the air.

"Ritz, send your men back to the windows. Shoot any Unifieds you see trying to run away. I want them pinned down in the building."

"You want me to herd them into the building?" he asked.

I managed to say, "Listen to me, Ritz," before I noticed all of the U.A. Marines crowded around me. Dozens of them. At first I thought I'd been spotted, but most of them ran past me and around the corner. One of them stopped and put out a hand to help me climb to my feet. If he'd known who I was, he would have shot me; but I had created chaos. My grenade must have killed the Unifieds who'd shot at me; and the ones who were left only wanted to see what was going on.

If they saw me carrying a gun, they would have figured out that I was not one of theirs, so I ignored my M27 as the U.A. Marine pulled me to my feet. Without the glow of shields, his armor looked just like my armor. The only notable difference was the tube running along the outside of his right sleeve. I hoped he would not notice that my armor was not equipped to fire fléchettes.

"Listen, Ritz, the exercise is over. Their shields ran out of batteries, and they don't want a straight fight. As long as we can keep their Marines in here with us, the Unifieds won't blast the building with fighters and tanks. We need to keep them pinned down. Shoot anyone who tries to get away."

I blended in with a pack of Unifieds as they walked around the corner to inspect the damage from my grenade. Water gushed from broken pipes in the floor and ceiling. Wires and twisted strips of metal hung above my head. Body parts and pieces of armor littered the floor. Helmets had been blown from bodies, some of them with heads still inside.

"If we keep their men pinned down, they won't be able to hit the building without burying them," I said.

"Yes, sir, we're on it," said Ritz.

U.A. Marines cautiously sifted through the debris. Seeing their dead, they must have realized that their glorious war game had become a disaster. I had only killed a few of them, maybe thirty at most. A passel of men gathered around some of the fallen, gingerly kneeling beside one of the bodies.

With the Unifieds distracted, I allowed myself a quick glance out the nearest window. A sea of men in dark armor stood in moonlight and snow on the tarmac, just below the building. They were waiting for orders. They must have known that their assault had gone bad; so there they stood, trapped in a purgatory between attack and retreat.

Ritz's men opened fire with M27s. Firing in small bursts, they hit the outer echelon of the Unifieds, catching the milling enemy by surprise. Ritz's men had the high-ground advantage and better weapons. In the few seconds that I watched, I saw dozens of men collapse.

Hearing the renewed fighting, the Unifieds went to the window frame and stared down at the scene. Nobody noticed as I backed away; they were too busy watching the slaughter outside. Another few steps, and I turned and started for a hall. As I rounded a corner, I reached down and scooped up an M27.

It's not as glorious when we can shoot back, is it? I thought. *How do you like the war games now? How do you like your specking war games now?*

From where I stood, I could see along two sides of the terminal. I saw U.A. Marines standing by the window casings, staring out at the slaughter, helpless. If they had rockets, they could shoot the ceiling and cause a cave in; but they came armed with fléchettes instead of grenades.

One of the U.A. Marines looked back, saw that I was carrying an M27. He stood in a mostly empty hall. He glanced in my direction, started to turn away, then gave me a second pass. He probably tried to speak to me. When he realized he couldn't, he raised his arm.

I shot him in the head, then opened fire on the three Marines standing near him. Hearing the sound of gunfire, more Unifieds came running. I fired my M27 down the hall, turned and fired at anyone coming from the other direction, and ran toward the nearest stairs.

I'd been hit by fléchettes before. They cut through armor as if it weren't there. Between the poison and the shock, your body and brain stopped working in seconds. The last time I had barely survived. If it happened again, I might not be so lucky.

Three Marines tried to make a stand ahead of me. They were a hundred feet away. Two stood. One knelt. Their fléchettes bored through a vending machine as I ducked behind it. Hot drinks bled out of the side of the machine as I spun around its edge and squeezed off twenty rounds. I killed them, then I leaped over their bodies on my way to the stairs.

I pulled a grenade and tossed it behind me without looking back. The hall was long and straight like the barrel of a cannon. It would funnel the percussion and flames from the grenade.

I jetted up a full flight before my grenade went off, and the walls shook. A geyser of flame shot into the stairwell below me. Even if the flames had hit me, they would not have hurt me. My unshielded armor offered that much protection.

I was almost at the top of the stairs when I realized that my own men might shoot me before I could identify myself. "Ritz, I'm coming up the stairs," I said, and I gave him my location. Then I lowered my gun and waited by the door. A moment later, a team of Marines opened the way and led me in.

The terminal building might have been made to accommodate ten thousand travelers, giving them plenty of space to carry luggage. For ten thousand travelers spread across the two upper floors, the building would be spacious. I now had twenty thousand Marines crammed onto one floor and the roof. That floor had become an unholy zoo. Most of the men stood in the central lobby, crammed close together like passengers on a bus in rush hour.

There were no departure gates on that floor. The outer walls were a continuous observation deck. The inside had storefronts, play areas, bathrooms, offices, restaurants, and bars.

The men in the center of the building stood so packed together that they could not move without bumping into each other. That put them out of play. If the Unifieds came running up the stairs, my men would not be able to shoot or defend themselves without killing the clones around them. I surveyed the scene.

We were the clones, the unwanted golems, the Frankenstein monsters that had come home to roost. Men in dark-colored combat armor looked like monsters as I viewed them through my night-for-day lenses. Because of their helmets, their heads looked huge and misshapen, featureless at the front and flat across the top. In the blue-gray of day-for-night vision, the armor was the not-quite-black of shadows on cement.

I stood just outside the stairs with Ritz and a circle of officers. As I started to ask for a report, I saw something through the window. We all saw it. Every man on that side of the building must have spotted it.

I walked toward the empty casing for a closer look.

I switched from night-for-day vision to telescopic lenses and saw lights the color of honey glowing behind the trees at the far edge of the runway. At first I thought a second wave of U.A. Marines had arrived, a column of troops with fresh batteries powering their shields. By that time the snow had mostly stopped, though flecks of powder still hung in the air.

The artillery was far away and hidden by trees, I could not get a good look at it. On a still night like this, the sound of the engines carried clear across the runway.

"Specking hell," said Ritz.

"Son of a bitch," said another colonel.

"What do you think they have out there?" asked another officer.

"How the speck should I know," I snapped in frustration. "The bastards don't consult with me? I mean speck! They don't come to me for ideas!" I hated myself for berating the dumb speck, but I could not make myself stop. I felt cold claws closing around my gonads.

The bastards shot a flare into the sky. They must have fired the son of a bitch from a tank, or maybe a cannon. None of our shoulder-fired weapons could have hurled a heavy phosphorous canister all the way across the runway. The flare burned like a silver-red diamond as it rose to the top of a fifteen-hundred-foot arc, then hung in the sky like a still photograph of fireworks, its glare shining down on the building. We had men on the roof as well as the second floor. The light from that flare must have wreaked technological havoc on the men on the roof. The glare from that projectile would have been bright enough to shut down their night-for-day vision, but the runway remained as dark as a cave beyond it.

As the flare started to fade, the Unifieds fired a second flare. This one was silver-green. It hung in the sky directly over the terminal for nearly a minute.

The third projectile rose up like a mortar shell. Sparks bubbled from the shining ball as it climbed toward the sky. It slowed as it reached its zenith, then it exploded, sending out an electromagnetic pulse, and the world went black around me.

FIFTY-NINE

Earthdate: December 3, A.D. 2517

The invasion had broken down around us. There was no sign of the second wave. Freeman had vanished. We were trapped in a spaceport, cut off from the world; and the EMP the Unifieds fired over the spaceport had destroyed the electronics in our visors. Now I would not be able to say good-bye to Cutter if he arrived in time to see me die.

We no longer had night-for-day vision or any other kind of vision through our visors. We had no interLink connection. Wearing our helmets, we were deaf, speechless, and blind. We couldn't even wear them to protect us from the cold.

The frigid wind that blew in through the broken window casings burned my ears when I pulled off my helmet. I tossed the worthless plasticized shell out into the open runway. Ritz saw me. I thought it was Ritz, but I could no longer use the smart display in my visor to identify him. Whoever he was, he was standing where Ritz had been standing a moment ago. He threw his helmet out the window as well.

In the lingering glare from the EMP, I spotted men sprinting across the runway. I started to shout orders for our snipers to shoot them, but I had no means of contacting them. Fortunately, our snipers were alert and did not wait for orders. Rifle fire tore through the calm of the night.

They had flares, but so did we. The snipers on the roof shot them in every direction. The first volley was uncoordinated. Dozens of phosphor-burning projectiles arced into the night sky turning it bright as day in some spots while leaving it dark in others. The light from the flares exposed the bodies of the hundreds of Unified Authority Marines we had slain.

I saw the carnage and wondered how long we could hold

out. The Unifieds had regrouped. We were like a tiger caught in a tree. So long as we held thousands of their men trapped in the bottom of our building, the Unifieds would not pull in their heavy artillery to finish us. They could send gunships to try and gut the top two floors with their chain guns; but we had already proven that we could defend ourselves against gunships.

So many shielded tanks had gathered on the far side of the runway that the forest glowed. If my visor still worked, I could have used the telescopic lens to scout their numbers. If I'd had a helmet on, I would not have worried about the cold numbing my face. The Unifieds had to fire that specking EMP.

The worst part about not wearing a helmet was trying to communicate. Every goddamned man in the terminal looked so specking alike. If I accidentally called Chris Nobles "Ritz," I could trigger a death reflex. Fortunately for everyone, it was so damned dark in the terminal building that no one saw anyone else clearly. In case the guy standing next to me was not the officer I expected, I would have an excuse. I said, "Those bastards stole your idea, Ritz."

He snickered, and said, "Assholes."

I heard another Marine bitching, but I did not know his name or rank without my visor. He said, "It's specking cold in here. Bastards. My ears are specking freezing."

We were in a powder keg with a fuse just waiting to be lit. The Unifieds had us at their mercy, but they did not know how to strike the final blow without killing the natural-borns we had trapped below us. A tank fired a few warning shells that shattered the runway a few yards from the building, but those shells were idle threats. Time passed slowly.

If they'd had shielded trucks, the Unifieds could have driven right up to the building to haul their men home. Apparently, they did not have shielded trucks. Nor did they send in more teams of men. Like us, they probably had no idea why the shields had failed, and they did not want to risk losing more men.

The sun started to rise. I was on the western side of the building, so I did not see it rise over the trees. I saw blue-and-pewter veins forming along the edges of the black sky; and then I saw fighters circling the runway.

CHAPTER SIXTY

The fighters did a flyby just a few hundred feet above the ground. There were three in the formation, either Phantoms or Tomcats. Who could tell at those speeds? They flew over our heads at thousands of miles per hour.

A few men fired guns and rockets at the fighters; but that was a waste. By the time they located the fighters, it was already too late to shoot. Looking out the second-story window, I could not see the U.A. fighters or the men who'd fired at them. I heard the engines and felt the sonic booms. As the noise of the fighters died down, I heard gunfire and the shouting.

Outside, the darkness slowly gave way to a gray morning sky filled with low-hanging clouds that threatened rain or snow. The glow of the shielded artillery faded in the light. The trees looked like shadows in a faint golden haze. Bodies still littered the runway.

"They're not coming back to get us, are they?" one of the clones asked. I thought he might be Ritz. No one else acted as casually around me.

"That depends who you mean by 'they,'" I said. "If 'they' includes the Unifieds, then yes, they are definitely coming for us."

"What about our second wave?"

"Just because we haven't heard from them doesn't mean they aren't out there," I said. "Without the interLink, they have no way to contact us."

Ritz, if it was Ritz, held his M27 over his shoulder, his finger still over the trigger, and said, "Whatever comes, we fight to the last."

"Oorah," I said.

"Semper Fi," he answered.

We were both full of shit and bravado.

The fighters screeched past the window so fast that I saw nothing more than a blur. Moments after they passed, the boom from their engines tore through the air. If they hit the roof with a missile, the right missile, they could cave it in without demolishing the entire building. Sure, they'd lose some of theirs as well; but losing Marines had always been an acceptable price to the Unified Authority. At least, it had always been acceptable when those Marines were clones.

"General, do you think they have already landed the second wave?" asked an unknown clone. He sounded desperate.

"For all we know, they've already landed and captured the capital without us," I said. It was true. I did not think it was likely; but without information coming over the interLink, who knew?

Only at that moment did it occur to me that Freeman might have failed. He might have only shut down one or two of the missile bases. Maybe there were more bases than he thought. Cutter might have flown the fleet into an ambush. So many variables. So many reasons why the second wave might never arrive.

Across the runway, a strange thing happened. A flying snake darted out of the trees. It was twenty feet long with a body that reflected the sky like a mirror. It fluttered and swirled in the air, flying in an erratic pattern that twisted and spun. The air dance only lasted a moment, then the Unifieds shot Freeman's drone to pieces.

"Freeman," I whispered. How long had he been out there, hiding in the woods, watching? I understood his message, though.

Several of the men around me asked, "What the hell?"

"That," I said, "is the signal."

Even as I spoke, a wing of fighters passed overhead, a wedge-shaped formation with six jets followed by two formations of three.

Across the runway and over the trees, the fighters put on an air show. The three fighters in the first formation split apart, each fighter crossing another's path, creating a braided vapor trail. The six fighters bringing up the rear split as well. They fired rockets, filling the sky with starbursts and smoke trails.

Inside the building, all went silent as the men near the windows struggled to understand. A moment later, they cheered. They screamed. They fired their guns in the air.

For the Unifieds, the battle had taken on a frantic turn. Jets from the Enlisted Man's Empire had entered their skies.

Desperate men turn to desperate measures.

First came the teakettle screech of an incoming shell, then the blast that shook the building, followed by the rumble of distant cannons. The shell hit the roof. Tiles fell from the ceiling, hitting men and shattering. Light fixtures dropped partway out of the ceiling as well, then dangled from wires over our heads. Clouds of dust billowed out of the walls, but those clouds vanished when broken pipes began spraying steam and water.

That first shell had been small, a test to see how hard they could hit the top floors without bringing the entire terminal down on the natural-borns trapped below. The second shell followed after another minute. This one slammed into a corner of the building like a hammer striking a sand castle.

The roof collapsed. It simply fell in, taking down a twenty-foot section of wall and crushing men beneath an avalanche of debris. As the smoke and the steam cleared, I saw open sky instead of ceiling.

The third shell hit a few seconds later.

The second wave of our invasion must have landed. The Unifieds could no longer hold our ships off. There was no longer any doubt that we would win the war, but my men and I would celebrate posthumously.

Without my helmet's electronics, I could not communicate orders across the ranks, so I communicated with my officers the way commanders had been communicating since the days of clubs and muskets—I screamed at the officer nearest to me and he screamed at the man closest to him.

"We're taking the bottom floors," I yelled. "Get your men! Go! Go! Go!"

I did not wait to see how they would react. I did not wait for my message to get through the confused and scared men crowding the halls. I ran to the nearest stairwell, and I screamed "Move it! Move it, Marines!"

One of the things I liked best about cloned Marines was the way they responded to commands. Hearing, "Move it," they did not stop to ask what they were to move or where they should move it to, they simply grabbed their guns and followed me into the darkness.

The stairwell did not have windows, and the lights were out. Even the emergency lighting had failed. I'd had a helmet with night-for-day vision the last time I'd taken these stairs. I never stopped to think about lights. As we clambered down the first flight of stairs in total blackness, I missed my helmet, with its many lenses.

I rounded the landing, the rattle of boots clattering against the stairs filling my head. If I fell, they might trample me, but I didn't care. I had my gun and my enemy and my combat reflex. I was in control this time, but I was more than ready to kill.

We ran past the doors to the first floor. If the U.A. Marines still held it, I did not care. They could have it. Their fighters and artillery were about to blow the stuffing out of this building. If the U.A. Marines wanted to ride the avalanche to the tarmac below, they had my permission.

As I started down the next flight, I saw a sliver of light in the shadows below. My men had set off charges in these shafts to make it harder for the Unifieds to attack us. Now we found ourselves running down the ruins of our work. I leaped breaks in the stairs, ignored holes in the walls and the groaning of the metal rails along the stairs. Somewhere in the back of my mind, I hoped the wall did not cave in on me.

I would be vulnerable at the base of the stairs. Give or take a thousand, fifty thousand Unified Authority Marines waited for me down there. They might not have shields, but they had numbers.

"Stop!" I screamed, but the sound of a thousand armored boots ground my voice to powder. "Stop!" But they could not hear me, and they would not stop. If I stopped, I would be trampled by my own Marines.

The same thing might have been happening in every stairwell in the enormous terminal building. I had over twenty thousand Marines, we were preparing to rush the enemy, we'd traded our thought processes for the mentality of a controlled mob.

I jumped a broken flight of stairs, landed badly, and tumbled into a wall. One more flight of stairs, and I would be on the ground floor, surrounded by U.A. Marines. The speckers would kill me. They would shoot depleted uranium darts through my skull, through my face, through my armor. The poison would not even have time to kill me as their fléchettes riddled my heart and drilled into my brains.

The breaks in the stairs behind had slowed the front of the herd; but the men in the back kept pressing. Some men leaped the chasm as I had. Some leaped and failed. Some tried to stop, and the men in the back pushed them over the ledge. They did not have far to fall, but a pile of squirming bodies began to form.

I ran to the door, reached for a grenade, pulled the pin, threw it low and hard, then I closed the door and fought halfway up the flight of stairs. My pill must have hit a wall or maybe a person. It did not go far. When it exploded, the percussion caused one of the walls at the base of the stairs to cave in. Had I waited by the door, I might have been crushed.

A cloud of dust filled the stairwell. Then came the fléchettes, like raindrops in a storm, only flying up, not down. The needles struck the cinder-block walls and bored into them. The darts hit men and metal stairs. I threw another grenade through the broken wall. This time there was nothing to block percussion. The explosion was deafening. Its force knocked me on my ass, but the hail of fléchettes slowed.

The sound of the explosion echoed off the walls of the stairwell. God, the battle was loud. It had never bothered me when I had a helmet.

One of the men standing behind me lost his footing. He landed on his armor-covered ass and slid down the stairs, making a clacking noise—*tak, tak, tak, tak*. He slid to the bottom of the stairs and climbed to his feet.

I saw the whole thing clearly. The man climbed to his feet, then dropped to his knees as fléchettes drilled through his gut, chest, and groin. Some of the needles passed all the way through his armor, both front and back. The man fell to his knees, and shots hit him in the face, shredding his cheeks. His eyes splattered. His forehead split as he fell face-first to the floor.

Despite the explosions and the dead Marine, more men gathered behind me, forcing me down the stairs. Without the interLink, I had no more control over this tide of cloned humanity than I would have had over water breaking through a dam. If I did not stay ahead of them, they would crush me.

I had no other choice. I scrambled down the stairs and dived through the hole in the wall, landing on my face in the shallow crater from my grenade. I had the briefest glimpse of a sea of natural-borns wearing combat armor, then other Marines began falling on top of me. The first one fell on my back, his head right above mine, driving my face into the rough concrete. The next man fell on him and slid forward, over my head. That second man probably saved my life. Moments after he landed on me, blood began trickling from his armor. The fléchettes left small exit and entry holes, but blood ran from those holes in steady streams. An inky, sticky puddle began to form around me.

Blood has a unique scent, a tinny, subtle smell that is not unpleasant on its own, but it comes with a rush of memories tinged with death and rage. Lying prone, with limbs and armor pressing down on me, I felt suffocated and trapped by the scent of blood. I heard men moaning and shouts of pain. A man right above me fired his M27. He fired a long steady burst. Other men fired, too.

I crawled forward, trying to pull myself from beneath the pile of men the way a snake might wriggle out of a collapsed den. Clamping both my hands around my M27, I used the butt like a paddle or maybe a crutch.

The fighting continued. Men died as I wedged my way out from under them. Some of them slumped to the floor like laundry, like wet towels waiting to be cleaned. Others fought. I kept low to the floor as bullets and fléchettes passed above my head.

Freed from the pile, I rolled to a clearing, using bodies as palisades as I rose to an elbow and sprayed bullets into the ocean of men. I lay on the floor under a ghillie suit of limbs and corpses, and I fired ten-second bursts, hitting ankles and thighs. Men fell, and I aimed at their faces.

I could not look back to see if my men were trapped in the stairwell. I had to keep firing. When I ran out of bullets, I did not stop to reload. With dozens of dead men heaped up around me, there were plenty of guns on the floor, some wet with blood. I had to pull one out of the hand of a dead Marine. Such things did not bother me. I did not think about them.

I did not need to aim; the Unifieds were everywhere. I faced forward and pulled the trigger. Men died.

Against a force with fifty thousand men, a man with a gun is little more than a nuisance. Screaming and shooting and insane with rage, I might have killed fifty men. I pulled a grenade and lobbed it high, over the heads of the Unifieds. I heard it explode, but I did not see the results.

And then came the apocalypse. It was not a grenade or a mortar or a rocket. Those are small weapons designed to kill men. This was a bomb. Something big. Something meant to fell cities.

It created a blast so powerful that the floor bounced beneath me. It was like lying on the surface of a kettledrum while a drummer beats it with a sledgehammer. The entire pile of bodies bounced six inches into the air; and when I fell back down, I landed on a dead Marine.

The blast must have been a U.A. shell, or a bomb, or maybe a missile. The next blast was even more powerful. All the men and bodies around me flew two feet in the air; and when we landed, the world returned to silence.

The shooting stopped.

I sat up. Still clutching my M27, I searched the floor.

The walls were covered with blood, and there was blood splattered on the ceiling. The sound of the explosion rang in my ears. Blood and dust still coated my face.

From where I sat, I could stare out to the runway. I could see the flames and the wreckage of tanks and trucks. Thick tails of smoke twisted from the flaming vehicles.

The fighting had stopped.

It took an act of supreme violence to bring the fighting to an end, an act so brutal that it stunned men into helplessness. Rising to my feet, I did not know if the caravan of destroyed vehicles belonged to the Enlisted Man's Empire or the Unified Authority. It could have been ours. It could have been theirs.

At the moment, it didn't matter.

The shooting had stopped, but no one laid down his gun. We could not disarm the Unified Authority Marines without removing their armor. My Marines held their M27s tight. They were ready to keep fighting. If one man fired his weapon, everyone else would follow. The feeling in the air was tense. It was like standing waist-deep in a pool of gasoline and holding a match.

A wave of fighters flew by, escorting the bomber that had delivered the message. The Enlisted Man's Empire now ruled the skies.

We never did invade Washington, D.C. The spaceport was as close as we came. When Freeman destroyed the missile defenses, the Unified Authority collapsed. Cutter had to drop a bomb on the forces massed around the spaceport to get their attention, but Tobias Andropov had already surrendered.

EPILOGUE

Earthdate: December 10, A.D. 2520
Location: Earth, the Enlisted Man's Empire
Galactic Position: Orion Arm
Astronomic Location: Milky Way

If the Bible is telling the truth, Moses tapped his rod against the shore of the Red Sea, and the waters split into a path. There's no point denying that that was a miracle. Jesus turning the water into wine, Peter walking on water, three guys spending a night in a blazing furnace without getting burned . . . all events that qualify for miracle status.

If Scott Mars had seen the battle at the spaceport, he would have called it a miracle. I'm not so sure.

The batteries that the Unified Authority Marines used in their armor ran out of power. The batteries gave out because the power spiked every time something touched the shields. In order to rush our position, the U.A. Marines crossed the runway during a blizzard. Snow landed on their armor and drained their shields.

It wasn't like Moses splitting the Red Sea or Peter walking on water. If the Egyptians had used water-soluble glue to attach the heads to their spears, and Moses had led them through a rain forest, their spears would have fallen apart. Would that have been a miracle?

So Lieutenant Mars, the "born-again" clone, prayed for a miracle, and we survived a battle against Unified Authority Marines because they didn't realize that their armor would react to the snow. Mars would probably say that God sent the snow.

I've always thought of miracles as singular events. God did not cause the Red Sea to split every year on the anniversary of

Moses's miraculous escape; but He sure as hell repeats the miracle of the snow every winter. We were just outside Washington, D.C., in early December. It snows there every year.

The weather changed the course of history, not God. At least, I don't think it was God. I'll explain that to Mars if I ever see him again. If he's alive. If God was as kind to him as He was to us.

Maybe in his "ineffable way," God sent the equivalent of a blizzard to help Holman and the Enlisted Man's Fleet as they delivered refugees to Terraneau. Andropov sent the entire Earth Fleet to the Scutum-Crux Arm. The Unifieds' fleet had faster ships with better armor. They had more fighter carriers than Holman. Could Holman have turned it around with his torpedo-wielding fighters? It would have taken a miracle.

When Tobias Andropov surrendered Washington, D.C., he must not have thought the defeat would last. He probably expected that the victorious Earth Fleet would return from Terraneau. *His* miracle never materialized.

The Earth Fleet never returned. Sometimes I stay awake at night, wondering what happened at Terraneau.

The first few days after we captured Earth, we had kept our fleet on high alert. Nothing happened. After a week, we realized that the Earth Fleet would not return and cut back our patrols.

And then we turned our thoughts to the Avatari. We knew that the murderous bastards planned to fill our atmosphere with tachyon particles and incinerate us; but without Sweetwater and Breeze, we did not know when. Andropov turned over the computer that once housed the scientists; but the men and the virtual space station in which they lived had vanished.

Without our barges, evacuating the planet was unfeasible. We inherited an impressive civilian fleet when we captured Earth, ships that were big and slow and comfortable. But those ships only traveled at ten million miles per hour, making it a twelve-hour flight to Mars and back, plus time for loading and refueling. With over fifty million people living on Earth, evacuating the planet did not seem possible.

In those first weeks after we captured Earth, I spent a lot of time thinking about Solomon, the planet on which so many people had died. We did not warn those people. We let them go about their lives completely unaware that death was around the corner.

Death comes quickly at nine thousand degrees. Those people might not have even had time to note the change in the temperature before they turned to ash. It was a comforting thought. Since we could not evacuate Earth, Cutter and I decided to keep its upcoming destruction a secret. It was Solomon all over again, only this time I was on the planet. Cutter remained safe on his ship.

Freeman and I spent days, then weeks, on edge. But, just like the Earth Fleet, the aliens never returned.

Miracles followed miracles in those days. Moses parted a sea, Peter walked on water, Earth survived to greet another year.

In the days after the first Avatari invasion, the Unified Authority sent its SEAL clones along with the Japanese Fleet to hunt down the aliens. When the Avatari never materialized, I decided that the SEALs had probably accomplished their mission.

Miracles never struck me as particularly miraculous when men died to accomplish them. The aliens never returned. Neither did the Japanese Fleet. If God was revealing His power, He allowed a lot of good men to die in the process.

AUTHOR'S NOTE

For any of you who are interested, I thought I might take a moment to talk about the construction of this book.

After writing the epilogue of *The Clone Empire*, I knew that *The Clone Redemption* would follow two story lines. If everything went right, the stories would wind themselves around each other like the strands of a double helix. My plan was to write both stories simultaneously; but as I began writing, I found it hard to switch from Harris to Yamashiro and Illych.

To make life easier, I decided to write two separate novels, then intertwine them. As I wrote the Harris side of the story, I created a calendar, then I referred to that calendar as I started writing about the Japanese Fleet and the SEALs.

I finished the first draft and polish of the Wayson Harris side of the book sometime in August and jumped into the other side of the book with absolutely no plan for where it would go. I knew that the Japanese had located the Avatari's solar system, and that was it. So I started writing and let the story take me where it wanted to go.

I finished writing the Japanese side of the novel on October 7, had a short night's sleep, and began weaving the two strands together on October 8. That is what I am doing right this moment.

I wrote this book with certain misgivings. As I started writing it, *The Clone Redemption* was meant to be the end of the Wayson Harris saga. The crafty Liberator clone has already lived three novels longer than I'd intended. I did not know in advance how the book would end, but I suspected that Harris would survive.

Now, though, I see intriguing possibilities. As *Redemption* ends, we are presented with a galaxy shared by three fledgling empires, all unsure if any neighbors exist. I'm not entirely certain about what happened at Terraneau, but I suspect there are survivors in the Scutum-Crux Arm.

I admit, I am intrigued. I like the idea of nations that have superior technology but lack the ability to renew it. Once their ships fall apart and their generators die, the Japanese on New Copenhagen will have a Bronze Age civilization. Ditto for anyone who landed on Terraneau. Back on Earth, Harris has factories, schools, and scientists; but what happens as his clones retire and die? Who will run the planet?

You can't possibly think Tobias Andropov is going to honor the surrender!

If the stars line up, and my editors at Ace are willing, there may be more Harris stories yet. If my editors have not deleted these paragraphs from my notes, I would say those novels are a distinct possibility.

If they do arise, however, I doubt they will be titled *The Clone* [fill in the blank]. Harris and the SEALs would certainly play an integral role in any future endeavors, but there are no clone farms anymore; and I don't imagine Harris has any interest in rebuilding them.

As always, I want to begin by thanking my editor, the lovely and talented Anne Sowards at Ace Books. There would not be any books without Anne's help, and I wouldn't know Anne if it weren't for my agent, Richard Curtis. Thank you, both.

When I first came up with the idea of returning to the "Boyd Clones," as they were originally known, I had meant to give them their own series. Then, as I wrote *The Clone Empire*, I decided to include them in the final pages. Had it not been for Anne, I could never have done that effectively.

Stephen King once wrote, "To write is human, to edit is divine." Truer words may never have been written.

And speaking of editors, I want to thank the people who have helped me throughout the Harris adventure: my wife, my parents, and most especially my good friend Rachel Johnson.

Also, I want to thank you, my readers. Harris would never have made it to a third book if it weren't for those of you who took an interest. He and I will forever be grateful.

Steven L. Kent
October 7, 2010

From national bestselling author
WILLIAM C. DIETZ

AT
EMPIRE'S
EDGE

In a far-distant future, the Uman Empire reigns, conquering worlds across the stars and beyond, ruling with a benevolent hand . . . and an iron fist.

On one planet, the remnants of a violent, shape-shifting race called the Sagathies are kept captive by Xeno cops, who have been bioengineered to see through the aliens' guises. Still, sometimes one manages to escape.

Jak Cato is a Xeno cop. He's returning a fugitive Sagathi when things go horribly awry. Saved from being slaughtered with the rest of his men because he is drunk, Cato must now become the hero he was created to be, recapture the Sagathi, and exact revenge. . . .

Praise for the novels of William C. Dietz

"A tough, moving novel of future warfare."
—David Drake, author of the Hammer's Slammers series

"When it comes to military science fiction, William Dietz can run with the best."
—Steve Perry, author of the Matador series

penguin.com

From National Bestselling Author
MIKE SHEPHERD

. . .

The Kris Longknife Series

MUTINEER
DESERTER
DEFIANT
RESOLUTE
AUDACIOUS
INTREPID
UNDAUNTED
REDOUBTABLE
DARING

. . .

Praise for the Kris Longknife novels

"A whopping good read . . . fast-paced, exciting, nicely detailed, with some innovative touches."

—Elizabeth Moon, Nebula Award–winning author of
Kings of the North

penguin.com

Ace Books by Steven L. Kent

THE CLONE REPUBLIC
ROGUE CLONE
THE CLONE ALLIANCE
THE CLONE ELITE
THE CLONE BETRAYAL
THE CLONE EMPIRE
THE CLONE REDEMPTION